DM

A BARGAIN SEALED WITH A KISS

"You will give me a kiss to seal our bargain, *oui?*" Rolf asked as he stepped closer.

Merlyn stiffened and backed away.

"Ah, ah, ah, my little pagan. You made a pledge, and I will hold to my part of the agreement only if you hold to yours."

He drew her close. As his mouth descended toward hers, his hazel eyes were bright with triumph . . . and something more subtle, yet infinitely more profound.

Merlyn held his gaze, unable to look away. His lips touched hers, firm but gentle. Gentler even than the first time. So delicate was his touch that she relaxed, quite against her will. And when he softly whispered her name, she felt the last of her defiance slip away. . . .

LINDA LANG BARTELL

TENDER WARRIOR

ZEBRA BOOKS
KENSINGTON PUBLISHING CORP.

I wish to thank my friend and peer,
Judith E. French,
for her unflagging support when I floundered
and her ready ideas when I was in need.
She also knows more about farming
than this city slicker ever will.

Thanks again, Jude, from "Moi."

ZEBRA BOOKS

are published by

Kensington Publishing Corp.
475 Park Avenue South
New York, NY 10016

First Printing: November, 1992

Printed in the United States of America

Prologue

Northern England, 1075

They came out of nowhere.

The savage Scots tribesmen swept over the Anglo-Saxon village in a tide of blood and fire, their fearsome ululations piercing the September air. Wild-haired, many of them bare-chested and bare-footed, they overran the settlement like a swarm of famished locusts. Most were on foot, some on shaggy ponies; they caused devastation wherever they moved, for it was almost dusk, the time for retreating not attacking. And they'd caught the villagers off guard.

Cold metal flashed silver in the waning sunlight as they brandished sword and spear, battle-ax and dagger, overwhelming the astonished villagers in one short, swift sweep. A pitifully one-sided battle . . .

A woman emerged from the wooded area to the east, a girl child skipping along beside her. The woman caught a glimpse of the moving bodies at the same time the battle cries reached her ears.

Her instincts shrieked in warning, and she instantly drew back into the sheltering thicket, flattening herself to the ground and forcing the child to the forest floor with her.

"Mamma," the child mewed softly in terror. The woman crushed the small face into her chest, her arm holding the minuscule body to the fragile shield of her own with the strength of fear and fury.

"Be silent!" she hissed, the virulent sibilance sounding foreign and faraway to her own ears. She tightened her bone-snapping grip on the little girl, reinforcing her desperate command, and dared to raise her face from the ground to peer through the foliage.

The partially rebuilt village provided little cover for the few old men and young boys who fought to protect the pitiful cluster of shelters they called home. And the women . . . Sweet God in heaven . . .

Flee . . . run! the woman screamed silently, her heart jarring a frenetic tattoo in her chest. She dared not reveal her position, or God knew what they would do to her . . . and, more importantly, to the child. She lowered her head and buried her face in the little girl's hair, fused to the ground. Familiar images were seared into her memory, refusing to scatter as she shut her eyes; snatches of fighting, of gleaming weapons, remained vividly before her; the grunts of men and screams of animals invaded her senses; the stench of blood and smoke; the metallic taste in her own mouth as fear rose up into her throat, threatening to cut off her breath.

Please God, make them go away. . . .

She dug the earth with broken trowel until her energy ebbed, until her arm muscles burned so acutely that she could do no more than halt her efforts. She sat back on the damp ground, tossing the long matted mane of her hair out of her face and

6

breathing heavily from her exertions. One grimy undersleeve rid her brow of sweat, while smearing the dirt already spattered in small beads thereupon.

The press of tears gathered behind her eyes, but she savagely willed them away, stabbing the near-useless trowel into the ground beside her. Crying was a sign of weakness in a thane's widow, even though she knew there were few around to see it. The remaining populace of Renford had scattered into the woods and hills after this last raid. Thieving, marauding Scots, supposedly Anglo-Saxon allies, but always ready to take plunder from Norman and Anglo-Saxon alike when they could get away with it . . . And if not them, then the Danes.

Everybody wanted England.

"A curse on them all," she muttered, and raised her fist to the cloud-laden gray skies. A peal of thunder was her answer, and a silver stitchery seamed the heavens directly above.

If any of her people were watching from nearby, of a certainty they would think her mad. *And let them,* she thought, a spark of defiance flashing in the dullness that numbed her soul. Let them all think her mad, then they wouldn't come to her for answers she didn't have. Then mayhap they would allow her to grieve in peace for her husband and family . . . and for her dignity, reft from her beneath a rutting Norman who'd left her for dead a year ago.

Tears glimmered along her lower lashes and bile burned the back of her throat at the memory, before she shied away from it. Not now . . . Later she would cry. Later she would crawl into the rotting hollow log that had sheltered her the night before, allowing her pain and anger to pour forth in hot, salty tears. It was the only thing that eased her anguish. . . .

And her love for her child.

A fierce protectiveness rose up within her, renewing her sapped strength, firing her determination.

The woman threw a furtive glance over her shoulder in the direction of the crude shelter that still hid her little girl. The child was relatively safe where she was, and certainly now accustomed to obeying her mother's terse instructions to remain quiet and out of sight. But these were unpredictable times, and one could never be certain of anything. . . .

One, two, three more bodies after this, she counted slowly and methodically, deliberately diverting her thoughts from her child, and the grisly task would be finished. It was the least she could do . . . give these, her people, a proper burial. It did not matter to her that the Scots could be lurking about still, ready to strike again, for there was little else they could take from the ruins of her village.

She'd been the only one who'd dared to return to what was left of it. Why not? There was nothing else they could do to her save kill her. Physically, that is, for she already felt dead inside. Yet she must live to protect her daughter.

The thought roused her once more, and she pushed her weighted limbs into action, ignoring the stink of death that threatened to relieve her stomach of its meager contents. "You'll not fatten the scavengers," she vowed softly to the dead. "Mayhap you're better off," she added, "for the pitiful harvest is destroyed, the few animals butchered and eaten where they stood, or scattered. There will be naught to eat the winter long."

Rolling the first of four bodies into its shallow grave, she hazarded a glance at the corpse's face. Somewhere inside, another piece of the woman shriveled and died, for this young man had offered to wed her after her husband's death. "I'm not a thane, only a humble freeman," he'd told her earnestly. "But I can provide for you and protect you in these uncertain times."

That was before this latest butchery.

"Well, you didn't!" she accused the still form. Emotion clotted in her throat and several tears traitorously tumbled down her dirty cheeks. They splashed onto the corpse's stiff, cold hands as she arranged them across his blood-matted chest, and the hopelessness of her situation washed over her with all the devastation of a bloodthirsty horde of the Bastard's mercenaries.

She hurriedly covered the body, clumsy with exhaustion, shaking with the last remnants of anger. She moved to begin the next grave, clinging to her anger like a lifeline, for it was the only thing that kept her functioning; the only emotion that made her feel any kinship with what little was left of humanity in the entire area.

She wasn't dead yet, by God. And as she lived and breathed, no one would touch her daughter.

Chapter 1

"Sweet Jesu, but he has consigned me to hell!"

Rolf de Valmont's low, frustrated exclamation lingered in the silent great hall at Conteville. One of the dozing mastiffs stretched out among the rushes nearby stirred lazily, then stilled, leaving the spit and snap of a small hearth fire unchallenged in the late night quiet.

The agitated knight thrust his long legs out before him from his position on a settle, kicking a clean-picked venison bone into an arcing path through the air in the process. He watched with perverse satisfaction as it landed with a soft rustle, his narrowed eyes contemplating it as if it were the object of his ire.

"I hope that was not meant for our good duke," said a masculine voice from nearby with a contrasting calmness . . . and a touch of subtle humor.

Valmont swiveled his head aside to scowl at the speaker of those suspiciously placating words. "I would not admit to such treasonous thoughts to anyone but you, Hugh. 'Tis all so easy for you to make light of this, but surely you remember the wasteland my lord William made of the entire area

11

between York and Durham. Seasoned knights that we are, we rode through there on the way south from Scotland three years past as if pursued by demons, sickened by the carnage."

"And so we did. But 'twas more to spare Brenna the sight, *mon ami*, than anything else," Hugh de Conteville answered. "And if I seem to take this news with more equanimity than you, 'tis because it will make you a baron in your own right instead of a landless younger son of one."

At the mention of Brenna, Rolf felt the old familiar ache center deep in his breast. Brenna of Abernethy, Hugh's lovely Scottish wife . . . and the only woman Rolf had ever loved. Not only had he been sentenced to a lifetime in battle-scarred, rebellious northern England, but also to a permanent separation from the woman he'd quietly worshipped from afar for the past three years.

A hand on his shoulder pulled him from his maudlin musings with a start. He looked up into his best friend's face and felt a sinking sense of loss along with his guilt, for he might never see Hugh again, either. So much for aggressive, complicated Norman politics.

"'Tis not the end of the world," Hugh said gently.

Rolf stared morosely at his crossed ankles. "Aye, but it is! 'Twill be a millstone about my neck . . . and I will never see Normandy again."

Hugh sighed and squeezed his friend's shoulder. "You are looking at this the wrong way." He raised a sandy eyebrow chidingly. "Come, come, Valmont. You are a Norman knight with no lands. Here is your chance to build your future. . . . You cannot be one of Geoffrey fitz Osbern's retainers forever. What matter that it is across the Channel? William needs you there even more than he needs you here." He pressed a cup of wine into Rolf's hand.

"To be baron of a pile of bones?" Rolf returned with a grimace. "A veritable wasteland? To resurrect some semblance of prosperity out of nothing? Out of a stubborn, hostile people—if there are any left!—with their lands laid waste by both Normans and Scots alike?"

Hugh moved to stand before his friend, his expression sober now. "There is more to this, I suspect, Rolf," he said quietly.

Rolf took a deep draught of wine before he answered, his eyes avoiding Hugh's. "Aye. I've no wish to leave you. I love you like a brother. And . . . and . . ." His words faltered, then failed, for he dared not voice the other reason.

"I know. But what use to pine after that which you cannot have?" The Lord of Conteville's expressive eyes communicated understanding and the rare compassion for which he was known and respected.

Rolf raised misery-muddied eyes to him. "You know?"

Hugh nodded. "And I understand, for I was once half in love with another man's wife myself. But you will not heal your troubled heart, nor, mayhap, make a life for yourself with a family of your own if you do not do as William bids . . . if you do not take up his offer."

Hurt and guilt threatened to overpower the younger knight. So Hugh had known all along. God's blood, but he'd surely worn his heart on his sleeve! He raked the fingers of one hand through his thick chestnut hair, then said, in a final stubborn protest, "I'm needed here to fight his enemies in France. . . ."

"Papa?" inquired a sweet child's voice from the shadows.

Both men looked up at the sound. A toddler with red-gold curls and sleep-flushed cheeks stood uncertainly at the perimeter of the firelight, a forefinger stuck in his tiny mouth. "Papa, I—" Before he could say any more, one of the hounds roused himself and trotted over to the child, sniffing the small, tear-streaked face and causing him to break into a watery smile.

"Jaimie," Hugh said to the child as he swung away from Rolf. "What do you here, *cher?*" He strode toward the little boy and scooped him up into his embrace, planting a kiss on his minuscule forehead. "Can you not sleep?"

Jaimie shook his head. "Demons . . . demons art in our chamber." He buried his face in his father's neck and clung tightly.

"Ah, I see, my precious one. Well, you can sleep with the men here in the hall until Uncle Rolf takes his leave. Then we will chase those demons away."

"There's no need to wake Brenna," Hugh said to Rolf as he joined him on the settle, positioning Jaimie comfortably against the pillow of his chest. "She's only just discovered that we are to have another babe, and I'd just as soon let her sleep while she may." He kissed the top of his son's bright head. "Sleep now, *mon petit.*"

Jaimie regarded Rolf with somber blue-gray eyes before closing them obediently. The dark-haired knight reached out a callused swordsman's finger to gently graze the child's silky cheek, a sudden longing moving through him.

"You will have your own one day, mark me, *mon ami.* And to prove my faith in your future, I will give you any of my best stallions—you may take your pick—and a brood mare to go with him. I'll also throw in several sacks of seed to begin planting in the

14

spring." He paused. "If you will stop and see Roger and his family in Wessex, I guarantee that my brother will add to your supplies. You saw how Derford was already prospering three years past."

Rolf watched the child sleeping in Hugh's arms, his lowered lashes hiding his eyes. "I know naught of planting," he admitted. "I am a chevalier."

Hugh smiled. "What you don't know your people will teach you, for they are, most of them, tillers of the soil."

"If there are any living souls left north of York." Rolf swirled the contents of his cup, transferring his attention from the dozing child in Hugh's arms to the bloodred wine. "I leave in two days. Better to get it over with it than to linger needlessly."

"I knew you'd come to your senses."

Rolf shot a look at Hugh, noting the warm humor in his eyes. He smiled sheepishly in response. *"Eh bien,* 'tis not as if I will never see you again. . . ."

"What's this about leaving?" inquired a woman's voice from the shadows. Brenna of Abernethy moved forward into the rushlight, clad only in a shift. Her tumbled auburn tresses caught the light with her movements and turned the deep tones to fire-red.

Rolf felt his chest tighten with suppressed emotion. "Good eventide, Brenna," he bade her.

"Eventide is long since past, Rolf de Valmont," she teased. "Hugh will fall asleep on his horse in the morn if you dinna allow him to go to bed. He has harvesting to attend to."

Hugh laughed softly. "Six and thirty . . . and the wench thinks I'm ready to be put out to pasture."

Brenna reached for the little boy, and Rolf smiled at Hugh's words. His eyes, however, were on his best friend's wife. Behind his merriment, Rolf stared unabashedly at her vivid, exquisite face, memorizing

15

every detail.

"Are you here on some secret mission, my lord knight," she asked with an answering curving of her mouth, "or for the sole purpose of imbibing Hugh's favorite wine?"

Rolf sobered. He looked at Hugh, but the Lord of Conteville seemed inclined to let Rolf give his own explanations. "I leave for England. William has granted me a fief in Northumbria."

The smile slid from her features, leaving a stunned look. "You are leaving Normandy?"

"'Tis good to know that I will be missed."

But even as he said the words, he was noting the look that passed between husband and wife. Hugh, steady as a rock in temperament and good-natured to a fault, obviously communicated assurance to Brenna, for when her eyes returned to Rolf, she seemed collected once more. "We will miss you, but 'tis your chance to become a baron in your right."

"So Hugh has generously pointed out."

She gently lay the sleeping Jaimie on the settle as Rolf stood. "Will you let me give you the kiss of peace?"

Rolf took her hands and glanced at Hugh. "You have to ask *me?*"

"Hugh wouldna' object." A blush tinted her cheeks. She stood on tiptoe and kissed him lightly on the mouth, then squeezed his larger hands in her own. *Adieu,* Rolf, and God go with you. Promise you'll return to us someday if you are able."

Hugh stood and came to join them. He put his free hand over both of theirs for a moment. "I've half a mind to accompany you, Rolf," he said unexpectedly.

Hands dropped as Brenna and Rolf looked at him in unison.

"Eh bien, you both would expect me to ignore

16

such a challenge? 'Hugh will fall asleep on his horse,' I believe the lady said of me."

His feigned offense did not fool Rolf for a moment. He was only jesting. Disappointment extinguished a whisper of hope.

"And why not?" Brenna said into the sudden silence, her face lighting with enthusiasm. "The harvesting can be completed without you . . . 'tis half done already. And Rolf . . ." She looked at Rolf, her beautiful blue-gray eyes alight, "Rolf would welcome your company, I warrant."

Hugh studied his wife, reaching out one hand to touch her cheek. "And 'twouldn't be for so very long. . . ."

Brenna touched her hand to his. "'Tis our second bairn, Hugh. And 'tis not as if you would be leaving me alone. Lady Katherine and Guy de Montrain will be here."

"Aye, *mon coeur*. My lady mother is as capable as I. She ran Conteville while we were in England, and in Father's absence before his death. . . ."

"And Guy is more than just a dependable castellan. . . ."

The whisper of hope rekindled and grew. "You would do that for me?" Rolf asked.

Hugh gave his friend a penetrating look. "How could I do less, *mon ami*? And if you need more, I will gladly give it. I'll remain with you at least a few weeks to help you establish yourself as lord. Between Roger and myself, we will supply you with everything you might need . . . including moral support."

Rolf thumped Hugh on the back, the heaviness surrounding his heart easing for the first time since he'd received Duke William of Normandy's missive.

*   *   *

The mounted party thundered across the lush green Norman countryside, the rumbling hoofbeats of their destriers resounding across the hills and meadows, over copses and woodlands, causing the very earth to tremble. Clods of grass and debris went flying; small field and forest creatures scuttled for their lives before the huge war-horses; sweetly-warbling birds suddenly rose up in mad confusion before winging away in raucous protest.

The sun relected off their chain mail, glinting off their helms, flashing off the sprays of water that geysered upward into the balmy air as they forded rivers and rills, their pace rarely breaking.

Northeast from Conteville, where they'd been given a send-off worthy of Duke William himself, they traveled through the mighty duchy and then into Flanders to Calais, across from Dover . . . Rolf, Hugh, three lesser knights—one in Rolf's service and two in Hugh's—ten men-at-arms, and three pack-horses.

"I see you've not lost your aversion to crossing water," Hugh had commented dryly when Rolf informed him in the early morning hours of the day they departed that they would not set sail from the mouth of the River Dives in Normandy.

"I told you once before. No knight in his right mind would rather cross more water than he could possibly help."

"Aye . . . and so you did."

Rolf had added, in the face of Hugh's amusement, "The Channel is unpredictable at best, and Calais little more than a stone's throw from Dover. Why take unnecessary chances?"

"But then we must travel southwest to Derford . . . and Roger."

Rolf had shaken his head stubbornly. "I'd rather

face the perils of any ride overland than over water."
He raised an eyebrow. "I also am not under God's
special protection . . . never having lived among the
monks at Cérisy-la-Forêt, as you did."

They had both given in to a bout of laughter then,
of shared camaraderie and pleasant remembrances.
"We made excellent time from the south of England
to the River Dives, as I remember," Hugh defended his
actions of three years past, when, for expediency, he'd
chosen to cross from England into Normandy, with
Brenna and Rolf, by a riskier route than Dover to
Calais. He sobered then, although it was obvious that
he could not quite squelch the sparkle of amusement
in his silver eyes before adding, "One only has to pick
the right boatman and then, of course, still the
waters."

A smile touched Rolf's lips beneath his nosepiece
as he relived their departure that morning. Even the
boatman had been apprehensive about crossing the
wider stretch of the Channel with three passengers
and three horses. But the water had remained calm
and their crossing uneventful.

Aye, Rolf mused, 'twas easier to reminisce about
the past than to speculate about what awaited him
in the very near future.

Well, Roger de Conteville had lived in England
since the great battle at Hastings nine years earlier.
From what Rolf remembered of his visit three years
past with Hugh and Brenna, the village of Derford in
Wessex had begun to prosper again under Roger's
guidance. And then, too, Liane was Anglo-Saxon.
Surely it would be well worth going out of their way
to see them, not only for friendship's sake or because
Roger wanted to see his twin, but for what Rolf could
learn about England and its people. Perhaps this was
all for the good, as Hugh had implied, even though it

meant being separated from all he knew and loved.

But even in his most optimistic moments, as he rode toward Calais with his best friend at his side, Rolf was besieged by doubts.

"By the rood, 'tis Hugh! And Valmont!" Roger de Conteville threw his arms about his brother, chain mail and all, and nearly lifted him off his feet.

"Mon Dieu, but you'll unman me . . . or both of us," Hugh laughed. "Save some of your exuberance for Rolf here."

Roger stood back and looked at his brother. He flipped off Hugh's helm and studied his face, his own eyes full of emotion. "How dare you ride into my village without so much as a warning!" he exclaimed, his voice husky. "I'm getting too old for such surprises."

Rolf coughed behind his hand as he sat his horse. "Comments like that will only spur Hugh on to reckless behavior, Roger. Better to tell him how fit he looks for his years."

Rolf dismounted and received Roger's kiss of peace. "You look well, Roger," Rolf told him.

"And you also." Roger turned aside and called out to a dark-haired lad of about eight years. "Brian, fetch your mother. We have important guests."

"Aye, Papa," the child replied, and ran through the palisade gate toward the village.

"He was little more than a babe when I saw him last," Hugh said.

Roger put one arm about his brother's shoulders, the other about Rolf, and led them through the palisade and toward the manor hall. "Well come, all of you," he threw over his shoulder to their companions. "Come in and take some refreshment."

They passed through the compound, which contained several outbuildings, including stables, a granary, and a small stone church. A great elm spread its branches over a patch of emerald grass between the gates and the manor doors at that end of the great wooden building.

Once inside, Roger called for wine, bread, and cheese. As several servants scurried to do his bidding, he motioned for Hugh and Rolf to be seated at a long trestle table that was immediately set up for them.

"Thank you, nay," Hugh said with rue. "I need to stretch my legs after sitting almost constantly since leaving Conteville."

Rolf looked at Roger and shook his head. "Surely you understand, Roger, that your older brother stiffens with age."

"Older by moments," Hugh said with a grin, taking no offense. "And if age stiffens me, then so be it." He accepted a cup of wine from a servant.

"What brings you to England?" Roger asked. "And how is Brenna? Have you any children?"

"Brenna is well. She sends you and Liane her love. We have a son, Jaimie, and she is to have our second child in the spring."

"*I* bring Hugh to England," Rolf added. "Duke William granted me lands in Northumbria."

Roger paused in the act of raising his wine to his lips. He looked at Rolf, then at Hugh, his expression sobering. "Northumbria?"

"Aye—"

"Roger, who? . . ." Liane entered the hall with Brian and a blond little girl and boy trailing after her. She stopped in mid-stride as she recognized the fair-haired knight standing across from her husband. "Hugh?" she whispered, touching her fingers to her mouth in wonder. "Is that you?"

21

"None other, *chère*," he answered with his beautiful smile, and went striding up to her.

She threw her arms about his neck, ignoring the mailed coif that he still wore as it dug into her cheek. He whirled her around before setting her on her feet again and holding her at arm's length. "You're just as lovely as ever, sister. You still hold me in thrall."

"Oh, Hugh!" She reached to unfasten his coif and ruffled his hair affectionately. "You sound more and more like your silver-tongued brother."

"Never!" he denied with a shake of his head. "'Tis just that you were my first love . . . and you saved my life as well. I am forever indebted to you."

"The abbess saved your life," she answered with a smile. "I but changed your bandages and stood vigil. . . ."

"Are you my Uncle Hugh?" inquired the little girl standing beside her mother.

Hugh turned his attention to the children. He squatted down beside the two youngest. "You must be Alais," he said, smoothing back her tumbled curls.

"Aye," she said shyly. "And this is William—we call him Will." She studied Hugh with clear gray eyes exactly like his own. "You look just like Papa."

Roger came up to them and swept Alais up in his arms. "How can you say that, child, when 'twas settled long ago that *I* am ever so much handsomer than my brother."

"I said that Hugh was every bit as handsome as you, Roger," Liane reminded him, "and that the only thing that gives you away is your arrogance."

Hugh threw back his head and laughed heartily, as he'd done once before, long ago. "We'll never let you forget that, Roger."

Rolf came up to them. "I think you are the stuff of legends, my lord," he told Roger. "I would rather be

22

called 'arrogant' than 'Hugh the Pious.'"

There was an awkward moment of silence then, and suddenly Rolf wished he'd kept his mouth shut. Roger had taken offense at Hugh's mortal enemy, Philippe de Bellême, calling Hugh such, while Hugh had accepted it with his marvelous equanimity. Obviously, Roger still took umbrage at such name-calling.

Then, unexpectedly, Roger's mouth softened into a tolerant smile. "And so would I, Rolf. And so would I."

Liane turned to Rolf and took his hand. "Well come to Derford, *Sieur* de Valmont," she bade him warmly. "Let me speak to my servants about the evening meal and the seeing to accommodations for your retainers. Then you and Hugh can tell us what brings you to England . . . and news of Brenna and Conteville."

"How is Kerwick?" Roger asked his wife after touching his lips to her cheek in greeting.

"We set his leg," Liane said. "But he is getting older and more stubborn each day. Nedra will have all she can do to keep him off his feet."

"A broken leg?" asked Hugh. "I believe the pain of putting pressure on the limb will be all the deterrent he needs, stubborn old man or nay."

An hour later, they sat at the board, the other men of their party at a second table, and traded three years worth of news.

As wine and conversation flowed within the great hall, Rolf took in the beautiful tapestries adorning two of the walls, the clean, sweet-smelling rushes that had obviously been freshly laid, the efficiency of the servants, and the contentment of Roger and Liane with their lot.

He observed the love that bound Hugh's brother

and his wife, and their pride in their home and children, and felt the increasingly familiar ache within him. He longed for this, he suspected, even as he acknowledged his love of battle, his delight in the challenge of besting an opponent, whether through the action of swordplay or the strategy of siege. Could he ever have both? he wondered. Or would he find such happiness with a wife and family that he would need nothing more to be fulfilled? Roger had his raven-haired Liane, and Hugh had his Brenna. What awaited him? Rolf wondered, torn between his feelings for Brenna of Abernethy and his half-formed hope of finding his own love.

"What think you, Rolf?" Hugh was asking him.

Rolf wrenched himself from his ruminations.

"Aye, Rolf," Roger said, leaning forward over his trencher. "Would you mind one more man in your party?"

"One more?" Rolf repeated uncomprehendingly.

Roger shrugged apologetically. "Liane would never forgive me if I didn't at least accompany you . . . offer to help you help her people to rebuild."

"Aye," Liane said earnestly, her blue-green eyes full of entreaty. "The north was wasted by William, so we all know. I should be forever in your debt if you would allow Roger to go with you and see what he could do. We can provide a milch cow or two, perhaps a pair of oxen . . . and seed and any extra farm implements we could spare."

Rolf suddenly felt as euphoric as if he'd imbibed an entire cask of heady red wine. Would he mind? Would he mind any offer of extra help?

"I would be honored, my lady Liane, to have Roger accompany us. And I can pay you at least something for your supplies. . . ."

"What?" Hugh said, the good humor in his eyes

belying his exclamation. "When you offered me naught for Charon, magnificent destrier that he is, or the fine brood mare I gave you?"

"Charon?" Roger cut in. "Could he be a son of Styx? The horse you *stole* from me? If so, then Charon—clever name, by the way, Hugh the Scholar—is actually *my* gift to you, Rolf."

Rolf looked from Roger to Hugh. "You stole Styx?"

Hugh shook his head. "'Tis well past time to retire the jest, brother. You had Brenna convinced, but I'll not allow Rolf to believe it for even a moment."

Roger sighed in affected resignation. *"Eh bien,* I know when I'm bested." He sobered then. "But the situation in Northumbria is nothing to jest about. I suspect William picked you because of your skill with sword and lance, your reputation for valor. You will need not only to rebuild, but to protect your fief from Scot and Dane alike."

"Aye," added Hugh. "With William fighting his enemies across the Channel, he needs dependable and loyal men in England. He pays you a compliment, Rolf, by sending you to the troubled north."

"Waltheof, son of the late Earl Siward of Northumbria, retains much influence in the north still and, as husband to the duke's niece Judith, has William's trust," Roger told them. "But one by one the English nobility have turned against William . . . and been destroyed. Let's hope that Waltheof of Huntingdon knows better."

Rolf followed Roger's glance at his wife. "This past summer Malcolm brought his men sweeping down from Scotland to wreak devastation from the Tweed to the Tees. William has yet to punish the Scottish king."

Distress darkened Liane's eyes at her husband's

words. "Surely Waltheof will see the wisdom in loyalty," she said. "There has been naught but slaughter and destruction in the north for the past six years. How can the people withstand any more raids or rebellions? Needless loss of life and property? They must submit . . . band together under a strong leader to fend off any more incursions from the Danes or the Scots." She looked at Rolf, the bright light of hope dawning in her eyes. "With you to help them, to lead them toward prosperity, surely they can eventually recover."

What could he say to that? Rolf thought. With so generous an offer of help from both brothers, how could he ignore the appeal in Liane's eyes? And, after all, he acknowledged, this was to be his home. It would be in his own interests, as well as those of William and his English subjects, to do his best in stabilizing the area he'd been granted.

He looked first at Hugh, then at Roger. How could he fail with two such knights at his side? And men-at-arms? And supplies?

You cannot fail, a voice told him.

Nay, I cannot, he thought. I will succeed in this venture . . . or die in the attempt.

Chapter 2

They rode for three days, slowed considerably by
the livestock and carts of goods. During some of the
journey the men relived old times, but the farther
north they traveled, the more Rolf lost himself in
memories of the trip from Scotland to Wessex with
Hugh and Brenna . . . and then on to Normandy and
the months following, when he'd finally admitted to
himself that he loved Brenna. In an effort to deny his
feelings, he'd persisted in maligning her to Hugh.
But, evidently, Hugh knew better than Rolf himself
of his true feelings toward Brenna. Hugh, the monk-
turned-knight . . . wise, even-tempered, compassionate, steady as a rock, and with a sense of humor that
endeared him even more to Rolf. Yet woe to the man
who mistook the fair-haired knight's characteristics
for weakness. There wasn't an intelligent man in
Normandy who would cross Hugh de Conteville
deliberately . . . and Brenna of Abernethy had fallen
in love with him for the exact traits that bound Rolf
to Hugh as closely as a beloved brother. Brenna . . .
Why couldn't she have been his?

Rolf pulled himself from his memories, for it was
futile to relive the past. Brenna of Abernethy had

never been his . . . *would* never be his, and he was a fool to allow his thoughts to follow such a course simply because he and his party were approaching northern England. And Scotland.

"'Tis preferable to dwelling upon *this*," he muttered to himself as he allowed his surroundings to register in his mind. Leveled villages, burnt fields, rotting corpses . . . and the stench in the September heat. Sweet Christ, it was nauseating, even to one inured to the sight and smell of death.

They'd passed through York just after dawn, appalled at the devastation all around them, and stopping only long enough to ascertain the exact location of Renford and Lexom, the two villages that would be within Rolf's jurisdiction. Lexom was two leagues north of the Tees, while Renford, the larger of the two, was on the southern bank of the river itself.

Roger had given an emaciated old man a sack of apples and a small package of dried beef for the information. Immediately, the Anglo-Saxon and his companion, a small, thin boy with straggly blond hair, had scuttled away and disappeared into a stand of trees with their treasure.

"If there were any more English left alive," Rolf had observed grimly, "we should have needed an added guard for the supplies."

The easy camaraderie that had prevailed among the three knights had decreased in direct proportion to their proximity to Northumbria. Banter had been banished by the sights that increasingly greeted them, until a silence that was every bit as unnatural as the quiet around them held sway.

With a rising sense of foreboding, Rolf withdrew once again into the haven of his memories.

*   *   *

From the sheltering thicket, the woman watched the Normans ride into the ruins of what was once her home. Three knights astride their awesome destriers led the contingent, two on animals as ebony as the night sky and the third astride a mount as pale as newly fallen snow. Nearly a score of men-at-arms followed behind them, and in their wake two heavily laden supply wagons pulled by a pair of brown and white oxen. Two cows and three extra horses brought up the rear.

Sunlight glanced off their steel mail and weapons, their helms with protective nosepieces making them look even more fearsome, more inhuman. The pride and utter confidence in their bearing alone declared them Norman.

Terror and fury collided within the woman's breast, one rooting her to the spot, the other fighting to propel her into their midst with claw and tooth bared, like a wild thing driven to desperate action, even if it meant self-destruction.

Food.

The word crept quietly through the tumult of her thoughts, and her mouth suddenly watered as she envisioned what precious commodities undoubtedly lay hidden beneath the canvas that covered the carts. Several casks hung suspended from their sides, and she suddenly had the most uncharacteristic urge to laugh aloud at the thought of the precious Norman wine—a frivolous thing to her mind—brought to an area where anything but water was unobtainable. Fools! Did they think to have a celebration in the middle of hell?

Rolf signaled a halt. All three removed their helms, and the dark-haired knight rested his hand on the cantle behind him, surveying what was left of deserted Renford within the hacked and blackened remains of the wooden palisade that surrounded it.

"Dieu au ciel," he said in disbelief. "There's no one here!"

The men followed his gaze, then Roger looked directly at the place where the woman crouched among the brush and briars. "They are either all dead or afraid to return."

"Or hiding from us," Hugh said with rue. "One can hardly blame them." '

"So what am I to do now?" Rolf asked, his voice edged with irony. "Announce that the new Lord of Renford bids them come out and populate his village?"

Hugh nudged Styx's sides and moved the black courser close to Rolf. "We will round them up," he said in a low voice. "Do not despair, Rolf. Rather, save your pity for the English."

Rolf turned his head aside, properly chastised, but the mutinous set of his mouth betrayed his bitter disappointment.

"Come out from there!" Roger suddenly commanded in English, his eyes on the quivering thicket to their right. "We'll not harm you."

Roger and Hugh followed his gaze. A long, taut silence prevailed. Rolf's hand went to his sword hilt, his eyes narrowing. . . .

She came at them suddenly, a thin wraith in tatters, materializing from the forest. As if bent upon mayhem, she clutched a broken trowel in one upraised hand and pointed at Rolf with her other.

"Begone from here!" she shrilled in a voice that raised the hackles on his neck. "Begone from this land of pestilence and starvation, lest ye too are cursed!"

One eye glinted at him from beneath the filthy tangle of her hair, the other hidden by dark, matted tresses. Unease slithered over Rolf like a serpent.

Don't be ridiculous, he scoffed at himself. *Only the superstitious believe in curses.*

But Hugh was speaking before Rolf could open his mouth, diverting the crone's attention away from the bemused chevalier. "We mean you no harm," he said placatingly as he gestured toward the rest of the contingent.

"'Twill be a cold day in the devil's domain before any Norman comes here with aught but evil intent!" she accused, her visible eye slitting with loathing. "Get yourselves from here, Norman, for there's naught left for the taking but barren fields and rotting flesh."

"We bring you your new lord," Roger told her in near-perfect English, "and supplies with which to rebuild your village."

She cackled eerily, causing Rolf to shift in his saddle. *Who was this hag?* he thought, *And how dare she accost them like . . .*

"So that the Scots or your own countrymen can raze it again?"

"'Twas the price for your rebellion against Duke William," Rolf informed her, a self-righteous edge to his words.

Roger threw Rolf a frowning glance and shook his head. "Your lord, Rolf de Valmont, will protect you." He inclined his head toward Rolf.

Merlyn glanced at Rolf as if he were no more than a fly. Indeed, after his careless, dispassionate words, she could have easily swatted him into oblivion like some bothersome bug.

As it was, the dismissal in her expression was irritating in the extreme to the chevalier.

31

"How are you called, old woman?" he demanded, his mounting ire exacerbating his already halting Anglo-Saxon and accenting his impatience.

Ignoring Rolf, she sidled up to Roger because he spoke her own language so easily. "Merlyn," she told the sandy-haired knight. "I am called Merlyn," she rasped.

Roger's destrier pranced uneasily at her approach. "Stay back then, Merlyn," he warned, his hands tightening on the reins. "Odo here does not know you."

"He knows I'm the enemy, Norman. *English*. And to be stamped out like a lowly insect according to your duke." Her eyes glittered with hatred. Rolf nudged Charon's great sides and moved closer to her. Merlyn slanted him a look that he could have sworn held fear, yet she held her ground. "Isn't that what your kind seeks to do? Isn't that why you're here?"

Rolf slid to the ground and approached her, removing his helm as he came to stand before her. His dark hair was plastered to his forehead beneath his mail coif, adding to his fearsome appearance. "Nay. We are come to help you. . . ."

She turned on him fiercely, jabbing the still upraised trowel toward him for emphasis. "*No one* can help us!" she hissed. "'Tis too late! There's naught here . . . naught!" She waved both arms wildly. "Begone, begone!"

Charon snorted and tossed his head nervously at her sudden gesture, his silky black mane ruffling with the movement. Rolf reached behind him to grab the destrier's reins. "Easy, old woman, around our horses. Didn't Sieur de Conteville just tell you that?"

Merlyn scrambled back, keeping her shoulders hunched like an ancient one, her eyes riveted to the great black destrier. "Aye, and so he did. Satanic beasts . . . I've seem them bring down men at the command of their masters. Demon seed, just like those who ride them.''

Rolf resisted the temptation to roll his eyes. ''Where are the rest of your people? The other villagers?''

''Are you *blind*, Norman?'' she demanded, then wished she hadn't spoken quite so derisively. After all, he could easily cut her down where she stood with one sweep of his great broadsword. . . .

And she had to remember Raven. Raven, her child. Stigand's child. God help her hold her temper, her seething hatred for these bloodthirsty Viking descendants.

''Not *yet*,'' Rolf bit out, ''but—''

''Merlyn,'' Roger interjected, ''do you mean that all the villagers are dead? You're the only survivor of Renford?''

Merlyn tipped her head at him, considering him carefully . . . and her options, which, at the moment, appeared almost nonexistent. He seemed more levelheaded than the dark-haired devil. So did his fair-haired brother . . .

''Tell me first what you want of us,'' she answered slyly, refusing to show her acute misgivings, in spite of what she perceived as an extemely precarious position.

''Roger told you once,'' Rolf replied, reining in his impatience with an effort. For some inexplicable reason, this woman was as irritating as a thistle in his chausses. ''I am come to Renford as your new lord, to pro—''

A high-pitched shriek rent the still air, causing every man in the party to go for his sword. A tiny animal scurried from behind one narrow stretch of charred stockade and directly into the road before them, yelping as it darted between the great hooves of the war-horses.

Caught as he was among the three destriers, Rolf moved to mount Charon before he could be brained by one of those platter-like, flashing hooves.

"Raven!"

The horror in that one word froze him in mid-motion, and Rolf caught movement out of the corner of his eye. Hugh reached down to grab Charon's reins, and Rolf, with a lightning-quick movement born of pure instinct, bent to swoop up into his arms a small form of flesh and blood. He flung himself to the side of the road, away from deadly hooves, shielding the child with his own body and awkwardly but effectively cushioning her fall to the rutted ground.

The commotion ceased as abruptly as it had begun, the dying whimpers of the puppy suddenly sounding strident as the shouts of the men and the shrilling of the destriers died away.

The small, trembling body beneath Rolf struggled out from under him, crying softly, "Thor . . . Thor!"

Rolf released her and rolled to a sitting position, his scabbard poking into the road beside him like the broken spoke of a wheel, his sword still sheathed. He looked into blue eyes, shining with tears, in a small, heart-shaped face. "My . . . puppy," the girl-child murmured brokenly in English, seemingly more concerned about the dog than about the mailed warrior sitting beside her.

Rolf made to stand then, feeling utterly foolish . . . only to look up into Merlyn's panic-stricken face. "Don't touch the child," she warned him in a strange voice, the broken trowel pointed right at his belly.

"Enough," Roger said from behind her, knocking the pitiful weapon away and taking hold of her wrists. "You've no need to threaten Rolf . . . or any of us. We'll not harm you—any of you. You have my word."

Hugh came up to them, the unmoving puppy cradled in his arms, his expression full of pity.

Merlyn looked at her daughter, her eyes dark with anger and frustration, but Raven was weeping over Thor. She reached out tiny dirt-stained fingers to stroke the animal's still-warm side.

"Je te trouverai un autre," Rolf heard himself tell her, then realized he was speaking in French. He gruffly translated, "I'll find you another," feeling foolish.

As Merlyn's gaze clashed with his, it occurred to her how very strange it was—how very strange, indeed—to see three Norman chevaliers standing in the middle of a road in battle-torn northern England and comforting an Anglo-Saxon child over the loss of a pup.

In fact, the word *strange* was totally inadequate; bizarre . . . dreamlike . . . eerie, were more fitting.

The little girl looked up at Rolf. "There are no dogs about, lord," she told him on a stifled sob. "They were killed or driven away." Fresh tears sheened her eyes and her lower lip quivered. "Or eaten."

"After all the death you've seen," Merlyn told her with tight-lipped severity, "you lament a *cur*?" Roger had released her hands and she hobbled over to Raven, a finger shaking in the little girl's face. "You disobeyed your . . . elder," she charged. She was hard pressed to keep her voice to a cackle, so great was her relief. "You were to stay where you were until you were told otherwise!" Her fingers wrapped about one of Raven's wrists, the force in her desperate grip causing the child to wince.

All the anger and dismay, the fear and uncertainty Merlyn was feeling at that moment, must have communicated itself to Raven, for the little girl's other hand fell away from the puppy in Hugh's arms and her lashes lowered, her gaze seeking the ground. Heat crept up her pale cheeks. "A bee stung 'im," she whispered. "And he was hurt . . . and afeared."

"And now he's dead!" Merlyn snapped.

"Bryce," Rolf called out, quite unexpectedly wishing to put an end to the child's guilt and anguish. His young squire handed Charon's reins to a retainer and stepped closer. "Aye, my lord?"

"Help the child bury the dog." His eyes met Merlyn's, and something deep within him stirred at the unguarded misery in her dark blue eye . . . which quickly disappeared at his probing look. He'd thought her to be brown-eyed, so dark did the hue appear from a short distance. And her skin—at least what he could see of it—was as sun-darkened as the meanest peasant. Now, however, the true color of that single orb was apparent, and it dimly registered in the back of his mind that an old woman's eyes would have probably been faded. . . . "And beware of hostile Saxons lurking about."

"'Tis more likely Scots ye'll encounter. There be little spirit in those of us who were spared," she said, her voice curdled with bitterness as she watched Raven follow Bryce, the pup now in his arms, to the edge of the forest. "And ye've no business tellin' the childie ye'll find 'er another dog, Norman. 'Tis cruel te raise her hopes. . . ."

"Are you her mother?" Rolf asked suddenly, studying her through narrowed eyes, noting that the flesh of her face, grime-streaked as it was, appeared to be smooth for that of an old woman.

She cackled and cocked her head at him, screwing

36

up her features as she guessed the bent of his thoughts. "Nay. I'm only Merlyn. . . . What man would have a woman they say is touched in the head? Some say I have the Sight. Others say 'tis madness, rather, that moves me."

"You hardly seem mad to me," Roger said, a thoughtful look on his face. "Mayhap 'tis a ruse to discourage us from stopping here?"

For a moment so fleeting it might have been imagined, Rolf thought her expression wavered. Her mouth shifted slightly, and emotion flared in her eye but then was gone.

Hugh came forward then and spoke. "What happened to your other eye, Merlyn?" He slowly reached forward and she allowed him to gently brush back the tangled hair that hung over the right side of her face. The area around the eye was red and swollen beneath a dried layer of what appeared to be mud. The eye itself appeared to be held closed by the crude dirt dressing.

For a moment, Merlyn responded to Hugh's gentle touch, the compassion in his eyes, then remembered herself. She pulled away and averted her head. "It festers," she told him in a scratchy voice. "My mother was a healer; she taught me of poultices and the like."

"It should be cleansed, then redressed," Hugh told her quietly, "but not with mud. I know something of the art of healing."

Her eyes on Raven once more, she answered, "I'd wager that you are much more adept at inflicting wounds, Norman. . . . Hurry, childie," she called to the little girl. "We must go home."

"And where is home?" Rolf asked, crossing his arms over his chest and leveling his sternest look at her.

Merlyn looked about her, several emotions passing

37

over her features, before she answered. "The *weald* now. We abide with the beasties in the woodlands, for to reinhabit Renford is to invite death. But we've nowhere else to go." She slanted a look at him. "Get yourself from this place, Rolf de Valmont, ere ye, too, end up cursed . . . or carrion."

Raven came scurrying back to the group, throwing a yearning look at the loaded wagons. She took Merlyn's extended hand obediently and stared shyly at her bare toes.

"*Tu as faim, petite?*" Rolf asked her. "Are you hungry?"

"Aye," she said softly, making a circle in the dust of the road with her toe.

Rolf signaled to one of the men beside the first wagon.

"Are there just the two of you?" Roger asked Merlyn.

"A few more than that, though I don't ken for certain how many. But ye'll not find them, for they're not so bold as Merlyn. . . . They'll not be foolish enough to expose themselves to Normans." She pointed a bent finger at each one of the three chevaliers in turn. "An' they've not the Sight, so they'll take no chances." She chuckled softly, although her heart was bumping up into her throat with fear. Would they let her go? she wondered, her grip tightening on Raven's hand.

Movement caught Merlyn's attention, and her gaze skittered over to her blind side in alarm. But it was only the youth Bryce striding up to her. He handed her a bundle of what looked like food. Raven's eyes lit up, and she looked questioningly at her mother.

"For you and the child, *old* woman," Rolf told her. "And for every person you can bring to Renford, I'll give you more. Do you understand?"

"Think ye that ye can *buy* us?" she asked, hatred honing her skewed features.

"It depends," he answered, glancing at Hugh and Roger, "on how hungry you are. And how great your love for the child."

He watched her scrabble away, wondering just how old she was. And just how "mad."

Renford was indeed deserted. There was no sign of anyone after Merlyn and Raven disappeared into the forest. Even the creatures that normally abounded were unnaturally quiet.

"We're being watched," Rolf said to Hugh later as they helped the men clear the debris from the grounds within the battered stockade, then brought in the wagons and animals. "Why else the silence?"

"Aye," Hugh agreed wryly. "But by whom? Let us hope 'tis the homeless Anglo-Saxons and not the marauding Scots."

Rolf patted his sword, which he still wore, in spite of having removed his mail as they labored in the early September heat. "They'd be no match for us . . . naked, screaming savages. We already know they prefer to single out defenseless farmers." His features twisted with contempt at the very thought.

"You of all people know better than to under-estimate the enemy," Hugh answered, but a corner of his mouth quirked suspiciously, as if he were satisfied with Rolf's reply.

"And that includes the woman Merlyn," Rolf said as he straightened a moment from trimming a newly cut sapling for a stockade post. His damp tunic and chainse clung to his perspiration-sheened skin. He ran a forearm across his brow and looked over the remains of the village with a thoughtful cast to his features. "I don't trust her. . . . There's something odd about her." He glanced toward the forest, his eyes narrowing against its density.

"Win her trust, and you'll discover what you want to know," Hugh advised. "And if you gain the old woman's trust, I think any others around will follow suit sooner or later. You must be patient, Rolf," he added.

Rolf bent to the sapling again. "Patience, *mon ami,* is not one of my virtues."

Hugh bent to help him. Hand over hand, they eased the green pole into an upright position. When it was secured, the fair-haired knight said, "Then you would do well to cultivate some. 'Tis necessary in a leader of men, be they warriors . . . or farmers."

Half a mile away, a small group huddled about the hollowed log that had sheltered Merlyn and Raven many a night. It wasn't cold, but several shivered from fear more than from the cool evening breeze.

There was no fire, only a small pitch torch providing enough light to identify one another beneath the night-blackened canopy of trees. The food in the bundle the Normans had given Raven was gone, shared equally among them by their dead thane's wife.

"You need a husband!" one young man insisted, his voice strained with urgency in its low pitch. The breeze ruffled the shreds of his tattered tunic like so many flapping feathers.

"I need no man!" Merlyn blazed at him, causing Raven, who was tucked beneath her arm, to stir. "Beyond brute strength, a man can do naught more than I, we've seen proof enough of *that."*

"Bryan's right, Merlyn," said a mouse of a woman,

her straight brown hair whipping across her face with the shifting wind. She tucked a hank behind her ear with thin fingers, and Merlyn noted the shudder that moved through her. "Would that I had such an offer," she told them. "A woman needs a man to fish and farm and protect her from—"

"As your Edric did? As Stigand did?" Merlyn demanded under her breath.

An old, old woman on the perimeter of the small group glanced through milky eyes at Merlyn in the dancing torchlight, but she said nothing.

"You've no right to speak ill of the dead, Merlyn," Bryan defended the dead men. "One day you'll find you've taken on too much. . . . Those Normans may be barbarians, but they're not all lackwitted. Especially any that the Bastard sent to rule in Northumbria."

"Aye," Merlyn said. "Northumbria, with its leveled villages . . . its skeleton-strewn roads and famine-ridden lands. 'Tis a challenge for any intelligent and enterprising warrior." Sarcasm saturated her words.

"A woman can do aught that a man can . . ." said the old woman with the cataract-glazed eyes unexpectedly in a soft, mewling voice. Her eyes met Merlyn's. ". . . can wield any rod but one, Merlyn, and we've other men to do that." Someone snickered, and the short-lived sound of levity echoed eerily about them.

Ignoring it, the ancient woman, who was the late Stigand's grandmother, glanced about the circle, her eyes squinting against the shadows. Her long white hair, hanging loose down her back, stood out against the night. "The child is right," she said to Bryan. "And you would do well to support her, rather than cause her grief because of your male pride."

Bryan's mouth settled in a sullen line, and he stared stonily into the night, put in his place by Elsa. The mouse-haired woman, Marthe, scooted over to him and put a hand on his shoulder. "If Merlyn is so brave and strong, let her drive the Normans from our lands. And the Scots. And the Danes."

"A brain is always worth more than brawn," Merlyn said in her own defense, wishing Bryan—or any of the others—would take Marthe to wife and give them a respite from her whining wishes and empty challenges. She'd already shared most of their beds, Merlyn would have wagered anything, and she wondered how long it would take the men to realize that they couldn't afford to be as selective as before tragedy had struck.

"Give them some time, I say," said a middle-aged man with one leg.

It was the first offer of advice from Cedric, who'd lost his leg, then his family, to the Normans, and what little remained of his spirit to the savage Scots.

"What do you mean?" Merlyn asked, giving him her full attention.

"I watched from the trees," he said, his expression bleak. "I heard every word. Mayhap they can be trusted—to a degree. Let's wait . . . and watch. If they are cruel and truly care naught about our people, then we can either leave here . . . or murder them in their sleep."

The absolute lack of emotion in his voice raised the hair on the back of Merlyn's neck. Cedric . . . the wonderful father and loving husband. The capable farmer and defender of all that was his. Stigand's good friend . . . Now a shadow of what he once was in body and spirit.

Yet he had spoken.

"The twin brothers . . ." Merlyn said with a frown

of concentration, "they seem sincere. And they speak our tongue well, especially the one who rides the white beast." She shook her head slowly. "But Valmont, dark-haired and dark-tempered . . . he's to be the new thane?" The corners of her soft mouth curved downward with distaste. "He belongs on a battlefield, that one, not on a plot of freshly tilled land, or in a quiet, scented orchard. . . ." At the wistfulness in her last words, a hush fell over the group, with only the wind moaning through the trees, as if lamenting their desperate situation.

"Leave here for where?" Bryan asked Cedric in stringent tones. "And who will murder them in their beds?"

"Give them a little time—"

"How *much* time?" Bryan cut Cedric off. "Time enough for winter to set in? Then we pray that they will share their food with us? That they will allow us to fish in the Bastard's streams? Hunt in his forest?"

Cedric shook his head, his expression unreadable. "A few weeks, naught more. A few weeks, and then . . ."

Merlyn looked at him, suddenly catching a fleeting glimpse of the old Cedric in the set of his shoulders, the tone of his voice. "And then?" Merlyn pressed.

"And then I will show you myself how to get rid of them."

Chapter 3

The feeling of being watched persisted the next morning, but several men stood sentry as Rolf listened to first what Hugh, and then Roger, had to say. They were evaluating the damaged village and offering suggestions about everything, from rebuilding, to new crops, to defending the area. When they'd given their recommendations for Renford, Rolf felt some of the old enthusiasm return at the thought of activity and, in all probability, a skirmish with Scots . . . or anyone else who dared encroach on his newly granted lands.

If he could do nothing else, Rolf acknowledged with grim determination, he was certainly more than capable of defending and maintaining a holding against an enemy.

The rest, he hoped, would fall into place. If not . . . well, he would think about that when the time came.

"What think you, Rolf?" Hugh was asking.

"I think," he answered, pulling his thoughts back to the immediate problem, "that a stone manor house—heavily fortified—would be wisest. We can use the foundation and basic structure of this one for now. A castle would take years to build, and much manpower." His mouth twisted. *"Manpower* we don't have. The sooner 'tis restored, the better for all."

"It seems to me," Roger observed, "that, as imperative as is a fortified shelter, you've an even more immediate problem."

Rolf de Valmont, fearless and skilled chevalier, brilliant tactician in war, instantly knew what Roger meant. "Indeed. The area must be routed of Scots . . . or even Norman deserters and renegade Danes. I cannot expect these people to cooperate the least bit when hidden danger could be in any given place at any given moment. They've lost too much already."

He missed the surreptitious look of what was obviously delighted approval that Hugh and Roger exchanged, his mind awhirl with various plans to ensure the safety of the surviving Saxons he could round up.

"You can use what's left of the old manor house while we restore it," Roger said, "and add a few improvements. 'Tis still warm enough to need only a temporary roof to keep out the rain. Meanwhile, any villagers can stay in the hall of the manor for safety and shelter as long as need be. Since, fortunately, the destruction is not so far-reaching as we first thought, their cottages can be rebuilt where they stand, unless you prefer a different plan."

"Nay." Rolf squatted and drew a rough diagram in the dirt of the road just outside the manor gates. "The original plan is good, don't you think, Hugh?"

Hugh nodded.

"There need be no difference then, except for the manor house and the increased village fortifications."

"But is there a quarry nearby?" asked Myles de Mortain, a knight in Rolf's service. "I've seen little of

45

stone about."

Rolf stood, letting the stick fall to the ground. "We've not been here long enough to see much of anything," he said with a grimace. "But we must secure the area before we can do aught else."

Merlyn was dismayed by the snatches of what she'd heard.

"What did they say, child?" Elsa whispered into her ear.

"They're going to comb the forests and fields to rid Renford and the surrounding area of any Scots . . . or other threats to us."

Elsa's white eyebrows raised. "A good idea:"

Merlyn clutched the woman's thin arm. "Nay! They'll find us, don't you see? And Bryan and Cedric and the rest aren't ready to meet them face to face . . . to trust them not to murder us!"

Elsa placed one gnarled hand over Merlyn's. "The Bastard may be many things, Merlyn, but he's no fool. If we can convince these men he's sent that the rebellions are over, perhaps we can escape with our lives and return to some semblance of normalcy."

"Then I will return to the land of the Cymry, my mother's land. Surely I can find peace and safety there!"

Elsa shook her head. "You'll find naught of either, child, for the Welsh have no more liking for the Normans than for the English. They're fierce fighters, your mother's people, and will die before they allow the Normans to subjugate them." She pursed her lips thoughtfully and added, "And what of Raven? This is home to her. . . ."

"And what kind of home is *this?*" Merlyn asked as her gaze went to Renford before them through the camouflage of foliage. A hint of hysteria penetrated her words. "She has known too much of cold and hunger, violence and death, in her short life."

Galvanized by thoughts of Raven's safety, Merlyn said in a soft but fierce voice, "I'm going to speak to them. If they allow me to leave freely, then all the better. If you see that they detain me, then go and warn the others of their plans, Elsa. Will you do that?"

"If 'twill set you at your ease, but rather let *me* go. I am old and feeble, and have no child who needs me."

Merlyn stubbornly shook her head, her mouth set in a thin, hard line. "Nay. Raven needs you should aught happen to me, and you've more wisdom and vision than I will ever have. I pray you, Elsa, promise you'll retreat and warn the others if necessary."

Obviously seeing that she had no choice in the face of the younger woman's sound reasoning and determination, Elsa nodded her head with resignation. "I'll be right here, watching and listening. If aught goes awry, I'll do as you say. But have a care, child. . . ."

Merlyn squeezed her hand, then carefully made her way toward the periphery of the forest. There were few dead leaves to crackle beneath her bare feet this early in September, yet she felt as if she were announcing her presence with the blast of a horn.

Without warning, a large hand came out of nowhere and grabbed her by the arm. A deep male voice said something in clipped Norman French, and a platinum-haired giant pulled her out from the trees.

Merlyn found herself ungently propelled toward Rolf de Valmont and his two friends.

In spite of her alarm, close up and without his forbidding steel armor and helm, she had to acknowledge that Rolf de Valmont was a splendid figure of a man . . . if one liked a man's hair shorn up the back of his neck to his ears, and no beard or moustache.

The other two are fair of face and form, as well, a perverse imp offered, *and kinder.*

The errant and completely irrelevant thought caused her a moment of confusion. But only a moment.

"Do your men make a habit of frightening old women and dragging them from the *weald?*" she asked, concerned that the exceptionally tall Norman beside her might discover Elsa if he returned to the spot where he'd found her.

"Release her, Myles," Rolf said. Then, to Merlyn, "He was told to be aware of *any* activity in the area. How are we to know the difference between skulking Scots and skulking Saxons?"

"I was not *skulking* on my own lands!" she snapped, forgetting she was supposed to be a landless old woman, not the late thane's wife.

"This is not *your* land! 'Tis the king's—"

"My king is dead!"

Rolf opened his mouth to retort, then paused. The breeze had shifted, bringing the overpowering stink of garlic with it. His eyes narrowed at Merlyn, even as his senses went reeling from the smell. A small pouch hung by a cord about her neck.

She stared defiantly at him, essaying to keep her features screwed up in the face of his momentary dismay.

Roger de Conteville glanced at his brother. Hugh met his gaze, immediately canting his head aside to cough and then clear his throat vigorously behind his hand.

"You and your people still hold your lands, but of Rolf now," explained Roger, "and Rolf holds them of Duke William . . . who holds them of God."

"There are many who will not accept that."

Recovering his tongue, Rolf said, "And 'tis exactly why so much of Northumbria is a wasteland."

"Tell me how you've been surviving with no crops," Roger said, steering the conversation to slightly safer ground. "Or have you some grain and other supplies stored against such a time as this?"

Without thinking, Merlyn flung her hair from her face, for the area about her muddied eye was becoming almost unbearably irritated. "Who could have ever envisioned such a time, Norman?" she answered with what sounded suspiciously like a sneer. "Never have any people done to another what yours have done to mine! You and your ilk have destroyed almost an entire generation of English here." She put one hand to her bent back, wishing she could stand upright for a few moments to relieve the cramping and aching that was causing her to tremble from the prolonged strain.

"Come . . . sit," Rolf invited, and before anyone could stop him, he untied the sleeves of his tunic from about his waist and laid it on the road at her feet. He took Merlyn firmly by the shoulders, mentally noting how slender they were without feeling bony or gnarled, then pushed her down before she could brace herself against him.

His eyes met hers . . . that is, the *one* that was unobstructed by mud, and once again, he noted the clear, deep blue of a cloudless sky at dusk.

Then the odor of garlic wafted up to him, invading his nostrils and sending him straightening with alacrity. He towered before her, arms crossed, feet spread, his intention to intimidate her apparent.

Merlyn, too, was caught up in something she didn't quite understand for fleeting moments. His hands on her shoulders, his very fine green-brown eyes looking into hers with something more than impatience and hostility ... or was it her fevered imagination?

And then he stood so quickly, as if he couldn't bear touching her and had remembered that fact belatedly.

The garlic, you wantwit! 'Tis hardly attar of roses ... or do you seek to charm him?

"We have apples and berries and nuts and ... a hare or two," she said with dull—and inexplicable—disappointment. "And fish from the Tees—" she inclined her head toward the east side of the village. "And turnips ... They grow about the edges of the fields, reseeding without our help."

"What about boar?" Roger asked. "Boar abound in England. Good eating, and plenty of meat for more than one meal ..."

She slanted him a sly look. "Are ye tryin' to trick me into admitting we've been hunting in the *king's* forest?"

"Nay. I'm being practical. Who among your people would ever betray you for trying to stay alive?"

Merlyn's gaze lowered. "We've tried fattening boar on acorns—the precious little that aren't immediately eaten—and thus far, they've only managed to grow plump and *still* evade our spears." She wouldn't tell them about their pitiful stores buried beneath the ground ... or the few hens and one precious rooster.

"No pigs or sheep?"

She shook her head, willing away a sudden, unwelcome urge to weep. "Butchered, most of them . . . or scattered through the *weald.*"

There was something about her slumped shoulders as she spoke that affected Rolf in a way he hadn't anticipated. He hunkered down before her, taking scant notice of the other men drifting away to their tasks. "Would you like boar meat for supper, Merlyn?"

"Aye! With *your* eyes in its head on a serving dish, fool, for your duke will strike you blind if you hunt his boar!"

"If he learns of it, then 'twill be your doing."

She gave him a strange, considering look, briefly torn between the thought of succulent roast boar and the fact that the man who was offering it to her was her mortal enemy.

"I'll kill you a boar, old woman," he said quietly. "To feed Raven, and—'"

"Only to have you discover our camp when we light a fire to roast it, Norman? I think not!"

"Do you really think that you can hide from us? We are not so inept as that. And neither are we deaf. You'd have to behead that self-inflated cock to keep him silent in the morn. . . . Nor are we stupid. What use to kill the very people whom I've been sent to rule? What is a baron—or a thane—without his people?"

She sent a stabbing glance at him before she bent her head again and said with soft vehemence, "You are the enemy!"

Rolf shook his head, more to dispel the stink of garlic—which was making his eyes cross, or so it felt—than in disagreement. "None of us in this party is your enemy. Unless . . ." He paused deliberately.

Merlyn lifted her one-eyed gaze to his with curiosity. Why, he had *tears* in his eyes. . . .

'Tis the garlic, fool. . . .

51

". . . you raise your hand against us."

He stood then, before the tears could dribble down his cheeks. "By the rood, woman, *must* you wear that foul-smelling amulet?"

"It wards off disease, Norman," she told him flatly. "And other, more offensive things . . ."

But Rolf wouldn't take the bait for once. "Rolf. My name is *Rolf*, not Norman, and you'll call me as such." His patience was fast fading. "And you weren't wearing it yesterday."

"The cord was brok—"

"Never *mind!* Do you want boar or nay?"

"Will ye share with us, *my lord Wolf* . . . or will ye slay two animals while ye're about it?"

My lord Wolf? Rolf had the distinct feeling that she was laughing at him, and it irritated him in the extreme. Who did she think he was? Some Norman serf who had bread for brains and mush for muscle?

He opened his mouth to deliver a scathing reply, then realized how silly he was being. What was his reputation to this woman? This woman and her people, who had lost everything, no matter if it was because of their rebellion against Norman rule . . . They, no doubt, had never invited the Scots or the Danes into Northumbria to terrorize them, and there were quiet but distinct echoes of disapproval of the unheard-of barbarity William had employed in northern England. Rolf had even heard William's brutal campaign in the north branded as "an act which leveled both the bad and the good in one common ruin." In other words, some believed that William had carried his quelling of the rebellions too far; thus, as was obvious to anyone who cared to notice, the literal wiping out of an entire generation of English and the making of a desert of the land.

And what matter if she anglicized Rolf to Wolf? his

52

reasonable side persisted. *After all, haven't you been speaking in English since you arrived?*

The look on Rolf's face as he pondered these things (while still straddle-stanced before Merlyn) made her wonder if she had pushed him too far this time. His sword belt with sheathed sword and dagger were still about his waist, even though he was clad only in chainse and braies. It would take little to cleave her head from her body if he chose to do so. She'd seen it happen before . . . for less reason than she'd just given him.

Merlyn rose to her feet, then felt his hands taking hers. How odd, she thought, that he should help her. Unless . . .

She tilted her head toward him, studying him suspiciously through her tumbled hair and mud-tipped lashes, her hands instantly curling into claws like the gnarled old crone she was portraying, her back remaining semi-stooped.

This one, she reaffirmed in her mind, was going to make her life hell on earth. No matter how bad it was now, it would only get worse. She suspected that, even were she not affecting a disguise, she and this Wolf would mix like oil and water.

And he had no interests but his own. His reputation. His prowess. His wealth, of a certainty, as well. Wasn't that why his bastard duke had invaded and conquered England? For wealth and power . . .

Mother of God, she thought bleakly as she turned her head toward Renford and caught sight of the two sandy-haired brothers talking to several of their men. Why Rolf de Valmont instead of Roger or Hugh de Conteville? Why? . . .

The thicket immediately behind them quivered as if coming to life, then parted. Elsa stepped into their

53

midst, like a fragile, pale-haired queen, the grandmother of the late Stigand of Renford. She blinked in the bright sunlight, yet maintained a dignity born of blood ties to Alfred the Great and years of experience turned into wisdom.

She looked unflinchingly at each man, then Merlyn, before her pale gaze returned to Rolf. "I am Elsa," she said without hesitation. "And now you owe Merlyn another sack of food."

Rolf knelt for the final blow. There was absolute silence around him, as Hugh and two others stood stock-still. Even the two hounds were quiet, expectant, although they stood stiff-legged, their teeth still bared, their hackles raised.

The boar, more than nine hands high and obviously well fed, leveled his piercing porcine stare at the man across the clearing from the thicket where he'd been sheltering. From this distance, his four small, sharp tusks gleamed dully in the muted forest light . . . lethal weapons capable of tearing a man into pieces.

Suddenly, it came charging at Rolf, its small red eyes fastened on his face as it roared its life-or-death challenge. Rolf braced himself automatically for three or four hundred pounds of animal to slam into him.

His senses were at key pitch. Excitement thundered through his veins, his hunter's instincts honed to perfection as he locked eyes with his quarry.

The ground shook as the boar's short, powerful legs and hooves pounded the earth, plunging him toward his enemy. Its pale tusks were a blur now, and its coarse, grayish black hair stood on end in a menacing ridge that ran from between its ears to halfway down its back.

It was fast and ferocious . . . outweighing the man before it by two hundred pounds. It was also fighting for its life.

Rolf felt sweat beading his brow, his palms were moist from the warmth of the late day and his own exhilaration. *Easy, easy, easy.* . . . he told himself as the distance between him and the boar closed.

And then it was striking, hurtling its long body straight at him, jaws gaping beneath its ugly, sneering snout.

Just as the tip of Rolf's lance was inches from the boar's head, a crow flapped its wings directly overhead. As the animal's fetid breath seared across Rolf's face, as his lance tip penetrated the front of its mouth, it unexpectedly lurched its head upward toward the distracting flurry overhead, as if sensing another danger besides the man.

The spasmodic movement of its heavy body forced Rolf to tilt his lance toward its chest. His crouch all but destroyed, he felt his feet pulled from under him as the beast soared over him, catching one of his arms with its wicked tusks.

He rolled to the right and scrambled to his feet, prepared to finish with his dagger. As he unsheathed it, however, the boar hit the ground with a mighty shriek and collapsed, huffing horribly in its death throes.

Hugh stepped in quickly to end its suffering.

"God's wounds!" Rolf swore, looking down at his bloodied arm. It was numb now, but he knew from experience that pain was only moments away. And his right arm, yet . . . Of all the foul luck.

"Even the cursed crows are hostile in this godforsaken place," he grumbled under his breath. He walked over to Hugh and set his right foot to the boar's shoulder while he pulled out the lance with his left hand.

"You insisted on killing both boars," Hugh reminded him as he peeled back the sleeves of Rolf's tunic and chainse to examine his arm. "Myles or I could have taken this one . . . or even the one you killed earlier."

Rolf glared at him from the cover of his lashes before lowering his gaze briefly to his bloodied arm. "What? And take away my only reward thus far for becoming a baron?" Silently, however, beneath his half-serious quip, he was desperately trying to hide his aversion to the sight of his own blood. God's teeth, but he had the stomach of a woman! He was inured to battlefields strewn with gore and mangled corpses, yet a glimpse of his own blood could make him queasy. So rather than have his wounds seen to immediately, he tended to ignore them—at least the more minor ones—for as long as he could get away with it.

No one knew—not even Hugh—of this weakness . . . or if he did, he never let on. But that was Hugh's way and one of the reasons Rolf loved him like a brother. Why couldn't he be more like Hugh? Hugh wouldn't vomit at the sight of his own blood, Rolf knew from experience.

"You've the courage of ten, *mon ami,*" Hugh was saying to him as Bryce and Miles came up to truss the boar. "And the common sense of a green youth." The hounds eagerly sniffed around the dead animal, growling softly in the face of their dead prey as Rolf dragged his eyes from his arm and looked at Hugh. He could never take offense at anything Hugh said.

"Because I took one away from you?" Rolf said churlishly, then acknowledged how childish he sounded.

Hugh laughed softly and met his frowning gaze. "Nay, Rolf de Valmont. Rather because you could have robbed Renford of its new lord." His smile dimmed. "And they need you so very badly."

"And why do you think I *did* this?" he asked, suddenly feeling inexplicably guilty.

Hugh glanced up at him again, his eyes bright with rue. "You'll not be much good now, friend, in any capacity, until you're healed." He glanced at the other two men struggling to lift the branch to which the boar was now tied by its legs. "Can you make it to the village?" Hugh asked them.

Before either could answer, Rolf broke in, "Nay! We go to the Anglo-Saxon camp. I would give this to the crone *myself*."

So fierce was the look on Rolf's face that Hugh, obviously deciding to concede to his friend's authority in his own barony, nodded his head before easing Rolf's arm back to his side. "Shall I go with you?"

"Nay. I've Bryce and Myles. You can take the dogs."

The sun was getting low, the *weald* darkening with growing shadows as Merlyn combed the last of the tangles from her damp hair with her fingers. She was taking an enormous chance, she knew, especially with Valmont and his men staying in Renford. But to Merlyn, a clean face and hair was worth the risk, at least once in a while. The stain had to wear off, but the taint of garlic . . . She made a face. By the end of the day, she felt as if they would bury her in a shroud of garlic skins.

Her belly rumbled, and she remembered the sack of food Elsa had earned them. Its contents were long gone.

Just then, Raven came crawling over to her mother, obviously trying to make as little noise as possible, but also spurred on by fear. "Mamma," she whispered as Merlyn scooped her into her arms. "Bryan bid me tell you they're coming!"

Her words sounded strident in the sudden silence that enveloped them.

Merlyn tensed. "Who's coming?"

"The Wolf . . . an' two others. Bryan said we should slay 'em, for they are only three, but Cedric said nay!"

Sweet Mary, Merlyn thought, panic surging through her. "Stay here," she ordered the little girl softly, and pressed her against the interior of the end of the log.

Clutching the blanket about her, Merlyn dug her fingers into the damp humus from around her feet, smearing it over her face and neck. She threw her long tresses forward, grabbed another clump of soil and leaves, and raked it with desperate movements through her hair.

With one last hurried look at Raven, she hunched her shoulder and awkwardly made her way to where the child had pointed. Her left eye was free of its mud pack, but was burning and tearing beyond belief from irritation. The flesh around it felt warm and tight. Swollen.

I'll no doubt *really* lose it, she thought with a sense of fatalism, and all for naught.

Save your pity for the others.

She thought of those who depended on her and, once again, drew upon an inner wellspring of strength and resolve.

He was standing in the dying light of day, a dark

58

silhouette against a dimming background. Most of her people never ventured about the forest at night, for fear of wolves and spirits.

But not *him*.

"Merlyn?"

His voice sounded low and raspy, as if he was tired . . . or hurt.

Her tongue clove to the roof of her mouth for a moment, for if he so chose, he could destroy them all, pitiful lot that they were now.

'Tis too late.

"Aye, Norman. What can ye want here? Get thee to your bed and leave us in peace." *How did you find us?* she screamed silently, but held her tongue. He'd spoken the truth earlier in the day when he'd told her that he and his men were not stupid.

". . . brought you fresh boar," he was saying quietly.

Stars sprinkled the sky, winking down at her . . . dimples of laughter dotting the heavens, Stigand used to tell her.

There are no smiles in the sky this night, only stars as cold and distant as death, and standing beneath them, a stranger . . . an enemy of immense strength, his numbers legion. . . . He has only to send a message to his duke.

"We want naught from you."

One of the men at his side shifted. Alarm went skittering down her spine. She hoped to God that he couldn't make her out clearly in the crepuscular light.

"Elsa has no such qualms."

His audacity was outrageous, and Merlyn could have sworn that she'd heard a muffled sound of levity behind her. Impossible. Her people had forgotten how to laugh.

59

"Why must *you* remain here?" she asked, voicing her innermost thoughts.

"You'd rather accept fresh meat from Hugh or Roger?" His tone was a mixture of disbelief and . . . amusement. He remained standing where he was, however, squinting against the encroaching darkness.

"They are . . ." She stilled, afraid of offending him once more as caution reasserted itself.

"They are both barons in their own right—one in Normandy, one in the south of England. They have other obligations . . . and families."

His voice sounded weaker, as though speaking was an effort, yet his words had the definite ring of authority. In the silence that stretched between them, personal pride and a sense of responsibility waged a ferocious battle inside Merlyn.

"As much as you may hate me, old woman, you could do much, much worse. I would advise you to consider accepting me as your new lord . . . and persuading the others to do the same."

With that, he turned on his heel and began to walk toward Renford, still flanked by his two men. "Enjoy your boar, Merlyn," he threw over his shoulder before he disappeared into the trees. "And light your fire. You'll find boar meat tastes much better roasted."

Chapter 4

The rooster crowed, and Merlyn nestled deeper into the blanket, her mind still steeped in dreams of the mouth-watering aroma of roast boar, the tantalizing taste of it, the indescribable contentment of a full stomach.

She instinctively pulled Raven closer in her sleep, instead of being jerked into awareness and the ever-present fear that normally haunted her sleeping hours as well as her waking ones.

Your new lord, Rolf de Valmont, will protect you.... We bring you supplies with which to rebuild your village....

Round and round the words went in her head, oddly reassuring.

We'll not harm you—any of you.... You could do much, much worse.... Enjoy your boar, Merlyn.... Enjoy your ...

"Merlyn, wake up!"

It was Elsa.

"What is it?" Merlyn hissed in alarm, almost bumping her head on the side of the log, so quickly did she waken and sit up.

Raven stirred and whimpered softly in her sleep.

Elsa put a bony hand upon Merlyn's arm. "Naught is amiss, child. But you've slept too long on your full belly." She grinned with genuine humor, revealing several missing teeth.

"And you've not smiled thus in many months, Elsa," Merlyn answered, putting one hand to her stiff back. "Good food agrees with you, too."

Elsa's gaze rested briefly on Raven. "And the wee one, as well." She looked back at Merlyn. "'Tis time to go see what our Wolf is up to in the village. Bryan has already—"

"Bryan?"

"Aye. He gave his word to Cedric that he wouldn't reveal himself until he spoke to you."

"Nay. He will do something utterly foolish and give me away. . . ."

"He cares for you, child."

"He will get me—all of us—killed with his quick temper and arrogance. And what do we really know of him? He's from across the river . . . from Lexom. We know little of him or those with whom he lived."

As she spoke, Merlyn slipped from the tattered blanket about her body and struggled into her own clothing. A sharp pain stabbed through her back and she bit her lip, her motions ceasing for a moment. God, how she hated this moldy, decaying shelter! She'd cleaned it out as best she could, but it was damp and chill and smelly. Raven had sneezing fits every morn.

She felt Elsa's eyes upon her, pulling her from her musings. But the old woman only said, "Let Raven sleep while you're gone."

Merlyn nodded, grimacing at the smell of garlic emanating from the clothing. Lastly, she lifted the small pouch containing the offensive bulbs from beneath an oiled skin cover and slipped the cord over her head.

Afraid of waking Raven with the potent smell, she crawled from the log. Elsa handed her a small chunk of cold boar meat and a wedge of rather dry cheese the Normans had given them the day before. Merlyn washed it down with water, then hurried to finish the hastily begun job on her hair and face the night before.

Elsa took hold of Merlyn's chin and tipped her face toward the morning light. "The eye should be kept clean now. We don't want it to fester."

"I can wear a patch," Merlyn said.

"Or you can leave it as it is. 'Tis red and swollen. With your hair hanging over it, they'll be none the wiser . . . especially if they haven't guessed by now."

Merlyn's gaze met the older woman's, a frown drawing her dark, slender brows together. "If they suspected, why wouldn't they have said so?"

Elsa shrugged. "What harm for now? I think they know . . . except for our Wolf. . . ."

"He may be *your* wolf, but he's not mine!"

"And it won't be long before he guesses," Elsa continued, as if Merlyn hadn't spoken. "I heard the tone of his words yestereve." She watched as Merlyn adjusted her clothing so that she could bend forward.

"Cedric?" Elsa called over her shoulder.

The man came limping toward them, a crude crutch beneath his left arm. "Aye?"

Marthe followed in his wake, and Merlyn could not believe how quickly the woman's love interests changed. As soon as Bryan was absent from the camp, the mouselike widow shadowed Cedric.

"What think you of padding to make Merlyn appear stooped? Her back ails her after hours of holding such an unnatural position."

"'Tis a good idea," Cedric agreed. "Yet what if it

slips . . . even gives her away?"

"Oh, aye," breathed Marthe, her eyes like saucers. "Your hump could end up round your backside, or—"

One corner of Cedric's mouth quivered, something unheard of these last months. But Merlyn was impatient with the other woman. "Or I might even stumble over it!" she said with exaggerated horror.

"We can make it much more secure than that," Elsa said, casting a look at Marthe.

And so, with Cedric's "Have a care with Bryan, Merlyn" echoing in her mind, she walked the short distance to Renford without her mud plaster and with a new hump.

"And see what ails our Wolf," Elsa had advised her. "He was hurt."

Hurt? What did she care? Mayhap he would die, then they would all go away and . . .

And what? Leave you to the Scots or Norman deserters? Or land-hungry Danes?

"We can—we *will*—rebuild," she muttered under her breath. "We need no one, and least of all the Normans."

But deep down, she wasn't at all convinced, and a niggling worry made her move, hump and all, more quickly than was her wont as Merlyn the crone.

He was herding the two cows into a newly thatched shed with small pen outside the manor house. His right arm hung limply at his side, while he wielded a stick like a mighty sword with his left.

"*Allez . . . allez-y*," he commanded the animals as if they were his men-at-arms. The first cow, a brindle, looked at him with its large, dark eyes and continued to calmly chew its cud.

"What's her name, my lord?" Bryce asked him, holding a nail between his teeth as he made certain the fence about the shed was secure.

Rolf glanced over at him, bemused. "Name?"

"Aye." The squire removed the nail and gestured toward both cows. "It seems to me that they mind better if you use their names . . . just like the hounds."

"Ah. I see. And have we named our chickens as yet, Bryce?"

Bryce flushed. "That I do not ken, Lord Rolf. Don't know much about . . . fowl." He turned away, as if he'd said enough.

"Merlyn."

Bryce turned back. "My lord?"

"We'll name her Merlyn . . . what think you?"

"Excellent choice," commented Myles, who was putting finishing touches on the shed itself.

Bryce raised his eyebrows and nodded, then grinned. "Aye. She has a lump between her shoulders. . . ."

"And she's obstinate as an ass," Rolf agreed. "Just like her namesake."

Myles grinned from ear to ear as he continued his task.

Bryce, obviously warming to the game, scratched his head. *"Voyons* . . . let's see . . ." He bent over with an exaggerated squint at the cow's underside. *"Eh bien,* she's got—"

"Udders!" Merlyn snapped from behind them, ire overcoming caution. "Where do you think the milk comes from?" She'd crept up on them, astonished at how easily she'd accomplished it. "And where are your guards? I sneaked up behind you as easily as up to a sleeping babe, and ye were so busy making jests that ye never noticed. Why, what if I'd been a Scot bent upon mayhem?"

Rolf leaned the tip of his staff on the ground and stared at her, deciding upon another tack. "Scots don't send old women with humps into the woods on scouting missions." He smiled engagingly. Why not? It always worked on other women. Maybe he could soften her up.

"I see ye take your new position as lightly as ye take marauding and conquest."

The charming smile slid from his face and was replaced by a scowl. "We combed the woods around Renford yesterday. I would never have left your camp unguarded last night—let alone my own—had we not already secured the area."

To her dismay, she realized she hadn't thought of that. They'd been so overjoyed to have fresh meat—to be able to light a fire and cook it and also keep the wolves away—that they had been careless. Careless in the same manner that she'd accused him and evidently been wrong . . . In assuming the enemy to be the Normans, they'd neglected to consider other, even more threatening dangers beyond the light of their precious fire. In the wake of Rolf de Valmont's offering, she'd relaxed her guard. And so had the others.

"Where are my lords Hugh and Roger?" she asked, seeking to change the subject. She stepped forward before Rolf could answer, saying something unintelligible to the brown cow behind the brindle, then slapping it on the flank. The animal placidly walked into the pen, and the brindle followed.

Unthinkingly, Rolf cradled his right arm while he studied, with narrowed eyes, first Merlyn and then the cows.

"What happened to your arm?" Merlyn asked.

"'Tis just a scratch," he answered, essaying to

66

discover just how she'd accomplished the penning of the cows. Was she a witch, with a bizarre incantation she'd mumbled? Hadn't she said her mother was a healer? Hah! More likely a witch . . .

"Where are you from?" he asked suddenly. "You're dark-complexioned, not fair like the Saxons or Danes. And your hair—"

"—is rather like yours," she cut him off. "And yours isn't blond like your Viking ancestors. Where are *you* from?"

"I asked you first, you viper-tongued crone!" he said shortly, his thoughts of charming her forgotten. "And obviously, since you're so fond of calling me Norman, you must believe that I hail from Normandy."

Ignoring his second comment, she told him, "I am part Welsh. . . . I told you my mother was a healer."

"And to some, there is little difference between a healer and a witch." He stepped closer to her, then caught the now-familiar but still repulsive odor of garlic and checked himself. "As I remember, you put a curse on us when we first arrived."

Merlyn was relieved that he'd halted his steps, for she felt particularly vulnerable without her "mud poultice" to hide her left eye and part of her cheekbone. His looks were becoming increasingly suspicious, and Merlyn got the distinct impression that he missed nothing when he studied her as he was doing now. "If I tell you that I'm a witch, will you leave here?"

"Nay," he answered softly, "but I may have you burned alive."

He watched with contrary satisfaction as the blood left her face . . . her rather youthful face, in spite of the dirt and snarled hair . . . and the way she held her features unnaturally skewed as if her life depended on it.

"I put no curse on you or the others when first you arrived," she told him in a cackling voice with less than her usual bravado. "I merely told you to leave before you became cursed as we were. The entire land is cursed."

"What did you say to the cow, then?"

She looked blank for a moment, and her features relaxed a little in her confusion. "Oh . . ." she said belatedly. "Why, 'twasn't *what* I said, but rather to *which* cow I said it. She was the lead cow. . . ."

Rolf, more concerned about the strange words he'd thought he'd heard than as insignificant a matter as one cow over another, repeated, "What did you *say* to the cow?"

"Why, I spoke to her in the tongue of the Cymry."

"Welsh."

"Aye."

Bryce, who'd begun stacking hay for the cows, glanced sideways at Myles. *"Ces vâches Anglaises sont bien intelligentes, n'est-ce pas, si elles comprennent le Gallois."*

Myles roared with laughter, startling Merlyn, and Rolf grinned at Bryce's words, especially since the joke was on Merlyn and her bilingual cows. In fact, he would have laughed outright himself if he suddenly hadn't felt so *warm*. He glanced up at the sky. It was a mild but overcast day . . . and he'd done little this morn because of his arm, save try to herd the two cows into the pen. Why was he sweating as if he were in full armor?

". . . are my lords Roger and Hugh?" she asked him once more, choosing to ignore their hilarity since the jest was obviously at her expense.

"Lexom." He sat down on a discarded fence rail, feeling dizzy. He ran his left arm across his forehead.

68

"Have we any water?" he mumbled to Bryce, feeling suddenly like someone had clubbed him with a mace. His eyes burned, too.

As Bryce poured him a cup of water, Merlyn cautiously hobbled closer.

His eyes met hers over the rim of the cup. "Sweet Jesu, wench, get rid of that pagan amulet!" he said irritably, feeling faint. Then an idea came to him through the fog. "'Tis my arm, undoubtedly," he muttered, slanting her a sly glance from lowered lids. "Hugh neglected to examine it before he left for Lexom." The truth was, Rolf hadn't allowed Hugh near his arm that morning. He'd told his friend that it could wait until Roger and he returned later in the day, feeling squeamish at the thought of his own exposed wound that early in the morn . . . and before breaking the fast, yet.

Merlyn edged closer, suddenly concerned. She knew now that neither of the Conteville brothers could remain in Renford, much as she might prefer it. And if Rolf de Valmont perished, surely William the Bastard would send someone infinitely more un-desirable . . . more undesirable even than *him*.

Rolf watched her approach from beneath his lashes, like a wolf eyeing a helpless hare sniffing at a beckoning patch of greenery.

He handed Bryce the empty cup and glanced up at Merlyn guilelessly.

She caught the full force of his splendidly hewn features: the deep-set hazel eyes beneath thick dark lashes, the proud jut of his nose and chin, his high cheekbones, now fever-flushed. And his beautiful, sulky mouth.

Merlyn would have wagered her new hump that he'd left a long trail of trampled hearts back in Normandy.

"Your wife should be caring for you and not I," she said, suddenly needing to know if he had a spouse in Normandy for whom he would eventually send.

"Is that an offer?" he asked with a lazy smile, enjoying the leisurely study he was afforded as Bryce helped him remove his tunic. He concentrated on Merlyn's face, rather than his lacerations, as she scrutinized his lower arm. "You'll forgive me if I prefer younger, cleaner . . . and pleasantly perfumed wenches, won't you?"

But Merlyn's attention was on his injuries. With gentle fingers hard pressed to keep their unnatural, clawlike positions, she pushed back his chainse sleeve. "Even were I younger," she muttered, "there's no need for fragrance in hell, Norman. If 'tis powdered and perfumed ye want, go back to Normandy."

She looked up at Bryce. "It festers . . . at least what I can see. Boar tusks are filthy . . . small wonder he's fevered."

Myles, not as tactful as Rolf's young squire, looked over and said bluntly, "And small wonder if he's not punished by my lord William for killing a boar for you. And I heard naught of thanks last eve, either."

Guilt colored Merlyn's cheeks beneath the grime. "Our thanks, my lord, for the food you provided . . . and from your wagons, as well."

Rolf watched the color creep into her face with unwilling fascination, noting, once again, how smooth her skin looked beneath the dirt, even though it was dark as walnut stain. . . .

Walnut stain?

He reached out to touch one of her hands as she carefully probed the swollen flesh of one edge of the longer gash. Merlyn jumped, losing her balance and falling backward as memories of rape rampaged

70

through her mind in the wake of his gesture.

"Don't touch me, Norman, or ye'll rue the day!" she threatened with an uncronelike squeak, her voice shaking, as she scrambled back.

Through a haze of discomfort, Rolf was not only taken aback by her swiftness, but by the violence of her reaction as well.

He'd also caught a glimpse of slender calf and ankle . . . pale as alabaster, not swarthy like her face, neck, and hands.

He sensed a strong fear—no, a *terror*—in the woman who called herself Merlyn, and for the first time since meeting her, Rolf wondered exactly what had happened to her in the recent past.

He also wondered why she was trying to disguise her appearance.

Merlyn scrambled to her feet, her face flushed with anger at herself. She was trembling like a leaf and furious at her overreaction. Nonetheless, however, she was ready to retreat to the "safety" of the Saxon camp.

"Merlyn," Rolf began, attempting to make up for his inadvertently bold gesture.

She held up one palm toward him, as if to ward him off, and crept backward toward whence she'd come. "You can wait until they return from across the river," she said, "for I must go back. . . ."

"What?" the blond giant, Myles, said, straightening from his work. He moved toward her, his patience obviously at an end. Merlyn froze to the spot, her will temporarily deserting her. As his huge hand clamped about her upper arm, he said, "They could be gone for hours, old woman. If Rolf suffers from a festering wound, 'tis because of his efforts to feed you. By all the saints, you owe him at least the consideration of tending him!"

71

His pale blue eyes were icy cold beneath the shock of his white-blond hair, and Merlyn stared up at him in awe, slack-jawed.

"Now, Myles, you'll frighten her to—" Rolf began.

"Unhand her, you filthy Viking!"

The voice penetrated Merlyn's brain. God help them all . . . Bryan.

She craned her neck toward the woods, feeling gooseflesh rise at the sight of him advancing toward them with a rusty-tined pitchfork.

He would have looked comical if his face hadn't been contorted with rage. And the proof of his temper through this foolhardy behavior brought reason rushing back to Merlyn.

"Don't harm him," she appealed to Rolf, who had heaved himself to his feet. "He's but a youth and—"

"I'm a man grown, Merlyn," Bryan snarled, and stepped closer to Myles. "Release her *now*, before I skewer you and roast you like your boar!"

Merlyn paled at his words. He was speaking to one of the Bastard's own, not some ill-trained farmer who couldn't wield anything more threatening than an ancient pitchfork.

Rolf grabbed his sword with his left arm and advanced straight toward Bryan. As he passed Myles, he said, *sotto voce*, "Let her go . . . and stay where you are."

Myles instantly obeyed.

When Rolf's sword was inches from Bryan's pitchfork, he spoke. "I am lord here, boy, and when you point a weapon at my man, you point it at me. Do you understand?"

Bryan's expression lost some of its ferocity as the gleaming tip of Rolf's sword loomed much too close for any sensible man's comfort. But he stubbornly clung to his pitchfork . . . and his anger. "Release her, and we'll leave," he insisted.

"And *you* drop the pitchfork," Rolf said softly.

Tense as the situation was, Merlyn was very aware of Rolf's quiet but steely authority. Gone was his impatience, his frustration at small setbacks, his erratic temper, replaced by the deadly calm of a man who knew exactly what he was doing; he exuded confidence. True, he had only a youth with a pitchfork as an adversary, but there was something about his stance, his attitude, his mien, that suggested to Merlyn that here was the reason William of Normandy had chosen Rolf de Valmont to secure and defend Norman lands in the rebellious north of England.

"Please, Bryan," Merlyn said. "I am unharmed."

Rolf cast her a look askance, a furrow skimming across his sweat-beaded forehead. "Is this your son?" he asked.

At the look of purest indignation that suddenly appeared on Bryan's face, Merlyn had the wildest urge to laugh aloud, then mastered it and got a grip on her wits. *Please, Bryan . . . don't tell them,* she exhorted silently.

In that moment, with an upward swipe of his sword, Rolf knocked the pitchfork from Bryan's hands. Bryce, who'd been standing at the ready, reached in to grab it and place it safely beyond Bryan's reach, while Myles placed his great hands on his hips and glowered at the Saxon youth.

"And I thought to be bored in Northumbria," Rolf muttered, more to himself than anyone else, "among other things." He handed his sword to Bryce, who replaced it in the scabbard leaning against the pen. "Lock him in the granary," he said to Myles.

"L—lock him?" Merlyn sputtered, her voice

dangerously close to its normal pitch and smoothness.

Rolf stepped toward her and shook a finger in her face. "Think you that I would be careless enough to let him roam free after he tried to skewer us?"

"But he's only a . . ." She let her words die as her eyes met Bryan's. Oh, yes, she thought. Proving his manhood was more important to him than protecting her identity.

The fury in Bryan's hazel eyes, in turn, fired her own anger. "Aye. He could have done much damage," she croaked. "'Tis better if he cools his heels in the granary."

Before Bryan could do anything but open his mouth, Myles was ungently propelling him toward the empty granary.

"Will you tend my lord?" Bryce asked her, his worried gaze going to his master, who had reseated himself on the ground, his head resting on his uninjured arm crossed over updrawn knees.

"Aye," she said after a moment's hesitation. "If he gives his word not to touch me."

Rolf raised fever-bright eyes. "You have it," he said.

"Then I'll need clean water and cloths," she told Bryce, and began to gather kindling for a small fire, acutely conscious of the man who sat watching her unwaveringly.

"He isn't ready for this."

Hugh smiled at his brother's words beneath the nosepiece of his steel helm as they forded the Tees River. "Oh, but I think he is. Baptism by fire, as they say, and long overdue. He needs only to learn a bit of patience and—"

74

"And how to deal with a conquered, bitter people . . . people who make their living from the soil, and not pillaging the property and spilling the blood of other men."

Hugh studied his brother as their horses, midnight and alabaster, splashed across the shallow ford. He'd changed so much during the last seven years or so. Well, maybe not changed, but grown . . . in patience and compassion and tolerance. Some of that, Hugh acknowledged to himself, surely had come of marriage and children. But, also, his role as Lord of Derford had brought out the best in him, qualities that had always been there.

If someone had told Hugh years ago that Roger would be lord of two Anglo-Saxon villages, wed to a Saxon woman, and very successful, Hugh would have agreed that his twin could do it. But the degree to which Roger had accepted his "people" and they him was nothing short of a miracle. A miracle performed within a few short years, not a lifetime or generations.

"As you learned, Roger, and you were renowned for the very traits you vilify in Rolf. In, perhaps, all Normans."

Roger looked over at Hugh, then halted Odo on the southern bank. He removed his helm and wiped the sweat from his dripping forehead. As he began to unfasten his mail coif, Hugh followed suit.

"If Lexom is as badly off as Renford, I think we're roasting needlessly," Roger said, then was thoughtfully silent a moment. "Was I quite as . . . arrogant as Rolf? Quite as disdainful of aught that wasn't Norman?"

Hugh looked him straight in the eye and answered, "Worse."

Roger laughed aloud. "Was I truly?" He ran the

fingers of one hand through his hair, his smile slowly fading. "But things are so very bad here. . . ."

Hugh nodded. He reached forward and stroked Styx's silky ebony neck, a thoughtful expression on his features. "Aye, worse than I've seen anywhere. But there is a compassionate side to Rolf. . . ."

"No doubt because of his long association with you."

This time Hugh grinned. "No doubt." He dismounted and led Styx to the edge of the Tees to drink. "I believe Rolf will be good for these poor souls," he said, his gaze off in the distance as the stallion drank, "and they for him. They will teach him all he needs to know of things besides war."

"I hope you're right, *mon frère*," Roger said, coming up beside him. "There are such deep wounds to heal in any conquered land, but perhaps the very severity of the situation here—the need of these people for a leader and Rolf's need for stability—will work to everyone's advantage."

Hugh nodded. "Everyone's advantage save the Scots—or any other interlopers. You know what a fine warrior Valmont is . . . always was. The years since we were last in England have served to make him one of William's best, his skills honed to perfection while keeping Normandy's enemies at bay on the continent. Maine and Anjou and Flanders . . . and now France itself."

Roger nodded. "He will have any number of opportunities to prove his prowess with sword and lance, his mastery of strategy. But the real test will be in dealing with everyday problems—naught so exciting as the life of a chevalier."

"He will do it and do it well, mark me." Hugh slapped Roger's shoulder as their gazes met. "If you return to Renford two summers hence, things will be vastly different . . . and for the better."

Roger shrugged. "You know him better than I, although I think I'm a fair judge of men. If he will do so well, perhaps William will grant him the entire earldom of Northumbria."

"Or mayhap England, itself," Hugh said, his gray eyes alight with amusement.

"Aye. With Merlyn as his first lady."

Both men burst into laughter at the thought, sharing the jest within the close bond of brotherhood that time and distance couldn't diminish, nor the prospect of not seeing each other again for years, if at all.

"Let's get this over with, shall we?" Hugh said as he went to remount Styx. "By the time we return, Rolf will be begging me to treat his arm."

After they'd sobered, Roger was silent for a while again, nodding absently at Hugh's remark about Rolf. "There is more to Merlyn than meets the eye," he said.

"Indeed. You've had more experience with rebellious—terrified—Anglo-Saxons. What do you think?"

Odo flung his head aside, splattering Roger with droplets of river water. "Odo and I believe," he said as he gave the horse a look of feigned disapproval before wiping water from one cheek, "that beneath the garlic and the grime, she is a comely wench with enough courage for three. If Rolf can win her over, his task will be easier by far."

Hugh glanced over at Roger. "I'd wager that she was the wife of someone important . . . like the thane. Her protectiveness toward the few souls left is nothing short of heroic."

"Aye. And I have a feeling that she is as pretty as she is enterprising. . . . Look at Raven. Both are alike in hair and eye coloring, and Merlyn protects her as

77

fiercely as a female wolf her pup." He made to remount Odo. "How will Rolf take to being duped? And by a female?"

Hugh's gaze met that of his brother, an unholy gleam in his eyes. "I don't think he is. And I hope heartily that we'll still be here when *she* discovers her game is over."

Chapter 5

Rolf made it to the manor house unaided, but was grateful to lie down on a straw pallet in the cool, dim interior. The sound of hammers and the scrape of trowels, as several men worked at repairing the hall and making a few modifications, were only a distant buzzing in his ears.

"Have you any moldy bread?" Merlyn asked Bryce.

"Moldy bread?" he repeated, bemused.

"Aye. I can find some," Myles said, and strode toward the back of the hall.

"Build me a fire to boil water . . . quickly," Merlyn directed Bryce.

After one questioning look at her, then at Rolf's flushed face, the squire said, "There are always banked embers in the fireplaces," and hurried to do her bidding.

After a brief hesitation, Merlyn said to Rolf, "I need your knife to cut away the sleeve."

"Rather, I think, to slit my throat, *non?*"

Merlyn narrowed her eyes at him, feeling the urge to slap some sense into him. "I'm no murderess, Norman. I am Welsh and Anglo-Saxon. We do not kill for sport."

He closed his eyes for a moment, feeling too tired suddenly to spar with her. "'Tis in my belt."

She inched one clawlike hand toward its sheath, watching his face for any sign of change . . . for any change of heart. But he remained still, his long lashes shadowing his fever-dotted cheekbones as his eyes remained closed.

As soon as she began to slit his chainse sleeve, she felt his eyes on her again. But the swelling on his arm, which made her task all the more difficult, claimed her full attention.

"How old are you, Merlyn?" he mumbled, his gaze still on her face.

"Old enough to be your mother," she said. "Now close your eyes and save your strength."

When the sleeve was cut away, Merlyn glanced about for Bryce, her brow furrowed with concern. The youth was placing several clean cloths in a small pot he'd suspended over a now-active fire.

". . . not so weak as that," Rolf was saying in that high-handed tone she detested. "Hugh cleaned the wounds last eve and said he would look at them again when he returned," he said, without a qualm. What did it matter if he neglected to tell her the entire truth? She'd laugh him right back to Normandy if she knew of his weakness. If, that is, the old crone knew how to laugh.

What reason has she had to laugh? a voice asked him.

"Water," Merlyn said as Myles returned with a half loaf of green-black bread.

Rolf took one look at it and said, "God's teeth, man, where did you find *that?*"

"Someone left it for the mice," Myles answered with a lift of his eyebrows.

"No doubt the Scots," Merlyn said sourly as she set the bread beside her. "My people were too hungry to

80

leave half a loaf of bread uneaten.''

Rolf watched her minister to him, bleary-eyed as he was. But he only saw an old woman before him, and he was too uncomfortable to scrutinize her more carefully. He remembered the flash of pale leg, of smooth skin, but then her dark, tangled hair came into view—was it streaked with gray or mud?—and the smell of garlic invaded his nostrils. Judas! It was making his eyes tear.

He reached out with his wounded arm with a swiftness that caught Merlyn by surprise, grabbing the offending pouch in a death grip. Before Merlyn could move or speak, he'd jerked it free of her neck and tossed it toward the fire.

"'Tis making me retch," he gritted, turning his head away from both Merlyn and his arm.

"Lady Liane gave Rolf a small chest of medicines," Myles said.

Merlyn looked up at him expectantly.

"Roger's wife . . . she's Anglo-Saxon and knows much of these things," he explained. "Shall I bring it to you?"

"Aye. And bring me a cup of that boiling water, Bryce," she said over her shoulder in her cackling voice. "Then wring out several of the cloths and bring them here."

The cask of medicinals was a treasure to Merlyn— worth more than a basket of gold. She immediately picked out a bundle of willow bark, dropping several small pieces into the cup of hot water Bryce had placed beside her. "Willow bark," she said shortly.

"For pain?" Myles asked, his eyes on Rolf's face.

"Aye." She glanced up at the chevalier. "We will need to hold him down when I draw the—"

Rolf's eyelids snapped open. "Pin me down while you scald me? I think not!"

"Did I take your dagger to your throat, Norman?

Nay. Nor have I any intention of scalding you, but 'twill hurt."

"Think you that a chevalier of Duke William cannot take a little pain?"

Merlyn stirred the willow bark steeping in the cup of water without answering. Myles, however, put one hand on each of Rolf's shoulders, the set of his features grim. "'Tis for your own good, Valmont. *Tais-toi* . . . quiet now."

Merlyn lifted one of the rags with a smooth wooden wand she found among the medicines, held it aloft for a few moments while some of the steam rose into the air and curled toward the ceiling, then gingerly laid it over the two wrist-to-elbow gashes. Rolf started, but he bit his lip in an obvious effort to do no more. Merlyn carefully spread the cloth completely over the wounds, then looked at Rolf's face.

"I'm hale and somewhat hearty," he muttered, his face bathed in sweat.

"'Tisn't over yet," she informed him, ignoring his attempt at levity, then picked up the willow bark tea. "Lift his head and shoulders," she instructed Myles.

As she held the cup to Rolf's lips, he drank, his eyes locked with hers. "Drink it all," she ordered him, then motioned for Bryce to bring more water.

"Can you do the same with the other cloth?" she asked Myles. "We'll get Bryce to hold him down while—"

"I can control myself," Rolf insisted stubbornly.

"—I prepare the mold and the poultice," she finished as though he had never spoken. "Do it twice more."

Myles spoke to Bryce and the procedure was repeated, while Merlyn scraped the mold from the bread into a powder she caught with a small, empty mortar. After giving Rolf another cup of tea, Merlyn waited until the last cloth had been applied and removed. She sprinkled every last bit of the mold powder over both cuts, then applied a leaf-paste poultice over that.

Rolf wrinkled his nose. "Mold," he said disdainfully. "I suppose now my arm will be permanently green?"

Merlyn looked up from replacing the potions and unguents, herbs, bark, and wand in the medicine chest. "I could have used cobwebs, Norman. Fresh cobwebs from yon empty buildings, and 'twould have done just as fair a job."

"Thank you for sparing me that," he said, his eyelids growing heavy.

It was the last thing he remembered before he slipped into dreams of huge arachnids dancing around him like taunting eight-legged devils, draping him in shroudlike, suffocating webs.

When Rolf awoke, he thought at first that he was alone. He lay still for a moment, then realized he was thirsty. His mouth was dry as sand, but at least he wasn't feeling so unnaturally warm now.

Merlyn. Her hunched figure flashed in his mind's eye . . . an enigma if ever there was one: dark and pale, crippled and spry, ancient and youthful.

Witch. She was a witch, he thought with a frown. She was . . .

"So ye're awake, are ye?" a familiar voice cackled in his ear.

He started, the movement causing his arm to throb anew, but not nearly as badly as earlier. His eyes met hers—at least the one he could see, its twin hidden by the hank of hair hanging over one side of her face.

"Water," he rasped softly, catching the faint and familiar odor of garlic. "Bryce—?"

"—is busy, as is the giant. They've a village to rebuild . . . if any of you can be believed. Here . . ."

He raised his head and Merlyn slid an arm under his shoulders while he drank. He tried to study her face but she averted it, sloshing some of the water down his chin in the process.

"Are you giving me water or trying to drown me?" he asked darkly as, when the wooden cup was empty, she pulled her arm from beneath him with unnecessary haste. His head dropped to the pallet like a rock, causing his teeth to rattle. He muttered an oath, but Merlyn had already turned away to fuss among the assortment of vials and jars in Liane's donated chest.

The hall was deserted, as far as he could see. God's blood! Had they left him unguarded while *she* tended him? She could have slit his throat while he slept.

And been immediately put to death.

He ignored the voice of reason, wondering instead if he dared to sit up. He should have been out with Hugh and Roger or helping repair and rebuild the village, not lying abed like a helpless newborn with . . .

Save your pity for the English.

With Hugh's words whispering through his mind, Rolf attempted to sit up. Merlyn's fingers poked him in the chest like talons. Her strength was no match for his, but she had the advantage of surprise. He fell back before he could catch himself. His teeth snapped shut.

"God *damn* it, woman!" he roared. "What are you about . . . curing me or killing me?" He struggled to his elbows, the look on his face ferocious as he gritted his teeth against the searing pain shooting up his arm.

"I swear on my father's sword, if you touch me *once* more, I'll strangle you with your stinking garlic cord!"

84

"You burned it," she retorted, a flash of blue fire lighting her eye—or was he delirious?—before it was replaced by what looked like fear.

Merlyn scuttled backward to a safer distance in the face of his very real wrath. "Ye weigh as much as your brutish horse, Norman. Ye are thrice my size and weight, I wager. How can I be expected to hold ye like a babe?"

His expression relented slightly, although being considered as heavy as Charon wasn't exactly a compliment—unless one was a war-horse. "Why did you push me back down?"

"Ye cannot get up before morn."

His eyes widened and he opened his mouth to protest.

"Ask your Lord Hugh, then," she challenged. "If ye don't rest at least until the morrow, I'll not be responsible for your recovery."

He pointed one finger at her. *"You* are not responsible for aught I do." He stared at her, their gazes clashing, tension pulsating through the air. "Why are you doing this?" He canted his head toward his arm and then toward Liane's chest.

Merlyn shrugged lopsidedly but maintained her distance. "Ye gave us food last eve." She was silent a moment, her gaze going to the huge open doors through which portions of the forest could be seen, thus presenting him with the profile of the visible side of her face.

The purity of that profile was what absolutely gave her away to Rolf in that moment. There was no woman of her supposed age who could have presented so clean cut a chin, so dainty a tip-tilted nose, so sweet a mouth, and so delightful . . .

In her thoughts of Raven, not only had Merlyn turned her head to the side, but her expression softened of its own volition, the perpetual scowl easing. Completely oblivious of his scrutiny, she added quietly, "You saved Raven's life."

Thinking to catch her in that unguarded moment, he asked, "Is she your child?"

The question pulled her back to the situation. "Aye." Her gaze met his, and she scowled. "And so is Bryan, and Cedric, and Elsa, and every other miserable soul who looks to me for . . . something I cannot give them now."

His eyes held hers for long moments. "But mayhap *I* can."

One of the cows mooed plaintively from outside; the sound of pounding hammers and muted men's voices came to them from the roof of the hall and even farther away; birds shrilled from the treetops as if welcoming normal human activity once again.

Merlyn shook her head. "You and your kind are responsible for all this. The best thing you can do is to go back to Normandy."

"And leave you defenseless against the Scots—and anyone else who would rape England?"

"There's naught worth taking now," she said grimly, and swung away to move awkwardly toward the cauldron of water over the fire.

Rolf watched her, his expression thoughtful.

"Why are you called Merlyn?" he asked, in the wake of a new determination to prove her wrong in her assessment of what was best for her and her people, and thinking to steer the subject to safer ground.

"I know not." She steeped more willow bark in Rolf's cup, then added a dusting of another powder before stirring it.

"Your mother was a healer?" he asked as she handed him the tea.

"Aye."

"A legend says that once, long ago, there once was

another healer of sorts . . . a magician, a seer. He was advisor to Arthur, the Saxon king. His name was Merlin, too."

"I am familiar with the legend . . . I am English. Drink your tea while 'tis hot." She glanced at him through her tangled hair. "Merlin also means falcon."

"Small and fierce," he mused after his first few sips. "It suits you, I suppose. But 'tis still a strange name. . . ."

"So is Wolf . . . When are you going to release Bryan?" she asked unexpectedly.

"When he learns some manners." He yawned, feeling woozy and congenial. "Have you any sweet-tempered wenches about?" he asked. "And young? Who bathe in the river and brush their hair till it shines . . ."

He closed his eyes, succumbing to Merlyn's potion. "With sweet-scented skin and pretty names . . . like Brenna . . ."

The reverence with which he uttered the name, drowsy as he was, did something strange to Merlyn. Anger and resentment—and jealousy—rose within her breast. The latter she refused to acknowledge, but to the first two she gave free rein.

How could he speak of such things in a world that had been all but destroyed? How dare he wish for such frivolous things when men and women were fighting for their very existence every day?

And Brenna was a *Scottish* name, by God . . . another enemy.

His deep, even breathing told Merlyn that he was asleep. She narrowed her eyes as she studied his face at her leisure. A dark angel, this one, she thought. His sable hair looked black as night in the dim hall . . . and thick above where he'd shaved it off his neck. She'd seen fox-red highlights where the sun kissed it in the light of day, and a wave of unidentifiable emotion rippled through her.

His lips were parted slightly in his sleep to reveal even white teeth. Merlyn unconsciously ran her tongue over her own, tasting the film over them that made them look unappealing.

The Norman who had raped her had been bald and fat, with rotted teeth and rancid breath. The pressure of tears formed behind her eyes at the memory, and she squeezed her lids shut in an effort to block it out and stem the threatening flood.

She swung away hurriedly, anxious to get away from him and the disturbing effect he was having on her. She was just tired. And hungry again. And burning with resentment at his careless words about women.

Sweet Mary, but she wished she'd cracked his head hard enough to rattle his brains! Just enough to put them in proper order . . .

It never occurred to Merlyn as she hobbled out into the light of day that, for once, she hadn't wished him dead.

As Merlyn reached the edge of the forest, a flying body tackled her and sent her sprawling to the ground. She lay still a moment, trying to regain her wind . . . and guess who had thought her so great a threat as to flatten her without warning.

"Merlyn, be quiet!" Bryan commanded in her ear.

At the sound of his voice, the fleeting fear that it might have been a Scot or Norman deserter was immediately dispelled and replaced by anger. She struggled to sit up, pushing him from her with a mighty shove. "Get *off* me!" she said, her eyes narrowed at him. "What are you doing here? How did you get free?"

"No thanks to you! "Tis better if he cools his heels in the granary,'" he mimicked in a croaking voice. "Did you think a puny granary could contain me? I freed myself to come protect you."

"And I am not in need of your protection, Bryan Edmundson! We survived well enough before you came from—"

He grabbed her elbow and roughly steered her through the trees. "'Tis stupid to stand here and argue when *they* are about. We can get back to our camp and talk."

Merlyn balked, digging in her heels. "I won't be a party to your escape. They know exactly where to look for you, or have you forgotten so soon? You were willing enough to eat Lord Rolf's boar."

He released her arm. *"Lord Rolf?"* He gritted his teeth in obvious frustration, making those two words sound like an oath.

"Aye. And if you don't return to the granary, there will be a terrible price to pay, I tell you. We're dealing with Norman warriors who've been sent by the Bastard himself to restore order. They are now the law!" Merlyn thought of the power in Rolf's grip—and with his injured arm—as he'd grabbed the pouch of garlic and snapped it from her neck; of the speed and strength with which he'd relieved Bryan of the pitchfork. "They have hounds that can just as easily hunt a man as a buck or a boar. Would you want to be hunted like an animal?"

His expression bordered on doubtful for a moment, then returned to angry obstinacy. "You're afraid of them, but I'm not!"

She swung away then, refusing to argue futilely. "Merlyn," he said in her ear, his voice lowered. "I but seek to shield you. Why should you risk your life when—"

"Because Stigand was my husband. Most of these

89

are *my* people, and they look to me for leadership."

"A woman?"

She drew herself up straight, her hump jutting at right angles to her shoulders. "It can be done . . . has been done."

"You are no Boadicea."

She ignored his deliberate insult, wondering how he knew of that ancient queen. "If you don't hie yourself back to the granary, then I'll turn you over to them myself." Before he could reply, a sudden thought struck her, filling her with horror. "You didn't kill the guard, did you?"

Bryan's hazel eyes narrowed, and he tossed his dirty blond hair back from his face. "He was little more than a boy . . . a man-at-arms, so he boasted to me. 'Twas easy enough to win his trust and then dispose of him, Merlyn. You have so little faith in me."

"What do you mean *dispose* of him? And a lad, yet . . ." Terrible scenes of retribution flashed before her, knotting her stomach and causing her heart to pump painfully in her chest. So far they'd done little to anger Valmont and his party, but now, if one of the Normans lay wounded because of Bryan . . .

What use to kill the very people I've been sent to rule?

Rolf's words came back to her, shoring up her spirits somewhat. Surely she only had to tell them of Bryan's perfidy . . . that it was solely his doing. Mayhap she could even go the granary herself and tend the guard, if he was yet alive.

"Merlyn, I—I care for you," Bryan said, his voice softening, his eyes full of an emotion much warmer than anger.

She looked up at him, her thoughts disrupted. "You've a strange way of showing it, Bryan," she told him. "You could get us all killed with your foolish actions."

"Foolish . . ."

"Aye. Even more foolish than taking a pitchfork to the giant. Do you fear naught?"

"Not where you are concerned."

She shook her head, thinking him even more immature than before. "Then you are a bigger fool than I thought, for only fools and babes know naught of fear. Fear and caution do not signal a coward; my wise husband taught me that long ago." She turned back toward the road.

"Your wise husband is feeding the worms."

She swung back to him, her look so full of dislike that he relented. "I—I meant no disrespect. . . ."

"Then think before you speak, Bryan . . . in all things." She turned her back to him with an abrupt movement and began to walk away.

"Where are you going?"

"To see if I can help the man you hurt."

"What have you done to him?" inquired a deep— and forbidding—voice.

Apprehension feathered down Merlyn's spine as she held the young Norman's head in her lap. She slowly raised her eyes to Myles, searching for the right words.

"And to think we entrusted Rolf to your care," he added before turning to Bryce. "Stay with them," he told the youth, and strode toward the manor hall.

Merlyn looked at Rolf's squire. "I did nothing to him. . . ." She glanced down at the unconscious youth.

"Then who? . . . " He trailed off and looked into the open granary door. "Bryan—'tis his name, is it not?—did this if you didn't."

Torn between the inbred need to protect Bryan and the habit of telling the truth, Merlyn merely said,

"He will be fine. 'Twas merely a bump on the head."

Myles appeared at an open door of the manor and stepped into the light of day. He reached them with long, quick steps. "Rolf is asleep," he said, "and feeling cooler to the touch, as well." He glanced at the empty granary, then back at Merlyn. "You would shield the hothead? Attempt to make amends for his foul action?"

Merlyn couldn't meet his eyes, for wasn't she guilty of wanting to do exactly as Bryan had . . . and worse? "I am not responsible for Bryan's actions, Norman, but I would not see this lad harmed for following his lord's orders. The Wolf would, indeed, be a fool to allow Bryan his freedom in light of what he did."

"And where is your Bryan now?"

Merlyn bit her lip in hesitation, but Bryce answered, "No doubt hiding in yon woods."

"Or behind Elsa's skirts at the camp," Myles added with a twist of his lips.

"Let him be," Merlyn said. "I pray you, he'll not—"

"Think you that my lord William conquered England by treating treachery with kindness? Only a fool would be so careless."

Merlyn shook her head as her eyes met his. Hard pressed to keep her face screwed up (for her muscles were beginning to ache from the prolonged effort), she said in a thin, ragged voice, "I have no doubt that the Bastard would never resort to kindness. Ye have only to look around."

The unconscious man-at-arms stirred in her arms, claiming Merlyn's attention before Myles could respond.

But it was Bryce who spoke. "My lord Rolf would never allow a man who raised his hand to him to roam freely. He will be found and punished—as much for Sieur de Valmont as for Michael here."

"And I will take particular pleasure in skinning him alive," Myles warned, fingering his dagger thoughtfully.

Merlyn's face contorted with horror, for she had no reason not to believe what this giant threatened. Yet what could she do? Stigand would not have stood for a man who had threatened him—or any of his men—to remain at large; and especially after injuring his guard and escaping, no doubt, only to create more mayhem.

She looked down at Michael, who groaned softly as his lashes began to flutter. *Hasn't there been enough destruction and death here?* Merlyn silently asked a God who seemed to have turned his back on the English. *When will it ever end? When could they return to some semblance of normalcy?*

And, for the hundredth time, she wondered why the enemy had been sent to them, when all of York and Durham was in ruins.

The most ironic twist, however, was that Bryan had been a stranger to them all only a fortnight before Rolf de Valmont and his contingent arrived. Now, he was only making things worse for them, and here she was, actually *shielding* the man.

". . . me get him to the hall," Myles was saying to Bryce. As they moved toward Michael, Merlyn hastily got to her feet and scrambled away, a dark foreboding forming over her head like a thundercloud.

Chapter 6

They found Bryan's body the next morning. The wolves had gotten to him before either Father Francis—a priest who'd joined them the day before—or Cedric.

"I *knew* they were evil," Merlyn declared bitterly when they had returned with the young man's body. "I knew they would kill poor Bryan."

"We have no proof, daughter," Father Francis consoled her. "We all know what a danger wolves are in the *weald*. He must have lost his way."

"Bryan may have been impulsive and rash, but he wasn't dull-witted," Merlyn answered with a shake of her head. "He knew exactly where we've been hiding."

Cedric was examining Bryan's body. He said nothing for long moments, intent on his task. Then, with an awkward movement, he hauled himself upright on his crutch to balance on his good leg. "The back of his skull was crushed," he said. "Then, evidently, the animals found him, he could have been yet alive."

"A mace," Merlyn muttered. "The Normans use those ungodly weapons upon their victims. Bryan

94

never knew what hit him."

"Every weapon known to man is ungodly," Father Francis told her, his fold-draped face reminding Merlyn of a bloodhound's. Father Francis was from Richmond, and he had traveled throughout the countryside in search of scattered, starving Anglo-Saxons. He was obviously accustomed to a fairly good life, for his entire body—or at least as much as Merlyn could see—was made up of folds of skin where, obviously, he'd once been well-rounded. No religious abstention for him, she decided wryly.

"Wickedness comes this way," Elsa said suddenly, her pale eyes trained unseeingly upon the forest across the small clearing. The breeze played with her hair, molding her tattered clothing to her fragile frame.

"'Tis here already," Merlyn answered, keeping Raven's face averted from the now cloth-draped corpse.

Elsa shook her head slowly. "Nay. 'Twas not the Normans who killed Bryan. Nor are they here to harm us, I *feel* it. They are our only protection against . . . what comes."

Unease slithered through Merlyn, settling in her middle like a coiled snake. She glanced at Cedric, but he was watching Elsa. Marthe was clinging to Father Francis, her great, nearsighted fish-eyes bulging with alarm in her freckled face.

What could be worse than the scourge of England? Merlyn wondered. The Scots? The Danes?

The birds were suddenly unnaturally quiet, the breeze soughing through the trees like a sibilant dirge as they all stood looking at Elsa. . . .

"Will you not see how he fares?" Elsa asked Merlyn

as they wrapped Bryan's body in preparation for burial.

Merlyn's eyes met hers, angry defiance shining in their ink-blue depths. "Valmont—all of them—can go to the devil for all I care!"

Elsa shook her head and sat back on her heels. "They are not responsible for this," she said. Her eyes narrowed at Merlyn then. "Can it be, child, that you are afeared of believing them aught but evil? Especially the one called Wolf?"

Merlyn's eyes widened in reaction before she tucked in the last corner of the shroud nearest her. "What Norman isn't? Valmont has no worth save on a battlefield—if his cohorts are to be believed. What use have I for such a one?" But her eyes would not meet Elsa's.

"You cannot keep up this pretense forever. I wouldn't doubt but that they have already guessed you are not what you seem, but only indulge you for the time being. 'Tis one more reason to believe in their good intentions."

Merlyn looked up in surprise, her mouth opened to retort. Then she remembered Rolf de Valmont's unwavering scrutiny . . . and Roger de Conteville's words, *You hardly seem mad to me. Mayhap 'tis a ruse to discourage us from stopping here?*

"I haven't been acting very mad," she admitted. "There are so many things to remember."

"And more than that. You are too young and fair to be convincing for very long, especially upon close inspection, child. The walnut stain is good, and your hair and mannerisms." Elsa shook her head. "But close up the truth is apparent enough to a careful observer."

Merlyn stood, stepped around Bryan, and helped Elsa to her feet. "Then I will convince them that I *am* mad enough to act the hag. Mad enough to believe I am an old crone who has no use for bathing, or neat, shining hair . . . or aught to do with grace."

Elsa merely nodded her head, her expression unreadable, although Merlyn had the distinct impression that the old woman was humoring her.

A commotion behind them caught their attention. Raven came running up to Merlyn. "Mamma . . ."

"*Merlyn!*" Merlyn corrected her in a low but emphatic voice.

"Aye . . . Merlyn, the Wolf comes! And the giant, too!"

Dismay danced across Merlyn's features and she automatically assumed her hunched position, distorting her features with a mixture of resignation and resentment (and, God above, was her hump properly in place? Was it there at all?). Not only was she forced to continue her masquerade, but at all times, or so it seemed, in light of Valmont's disconcerting habit of invading the camp at any hour of day or night. "Already they come to see their handiwork. No doubt Valmont only feigned illness yesterday."

"No one can feign a fever," Elsa said.

"Merlyn . . ." Marthe said as she came toward them, then stopped in her tracks at the sight of Rolf and Myles approaching. Her mouth fell open, like a gasping fish stranded on the riverbank, Merlyn thought, as she watched the other woman.

Merlyn slowly swung around, acutely conscious of Cedric and several others gathering near her, as if to offer their pathetic protection.

The two Normans were unarmed save for their daggers—either an indication of their utter lack of fear where Merlyn's band of survivors was concerned, or their confidence that the area was, at least at the moment, cleared of outside enemies . . . or both. A contradictory mixture of irritation and relief trickled through Merlyn's breast.

Myles was fairly somberly dressed, but Rolf . . . oh, indeed, Rolf de Valmont looked like a brightly plumed bird. At least to Merlyn. That fact, combined with what appeared to be Bryan's murder, prompted her to ask acerbically, "Do you seek to provide a target for our enemies, my lord Wolf, or are you merely displaying your frivolous Norman wardrobe?"

Rolf had shed his warm long-sleeved chainse, wearing only an emerald-green bliaud over a dun-colored shirt. He'd also foregone the roughly spun chausses and leather cross-garters normally worn over loose-fitting breeches, or braies. Except for the bright color of his overtunic (and his supremely confident demeanor, Merlyn thought darkly), he could have been a common freeman—a cottar or even a villein, like most of the others.

The poultice had been removed from his forearm, and beneath his three-quarter length sleeves (the right was rolled up past his elbow), the lacerations were clearly visible. Merlyn noted with a practiced eye that they were pink, not angry red like the day before, and his facial color had returned to normal.

Except for his eyes. As he came to stand before Merlyn, they reflected the brilliant hue of his tunic and looked as green as a lush spring meadow. Merlyn found her gaze clinging to his, quite involuntarily.

"Good morningtide, Merlyn," he bade her softly, for once swallowing his ire at her insulting words. "My arm is better." He glanced down at it and then back to her. "Hugh said 'twas well tended."

"And this is the reward for my services?" she asked, inclining her head toward the shrouded body lying upon the ground.

Rolf stepped closer and went to one knee before the still form. "Who is it?" he asked as he reached for the portion of the shroud covering Bryan's head and face.

"As if you didn't know!"

Her words were said with such venom that Myles stepped forward as if he would come to Rolf's defense.

"I told Merlyn that I didn't think you would bash in a man's head for the 'crime' of wanting his freedom," Cedric said as Rolf uncovered Bryan's face and then replaced the ragged shroud, "and then leave him half alive for the wolves."

Rolf straightened and looked at Cedric, taking in his missing leg. "He threatened Myles here with a pitchfork. No one points a weapon, however crude, at any of my men without punishment."

Cedric didn't answer, but Father Francis said, "Death was extreme in this case. . . ."

At the look on Rolf's face, he obviously thought better of voicing his opinion and fell silent.

"*I* am the one who decides just what is extreme punishment and what isn't. I may be unwelcome here, but I am lord of Renford and Lexom now, and I will not tolerate disobedience. Disobedience can mean death for innocents . . . for all of us," he added as he looked at each Anglo-Saxon in turn, trying to communicate the gravity of his message to them not only with the steely tone of his words, but with a grim determination shining in his eyes that had never before failed to pull into line any recalcitrant men under his command.

"So you admit that you killed Bryan," Merlyn persisted.

"I did no such thing," he answered, wondering in one part of his mind what was different about Merlyn this morn. "We've had two men searching for him since dawn, but obviously you found him first." He glanced at the body. "I regret his death, but if he'd remained in the granary until he'd come to his senses, perhaps we could have let him go." He shook his head, then looked up at the others. "As it was, his own rash behavior got him into trouble, then resulted in his death."

Why was he explaining himself to Merlyn and the others? Had he not said that he was lord? His word was law . . . unquestionable. At least that was how it worked in Normandy.

Myles was looking around, not even attempting to hide the fact that he was noting everything about the rudimentary encampment and its occupants. His strange blue eyes paused when they came to Merlyn, and a shiver went through her. He looked as cold and dispassionate a man as any she had ever encountered.

"Roger and Hugh have returned with several villagers from Lexom. They have agreed to abide in Renford for now, where they will be safe and well fed," Rolf told them. "I would have you do the same, for I cannot employ my men with rebuilding your village if they are constantly combing the forest in search of lost English as well as enemies. Renford was your home and 'twill be again, if you will cooperate." He looked at Cedric, then Merlyn. "I will provide you with venison for another day while you decide what you will do. I cannot be responsible for you if you will not learn to trust me and abide by my decisions. Neither can we reestablish a home and haven for you with any speed if you won't help."

"Trust must be earned, not given on command."

Rolf stared long and hard at Merlyn, who suddenly had the most inappropriate attack of itching in the area between her shoulder blades. "It seems to me that I have given you more cause to trust me than not. You said so yourself when you gave your reasons for tending my arm."

"Tending your wounds was not nearly so risky as putting myself under your protection."

"As I said before," he continued, ignoring her challenge, "I regret the boy's death. Myles can help you bury him if—"

"We need naught of your help!" she snapped, her irritability with his offer exacerbated by her discomfort. Also, she was testing him . . . hoping that maybe, just maybe, he was not quite as impatient as she'd first thought. Not quite as rash and quick-tempered . . .

Rolf, for once, did not disappoint her. "As you wish then." He squatted down and beckoned with one finger to Raven, who was peeking out from Merlyn's dark overgown. *Viens-ici, petite.* Come here and I'll show you the surprise I have for you." A corner of his mouth lifted, and his expression softened.

Raven bravely crept out from behind her mother, and Merlyn thought irrelevantly that Rolf de Valmont's smile could charm a babe from its mother's arms. Small wonder he had wrought such havoc with her senses when she'd tended him.

The child came to stand before him, her eyes wide with cautious curiosity.

Rolf motioned to Myles, and the latter handed him a sack he'd been holding cradled in one arm. Merlyn had thought it was food, but suddenly the contents of the sack began to squirm, then emitted several soft whimpers.

Rolf gently laid the sack on the ground between them. "Remember what I said when Thor was killed, *ma petite?*"

Raven nodded, her gaze fastened on the wriggling bundle.

"Eh bien, Sieur de Conteville found this little fellow roaming about the outskirts of Lexom." He tipped the sack, and a fawn-colored puppy came tumbling out to land at Raven's feet.

"He's *un peu maigre*—a little scrawny—but we'll fatten him up, *n'est-ce pas?"*

Her mouth a rounded O, Raven dropped to her knees before the animal and reached out to pat its tiny head. As the pup responded by eagerly licking her fingers, Marthe, who'd been eyeing it like a hungry vulture, exclaimed softly, "Food!"

Raven's fingers froze in mid-motion, and Rolf gave the woman such a quelling look that she instinctively stepped back and put one hand over her mouth. With the other, she clutched Father Francis's robe.

"I'll personally cut off the hand that extends toward this animal with aught but kind intent." Rolf reached to stroke the puppy's head, turning his attention to Raven. "What shall we name it? Thor?"

She looked up at him shyly, but the light in her eyes told him just how delighted she was. "Nay, Lord Wolf. It might bring 'im ill luck." Her face clouded at what was obviously the memory of the first Thor's fate, and something stirred deep within Rolf.

"We barely have enough for ourselves," Merlyn said in a brittle voice, alarmed at the way Raven was taking to Rolf de Valmont's outrageous charm and unadulterated bribery.

Raven looked up at her, a plea in her blue eyes. "Oh, Mamma, he can have . . ." She trailed off at the look on Merlyn's face at her slip of the tongue.

"He's too small to eat much now," Rolf said into the uncomfortable silence as he watched Merlyn intently. "You surely have aplenty with the supplies we've given you and the fresh meat."

"The battle between pride and need will win out in time, I suspect," said the normally laconic Myles. His words dropped like stones in a placid pool. "You took the boar Rolf killed for you," he added, "and the sacks of food. I doubt that you will refuse the venison—or aught else." He looked at Cedric, then Father Francis, with Marthe still cowering behind him. Elsa said nothing, her cloudy but shrewd gaze on Rolf, a look very close to satisfaction on her features. Myles glanced at the few others of their group, then his eyes came to rest on Merlyn. "Whether you will admit it or nay, you are already accepting his support. 'Tis merely a matter of degree."

Merlyn outwardly bristled at his words, although it was more for show than for anything else. What would Stigand have done? she wondered dismally.

If Stigand were here, he would still be thane, her stubborn side insisted.

But reason whispered, *Even Stigand could not have single-handedly held back the tide of Normans. You must consider these people and what is best for them now . . . not dwell upon that which is lost forever.*

"He's right," Cedric spoke out unexpectedly.

Rolf made to stand then, but Raven tentatively touched his hand. "Have *you* a name for the puppy, lord?" she asked earnestly, a frown of uncertainty flickering across her forehead. Then she glanced at Myles, who was even taller than Rolf, with his white-blond hair and a face as fierce as she had no doubt ever seen.

"Viking!" she burst out suddenly, then obviously remembered that this "Viking" after whom she was naming the dog was not supposed to be her friend; no Viking had ever done anything but strike terror into the hearts of the English. She looked down at the ground in silence.

"Or perhaps Gryff," Rolf suggested, thinking of Merlyn's Welsh mother and the fact that he was certain Raven was Merlyn's daughter. "After Gryffith, a famous prince of Wales."

"Do you mean Gruffydd?" Raven asked in an awe-tinged voice, her pronunciation of the Welsh name perfect. "Prince Gruffydd was a great man."

Merlyn couldn't believe the incongruity of such an insignificant matter as deciding upon a name for a hound in the devastated shire of Durham . . . where, in many cases, any dogs that could be found were slaughtered and eaten to hold starvation at arm's length for another few days.

It was just one more thing about Rolf de Valmont and his absurd and contradictory code of behavior that infuriated Merlyn.

Nor did she like the idea that he suspected, in spite of everything, that Raven was her child . . . and he could therefore use her as a weapon against Merlyn and, through her, the others if he so chose. His suspicions would also make Merlyn much younger than she wanted him to believe.

"Rolf is as good a name for a cur as any," Merlyn said with foolhardy boldness, desperation pushing her past caution.

Raven looked up at the suggestion, but the adults around her (except for her mother) looked definitely uneasy—some even appalled—at Merlyn's brazen words. Myles's hand went to his dagger hilt, his eyes slitting as they came to rest upon Merlyn. A muscle in his right cheek spasmed with suppressed anger as he waited for a command from Rolf.

But Merlyn's comment brought the response that she had half suspected it would; a response that would once again prove Rolf de Valmont incapable of any of the attributes she had observed in Hugh or Roger de Conteville . . . save skill with sword and lance.

A perverse gratification settled in her mind; but a worm of disappointment burrowed through her breast, mysteriously remaining there like a heavy stone pressing against her ribs.

Rolf stood, the question of the pup's name forgotten in the wake of this second insult. As he stretched slowly to his full height, he snagged her gaze with his. "You, *madame,* have the manners of a sow," he told her, "and the false courage of a fool. I suspect that had you been a man, someone would have rid the world of your troublesome presence long ago. On the morrow you will come—alone—to the manor house and apprise me personally of the group's decision. I will at that time," he added ominously, "have decided the punishment for your insolence." He glanced about him, his now-cold gaze lending no credence to his next words. "The *rest* of you are all welcome to return to Renford and get on with your lives." He looked down at Raven, his voice softening slightly. "And you, as well, *petite,* with Gryff here."

He made to swing away, then paused. "Don't forget your hump, Merlyn. It seems to have disappeared."

With that, he turned abruptly and moved away.

"Now you've angered the Wolf," Elsa admonished Merlyn when Rolf and Myles had disappeared through the trees.

"But yet he invited us to come back to the village—and all but gave his word that no harm would befall us," Marthe whined, twisting her hands in agitation. She looked appealingly (or as appealingly as she could look, Merlyn thought) at Cedric from where she still remained beside Father Francis.

Cedric rubbed his bearded chin thoughtfully, his eyes still on the spot where the two Normans had disappeared. "Mayhap he is as good as his word." He looked at Merlyn. "But I'll not leave here without you."

"Nor I," Father Francis added.

"He'll not leave you to live in the *weald* alone," Elsa said with a shake of her head. "There is a bond between you, albeit plagued by antagonism. You would do well, child, to nurture that bond, for whether you can abide him or nay, if he means well for your people, he should have your backing."

"But Stigand is dead!" Merlyn cried. "And I have only a handful of survivors here. What obligation have I to them—to you—now?" She flung the tangled mat of her hair from her eyes, frustrated defiance crackling through the air. "Do what you will!"

After witnessing numerous raids and the ensuing slaughter by Norman and Scot alike, after losing her family and most of her village, after weeks of food and sleep deprivation and now being forced to be on her guard even more constantly to affect this ridiculous, difficult—and, she was beginning to suspect, futile—charade, her wits were dulling. She was becoming muddle-minded, losing the edge that perhaps would have enabled her to do her people—and Stigand—proud.

Sweet Mary, she was even losing her daughter, the most precious thing in her world.

She put one palm to her brow, as if to press her troubling thoughts into oblivion, but it was not to be. Voices began to come at her from everywhere, and she thought that at last she was truly going mad. . . .

Until she realized the hum of low voices was a small group of men, women, and children emerging from the *weald* in the opposite direction of Renford in two's and three's, caution and relief mingling in their pinched faces as they approached Merlyn's group . . . and the smell of food over a cooking fire.

"There is a quarry just the other side of the river," Roger told Rolf. "I suspected as much because the church, tiny as 'tis, is made of stone, as well as parts of the manor."

"And Lexom wasn't hit as hard as Renford, according to one man," Hugh added.

"Aye," his brother said at Rolf's raised eyebrows. "'Twas undoubtedly because the people had no will to fight, with their thane in Renford. But, as you've seen, they're more willing to join us here than Merlyn's band."

"Merlyn," Rolf said sourly. "The wench is more trouble than she is worth."

"But you just said she tended your arm," Hugh reminded him. "And she did as good a job as any could have."

Rolf kicked at a drying lump of cow dung (Cow dung? he thought in disgust. You'd never find such offal on a battlefield. . . . *Nay*, his sensible side scoffed, *only human blood and gore . . . surely preferable to a warrior like you.*)

Hugh exchanged a meaningful look with Roger, while Rolf momentarily stared down at the stain on his shoe as they paused before the thatched cottage closest to the manor. "'Tis just that if it weren't for her, I know the others would already be here in the village where they belong."

Roger shook his head. "Not necessarily." He gazed around at the village, obviously satisfied with the progress the men were making. It was also obvious that he and Hugh would feel more secure about leaving Rolf with Renford in decent condition for defense.

"I don't exactly see Merlyn shackling them to her," Hugh said in support of Roger's words. "Which leads me to believe that she was—is—someone important to them . . . someone whose opinion they respect."

Rolf looked up at him sharply. "She is no old woman, this I know. And Raven is her daughter. But she must be mad to take such pains to disguise herself. And if she *is* mad, then why would anyone look to her for leadership?"

They resumed walking through the village, pausing to banter for a few moments with several men-at-arms taking their midday meal near the well on the village common. Two thin, haunted-looking young Saxons remained outside the loose circle of Normans, carefully consuming every crumb they had been given.

Rolf approached the two Englishmen. "If you are still hungry, go to the manor and tell Michael that Rolf bid you get more to fill your bellies."

One of the men nodded, a shadow of suspicion in his eyes, while the other just stared at the ground in taciturn silence.

"Are you well, Garth?" Rolf asked the latter.

"Derwick," he corrected sullenly, finally lifting his gaze to Rolf's.

"Derwick, then . . . are you well?"

"Aye," he mumbled.

But Hugh put out a hand to lift his chin. Derwick jerked his head aside. "Don't touch me, Norman," he growled. Defiance sparked in his eyes, then died, as his eyes met Rolf's again. He quickly dropped his chin and stared at the precious, half-finished piece of bread in one hand.

"Let Hugh look at you," Rolf commanded, his voice stern. "He meant you no harm."

Evidently, Derwick feared Rolf's wrath more than Hugh's touch, and he grudgingly allowed the latter to look into his face.

"Have you a wound of some kind?" Hugh asked him. To Rolf he said, over his shoulder, "His skin is too warm to the touch, the whites of his eyes red."

"Jesu," Rolf muttered under his breath, "he carries the plague, no doubt. Now we'll *all* die of it."

He'd not meant for Derwick to hear his words, but hear them he did. "Nay," he protested with a grimace. "I've not the plague." He raised one leg of his braies enough to reveal an ugly, festering wound. It had a noisome odor and seemed to be reaching up his leg with jagged red fingers toward more vital parts, even as they stood there staring at it.

"I didn't notice a limp," Rolf said sharply, appalled that this man had been working on his feet in the hot sun since morn. The wound was in worse condition than either of Rolf's the day before, yet Derwick had been laboring silently while he, Rolf, had remained abed until the next day. "Why didn't you say anything to me? To any of us?" The anger darkening his features was not directed at Derwick, but rather at the fear he saw in the Saxon's eyes.

He doesn't know you yet. . . .

"Would I have been of any use to you lying upon a pallet in the manor?" Derwick asked bitterly.

"Will you be any more so to me dead?"

"What use to you an Englishman?" Derwick asked with soft acidity. "A lowly tiller of the soil who failed his king in protecting his country?"

Rolf stared at him for a moment, taken aback by the savage self-recrimination in the man's voice, the desolation in his eyes. "You were at the great battle? You were in the *fyrd?*"

Derwick nodded. "I was one of the unfortunate ones. I lived to return. To this . . ."

Here was a side of the Anglo-Norman antagonism that Rolf had not dealt with personally in the past. He had never really given much thought to the feelings of the English. William of Normandy was his liege lord and Rolf fought for his duke unquestioningly.

At the same time, on the periphery of his mind hovered the fact that neither Hugh nor Roger was stepping in to smooth things over, to help take charge.

This was *his* barony, *his* problem. His burden to bear for the rest of his life . . .

God in heaven, it was enough to make him want to drown himself in a vat of good Norman wine.

Suddenly feeling virtually overwhelmed, Rolf spoke more harshly than he had intended. "Hie yourself to the manor, man. And don't return until you are fit to work." To Hugh, he said, "And send someone to fetch the shrew. I need you for things other than healing."

He turned his back to all four of them, moving away with quick, angry strides.

Chapter 7

Rolf stared unseeingly into the bed of pulsing embers in the completed stone fireplace at one end of the great hall. They seemed to take on a life of their own, with their wavering glow, the red-gold hue of hell-flame, taunting with their undulations, beckoning in the unwary, before merging once again into nothing more than harmless, incandescent coals.

In the deep and blurred shadows around the perimeter of the hall, everyone was asleep, except for the men on watch outside. The gloom extending out from the walls seemed to have swallowed their forms, but the soft snores and occasional rustling of pallets reminded Rolf that he was not alone.

Outside, the Saxons who had been trickling into Renford at Hugh's and Roger's urging also slept. Those who were still terrified of unseen enemies slept within, among Rolf's retinue, although Rolf wondered just how "safe" they actually felt among Norman warriors.

Derwick, who was closer to the fireplace, was visible in the muted glow from the flickering flambeaux. He groaned and uttered something unintelligible in his sleep, catching Rolf's attention.

The Lord of Renford sighed heavily and raised a mug of wine to his lips. He drank deeply, knowing full well that he was wasting the precious ruby-red liquid to drown his sorrows in an unprecedented bout of self-pity.

He dismissed the thought and rested his chin on his left fist on the trestle table, his wine-blurred vision only causing the terpsichorean embers to move faster and more erratically before his eyes.

He raised the mug once again for another long draught, then set it down and reached out to finger the jeweled hilt of Death Blow, the sword of his father and his grandfather before him. It was the only thing Richard de Valmont had left his youngest son. His lands had been given to his firstborn, his other war accoutrements (including his best destrier) and a decent sum of gold to his middle son. And Rolf . . . Rolf had gotten his sword.

He slid his fingers lightly over the polished steel of the unsheathed weapon resting before him, thinking that most third sons received not even a valuable sword.

But Rolf's father had evidently recognized extraordinary talents in his youngest offspring . . . the exceptional physical skills of a born fighter and the intelligence of a natural strategist, a leader of men on the battlefield who inspired them, leading them on to greater glory through courageous and aggressive example.

"But not in an Anglo-Saxon village," Rolf scoffed under his breath. "What do I know of farming? Of pigs and chickens? And *cows?*"

When Death Blow did not answer him, Rolf tapped the gleaming blade with one finger, as if prodding it to reply. His rolled bliaud sleeve directed his eyes to the gashes he had earned while procuring food for *her*.

He dismissed Merlyn from his mind.

"Are you laughing at me, big fellow?" he asked the sword softly.

The sword remained silent.

"You are no help this night, *copain*," he complained to the weapon. He leaned closer to it. "But I know why. You fear being replaced by a plowshare, *n'est-ce pas?*"

The rubies and sapphires in the hilt shimmered and winked at him in the leaping, flaring torchlight.

Sapphire. Like beautiful eyes ... The color of Merlyn's eye ...

Rolf shook his head slowly, as much to chase the thought of Merlyn from his mind as to let the sword know that he was onto its fears. The world tilted around him with the movement. *"Eh bien,* 'tis true, you know," he said in careful if unsteady English. "Can you till a field? Eh?" He shook his head again, then ceased abruptly as the world began once more to tip precariously. *"Moi non plus, mon ami.* Nor can I." He belched with gusto. "Not that I give a damn, mind you, but 'twould seem as though everyone else thinks I should."

He reached for the ladle beside a cask of wine further down the table, and refilled his cup. "You must learn to understand *l'anglais* ... English," he confided, "and speak it as well." He rested his chin and left cheek in his hand, so close to the table that he was almost prone. The fingers of his right hand were curled about the cup.

"Look," he directed Death Blow. "I can still use my arm ... 'tisn't *that* injured." He hefted the cup, which seemed to grow a little heavier each time, and drank. Wine dribbled down one corner of his mouth, and he absently swiped it away with one sleeve.

113

He was vaguely aware of a rustling sound behind him in the rushes on the floor. One of the two dozing hounds raised his head from his paws to look at what was causing the soft disturbance. Before Rolf could command his head to swing around, something was bumping against his ankles beneath the board, then nudging them. . . . And then what felt like a sharp tooth snagged his braies, causing a pinprick sensation.

"What the? . . ." he said.

"Lord," a child's voice said from behind him. "'Tis us . . . Raven and Gryff."

With an effort, Rolf lurched his head around, and, indeed, there stood the little girl. He squinted down at the pup playing with the ankles of his braies. "Why aren't you abed?" Rolf asked, slurring his words slightly and trying not to revert to his native French. "What do you here at thish hour?"

Raven reached beneath the bench upon which Rolf was sitting and grabbed Gryff by the scruff of the neck. She hauled him into her arms. "I was afeared that Marthe would take 'im." She hesitated. "An' eat 'im."

"Eat him? My gift to you?" He frowned, concentrating on who exactly this Marthe was. "An empty-headed, fish-eyed wench, that one."

Raven nodded. "Mam . . . Merlyn says the same." She looked up from the bundle of fur in her arms, a frown between her tiny winged eyebrows. "Can I leave 'im here, lord? I think he'll be safer."

The female hound brought from Normandy, Helga, meandered over to them and sniffed Gryff as he rested securely in Raven's arms. "Oh!" Raven stepped backward, trying to hold the puppy out of reach of the curious hound's nose.

"Helga won't harm him," Rolf assured the child.

"She just left her third litter in Normandy. Mayhap Gryff would be safer here for now, under her washful eye. She seems to like him."

Raven looked at him doubtfully, then bent to place Gryff among the rushes. Helga sniffed him thoroughly, while Gryff capered about her in an attempt to play.

"See?" Rolf said.

"Aye." Her tentative smile faded, replaced by concern. "Have you enough to feed 'im? I—I brought a bit of scraps to help out . . ."

She trailed off at the look that crossed his features, hurrying to reassure him. "'Twas part of my meal, lord. I took it from no one else."

"Didn't Michael bring you venishon this eve? There was more than enough for sheveral days. No need for you to give the cur your own meal!"

Raven stepped back from him, eyes wide, as his voice thundered across the hall.

Two guards immediately stepped through one of the great doors. Several other men who had been sleeping went for their weapons, sitting up on their pallets as if on cue.

Rolf waved one hand negligently. "Go back to shleep," he commanded. "There'sh naught more dangerous in this hall than a girl-child and her pup."

"And what of her mother?" Hugh asked quietly, emerging from the shadows behind Rolf, clad only in braies. "What happens when she discovers Raven missing and comes racing into Renford in a complete panic?"

The thought of Merlyn racing anywhere brought a smirk to Rolf's face. It quickly faded, however, as he contemplated Raven, then lowered his gaze to Gryff, who was nipping at Helga's back legs as the older hound started to return to her place before the hearth.

115

The puppy followed her naturally, then plopped down beside her in the rushes.

"That shettles that," Rolf said. "Your pup can remain here until you and the others come back to Renford, *si tu veux*—if you wish."

Raven brightened, in obvious agreement.

"I'll take you home, *chère*," Hugh told her. He looked at Rolf. "With my lord's permission, of course."

Rolf made to stand. The toe of his leather shoe caught the edge of the bench, almost pitching him to the floor. He hastily reseated himself before he appeared the laughingstock in front of his best friend—and anyone else who might be observing them from the shadows.

"Her home ish *here*," he corrected Hugh with a frown.

Hugh nodded. "And so it is, but for this night, I'll take Raven back to her . . . family."

Rolf watched them leave the hall, a dark frown between his brows. The child didn't belong in the wild *weald*. Nor did the others . . . There were wolves and other predators. And someone had murdered the youth Bryan. Rolf had noted the smashed skull in his cursory examination earlier that day.

His lids suddenly grew heavy. He lay his head on his left arm upon the table, the fingers of his right hand lightly caressing Death Blow's gleaming blade. "On the morrow," he muttered to the sword. "On the morrow, we'll shee just what stern stuff thish Merlyn is made of . . ."

But at dawn, it was Elsa and not Merlyn who arrived at the great door of the manor.

Rolf was stiff from spending part of the night at

the table—even though Hugh had helped him to his pallet later—and his head felt as if someone had cleaved it in two with an ax. Pain corkscrewed across his brow with every movement, therefore his mood was less than congenial when he came face to face with Elsa.

"What do you here, old woman?" he said when she entered the hall. "And where's Merlyn?"

"I would speak to you alone," Elsa told him calmly, folding her arms over her chest like a queen in tatters.

"Oh, you would, would you?" he asked, eyebrows raised. That only caused a sharp pain to zigzag across his forehead.

Elsa nodded. "Aye. Come outside." She swung about and exited the hall just as she had entered.

"Would you like me to speak to her?" Roger asked, although the less than enthusiastic tone of his voice told Rolf that Roger did not consider the task his to perform. "Or Hugh?"

Rolf went to shake his head and instantly stilled. "Nay. 'Tis up to me to take hold of the reins of authority." He stood then, waited a few seconds for the throbbing in his cranium to ease, and then followed in Elsa's wake.

"What's wrong with Merlyn?" he asked her without ceremony as they stood outside the manor in relative isolation. "Where is she?"

Ignoring his first question, Elsa said, "I risk her anger in coming to you first. She'll be here soon, but I would tell you a few things first."

Rolf nodded, then winced. He crossed his arms over his chest, imitating her, and waited.

"What ails you?" she asked, squinting up at him in the shadow of the hall's lower stone wall. "Too much Norman wine?"

He opened his mouth to agree with her, then closed it. Who was she to ask him for an accounting of his actions? God's wounds, you give these people a bit of food and they become as brazen as brigands.

Elsa nodded sagely. "That means not all goes well here, Wolf." She cocked her head and studied him through her pale eyes. "But if you win Merlyn over, you'll have a much easier time of it. If not, she may decide to leave, and the others with her, for she has much influence among her people."

"And just who *is* she?" he demanded in a low voice. "Who is she that she has such influence and respect?"

Elsa looked away, toward the dawn-dim *weald* and its receding shadows. The rising sun was turning the treetops to green-gold. Her gaze was on the middle distance, her mind obviously working. Rolf allowed her those few moments without interruption, sensing that she was about to explain the riddle of Merlyn.

"I cannot tell you who she is—was. You must learn that from Merlyn herself." She turned her gaze back to Rolf. "But I will tell you this, for I feel that you're a fair man . . . for a Norman."

Rolf took the backhanded compliment in stride, and his disappointment at her refusal to reveal Merlyn's exact identity, as well. Nor did his attention waver for a moment, either. He was anxious for any piece of information she could impart to him.

"Merlyn is not an old woman, although I sense that you've guessed that. Nor is she mad. Strong-willed, aye. Courageous, aye. Bold and impulsive, aye. But not mad, although she has had more than enough reason to allow herself to withdraw from life as we know it."

"Then tell me what you will," he said.

"She was raped by a Norman this winter last. She was a widow without a husband to protect her, although there were others who tried to stand in his stead for her. But they failed. And Merlyn was brutally beaten and misused."

Rolf was careful to withhold his immediate reaction for fear that it might make her change her mind about him. He didn't know why Elsa's opinion mattered so much, but it did.

Their gazes locked and then Elsa looked away, her withered cheeks heating with a blush that hinted at former beauty. Rolf wondered if she, too, had been likewise treated so abominably.

"I think the child helped her keep her sanity in those days immediately afterward."

"Raven is her daughter." It was a declaration, not a question.

"Aye. But 'tis all I can tell you." She looked over her shoulder. "I don't want her to know that I spoke with you. 'Twould just add to—"

"Just *who* is she then?" Rolf broke in, perplexed. "The widow of . . . the thane? That's it, isn't it? She was the wife of Renford's thane," he said in a low voice.

Elsa looked him straight in the eye. "Merlyn must tell you who she is herself. Ask her and not me. But, I pray you, remember what happened to her and treat her accordingly. She would have no qualms about leaving here if you were cruel or unjust . . . and the others would follow." She swung away, then added over her shoulder, "And it would take you years to populate this village—to prosper in any way—if word got out that the original residents—or what was left of them—fled in terror from their new Norman lord."

"Don't you turn your back on me with a threat

hanging in the air, Elsa," he warned.

She cast him a glance over her shoulder, then turned slightly. "'Tisn't a threat, merely a word to the wise. Now remember," she added, "Merlyn isn't to know you've spoken to me . . . or I'll never trust you again." Without another word, she moved toward the *weald,* with Rolf staring after her with a thoughtful frown.

Her disguise was perfect this morn. Even nature cooperated with her, spearing the world below the heavens with a sizzling bolt of lightning as she entered the manor. Thunder shook the very ground, and the bruised sky sundered and spewed forth torrents of rain.

Michael jumped at the sound and several Saxons crossed themselves, muttering among each other as they looked toward the manor door. Other men began returning from their work outdoors in the wake of the sudden deluge. Some came through the opposite door, while others gathered behind Merlyn as she moved into the hall, reluctant to interfere with her slow and dramatically orchestrated entrance.

Rolf was halfway up the newly begun stone stairway and speaking to the man in charge of adding an upper floor to the manor. He turned and watched her hobble in, her hump in place, one eye peering from beneath her filthy tresses, and he grudgingly admired the courage and determination that drove her to continue her daring charade.

She was raped by a Norman . . . brutally beaten and misused . . .

Courage moved her, Rolf surmised, but so did fear. And although it was not unusual for a husband to beat his wife, Rolf had struck a woman only once,

120

and that had been a disobedient serf who'd almost got him killed by her deliberate disregard of his instructions. He hadn't enjoyed it, either, as some men did, for he had no need to prove his manhood by striking a weaker female. That was bad enough, but rape . . . The thought enraged him, for he'd never had reason to rape a woman. There *was* no reason to rape a woman. Women had always been willing enough to come to his bed. If one wasn't, then he could always find another. Although of late, he had been comparing every female he met to Brenna, and they always came up wanting.

Brenna . . . He laughed silently at himself. He'd never done more than try to kiss her, yet she unwittingly claimed his heart now.

Rolf wrenched his thoughts from the forbidden and watched as Merlyn paused and searched the hall with her gaze. He moved down the stairs, every contact of his heel with the rush-strewn stone floor (to say nothing of each crack of thunder) renewing his headache. It was worse than the tenderness of his mending arm.

As he walked toward her, he watched her carefully and with new purpose. No matter what had been done to her, she had gone too far in her insults. No matter what her station before the conquest of England, she was nothing more than another woman now, and certainly one who should not be allowed to treat him with disrespect before the others. He could understand her reasons for the ruse, but whether she knew it or not, the reasons no longer applied.

She doesn't really know you yet. . . .

That warning again. It sounded more like Hugh than a part of himself. But it was true.

He stopped before her and noticed, peripherally, a

121

sudden silence settle over the hall. A silence that wouldn't be conducive to him reprimanding a seemingly harmless old woman . . . and a mad one at that, if anyone had cared to note her gestures and body contortions.

"Ye wanted me, lord?" she asked in that now-familiar cackling voice.

Why, even Elsa, who was much older, didn't speak thusly, he thought.

"Nay." He took her firmly by the elbow and steered her toward the kitchen at the back of the hall. The stench of garlic tickled his nostrils, and he caught sight of another pouch suspended from her neck. *That* was carrying things a bit too far, he thought. Had she no fear of or respect for him as lord? He'd flung the other into the fire. How dare she wear another in his presence?

His anger stirred apace with this added irritant to his aching head and queasy stomach. "I didn't *want* you, Merlyn," he said tightly, "only *summoned* you."

He felt her stiffen at the gibe.

"Where—where are ye taking me?" she asked in a suspicious voice, trying to pull back as they stepped out of the hall toward the separate kitchen.

To Merlyn's added dismay, Helga and the male hound Olaf had followed their progress across the hall, snuffling in obvious canine rapture among the folds of her garlic-scented skirts.

"Surely you know where," he answered curtly. "'Tis not as if you've . . ."

Or I'll never trust you again . . .

He trailed off.

Merlyn glanced at him sharply, then looked away, squinting against the driving rain. They would be soaked in the short time it took to get to the separate kitchen. That meant that her clothing would mold to her body, that some of the dirt would wash off. Thank God for the walnut stain . . .

The kitchen was in fair order, Merlyn had the presence of mind to notice, but not as clean as with a caring woman's touch. Although she hadn't done the cooking, she had always been in constant consultation with the cook, a Danish woman by the name of Elfgift. But Elfgift was gone now.

And in the center of the room, to one side of the chopping table, was a bathtub, the steam from the water spiraling toward the ceiling invitingly.

This wasn't, however, an offer to take a leisurely bath. Merlyn instinctively knew that Rolf de Valmont wanted to expose what he suspected. And, no doubt, because of her audacity the eve before.

Her eyes automatically went to the door opposite the one they had entered, her muscles tensing for flight; but Rolf's fingers closing about one forearm ended her half-formed intention to flee.

Just as well, she thought grimly, for a Norman retainer poked his head through that doorway and asked, "Do you need aught else, my lord?"

When he saw Merlyn, a shadow of distaste passed over his face, then was immediately gone. Merlyn would have dearly liked to dump him headfirst (and preferably in full mail) into the steaming tub for that look.

"You may tell Hugh and Roger if they'd like to see the unveiling of the real Merlyn, they may come to the kitchen. Otherwise, I'll only need some clean female's clothing from the chest Myles found in the bower."

As the retainer disappeared, Merlyn looked at Rolf, the beginnings of real panic stirring within her. "Bathing is bad for the health," she announced. "I never bathe."

"'Tis obvious."

The former Merlyn of Renford would have taken offense, but the crone would not. She concentrated, rather, on trying to talk him out of his intentions. "Then why this?" She inclined her head toward the wood-slatted tub, her trepidation rising with each passing moment. "Because of my remarks yestermorn? What if I apologize?" Panic raised the pitch of her voice, making the cackling natural now.

Rolf leaned one hip against the table and crossed his arms over his chest, right over left, to spare his bad arm. "'Tis much too late for that, Merlyn. Your first mistake was in thinking to trick us. We may come from a different land with different customs and language, but we aren't stupid. You may well be mad—which I doubt—but you are not as old as you would have us believe. Your second—and biggest— mistake was insulting me before my men and the others. Twice. Now remove your clothes and get into that tub." His voice lowered to a soft but stern command.

Her expression took on a wild, desperate look for several moments. Then she remembered she was Stigand's widow. Elsa's granddaughter by marriage. The daughter of Guinevere, healer and Druid priestess of Wales. What an insult to them all—to her people—to act with anything but dignity now that these invaders sought to expose her charade.

Yet the memory of her sexual abuse hung over her like a pall, threatening to overcome her reasoning.

Act mad, the voice of self-preservation prompted her. *'Tis your last chance . . .*

Nay. He already suspected that everything about her was a farce.

With shaking fingers, Merlyn removed the offen-

124

sive garlic pouch from about her neck and, to Rolf's satisfaction, flung it toward the great hearth. She would don it no more, she decided, for it was equally as offensive to her as, she suspected, it was to Rolf. She had merely grown somewhat accustomed to the stench.

Rolf watched her clawlike hands relax from their rigid, unnatural position, and he felt a secret satisfaction in the straight, slender fingers that were revealed to him. Her motions, which were now made with her own natural movements, took on a grace that was a pleasant surprise.

Her expression stoic, Merlyn stared at the wall before her as she raised her dark, ragged overgown above her head and let it fall in a heap to the floor. Clad in full-length chainse and shorter chemise beneath, she awkwardly reached behind her neck to unfasten the crude cord that bound her "hump" to her shoulder area.

Rolf unthinkingly stepped forward to help, and the look she gave him stopped him cold. "Don't come any closer, Norman, or I swear I'll take my own life!" She flung back her hair and stared at him with both eyes visible, acute dislike making their blue cast deepen to blue-black. "And there are ways aplenty here in the kitchen."

He remained halted in his tracks at the virulence in her voice. "But who would care for Raven?" he asked, trying to cover his surprise at the intensity of her reaction.

He could have sworn he saw distress pass over her features, as swiftly as a storm cloud racing across the sky, and then disappear. "Elsa is more than capable." Her voice was toneless.

"I would think Marthe better suited," he said, hoping to draw her from this strange mood.

It worked.

"Marthe?" Her eyes narrowed, her lips thinning with disdain. "Marthe cannot even fend for herself!" She removed the mound of twigs and rags that had made up her hump, discarding it with more force than necessary. It went skittering across the floor, and Rolf would have wagered Death Blow that the hateful look Merlyn gave it would have been the same had it been Marthe's head rolling across the dirt floor, as well.

Merlyn looked at him then and said, "Leave the room."

One dark eyebrow arched in mild surprise. "Just like that? Surely you jest."

"I jest about naught these days," she replied. "Rather, it seems to be your strong suit."

She was stalling, he surmised.

"Proceed, Merlyn, else I decide to provide you with a larger, although nonetheless appreciative, audience."

Her face turned ashen beneath the grime and stain, and Rolf immediately regretted his words as Elsa's voice returned to haunt: *She has had more than enough reason to allow herself to withdraw from life as we know it* . . .

God knows what she lived through, and here he was forcing her to strip off her clothing and then threatening to invite his men to view her bath.

"Kneel!" he said harshly, disgusted with his sudden weakness.

She went down to her knees obediently. Too obediently . . .

And then he saw the dagger, its glinting tip protruding from the edge of her left chainse sleeve. He watched with disbelief as her right hand slowly edged over to the left and, seeming to wring her hands in agitation, she eased the knife out from the sleeve and beneath the palm of her shielding right hand.

In that fleeting moment before he acted, he could not know if the weapon was meant for him or for her, but he didn't have time to decide. In a twinkling, he shoved himself away from the beaten and sand-scoured table, and rounded the closest end of the tub. Before Merlyn could even raise her gaze, he was squatting beside her, the fingers of his left hand securely shackling her right wrist.

"Look at me, Merlyn," he commanded softly, for he had already decided that Elsa was right . . . that he would do better if he had her on his side in this godforsaken part of England, no matter who or what she was.

"You have only to lean over the tub and wash your face and hair. If you choose to stink like garlic and wallow in grime, to continue to wear filthy, near-useless garments when, I suspect, much of what we've found in one of the chests in the larger sleeping bower would fit you perfectly, 'tis your choice. But I *will* see your face."

Chapter 8

Their gazes clashed in the taut silence. The muffled sounds from the hall, from the men still outdoors, faded as authority and obstinacy stood stalemated for a brief eternity.

Merlyn let the dagger slip from numbing fingers, wondering if he meant to snap her wrist in two. Even as she thought it, his grip eased.

"Don't ever raise a weapon to me again," he said in a soft, steely voice. "Nor to yourself. Do you hear me? No one will harm you while I draw breath. Do you understand?"

She said nothing in response, caught in the mysterious depths of his splendid hazel eyes, green-brown with gold flecks. Beautiful eyes, one part of her mind thought. She allowed herself the brief luxury of seeing him as a man, not just another Norman, and a tiny part of Merlyn urged her to take advantage of the impending bath and show him everything she had been . . . could never be again. Respected, responsible and, so it was said, comely.

Reason told her she was madder than Merlyn the crone for thinking such a thing. The man had to be a wizard to make her thoughts take such a turn. Or else she was truly losing her grip on reality.

"Can you make that assurance for the others as well?" she heard herself ask him.

"It seems to me," he said in a low voice, ignoring her question, "that you have not yet learned that I am not the enemy. The *enemy* . . ." he paused for emphasis, "is still out there," he said, inclining his head toward one of the doors. "He is our common enemy now, Merlyn . . . the one who killed Bryan."

She shook her head.

"*Oui*, 'tis true. And if you were half as concerned about the others as you pretend, you would direct your energy toward discovering this unknown adversary rather than stoking your hatred for me."

He reached his left hand toward the tabletop and presented her with a bar of what Merlyn could only assume was French soap. She had heard of it but never actually seen it. It lay upon his upturned palm before her, smooth and lightly scented, beckoning to her shamelessly, an utterly frivolous commodity in Renford. In northern England, period.

Rolf placed the soap in her hand and met her eyes again. "I'll be across the way. When you are ready, one of the guards will bring you over."

Just then the man who had been sent for clean clothes appeared at the door. Rolf glanced up. "Set them here, John," he directed. "And bring Merlyn back to the hall when she is ready."

He stood then and turned to leave. "There is toweling on the table," he added. "And you need not worry about privacy. My men are trustworthy."

Trustworthy? she thought dimly. Was there any such thing in these cruel and chaotic times?

Merlyn stared at the soap in her hand as if it were some foreign object. It *was* foreign . . . French, only talked about before but never seen. She raised her hand and dipped it into the warm water, sliding the pad of her thumb over the bar, reveling in its smooth, slick texture. And the scent . . . Lavender. It wafted upward toward her, caressing her nostrils, heady, enticing. Feminine.

The confrontation between common sense and pride was fierce and prolonged, but common sense won out. After a furtive glance at either door, Merlyn slipped out of her chainse and chemise and into the tub, sinking up to her chin in the warm embrace of the water.

How long had it been? Weeks? Months? With only the cold river for hurried bathing . . .

Merlyn blocked out the disturbing thought that Rolf de Valmont was trying to buy her trust with a bar of soap.

She luxuriated in the bath as the minutes floated by, letting her muscles relax, her mind drift, in spite of the fact that she was literally in the midst of a contingent of Norman warriors. There were also a few other women in the manor, she had noticed, and Anglo-Saxon men; yet somehow—perhaps it was a sixth sense passed on by Guinevere—she suspected that Rolf de Valmont was a man of his word. If nothing else, Merlyn suspected she would bathe undisturbed.

He had promised them boar meat, and he'd provided it. He had promised Raven a puppy, and he'd found her one. He had promised them shelter, and he was restoring Renford.

But could he provide for their safety and well-being?

She dismissed the question from her mind, refusing to think about what would happen after she returned to the hall.

As the bathwater began to cool, Merlyn finally

roused herself from its sinfully sweet spell. The bar of soap glided over her skin like cool silk. She experimented with it for a while, marveling at its texture and comparing it to the messy wood ashes she normally used, then began to scrub her face, proceeding all the way down to her toes. In spite of her knowledge of the staining power of walnut juice, she was dismayed at her brown hands and feet, and shuddered to think of the line where pale met dark at the bottom of her neck . . . like a ragdoll whose hands, face, and feet were stitched to a torso of contrasting color. Her cheeks heated at the thought.

She ducked below the water, cooling her hot face and wetting all of her hair at the same time. Washing it with the soap was easy, and she scrubbed her scalp until it tingled. However, the detangling, she acknowledged, would take forever.

Warm runnels of water trickled down her back and disappeared. If only the same could be said about her troubles . . . If only she could scour her mind free of horrible memories, her heart free of the dull, constant ache of loss.

By the time she was finished, she felt as if she were surrounded by lavender blossoms in a scented meadow. It seemed to have affected her mind, for she was almost content as she dressed in an old but clean bliaud and chainse that had escaped destruction in the half-burnt wooden bower. She'd been unaware of any of her personal possessions surviving the last fire, and her thoughts automatically went back to happier times when she'd worn the overgown.

Nay! she thought. 'Tis gone, past. Forever.

The yellow—and she had thought Rolf de Valmont a peacock in emerald!—linen overgarment and white chainse and chemise slid over her clean body with a soft sigh. The belt was gone, but it didn't matter. She was so stick-thin that she was glad for the fullness of the unbelted bliaud. It was clean and lightweight . . . and didn't stink of garlic. She had no shoes or hose, but what did it matter now? There were too many other, more important things to consider.

Lastly, Merlyn toweled as much of the dampness from her heavy hair as she could, before a lazy cooking fire in the hearth. But not all the tangles would slip free, and she had nothing but her fingers to use for comb or brush. She did the best she could, then decided she would have to cut it later. Most of the dirt under her broken nails was gone now, but her hands were still stained and chafed. The hands of an old peasant woman.

Stigand had called her hands elegant and had loved her dark hair; he would never have allowed her to hack it off. Unexpectedly tears glimmered along her lower lashes. She bit her lip hard, willing them away. Such an insignificant thing for tears. Englishmen had been slaughtered for attempting to overthrow the Usurper from Normandy, and here she was weeping over the prospect of cutting her hair.

And Stigand is dead now.

She balled her ragged and soiled clothing beneath one arm, swung around, and walked to the door.

Rolf watched her enter the hall, the antithesis of the woman who'd exited earlier. She stood straight and proud, her dark, damp tresses hanging down her back, pushed out of her face and away from her eyes. She looked neither left nor right but straight at him, and moved with a grace and dignity that were a far cry from the scrabbling, hunched Merlyn the crone.

As quickly as the skies had clouded up and delivered the deluge, just as swiftly did they clear and the sun return to its rightful place. Many of the men were already outside again, but Hugh and Roger stood talking to Rolf as Merlyn came through the door.

"She's lovely," Roger said under his breath as he watched her approach, "just as I guessed. . . ." He nodded. "No wonder she fought to maintain her guise. Beauty is not necessarily an asset in the world of the conquered."

Hugh glanced at Rolf and watched him study Merlyn. "I suspect the battle is far from over," he observed with a slight curving of his lips.

"Aye," Rolf said, recovering from the first shock of seeing the transformed Merlyn. "She has the tongue of a shrew, the temper of a termagant, and the stubbornness of an ass."

"To say nothing of being a consummate liar," Myles added with a grimace. "God knows what new fables she'll concoct to keep us in turmoil."

Rolf looked at Myles and grinned. "Why, Mortain, do you mean to tell me that you are afraid of a pretty wench? Or even an ugly one? A huge lout like you?"

Myles made a face. "Lighter skin and clean clothing change naught. But you'll discover that soon enough, Valmont."

"A woman hater? But I had thought to give her to you in marriage," Rolf pressed, a wicked glint in his eyes, "along with land of your own."

Myles glanced sideways at Rolf, then back at Merlyn. "I'll gladly take the land . . . but nay the wench. I'll find my own woman, *merci*."

Everyone but Myles burst into laughter, but one look at Merlyn and Rolf realized that the timing was poor. He saw her chin raise even higher, her eyes narrowing slightly. She obviously thought they were laughing at her.

Hugh evidently saw it, too, and moved forward to meet her. He bowed to her, a smile in his gray eyes. "The jest was on Myles," he told her. "You must forgive us our ill-timed merriment, Merlyn."

The suspicion faded from her features, but when she spoke to Rolf, there was no evidence of a sweet disposition to match her miraculously improved appearance. "Will it be safe for my people to return to Renford under your . . . protection?"

She held herself aloof and proud as Rolf's eyes searched her face, absorbing every detail of which he'd ever been suspicious. "Aye," he said slowly, consideringly. "They may sleep here in the manor if they so choose until their homes are habitable, and you, of course, will remain here as well."

She stiffened, clutching her dirty bundle with new tenseness and wondering why he would want her to remain in the manor for any purpose except a nefarious one. "I cannot do that."

"And why not?" He did not want to reveal his talk with Elsa, but there was another way. "I find it too coincidental that you are the right height for these clothes, *madame*, and so fiercely protective of your brood in the forest. I am guessing that you were wife to the late thane of Renford, and therefore your home is here."

Feeling as though she were being stripped of her last pitiful secrets, one by one, Merlyn answered, "While my husband was alive, aye. But not now. Not ever again."

"You need have no fears while beneath my roof," Rolf assured her wryly, even as he was admiring the fine features that were the perfect background for eyes as dark as the ink-blue northern seas. He watched as a blush crept up her darkened cheeks beneath his scrutiny. "And how long will your skin be two distinctly different shades?" he asked with a lazy quirk of his lips.

"As long as I choose to use the stain!" she snapped. "Now, back to the matter at hand. . . . I cannot remain under this roof. Raven and I can abide in one of the empty cottages and—"

The other three knights discreetly drifted away, leaving Merlyn and Rolf to settle things themselves.

"I need a female to see to the hall. As you can see, we are making improvements and enlarging it. I will be too busy with other tasks to see to the running of the manor. *You* are a woman—an unattached woman—with a child and no home. Since this was your home, you know how to manage it. It sounds the perfect solution to me."

"There is no such thing as a perfect solution."

He walked around her, looking her up and down like a prize destrier he was considering purchasing. "So you may believe, but you owe me, Merlyn," he added softly from behind her, close to her ear.

She started, his warm breath, so close to her ear, sending spurts of sensation all the way down to her toes. She refused to turn to face him, however.

"How so?" she asked in a not-quite-steady voice. "You are Norman; you owe my people reparation."

He stilled, struck by her outrageous statement. Until he realized it was the only defense she had . . . a last ditch attempt to preserve her pride, her people, in the face of what she believed he might ultimately do to them.

"Have you broken the fast?" he asked unexpectedly.

"Aye," she lied. For the last thing she wanted was to sit down at the same board and break bread with Rolf de Valmont.

He shrugged, his mouth softening to a rueful

135

smile. "Then sit with me anyway, Merlyn. I would tell you a few things about what we are doing to the hall."

She looked up at him as if he'd gone mad, her forehead furrowing with distrust.

He took her by the elbow, catching the scent of lavender soap that clung to her like a delicate mantle. Lavender had never smelled so sweet, he found himself thinking. He shook his head to clear it. "And I would ask you a few questions concerning life in Renford as it was."

She allowed him to lead her to the head table, noting that the hounds now paid her little heed, except for Gryff. The puppy came bounding up to her, his tiny tail waving furiously.

Merlyn ignored him, considering the dog a bribe for Raven's affections from the new Lord of Renford. She knew she was being childish by taking out her frustration with Rolf de Valmont on a dumb, innocent animal, but it was at least one vent for her anger and fear, no matter how small. Or infantile.

Rolf helped her over the bench with all the grace and manners of a proper lord, something she would not have expected from an uncivilized, warmongering Norman.

"What is it exactly that you want of me?" she asked stiffly, refusing to touch anything put before them on the table, although her mouth began to water at the smell and sight of food.

Rolf poured himself some wine, hoping it would chase the remnants of his headache away. As he broke a fresh, fragrant loaf of bread with gusto and set the unused portion back on the serving tray, he said, "I would make some changes here, but not in everything. I will keep what systems met with success under . . . er—?"

"Stigand," she murmured, a peculiar but familiar pressure bearing down on her chest at the thought of her late husband.

"—under Stigand's rule." Using his great slab of bread as a trencher, he speared a chunk of succulent venison onto it, the juice settling immediately into the thick, white bread. Someone here knew how to bake decent bread, Merlyn thought; manchet bread, made of the finest wheat that would not molder or sour as other inferior breads. They must have brought along good flour, among other things.

Bread is important in hell. The demons must be fed, chirped a voice.

"I have no desire to change things merely for the sake of changing them," he continued between bites of venison and bread.

In an effort to disregard the hunger gnawing at her belly, Merlyn said, "But you have already changed the manor hall when there was no need—"

His eyes sought hers, one of his dark eyebrows slanting upward, making him look like what she'd called him and his men earlier: demon seed. He washed down his bite with wine and then set down the mug. He took a long, slow look around the hall, and Merlyn's gaze followed his. When she'd taken it all in, she glanced back at him, only to find his eyes on her with a steadiness that was unnerving.

"A second story is necessary for bedchambers," he told her, "and most of the wood is being replaced by stone. 'Twill be safer then, until we eventually build a keep."

She nodded, her eyes going to his half-eaten bread trencher quite before she realized it.

"Manges-toi," he said, slicing off another chunk of bread with a clean sweep of his knife and setting it before her.

Merlyn shook her head dumbly as she watched him place venison and juice on the trencher.

"I command it," he said gently. "And I am your new lord."

She met his gaze fiercely. "Do you think to bribe me with food like you bribed Raven? And Elsa? Do you think to win me over with your charm and generosity until I fall at your feet and kiss them?" She stood abruptly and stepped over the bench. "Never!"

Rolf's limited patience was being stretched. Would this wench never yield? he thought. Did she want gifts and sweet words of assurance?

She has seen hell, reason reminded him. *You'll not win her quickly, and if you could, would* you *trust* her?

His fingers curled around her wrist, and he couldn't help but notice how delicate were her bones beneath his grip. Not those of a fragile old woman, but rather a small, slender young female. "It bodes ill for us, this disobeying of my command. And think of this: I have as much reason to distrust you as you do me. Even more so because I have been honest with you from the outset, whereas you tried to completely deceive us from the moment we arrived in Renford."

Merlyn regarded his hand on her arm, her thoughts clashing through her head. "I'll only ask you once," she said. "Did you kill Bryan or nay?"

He frowned. "I already told you that I didn't."

Her question, his answer, were only a sop to her smarting pride, and both knew it. Rolf was no leader of men for lack of insight. He recognized the question for what it was and released her arm as he added, "On my honor as a Valmont."

She sat back down, feeling like a fool. Color flagged her cheeks but he ignored it, urging her to eat as he took up his explanations regarding the changes taking place within the hall.

It was strange, this sitting beside a fair female, explaining his plans for the manor, for all of Renford. Rolf found himself inexplicably drawn to Merlyn, even as he'd been so before. However, where he'd been puzzled earlier, even appalled, the reasons were more apparent now. The intelligence and sharp mind were still there, even if the fear and anger remained as well. But here was a more subdued Merlyn than the crone . . . and infinitely more desirable as a woman.

Only days ago Rolf would have laughed aloud at the thought of an Anglo-Saxon woman holding any appeal for him. But this was no ordinary woman, he acknowledged with reluctant admiration. The same traits that had drawn him to Brenna of Abernethy— courage, mettle, intelligence—had attracted him to Merlyn of Renford now . . . had done so from the first, even while irritating him. Now, he realized, he didn't have to feel guilty or absurd about the strange and tenuous bond he felt had formed between them from the beginning. His ability to judge men (and women, in this case) had not failed him upon meeting Merlyn the crone. Rather, it had been her charade, her deliberate attempts to irk him and drive him away, that had angered and frustrated him.

He surreptitiously watched her eat as he spoke, still marveling at the difference between the former Merlyn and this one. What a strain it must have been on her, to assume the responsibility for those who remained from her village and anyone else who might have joined them, as well as that of her child.

Elsa had been right. If Merlyn left, the others would follow. And he could see why. And wouldn't he look the fool with an empty village?

Suddenly, he realized that she was watching him as

his monologue died away in the wake of his unsettling musings.

She held his gaze defiantly for a moment, then looked down, strangely silent. Was it because their relationship had subtly changed now that she had revealed who she really was? Was she, even now, fearing for her safety and that of her people even more than before? The shadow of fear in her eyes and been enough to answer his silent question.

"I need you to help me learn how to meet the needs of your people," he admitted suddenly, inexplicably wanting to smooth away the flush that brightened her berry-brown cheeks.

She looked up at him, startled, and he felt his heart slipping away in the blue-violet of her midnight eyes. What was he about?

"Then you'll need more than puppies, scented soap, and a charming manner," she said in a low, earnest voice when she'd recovered from the shock of his outright appeal. "If you are to be believed," she told him, the look of suspicion that tightened her features indicating she would not number among those believers, "then you must prepare yourself for, I suspect, the challenge of your life."

Merlyn rose from the bench then. "Thank you for the meal," she said with chilly politeness. "If the others are in agreement, we will return to Renford by dusk."

As Rolf watched her leave, he thought, indeed, that she was right; that he was about to embark upon a challenge like no other. And all his battle skills, all his experience as a chevalier of William of Normandy, would avail him nothing in this formidable and critical undertaking.

*　　*　　*

"'Twas stupid to kill the youth. Risky, too. We could have used him." Edward Smithsson's low-spoken words sounded like a premonition of disaster.

"He's already served his purpose. If we are to approach Stigand's widow, we must be certain that she'll not side with Valmont. That, even if she will not help us, she will not betray us." The second man, Will, paused before adding, "You saw enough of his behavior. He was not only angering Valmont, but he was alienating Merlyn. Not a good choice for our purpose."

Edward shook his head, prodding the slumbering fire into bright flames with a small tree branch. The flames cast his even features in red-gold. "If we are to use the promised help of the Danes to the fullest extent, we need a *man* working for us under Valmont's nose, not a woman."

"Waltheof said she was loyal . . . and intelligent. Someone who could be trusted. And Earl Waltheof was friend to Stigand of Renford." Will, small-built and darker-complexioned than his companion, shook his head. "You saw it. . . . The youth—Bryan—was rash and quick-tempered. He also was lovesick over the wench. I tell you, he could never have served us dependably."

Edward looked up from the flames, his long blond hair and beard catching and reflecting the firelight, his blue eyes narrowed against the brightness. "Then we will wait a little longer. Surely someone will appear who can act for us."

Will shook his head. "We haven't much time. And we must get to Merlyn before she's won over by Valmont."

Silence gathered in the small clearing, several miles southwest of Renford. The hiss and pop of the fire, along with the rustling of the leaves as the wind

141

whispered through the trees, were the only sounds to disturb the night. "Your words tell me that this woman is not firm in her loyalty to England."

Will's face darkened with annoyance. "Have you heard naught about Valmont? One of the Bastard's best, so 'tis rumored. Tall, good-looking, and irresistible to women into the bargain. What widow wouldn't be vulnerable before such a man?"

Edward glanced at Will. "And since when would a haughty Norman want a Saxon widow who has nothing to offer?"

Will, who was obviously getting impatient with his companion, shot him a look that communicated his growing offense. "Where have you been, Smithsson, for these past few years? How came Waltheof to choose you for the task if you knew naught about the affairs in Northumbria?"

"Waltheof didn't choose me . . . my lord Roger of Hereford did." His gaze met Will's over the fire, the flames bringing out the burning blue of his eyes. "I survived Hastings, only to watch while Norman mercenaries slaughtered my wife and two sons a year past. I had nothing to hold me down . . . and a festering hatred for all things Norman." His tongue was sharp as acid.

Will opened his mouth to reply, his expression softening, but Edward continued before he could speak. "Forgive me if I am cynical. I find it hard to believe that an English earl would put any faith in a woman against an adversary like the Bastard."

"Stigand of Renford had connections in Denmark, and Merlyn is part Welsh. Waltheof seeks to make use of anything Stigand's widow can provide. She is a natural leader, therefore we hope the local populace—or what is left of them—will rally around her, maintain their loyalty to her."

Edward nodded and tossed the branch into the fire, but he didn't appear to be convinced. "I *do* know that Valmont hates being here as much as he is hated. I doubt he will win anyone over, let alone a paragon of loyalty as you claim this woman to be."

Will stroked his bearded cheeks, his eyes narrowed thoughtfully as he turned his head away from the fire to stare off into the darkness around them. "Still, we cannot wait. Winter is almost upon us, and Ralph de Gael has the Bretons and many English behind his cause . . . *now*. Cnut of Denmark is also mustering a fleet—two hundred ships, they say. Time is running out for us."

Silence ensued for a time. "If no one else comes forth," Edward said softly, "then I'm ready."

Will sent him an expectant look and Smithsson shrugged, his mouth tightening into a thin line of resolve, his eyes as cold and hard as enamel. "I'll get the job done myself."

Chapter 9

They emerged from the *weald*, a ragged and weary-looking lot. Their faces were pinched, expressions ranging from guarded fear to outright suspicion imprinted upon their features, shading their eyes.

And Rolf noted that, consciously or unconsciously, they formed a protective cordon around Merlyn.

If any among his men doubted the ability of these English to make decisions, to defy their overlords, to flee back into the forest despite any edict forbidding it, Rolf was certain the doubt was dispelled by the way they held themselves, right down to the one-legged Cedric and the ancient Elsa. Anyone could see it, and Rolf de Valmont had not chosen his men haphazardly.

Pity seeped through him at the sight; yet a very simple, basic (if reluctant) pride also made itself felt. For these survivors were just that . . . the strong and determined, in spite of the decree of a pitiless providence. And they were to be the foundation of Renford.

While one small part of Rolf de Valmont wanted to weep with disappointment (for this pathetic little

144

band was almost exactly as he had evisioned any remaining inhabitants of the area between York and Durham), a sudden, if belated, attack of maturity and a new resoluteness to succeed as a baron in his own right made their presence known to Rolf in no uncertain terms.

He glanced at Hugh and Roger, and saw pity and genuine concern for these people—*any* struggling people, he knew—molding their expressions. And barely disguised admiration. The Contevilles were an integral part of the duchy of Normandy and, for the last nine years, of England as well. They were natural leaders and lords. Their combined experience and knowledge were nothing short of awesome.

And Rolf had less than a month to reap the benefits of their presence.

Hugh looked at Rolf as the fugitives came to a halt just outside the low stone wall separating the manor from the center of the village around the well. Their meager belongings were in crude bundles beneath or within their arms. Even Cedric carried his own, as did Raven.

As Rolf stepped forward and drew in a deep breath to speak, it came to him suddenly that these people still maintained remnants of pride. And pride he understood. No matter what their status, newly conquered or nay, he had no right to rob them of that. Perhaps another lord, but not Rolf de Valmont. And he knew he could say the same with certainty about Hugh and Roger de Conteville. That pride was, evidently, just as intrinsic in many of the lower classes and laborers as it was in the nobility, the chevaliers and, in perhaps more instances than was healthy, the sons of the church.

"Welcome back to your rightful home," he said to them, looking directly at each one in turn, just as he would while addressing the men who followed him into battle. "We have been repairing and rebuilding your homes as best we can, but 'twould be achieved more swiftly and, I suspect, to your better gratification if you could contribute to the effort."

The group murmured among themselves, some casting outright hostile glances at Rolf. He missed the subtle, silent exchange between Hugh and Roger that could have easily been interpreted as approval.

When he came to Marthe, she bobbed behind Father Francis's robe as she'd done earlier. This one, he thought, knew naught of pride (or anything else). She would not be an asset on anyone's tally stick, he suspected.

He held in a sigh. *Every village has at least one wantwit.*

Father Francis dragged Marthe out from behind him and hissed something into her ear, obviously having had enough of her cowardice.

And Merlyn . . .

She stood regally in the center of the loose semicircle, as calmly as if she were Matilde of Normandy, now Queen of England, not the vanquished thane's widow.

Raven unexpectedly smiled at him, revealing two missing teeth. A corner of his mouth quirked in a natural response before Rolf caught himself.

"Are you prepared to do homage and swear an oath of fealty to me?" he asked as he wrenched his eyes from the child's, then realized that he should have commanded it instead of making it a question.

"Have we a choice?" Merlyn asked, her voice hollow.

His expression darkened. Damn her, he thought. Why did she insist on making this more difficult than it already was?

"Non!" he snapped in a spurt of irritation. "You will take it before you do aught else. We can do it right here." He looked at Hugh, who took his cue and stepped forward.

He directed the English in that gentle, yet authoritative way of his, and Rolf watched as they formed a single line, strung across the front of the wall like so many bedraggled sparrows along a bare tree branch.

Twilight was approaching, and the other men who had been working in the village halted their work, one by one, and began returning to the hall for the evening meal. Many stopped to watch . . . especially the Normans, Merlyn noticed.

Let them!

She stared straight ahead into the distance, unable to envision anything but a great and ugly Norman keep on the far, northernmost hillock. Yet instead of representing safety from the Scots and Danes, it only caused Merlyn to think of it as a symbol of Norman dominance over the English.

Rolf was before her then, and Hugh helped her kneel. Rolf took both her hands in his and spoke in Norman French, then repeated it in English. It was basically a ritual of subordination, and after mechanically swearing to serve Rolf de Valmont for life, Merlyn allowed him to pull her back to her feet, indicating his acceptance of her. Then he kissed her full on the mouth, as was customary. But this was no purely symbolic kiss between lord and vassal. Rolf de Valmont took shameful advantage of his role and met her mouth with his lips slightly parted.

Lips that were warm and moist, gentle as the brush of a bird's wing . . . Yet there was something more urgent behind the kiss, Merlyn felt, and a queer feeling of physical arousal fired her blood.

Appalled, she jerked away, her cheeks aflame. His eyes held hers for a long moment, plumbing their depths, seeing into her very soul, Merlyn felt, for she had no disguise to shield her now.

Hugh de Conteville stepped up to them and held out a bible toward Merlyn. By placing one hand on it and repeating after Rolf, she vowed complete loyalty and fidelity to him, one part of her mind chastising her for giving in to Rolf de Valmont and his cohorts so quickly and without a struggle.

For the sake of life . . . of living it until it becomes intolerable and demeaning. And for Raven . . .

Rolf moved on to the next person, leaving Merlyn stunned, with contradictory feelings and thoughts churning within her.

Afterwards, they had a celebration feast of sorts, although Merlyn felt there was little for the English to celebrate.

Cedric unexpectedly said to her, "We must attempt to take some pleasure, however small, from this bid for peace and, hopefully, security." His dark eyes, normally devoid of emotion since the loss of his family, were more animated than she'd seen them in months. "I hope you know that you have my support, Merlyn," he added. He glanced away, toward Raven and Gryff, who were cavorting in the rushes with the two hunting hounds. "I know I've not been much help since . . . Well, I've decided that I have more to offer Renford—and myself—before I lay down and die."

Merlyn put her hand on his shoulder, something tugging beneath her ribs. "I thank you, Cedric. Your offer means so very much to me . . . and I'll always need your support." She gave him a smile of gratitude that lit up her features, and Cedric answered with a tentative smile of his own.

148

*　　　*　　　*

From a short distance away, Rolf watched her smile. For the very first time since coming to Northumbria, he saw Merlyn gift the world with her smile. And in spite of the walnut staining her skin, Rolf was reminded of the sun breaking through boiling clouds on a damp and dreary rain-washed day, as if assuring the world below that its benign warmth and brilliance was there . . . would always be there, merely hidden and not destroyed.

He felt an alien twinge of envy toward Cedric and immediately looked away. Envy toward a man with one leg? A farmer who was useless now?

Merlyn doesn't think him useless. How ungenerous of spirit, Valmont . . .

Merlyn looked around her, noting the distinct failure to mingle on the part of the Normans and the English. She wondered if it would ever change. If it were up to her, it would never be different. And the English would drive the Normans from their shores forever.

Elsa and Marthe came up to her, one reminding her of an empress and the other a buffoon. Marthe was gnawing on a venison bone as if she hadn't eaten in weeks, her fingers gripping it so tightly that they appeared bloodless beneath the grease.

"I'll *never* fill my belly," she said around the meat in her mouth.

Merlyn silently agreed with her, for the once-plump Marthe, indeed, had an appetite almost as big as that of any man.

Elsa glanced sideways at Marthe with a knowing lift of her white eyebrows. "And you'll never get a

149

man if all you think about is filling your belly."

Marthe's rapt expression suddenly turned sly. "Depends on what I seek to fill it with."

"True . . . true," Elsa replied with a nod. She looked at Merlyn, whose cheeks felt warm from Marthe's comment. Merlyn wondered if the woman was as stupid as she seemed or, as Stigand had once suggested, much of it was for show because she shunned work and responsibility.

"Your Wolf has outdone himself," Elsa said to Merlyn, her gaze scanning the tables of food and drink.

"Aye. He wastes now and will be wanting by mid-winter."

Elsa made a moue of light disapproval. "Give him credit, child. He surely knows just what he has and has not. He and his men are hunters, and I think the Wolf is capable of getting all of us through until spring planting."

Merlyn followed Elsa's gaze, and she had to acknowledge that while there was enough to eat for everyone, there would be almost nothing left over. Grilled fish from the Tees, venison, and fowl made up the main course. Some salted pork and beef brought in by the Normans was served with several sauces for dipping that cut the salt. Dried peas, beans, fresh apples, and fragrant bread accompanied the meat and fish, and although the quantity was not impressive, it was adequate.

To Merlyn it was almost overwhelming after weeks and months of deprivation. She found that she could not do the food justice, for her stomach had seemingly shrunk with time.

Norman wine and mead, which Merlyn assumed was for the villagers, was served to wash down the meal. The mead was, surprisingly, as good as her own used to be, she decided.

As she helped herself to another cup, Roger de Conteville came up to her (or was it Hugh). He smiled faintly as he asked, "Do you like my wife's mead, Merlyn?"

Merlyn looked up at him, an echo of fear shifting within her at his height and the fact that he was a male. A Norman male.

"You have naught to fear, *madame*," he assured her. "I am wed to Liane of Derford, an Englishwoman." He looked down into his cup for a moment before he spoke again. "I noticed you helping yourself to Liane's mead and thought it might bring you . . . some measure of comfort to know that 'twas made by one of your own."

His silver-gray eyes were stern, but also held a certain warmth and sincerity that she could not deny. He was much like his twin, Hugh, although outwardly more authoritarian, more arrogant.

Of course, she thought waspishly, Rolf de Valmont outshone both Conteville brothers in that respect.

"And is she content with her new lord and master? Her new life?"

"She is now," he said, his eyes darkening to slate with what Merlyn could only interpret as an affront. "We met upon the battlefield at Hastings, the poorest of beginnings. Now, I can say with certainty, she is happy as my wife and the mother of our three children." He glanced around the hall as he raised his wine to his lips and drank, then added, "Liane's people—*our* people—are content. How can they be anything else when Derford prospers? When they are well and fairly treated?"

They are under the Norman yoke! she cried silently, but merely nodded.

"Rolf will be fair, as well," he continued. "And although he's not as experienced at ruling as some, he will learn."

"And what happens when you and your brother—your men—leave here? When winter sets in and the supplies run out?"

"Most of the men will remain here. But you will have to help one another," he said soberly. "I will send anything I can spare from Derford until the crops come in, but I cannot guarantee that my men and the supplies will not be set upon by starving Anglo-Saxons or renegade Normans." He tilted his head aside and studied her from beneath raised sandy eyebrows. "And winter and early spring are lean for everyone even during the best of times, as you know."

"An impossible time for us now," she said bitterly, her voice lowering with urgency and despair.

"My brother Hugh will also try to help, although 'twill be even more difficult to send supplies safely from Normandy. But I have no doubt that Rolf will do it, he will see you through the next months or perish in the attempt."

Merlyn slanted a look at him, trying to decide if his last words were serious. They appeared to be.

"He won't abandon you . . . not Rolf. And, whether you believe it or nay, you are safer with him here than not."

Raven came running up to Merlyn, Gryff clutched within her small embrace, except for his dangling hind legs. She opened her mouth to speak, then stilled in confusion. "Mer—" she began after a moment. "Mamma," she corrected then, lifting the puppy up toward Merlyn, "Gryff's eyes are two different colors! Look . . ."

The dog wriggled from between her fingers and plopped to the floor, half hidden among the dirty rushes. Once free from Raven's unwitting stranglehold, he lurched to his feet and scuttled away from them, toward a Norman bearing a small cask of wine to the head table.

As man and dog headed toward a collision, a voice boomed, *"Rufus, halte-là!"*

Rufus stopped in his tracks, releasing the barrel and reflexively going for his sword. The keg hit the wooden floor and split with a loud thud, shaking the very planks beneath them and startling Gryff into a screeching yip. He was immediately doused with the spurting wine, as was Rufus, raised sword and all.

"Merde!" the Norman swore, wine trickling down his face and neck and onto his bliaud like blood from a spurting wound.

Raven launched herself toward Gryff, obviously thinking to protect him from a sword blow, and Merlyn looked on in horror as her daughter flung herself into the path of the startled warrior.

Rolf's hand swiftly clamped onto Rufus's wrist. *"Doucement!"* he said in a low, urgent voice. "Easy!"

Rufus relaxed immediately, but his annoyance was only too apparent. "Wasted a precious cask of wine," he muttered, "because of a cur and an English brat." He shoved his sword into its scabbard.

Out of ingrained habit, Merlyn reached for an empty vessel from the nearest table and moved quickly to the cracked cask. "Help me," she said to another woman nearby. She set the good keg on the floor and moved to lift the damaged one. As she and the woman bent to the task, Rolf moved in and stopped her.

She glanced down at his fingers about her forearm, and Merlyn was reminded of the ugly stain that still marked her skin in places, contrasting his hand and hers. A Moor, she thought . . . She surely must resemble what she imagined a Moor would look like.

Her eyes met his, her cheeks fiery.

"Do you realize just how precious this wine is?" Rolf demanded in a taut voice. She stared at his mouth for a moment. His lips were thinned with annoyance now, his cheeks touched with color from the wine he'd consumed.

It would be extremely foolish to let him slip under her guard, she knew. She had to keep him at arm's length, or she—all of them—would regret it.

"Do you?" he repeated.

"Not to us," she retorted. "And *you* were the one, I believe, who warned your man. He couldn't wait to draw his sword against . . . an English brat."

He searched her face, as if he couldn't believe she'd said what she did. "You jest!"

Her mouth tightened. "Who gave the hound to Raven in the first place? If you wish it, we can go back where we came from!"

He took her by the elbow and pulled her to her feet, leaving the other woman and Rufus to salvage what they could of the wine. "You're not going anywhere. You're *my* people now!"

The grim set of his features, the determined tone of his voice, the very words he'd uttered, made him appear ludicrous, he realized belatedly. Like a possessive child who considers everything within sight to belong to him and not to be shared.

To Merlyn it sounded like a shackle snapping shut around her soul.

She jerked her arm away. "I—*we*—belong to no one but ourselves! If you choose to treat us like your possessions, we can just leave!"

"You swore fealty to me!"

"In England, fealty is a bargain between two

154

parties. If you don't live up to *your* part, you have naught."

"'Tis not the Norman way . . ."

"We are in *England*. We have our moots—our courts. The hundred . . . and shire . . . and even—"

"Not under Norman rule!" His angry eyes bored deeply into hers. "I don't wonder now why William slaughtered so many in Northumbria. You are a stubborn, disobedient lot."

Merlyn paled beneath the stain at the reminder of the catastrophic killing in northern England, and Rolf immediately regretted his words. But not enough to take them back. He opened his mouth again and then caught sight of Raven, clutching Gryff to her and staring at him, her eyes wide with fear.

It tore at his gut, that look.

He noticed, too, the silence in the great hall. He wrenched his gaze away from the little girl and threw a quick look about him, noting that neither Hugh nor Roger—not even Myles—was coming forward to interfere. *Baptism by fire*, he thought with grim irony.

"Don't interrupt the celebration on my account," he said into the strained quiet. "I bid you enjoy what we have this eve, for we'll not be able to do it again until after spring. On the morrow, the work continues at twice the pace, for I'll not have my domain vulnerable to attack any longer than absolutely necessary."

Hugh came up to Rolf and Merlyn as several celebrants began to talk and move about them. He bent down to Raven, holding out a bright red ribbon he'd pulled from beneath his belt. "Look what my lady sent for you, child," he offered gently. "'Tis just like my lady Brenna wears in her hair."

155

Raven's attention was immediately snagged by the bright bauble, and her eyes trained on it as eagerly as if it were a handful of gold coins.

At the mention of Brenna, Rolf was doused with the reminder of what he had left behind in Normandy. For this.

Unexpected bitterness twisted through him. For a moment this morn he'd thought of Merlyn as a comely, intelligent woman, and had glimpsed a chance for them all to build a good and solid future.

As he allowed his pessimism free rein, his hopes, however ephemeral, were swept away, leaving only disappointment and frustration . . . a sense of irretrievable loss. Normandy and the uncomplicated life of a landless chevalier. Hugh and Brenna and peaceful, pastoral Conteville . . . all vanished before his mind's eye like so many whorls of mist into a clearing day.

"'Twas an unfortunate choice of words."

Rolf nodded but shrugged his shoulders negligently. "Mayhap. But an accurate one."

"It seems to me," Roger told him as he rubbed the blade of his sword until it returned his reflection, "that Merlyn is the one who definitely shows a lack of respect for authority. . . ." He looked askance at Rolf. "*Your* authority, specifically."

Rolf scowled at Roger. "She made no bones about asking why *I* had to remain here instead of either of you. Her disappointment was obvious when I told her that you both had obligations elsewhere."

Hugh was sharpening his dagger on a whetstone. Everyone else was abed, most of Merlyn's band electing to sleep under the stars rather than in the hall. Merlyn had made it clear as to her preference, having left as soon as she'd attended to Derwick.

The three chevaliers were at one end of the hall where there were few sleepers, and Hugh could see to any of Derwick's needs while Merlyn slept. The image of Merlyn, her pure profile limned by the fire as she'd tended the fevered Saxon, came to Rolf unexpectedly. He dismissed it from his mind, allowing his irritation the upper hand.

With a twinkle in his eye, Hugh looked at Rolf and said, "I say you beat her."

Roger glanced at him sharply, but Rolf's face lifted at the thought . . . until he met his friend's eyes. "Damn it, Hugh! 'Tis nothing to make light of."

"She's the fly in the ointment, isn't she?" Roger asked, looking steadily at Rolf.

"The ointment was bad to begin with. She's only added to its rancidness. I thought to put her in her place when I made her bathe earlier this morn, but the tables turned and . . ." His words died off as he remembered what had happened.

"You discovered what a gem you have right beneath your nose," Hugh said quietly.

"Gem? A backward Anglo-Saxon woman?"

As he said the words, Rolf realized that he was insulting Roger's wife. A slow flush rose in his face. "I'm sorry, Roger. I meant no insult to Liane."

"No offense taken. I felt the same way upon reaching England . . . until I met Liane."

"Not just any Anglo-Saxon wench, Rolf, but a thane's widow," Hugh continued. Derwick moaned in his sleep. Hugh looked over at him for a moment, but the Englishman stilled. "Do you want some advice?" he asked suddenly, his expression serious.

Rolf's mouth curved with rue. "For once I'm not sure."

"Wed her. Whether you win her first or nay, wed

her. You have more than enough attributes to win over a woman, even an Englishwoman. If she hates you at first, she will slowly come to realize that, as her new lord, you honor her in taking her to wife. Treat her well and you'll win over the rest of them, also." He began polishing his newly sharpened dagger, a thoughtful frown creasing his handsome forehead. "And the sooner the better. There's no time to waste."

Rolf grimaced. "Force her to wed me"—he snapped his fingers—"just like that." He shook his head. "Even were I willing, 'twould be no easy thing with such a one as Merlyn."

"You of all people must surely know that life is not easy," Hugh told him. "You've seen what William has had to deal with to keep his domain intact—on both sides of the Channel. If you want something badly enough, if 'tis important enough to you, then 'tis worth the effort and risk involved."

Rolf stared at the timekeeping candle, with its marks for each hour, before him on the table. A half-finished game of chess, discarded by Myles and John, stood nearby, its carved oaken figurines scattered. He dragged his gaze from the lowering orange-gold flame and looked up at his friends. "Do you really think I can do it?" He shook his head, doubt showing in his expression. "Do you really think it can be *done?* Here, under these circumstances?"

Roger nodded. Hugh rose to his feet before the whetstone and moved over to Rolf.

"*Oui, mon camarade.*" He put a hand on Rolf's shoulder. "As I said before, what you don't know, your people will teach you. If you combine your experience and knowledge with theirs, if you persist and keep your faith . . ." He raised an eyebrow meaningfully. "If you dredge deep down and tap

158

your tolerance and compassion, you'll do as well as anyone I know."

Rolf couldn't help but smile. "But you love me as a brother, Hugh. Would you ever tell me if I couldn't succeed at something?"

Hugh squeezed Rolf's shoulder. "You know I would. I'd not give you false hopes, ever. And my lord William would never have chosen you if he didn't believe in you, as well."

Roger's steady regard, his nod of affirmation in the wake of Hugh's words, gave Rolf's confidence an even bigger boost. *"Eh bien,* then we must take ourselves to bed. The celebration is over. On the morrow we continue our work. The time you have here is already passing too quickly."

"We can do much in a few weeks if we put our minds to it," Hugh said. "Look what we've done already. And I believe Merlyn's band will help make our task easier now that they've returned to their home."

Roger added, "And remember, Valmont, what I suspect you know but mayhap have neglected in your bashing heads with Merlyn: You can attract more with honey than vinegar."

Rolf began to laugh, then Hugh joined in. And, finally, Roger. When they'd sobered enough to speak, Rolf said, "I'd better remember all this sage advice, I think, for who will help me keep my wits about me when you are gone?"

"You've always managed well enough in the past," Hugh told him. "Don't sell yourself short."

"But remember this, too," Roger added. "If you haven't the respect and affection of those you rule, you have nothing."

Chapter 10

The days passed swiftly, too swiftly for Merlyn.

Rolf, for different reasons, too, would have slowed time if he could. But he threw himself into the restoration of Renford with a vengeance, determined that, no matter what, he would succeed in his venture, if for no other reason than to live up to Hugh and Roger's expectations.

And to prove to Merlyn, although he would never have admitted it, that he was just as capable as either of the Conteville brothers. The memory of her blunt question when he'd brought her the boar carcass remained with him like an irritating shadow: *Why must* you *remain here?*

The walnut stain had disappeared within a sennight, leaving only slowly fading shadows beneath her eyes, emphasizing her regal cheekbones and the haunted, almost ethereal look about her thin face. She slept many hours, a testament to her ordeal, and was distant and quiet around Rolf. She also kept out of his way whenever possible and avoided looking directly at him. He suspected this, too, would pass, and he was careful to give her no reason to fear or distrust him further. The one exception, however, was during the second week after her return to the village.

He'd heard two low female voices behind the kitchen one morn. One of them was Merlyn's, and it was obvious that she was agitated . . . angry. The other woman's voice was softer, soothing. It sounded like Elsa.

". . . would my lord Wolf say?" the older woman was asking Merlyn.

"I care not. 'Tis *my* hair and the . . ." He couldn't make out the rest, but it sounded desperately defiant.

Rolf swiftly rounded the corner of the separate kitchen, causing Merlyn to start. Elsa, too, looked up at him in obvious surprise.

"What is amiss here?" he asked with a frown.

His suspicions were confirmed as he caught sight of a kitchen dagger in Merlyn's hands, one hank of long black hair over the front of her shoulder.

"I forbid you to cut your hair."

The words were quiet but firm, brooking no opposition.

Merlyn grabbed the tresses draped over her shoulder and Rolf made a move toward her.

"Stay where you are!" she warned, an edge of hysteria to her voice. The weapon was pointed upward, its hilt clutched tightly in her fist.

"You would not be so selfish as to rob Raven of her only parent, which would happen whether you succeeded in killing me or taking the knife to yourself." He reached for the dagger. "Or would you?"

Distress clouded her face, and her reply was not at all what he'd expected from Merlyn of Renford. "But 'tis hopelessly tangled, even with Elsa's help I cannot free it." She sounded perilously close to weeping, and Rolf suspected she didn't want to snip off her hair any more than he wanted her to. Frustration was speaking.

"Here, let me," he said.

The look Merlyn gave him reminded him of a wounded doe as the hunter approached for the death blow. Even Elsa looked at him askance.

"I . . . *eh bien*, Hugh raises destriers and I have helped him care for them on many occasions."

"Destriers?"

"*Oui*. Hugh says I have a special way of grooming their manes and tails and—"

Outrage overcame fear. "Horses? Manes and tails?"

Before her anger could grow any more, Rolf took her firmly by the shoulders and sat her down on an empty wine cask. "Elsa, do you please ask one of the squires to fetch Charon's special comb."

Elsa complied, and Rolf began to gently run his fingers through the knotted mane. It was like snarled silk.

"You'll not use a horse's comb on me!" she said indignantly.

"Charon is well kept, if you fear dirt or vermin," Rolf said. "Although he might take exception to garlic."

With her back to him, Merlyn didn't see the half-smile that curved his mouth. She jerked as if slapped, winced at the hold he kept on her hair, then sat ramrod-straight, her back rigid.

"You wish to see me pampered and pretty, then, to better tempt your men?" she asked, her tone bitter.

Rolf's fingers stilled. "You'll not find a one of my men eager to harm you," he told her. "They were all picked for their loyalty, their willingness to obey."

The stiffness of her body remained, however, to Rolf's disappointment. Winning her trust wasn't

162

going to be easy. Why had he somehow thought that once she was back in Renford, it would be?

Patience, Valmont. She's been through more than any female ought.

Bryce appeared with the implement in hand, wearing a look of puzzlement. As he handed it to Rolf, Merlyn jumped to her feet.

Regarding the large-toothed comb as if it were a viper, she declared, "You'll not use an—an *animal's* grooming tool on me, Norman!"

Rolf pushed her back down onto the cask. "You can wash your hair afterwards."

The touch of impatience in his voice temporarily quieted Merlyn. She submitted to his attentions with her arms crossed over her chest and a tiny tendril of fear twining about her heart.

He was surprisingly gentle, Rolf de Valmont was. Yet the less discomfort he caused her, the tighter the feeling in her chest. Gentle and kind, Rolf de Valmont was more insidious a threat to her than had he been cruel; for he was in his prime and sinfully handsome, and had a magical charm about him when he so chose.

Stripped of her disguise, of the persona of the crone and her outrageous behavior, Merlyn felt naked, vulnerable. She wanted to fade into the background, let someone else take over the role she'd assumed, for, reft of her screen, she felt ineffective, helpless.

And Merlyn felt truly alone. She missed Stigand. She missed the security of a man beside her every night and every morn. She missed the companionship of a good husband. She missed the warm, comfortable love that had nurtured and sustained her up until her world was destroyed as effectively as a wave crashing into an unyielding cliff, breaking into a thousand scattered droplets of water, mere echoes of its former magnitude and might.

She felt like a droplet of that water pitched back into a boiling sea, lost and helpless, insignificant in the maelstrom all about her. Only Raven gave her the strength, physically and emotionally, to keep from disappearing altogether; from silently sinking into the abyss of oblivion.

"You'll not touch one hair on your head, nor defile your skin . . . or aught else while you are under my protection," he said low in her ear, pulling her back from her troubled musings.

She turned around, her eyes meeting his. "Pretty words, lord. But were you even half what you pledge, what happens when you are gone?"

The bleakness in her voice, the despair darkening her eyes, gave Rolf pause. For here, he suddenly realized, was the other side of a battered soul. She might dislike and fear him and his men, resent them for the death and destruction they'd wrought (no matter that 'twas because of their rebellions), but perhaps even more frightening to her was the instability and uncertainty of the future facing her. Surely someone of her position—wife and mother—would be afraid to succumb to the lure of that ephemeral entity . . . permanence.

Before he could voice any type of assurances—something he was not accustomed to doing—she spoke again. "These are naught but the fears of a weak and spineless female." Self-contempt weighted her words. "You will go about your business and I'll go about mine, Sieur de Valmont. Perhaps we can learn to tolerate one another with common goals between us."

The emptiness of her words struck Rolf once again, for he'd never heard a voice so bereft of hope.

He worked silently as he finished untangling the

last of her hair, then, in the guise of seeking any hidden snarls one last time, he ran his fingers through the long, dark silken strands. His fingers were so gentle, almost worshipful, that he thought for certain Merlyn would object, would pull her hair from his grasp and leave him.

But as the tough and fearsome Norman chevalier carefully splayed his callused swordsman's fingers through Merlyn's hair, she sat quietly, head bowed, before him. As one finger touched her cheek, it encountered a telltale wetness. An unnamed emotion rose within him.

He said nothing, however, for he didn't know what to say.

The unnamed feeling tugged harder within him, something alien but deep-seated. Something that wouldn't be dismissed or denied. He was half afraid to try and identify it, for he felt it so keenly that he thought surely it would decry him as weak, in some way, to the world.

Rolf suddenly knew the strangest urge to dry her tears. He watched her rise from her seat, thank him woodenly, then retreat to the hall. He didn't turn to watch her move away but remained standing where he was, comb in hand, picturing the way she moved, the way her glossy black hair hung down her back like liquid obsidian.

And the expression in her eyes, about her mouth . . . a hint of resigned futility. It didn't belong on her exquisite face, he found himself deciding, and he wanted to wipe it away. But there were so many things between them, even to make the meanest friendship a thing of difficulty, if possible at all.

Regret, a sense of loss, filtered through him, for Rolf de Valmont found himself wanting more than a mere friendship with Merlyn of Renford. And that was about as likely as capturing the moon.

Wed her. Whether you win her first or nay, wed her.

He shook his head to dispel the memory of Hugh's words of advice, then turned and strode toward the front of the manor. He surely was under some kind of bizarre spell cast by Merlyn the crone.

And his punishment for being a Norman in conquered Anglo-Saxon England was to pine for that which he could not have . . . again.

Absurd!

By the time two weeks had passed, most of the cottages, save for finishing touches, had been repaired. The fence surrounding Renford and the palisade around the manor house had been repaired, and the interior of the church had been cleaned and put to rights by Father Francis, Garth, and the rather questionable merit of Marthe's contributions. The altar cloth had been burned to cinders, but a simple wooden altar had been built to replace the one that had been destroyed, and several candles had been donated by Hugh de Conteville from his own village church in Normandy.

"By this time next year," Rolf had promised Father Francis determinedly, "the women will be spinning flax for a linen altar cloth."

Marthe had latched onto Garth since returning to Renford, and Merlyn felt pity for the unfortunate man. Rolf caught her watching Marthe, sympathy in her expression, and had smiled in understanding. She caught the curve of his mouth, but just as her eyes went to his, Rolf tactfully lowered his gaze, for Garth walked by, Marthe in his wake. The Saxon looked none too happy about his unwitting "acquisition."

"'Tis unfortunate for Derwick that he's almost up and about," Rolf commented as he walked past Merlyn.

He was rewarded by a soft, lilting laugh, the first he'd ever heard from her, and he was utterly enchanted. However, he kept moving, afraid to show her undue attention and distance her from him . . . from this small yet significant sharing of merriment.

Merlyn went outside to Derwick, who was sitting in the September sun beside the whetstone, sharpening their small, precious supply of farming implements.

"How are you today?" she asked him as she knelt to examine his leg. The whetstone stopped, the whir of stone against steel fading.

"Lady, you need not kneel to me," he said in a low voice.

She looked up at him. "We are all equal now," she answered. *"They* rule all of us." Her fingers gently glided over the healing wound. "You'll be fit to return to work in a few days. Your leg is nearly good as new."

"Thanks to you, lady." At Merlyn's frown, he added, "I cannot call you Merlyn when you were Stigand's wife. He was known in our village, too, as a wise and capable man."

She rolled down the leg of his braies and stood. "And he is gone. So is our old way of life."

"Only if we so choose!"

His low, earnest words brought a look of bemusement to her features. "You mustn't talk like that! 'Tis exactly why we find ourselves as we are now."

"Nay." He stood and moved closer to her. "If we had resisted more staunchly, Harold Godwinson would still be king."

Merlyn wanted to disagree with him, tell him that

167

Harold Godwinson's forces at Hastings had been exhausted from fighting Harald Hardrada of Norway at Stamford Bridge only days before . . . and that they'd been overpowered by Norman strategy and use of mounted knights, but the point was moot now. And Derwick had been at Hastings. He knew these things even better than she. "'Tis treason to talk so," she told him. "And what's done is done. Go back to your grinding, Derwick, for we'll have need of our tools in the spring."

"Aye." He sat down, his shoulders slumped. "Better that you had let me die, Merlyn, for we'll all of us starve during the winter, surely."

"And how can you talk of resistance when you envision us dying of hunger? *This* is where we can succeed if we are determined."

"Bah. You are under his influence already. But mark me, Merlyn," Derwick said, his words curdled with bitterness, "he will fail us. He will make slaves of us all, and he will fail us as leader."

"Then why came you to Renford?" she asked. "You came by choice, did you not?"

"Aye. And mayhap I had a purpose other than kissing Valmont's backside." But he said nothing more, returning to his task.

Merlyn slowly swung away with a frown, suspecting she knew exactly what he was talking about.

The medicinals that Liane of Derford had sent were much needed, and covered just about every ailment or injury that a village populace could have. Merlyn, however, had always employed several potions and brews handed down from her mother and grandmother, for which she hadn't all the proper ingredients.

One of them was an excellent cure for an aching head after too much mead or wine. She was also determined to find Ealdwyn's errant bees and their honey to eventually brew mead for her hardworking people. Some might say it was frivolous, but of a certainty Rolf de Valmont would never share much of his precious and limited supply of wine with the English over whom he was lord.

Merlyn ignored the memory of Norman wine that had been set out at the celebration the other day. Most Saxons preferred their mead, anyway, she thought ungenerously, and she would brew them some.

"Where do you go?" the Norman called Rufus, who was standing sentry at the gate, asked her in heavily accented English.

"My lord Rolf granted me leave to search for . . . medicinal herbs close to the village," she lied without a qualm. There was no real reason she had to apprise Valmont of her excursions about the immediate perimeter of Renford. Surely, in light of his assurances of having secured the area, there was no danger if she didn't venture too far.

The Norman stroked his smooth-shaven chin, his eyes narrowed consideringly. Merlyn didn't care for the way he took her in, from head to toe, but she hid her irritation . . . and tried to ignore the feather of fear that tickled the nape of her neck at his obvious male appraisal. He was yet another giant of a man, a typically tall Norman with bright red hair. But she would not show him her misgivings.

"Alone?" His auburn brows snapped together.

"Aye." She lifted her chin with pride. "'Twas my village . . . I know where I can go and where I cannot."

He looked doubtful for a moment, then shook his head. "Rolf wouldn't let a woman wander the forest alone with—"

"My lord Rolf," she cut him off, "told me himself that he had secured the land around Renford. Are you saying he's wrong?"

The man's brows shot up in momentary surprise, then lowered again in obvious ire. "I said nothing of the kind!" He glanced at the manor yard, then at the area about the well. When he looked back at Merlyn, his mouth was set in a grim line. "Stay close, do you hear? And if you are lying to me, you'll quickly regret it."

And good riddance to you, his eyes seemed to say, but Merlyn was already walking past, a basket slung over her arm. Ealdwyn the beekeeper was dead, the bees gone back to the wild. More than likely they had taken up residence in any tree hollows they could find. Hopefully, the trees weren't far away.

How she would induce them to give up their honey, she refused to think about just yet. If not today, then mayhap on the morrow.

Oak, beech, chestnut, ash, birch, and a conifer here and there surrounded her in their quiet majesty. The sounds from the village muted, then died, as she went deeper into the forest. The twitter of the birds, the soft, shuffling sounds of smaller animals on the ground . . . She paused, listening. Something was following her. It paused when she did.

Unease trickled through her. Surely it couldn't be anything so close to Renford. Surely Rolf was capable of . . .

Why was she defending Rolf de Valmont? Since when did she have any faith in him?

Since you have no choice. You came out of the forest at his command and placed yourself under his protection.

She loved the forest, resenting the fact that now,

with a Norman usurper on the throne, more and more of it was being included in the Royal Forest, where only the king or those granted special licenses could hunt. Even the wild honey of the forest was claimed by the Bastard.

"The honey was *ours,*" she muttered, "until they murdered our beekeeper and scattered the bees. I but seek to retrieve it."

She moved forward, straining to hear if the animal—or human—was still behind her. It was.

Self-reproach rose within her as she hastened to circle back to Renford: Why *did* you venture out alone? To defy *him?* To prove your courage and mettle? Now you'll reap the consequences of your stupidity. . . .

A hand on her arm stopped her in mid-flight.

She swung around, her flimsy basket raised in defense, her face a study in bleak determination. "You!"

Rolf de Valmont stood before her, Gryff under one arm. Relief swamped Merlyn, and anger followed immediately on its heels. "Why are you following me?" she asked, trying to put him on the defensive.

His green-brown eyes probed hers. "I wasn't following you," he answered. "Gryff here had gone after you. I was trying to catch him before a wolf did . . . or Marthe."

She completely missed the light of levity in his eyes, feeling, instead, a strange disappointment. "Why would a grand chevalier such as yourself bother chasing a stray hound? Have you nothing better to do?" The last words were more acerbic than Merlyn had intended, a result of her inexplicable irritation with him.

The humor softening his features disappeared, his lips compressed momentarily; then, as if he'd gained

171

control of his annoyance, his features relaxed again. He arched one dark, devilish eyebrow. "Rufus told me the pup was probably following you." He bent to set Gryff on his feet. The dog attacked Merlyn's foot with puppyish exuberance, gnawing on one of her bare toes.

"Stop it!" she hissed, jerking back her foot, only to feel even more keenly his tiny, sharp teeth clinging with a vengeance. Her face contorted with pain before the determined little animal lost his grip and plopped back to the ground with a soft grunt.

"He's fond of you," Rolf said, unable to remain angry with her in the wake of her plight. "Don't you like animals?" he queried with a straight face.

"Aye!" she snapped. "I love animals!" She glared at Gryff.

Rolf shook his head and glanced down at the pup, who was now licking the trickle of blood from Merlyn's toe. "He's got courage. He'll be a good bandog and protect you from wolves . . . or worse."

The pale-hued, minuscule mastiff sat down at last and looked up at Merlyn with his soulful, bicolored eyes, his pink tongue lolling.

"There . . . you see? You've hurt his feelings by saying you don't like him." He looked back at Merlyn. "Can it be that you dislike him because *I* gave him to Raven? And you can't abide the thought that the child might like *me?*"

The accuracy of his theory gave Merlyn a jolt, and for a moment she couldn't meet his eyes. "Do I need your permission, Lord Wolf, to continue my errand?" she asked, ignoring his unnerving question.

"I would think, as widow of the leader of your villagers, you would show more wisdom than that."

She stuck out her chin mutinously, her eyes darkening to a stormy blue. "There was no need for such precautions so close to Renford before you and your kind came and laid waste to populace and countryside alike. My husband and those he governed could take care of most threats. Evidently now, even though you informed me that this area is safe, you cannot be taken at your word."

He took her by the arm and steered her back in the direction away from Renford, his grip communicating his affront. "I only have so many men, *madame*, to patrol the *weald*," he said through stiff lips. "If the need to rebuild and fortify Renford wasn't so pressing, I would gladly spare more manpower to ensure the absolute safety of your leisurely excursions."

She rounded on him, yanking her arm from his grip and causing Gryff, who was following at their heels, to slam into her ankle with a yelp— which added nothing to her attempt at dignified outrage.

Before she could say a word, Rolf decided then and there that he preferred her this way—prickly as a briar thorn—to subdued and distant as she'd been since returning to the village. But he also had to admit to himself that he would have preferred her, even more, soft and compliant . . . and willing to lose herself in his embrace.

". . . hardly a leisurely excursion. I seek medicinal herbs and barks to supplement what Sieur de Conteville's wife sent along. And . . ." She trailed off, doubting the wisdom of revealing her other errand.

"And what?" One hand came up to brush back a flyaway wisp of her hair that the breeze gently blew across her cheek. Her skin beneath his knuckle was like satin, the strand of hair like dark gossamer, tickling the back of his hand.

His eyes held hers with so potent a pull that

Merlyn's thoughts went scattering with the breeze. "H—honey."

"Honey?" His gaze dropped to her mouth. Her lips were still slightly parted from speaking, and he caught a glimpse of white, even teeth.

He slowly raised his hands and cradled her cheeks with a touch so soft that it brought unexpected—and unwelcome—moisture to Merlyn's eyes.

She regained her senses as a thread of fear coiled through her. More powerful than the tenderness of his touch, the seeming sincerity in his eyes, were the images of a rutting Norman looming over her and . . .

"Merlyn," he murmured, the deep register of his voice as soft and soothing as velvet, "wed me."

The hush around them was like the benevolent silence of a cathedral, and in that fleeting moment Rolf de Valmont knew that he was falling in love with Merlyn of Renford. An Anglo-Saxon woman, who'd attempted to pass herself off as a hag, a termagant, a soothsayer, a witch, and God knew what else . . . this woman had unwittingly succeeded in pushing Brenna de Conteville's image from his mind in this moment. Nay, in all the moments since she'd emerged from her bath only days ago.

"For the sake of your people, wed me."

What had someone once told him? he thought with one rational part of his mind. The longer a man waited for love, the harder it hit him. . . .

Her expression suddenly turned sour. "Surely you are mad, Norman, to even think to ask such a thing."

He hadn't necessarily expected acceptance, although one could always cling to hope, but her words were like a slap in the face. Male pride reared up, causing him to delve into his darker side. "Nay, wench, *you* are the one who is mad to refuse my offer.

You'll not receive another from me."

Caution crept into her breast. He could have beat her on the spot, even put her to death for refusing his civilly worded command. But she couldn't find it within herself to wed a Norman, even for the good of her people. Besides, how could she know if he spoke the truth in that respect, in spite of his words? And how could she ever marry one of those who had killed Stigand? The rest of her family? How could she unite, physically or emotionally, with one of those who had vanquished and then ravaged England and the English?

"Then so be it," she answered. "Now, may I have your permission to proceed?" Her voice was still husky with emotion . . . and apprehension at what he still could do.

"Not unescorted."

"Then may I have an escort from the village?"

Instantly, Merlyn knew she'd made a mistake. While she meant no offense, only to allow him to return to his responsibilities in Renford and allow someone less needed to accompany her, she guessed by the look in his eyes that he believed she had no desire for his company . . . and fresh in the wake of her refusal of his offer of marriage.

"Perhaps Cedric," she hastened to add. "Or— or—"

The smile she'd given Cedric the eve of the celebration came back to sear Rolf's pride, piquing an uncharacteristic jealousy. "A one-legged man is no protection against a renegade or deserter."

"How little you know of strength and courage if that is what you believe."

Their gazes locked, and Rolf felt even more keenly a sense of loss at her refusal of his offer, for she was absolutely right. How wise she was for her years, he thought, and how petty of him to have said such a thing about Cedric of Renford.

"Nonetheless," he said with quiet conviction in the face of his newest discovery concerning Merlyn of Renford, "I'm afraid you'll have to settle for me this time."

And with a grim set to his features, he gestured for her to proceed along the path, with Gryff trotting along behind them.

Chapter 11

Just what she needed, Merlyn thought peevishly. Rolf de Valmont following her about like the pesky pup. How seriously did he take his role if he preferred accompanying her on a hunt for herbs and honey to overseeing his greater responsibilities?

Some lord he'll make! she mused as she tromped through the trees in irritation, completely ignoring both man and dog behind her. So perturbed was she that Merlyn almost passed by the partially hollowed tree where some of Ealdwyn's bees had made their home.

Rolf touched her shoulder, causing her to stiffen and stop. No doubt he wanted to . . .

"Look," he said, and pointed to a giant elm tree several steps back from the path. The faint hum of bees could be heard above the hiss of the gentle wind. If she'd been concentrating on her task, she silently chastised herself, she would have caught it before Rolf.

She followed his pointing finger, and sure enough, there was a hive in the hollow of the elm, slightly higher than the top of Rolf's head. Bees swarmed about it, which meant that the hive was overcrowded and the food plentiful.

Suddenly, an idea came to her. Her eyes took on an unholy gleam. She lowered her gaze for a moment, lest he divine her intent.

"Would you help me gather damp leaves to make a fire?" she asked sweetly.

Rolf looked askance at her upon hearing the tone of her voice. "What if they attack?"

"They only attack those on whom they smell fear." Her gaze met his in silent challenge.

"Alors," he said without missing a beat, "let's do it." He scanned the forest around them for a long moment, head canted; then, obviously satisfied, Rolf asked, "Where shall we build this fire?"

"Upwind," Merlyn answered as she searched for the proper spot. "There." She pointed to a place where Gryff was stalking a moth, belly to the ground, and bent to gather a basketful of leaves.

With Rolf's help, they had enough fuel in minutes, and Merlyn produced a piece of flint from a pouch in the folds of her bliaut. She noted Rolf's wariness when a bee would venture too close to him, but his efforts at nonchalance were admirable.

"'Tis a puny fire," he observed.

"Would you want to alert every renegade in Northumbria?" she asked with a raised eyebrow.

"Nay, of course not, but will it do the trick?"

Merlyn sighed and straightened from the newly lit fire. "Damp leaves cause smoke—"

"I am aware of that."

"—which will chase the bees from the tree. We do not, however, want to kill them, only make them sluggish, else we'll destroy this particular source of honey." She moved toward the elm. "I'll need a boost up to the hole, Sieur de Valmont."

He joined her with dubiousness and bent, linking his fingers to form a cradle for her foot.

178

He boosted her up and she warned, "Easy now," as the smoke enveloped the tree.

A new wave of bees swarmed out from the hollow in a black, buzzing cloud, but their movements quickly became sluggish and disoriented. Merlyn reached slowly into the hive. "Mother of God," she said softly.

"What is it?" Rolf asked, his eyes almost crossing as he watched several bees hover around his nose. He dared not move, for fear of causing Merlyn to fall . . . and his being stung.

"'Tis a huge hive . . . with an enormous honeycomb."

"Then—then take it all," he urged, just as Gryff yelped and scampered to the other side of the fire. "And be quick about it."

She was feather-light, but standing among a myriad of disturbed bees was not Rolf's idea of fun, no matter how pleasant it was to be so close to her—touching her—nor how easy she was to hold.

"'Tis not so simple as that," she said in a low voice. "They need enough to get them through the winter. . . . I'll not rob them of their food supply."

Rolf couldn't believe his ears. "And who is more important?" he countered with impatience. "Us or the bees?"

"To what purpose to use up our only source of honey thus far? To kill the creatures who can help feed us?" she hissed down at him.

Still smarting from her rejection of his proposal, Rolf felt like feigning a series of tremors just to jostle her and put her in her place, which, at that moment, he felt was on her backside on the ground. "We both know this honey won't feed us. Rather 'twill make the mead you and yours so love . . . to make your new life more palatable."

"Anything to that end would be welcome!" she

countered, tempted to fling a piece of sticky honeycomb right at his head. "If you were more civil, we would have a great deal less need for mead, wouldn't we? But I noticed that you brought aplenty of your Norman wine."

Before he could answer, Merlyn reached into the tree and gingerly pulled out a piece of honeycomb. Part of it was still sealed with wax, but the section damaged by her groping hand was oozing with honey. In spite of the insects buzzing around him, Rolf felt his mouth water at the sight, for he had an undeniable sweet tooth.

"Can you take this?"

"Only if I drop you," he said. *"Doucement . . .* steady now."* He lowered her to the forest floor, castigating himself for ever having thought to frighten her, and bent to retrieve the basket.

"Slowly!" Merlyn warned, but it was too late. As he reached for the basket, Rolf jerked, stung. "Ah! God's foot!"

"Put down the basket and move slowly toward the fire," Merlyn directed.

He looked at her through the haze of smoke and humming insects and began to cough. As he raised his hand to his mouth he was stung again, and he moved with alacrity toward the small, smoldering fire.

"Slowly!" Merlyn repeated, a touch of exasperation in her voice.

They only attack those on whom they smell fear.
The memory of her words shamed him as he retreated toward the fire. Yet a mass of woozy honeybees was a completely different type of adversary than that to which he was accustomed. Sword and lance were out of the question here.

Merlyn, feeling suddenly guilty, followed him to the fire and led him round the other side of it. By now, he was slapping at his neck and shoulders, waving frantically at the bees hovering around his face.

"Be still," she ordered him, taking his wrists in her hands and pulling them away from his face. "You're only making things worse by stirring them up."

Rolf opened one eye and peered at her, a scowl pulling down the corners of his handsome mouth. "They were supposed to be sluggish, I believe you said," he told her through set teeth. "If these bees are woozy, I warrant I'd be safer among their unsmoked comrades!"

He tried to slap away an errant bee still hovering around his face, but Merlyn held him back with a considerable amount of effort. "I told you to be still, Norman. Raven minds better than you do!"

At the look on his face, she hurried to add, "And 'twas *your* idea to accompany me, not mine."

The bites on his neck were turning red and starting to swell.

"Why have they not attacked you?" he asked suspiciously, prying her fingers from his wrists and moving even farther upwind from the fire.

Merlyn bent to examine Gryff, who was whimpering at her feet and swiping at his little nose with one paw. "I told you I come from a long line of healers . . . of Druid priestesses and soothsayers in the land of the Cymry. We are one with nature."

"A pagan, no less," he muttered with unmistakable sarcasm. "A Welsh witch . . . a pagan Druid. By the rood, how did your late husband find you?" In search of relief, he knelt and scooped up some of the fecund soil beneath the leaves covering the forest floor and applied it to his neck, welcoming the coolness.

"I was born in Renford. Rather 'twas my father who fell in love with my mother and took her by force from her land."

"The perfect way to begin a marriage."

"'Twas not political, but rather out of love."

"I see."

"My mother returned his devotion after a while and never spoke of returning to her people after that."

She fell silent for a while. Rolf sat with his back to her, the fire, and the dog, feeling like an utter fool. Well, he would just ignore the pain—he'd certainly suffered much worse—and wait until Hugh could look at the bites. He wouldn't ask *her* for any favor now.

The nooning horn sounded in the distance. "'Tis time to return," he said, "and eat." *Among other things*, he thought darkly, already planning his revenge for Merlyn of Renford. "Is it safe to move now?" he asked.

There was no answer.

"Merlyn?" He got to his knees and swung around toward the fire . . .

And caught a glimpse of flailing foliage and what he thought was a flash of the bottoms of Merlyn's bare feet disappearing into the tree vines and underbrush. Gryff suddenly emitted a high-pitched bark and Rolf lunged to his feet, his bee stings forgotten.

Too late. A cord was jerked around his neck from behind just as Rolf saw the puppy go down from a glancing blow to the head by a flying stone. He gripped the cord with both hands before it was pulled up against his flesh, matching his strength with that of his assailant.

It was a Scot, he would have wagered anything. A stinking, savage Scot, he could tell immediately. Or a half-starved, wild Saxon, stinking as badly as a Scot and more desperate.

Uppermost in his mind was Merlyn, however. He

had to overpower the intruder behind him and go after her before . . .

As his attacker moved closer to him in an obvious attempt to get a better hold on the rope, Rolf employed an old trick his eldest brother had taught him as a boy. He jackknifed forward, throwing his hips back into his assailant's midsection, and pulled the man over his head. The miscreant somersaulted through the air and was slammed onto his back at Rolf's feet, the breath knocked from his lungs.

After a glance over his shoulder, Rolf slit the man's throat with his dagger and plunged into the woods after Merlyn.

Merlyn struggled against whoever was dragging her into the *weald*. Every kind of horrible thought came to her in those moments: He would rape her, then kill her. He would kill her and then Rolf, before leading his hordes back to Renford, obliterating it once and for all. And Raven.

Even as she fought her attacker, sinking her teeth into his hand over her mouth and flinging back her head, hoping to do damage to his face, painful as it was, one small part told her to give up. The exhausted, ancient-feeling, world-weary part of Merlyn, the one that had experienced firsthand the worst of what man was capable in his darkest moments, urged her to succumb to what was obviously the inevitable.

Yet the stronger side of her, that of youth and the instinctive love for her child, love for her people, and, yes, love of precious life itself, wouldn't allow her to follow that other voice. And so Merlyn clung fiercely to her hold on life and fought with a frenzy.

The man finally dropped her flat on the ground, momentarily stunning her. Before she could draw breath, he was on top of her, his hand over her mouth. His long, wild hair and naked chest proclaimed him a Scot, and she felt his hips grinding into hers as he stretched her arms up over her head. His eyes were alight with an insane kind of triumph.

As Merlyn began to arch and buck against the man in an effort to unbalance him, he suddenly stilled, pressing his hand even harder against her mouth and nose. He raised his head and listened.

The pure pressure, the cutting off of all her air, made her light-headed . . . and panicky.

Without warning, he released her face and dealt her a blow that sent her to the brink of insensibility, teetering on the edge of the Stygian chasm of nothingness.

Merlyn was dimly aware of the weight of his body removed from hers as he jumped to his feet and swung away from her. He shrieked a battle cry, and that was all Merlyn remembered during the next few minutes.

Sounds teased her ears, distorted, undulating images danced before her blurred vision, and she could make out nothing more than violent movement and grunting.

A few savage expletives in Norman French finally identified one man as Rolf. Merlyn forced herself to her elbows and painstakingly crept backward, out of the range of their struggle. As her muddled mind and bleary vision began to clear, she saw a second man hovering at the perimeter of the crushed flora and opened her mouth to issue a warning. Only a croak emerged, however, and, to her horror, Rolf, who had seemed to be getting the better of the first Scot, was suddenly besieged by the other as well.

In the melee, Rolf had lost his dagger. Merlyn caught sight of it glinting crimson and silver on the light-dappled earth not far from her. It registered fleetingly that either it was his own blood staining the blade . . . or that of yet a third assailant.

Doom pressed down on her with crushing force, all but sapping her strength, freezing her ability to think; for surely if there were three or more men against one, it was all but hopeless.

The image of Raven's face flashed before her mind . . . sweet, beautiful child.

Merlyn pushed herself to a sitting position, ignoring the pain of her own bruises. *Please, God*, she entreated. *Spare us, this time*.

Strength flowed into her, propelling her on her hands and knees toward Rolf's dagger. Her fingers closed around the hilt, and another burst of life-giving energy surged through her. She spun around, half crouched, her gaze fixed on the three struggling men before her.

The dagger seemed to pulse with a life of its own within her clenched fist, bolstering her courage. She inched forward, oblivious to everything but the need to rid her lands of interlopers once and for all.

Rolf fought like one possessed, weaponless save for his powerful, battle-toned body. His lightning blows rained down on the first Scot, one striking the man's wrist with violent force. The battle-ax dropped to the ground, leaving the stranger momentarily stunned.

Rolf whirled, his back to Merlyn as she stood pressed against the meager shield of a beech. The second Scot brandished a sword and wielded it with skill, despite the impediment of the confining trees and undergrowth. Rolf dodged its deadly edge twice, thrice. He leapt with all the grace and litheness of a cat when the sword cut an arc below his knees. It whooshed malignantly as it bit the empty air.

Before the Scot could recover from his semi-crouch, Rolf dealt him a powerful uppercut to the chin. It lifted him off his feet and sent him slamming onto his back.

Rolf bent, snatched the sword, and whirled again.

The first man had regained his feet, as well as his ax, and was wielding it against Rolf's sword. The man's eyes shone with anger and bloodlust, his long, wild hair and shaggy beard adding to his savage appearance. Almost imperceptibly, he shifted his weight from one foot to the other, in obvious anticipation of a strike from either side by Rolf.

It was then that Rolf caught sight of Merlyn. In the heat of his frenzy, relief pumped through him. He could only hope there were no others hiding in the forest around them, for until he killed the man facing him, Merlyn was open to attack from any others who might be lurking nearby.

In the fraction of time it took to glance at her face, his blood turned to sludge in his veins, for her face was contorted into a terrible expression of grim intent as she crept forward behind the Scot, her footfalls as soft as any stealthy creature of the forest.

Beyond that, however, he couldn't give her any more consideration. Neither did he dare warn her to stay back, for that would give away her position—the very fact that she was on her feet and wielding what appeared to be his dagger.

The little fool, he thought as he parried his enemy's weapon with his sword. Why couldn't she just stay out of the way? Why must she distract him and . . .

The Scot swung his battle-ax again, parallel to Rolf's rib cage, its deadly whisper whining through the air. As Rolf jumped backward, Merlyn lunged toward the Scot's back, her timing slightly miscalculated as the man pressed his offensive. Rather than stopping his swing in mid-motion, the force of her weapon striking between his shoulder blades pitched him toward the retreating Rolf.

The cold tip of the steel blade kissed Rolf's flesh, causing a thin red line to sprout across his chest through the rent overtunic. Rolf grunted softly, more from surprise than from pain. But the look on the Scot's face was almost cause for laughter, he thought, for in the twinkling of an eye, his expression of ferocity transformed into one of absurd disbelief. Rolf took advantage of his surprise and, with a swift, savage movement, thrust the sword through his adversary's heart.

Rolf stood panting, leaning on his confiscated, gore-soaked sword, staring at Merlyn. The excitement of battle still shone in his eyes. It was obvious to her that he relished a good fight.

"We're missing the midday meal," he informed her solemnly. "Are you unharmed?"

"Aye." Trying to ignore the cutting remarks that sprang to her lips in the wake of his ridiculous statement, Merlyn concentrated instead on the laceration splaying across his chest.

"And what of your wound?" She stepped forward to better examine it, then lifted his right arm to look at his healing injuries from the boar. One was oozing blood near the wrist. "Had your men been doing their job, we more than likely could have avoided this."

He watched her approach and examine him, his eyes on her fine features rather than seeking the sight of his own blood. "And had you not decided to hie yourself off into the woods to hunt for *bees*, we could have spared ourselves . . . this, as well, and left my men to other, more important considerations."

Even as he said the words, the sound of someone approaching reached Merlyn's ears. Her eyes met Rolf's, alarm widening hers, before a low whistle sounded. "'Tis Myles, no doubt, looking for us."

Rolf sounded a similar whistle, and before long Myles and Hugh appeared along the path behind them.

"Scots," Myles spat as he discovered Merlyn and Rolf standing not a stone's throw from the path where the first dead man lay.

"Two more over here," Rolf said with a grimace for Hugh.

"I see you have things well in hand. But we'll circle around before returning, just to make certain," Hugh said. "I'm sure Merlyn can tend to your hurt before you even return to the village." Merlyn could have sworn he winked at Rolf, but she had been watching Myles as he nudged the skewered Scot with his shoe, half afraid that the latter would leap to his feet with his unnerving battle scream and attack again. Not only were these savages ferocious fighters, but they were also known for their trickery and deceit.

Myles just shook his blond head and returned to the path, muttering, "We'll leave them for the scavengers. They don't deserve burial . . . especially if they were stupid enough to build a fire for smoking out bees right on your lands."

Rolf nodded, then caught Hugh's eye. They exchanged a look that Merlyn did not miss, but she remained silent, refusing to let on as she bent to search for Gryff. "Gryff!" she called in a low voice, then chirruped a few times coaxingly.

"He was struck by a stone," Rolf told her, "as he went after the man who dragged you off the path."

Merlyn felt a sharp stab of guilt, and she listened intently for a sound . . . an answering bark or rustling of the undergrowth.

Rolf whistled. A woozy Gryff staggered on his short legs from beneath a cluster of dead vines, his coat matted with burrs and a lump on the side of his head. Rolf probed it with gentle fingers. Aside from the lump, the dog seemed well enough.

Hugh asked, "Shall I take the little warrior with us? The child will be relieved." Rolf nodded and handed Gryff to Hugh. They withdrew then, Hugh bending and, with his free hand, retrieving one Scot's sword from where Rolf had dropped it and the other's ax.

"We can't just leave them to rot out here," Merlyn said, more from a wish to rid the land around Renford of their stinking carcasses than from any need to accord them a decent burial.

"They'll be disposed of later," he said in dismissal. He bent to pull his dagger from the man's back. As he wiped it on the dead man's filthy, ragged breeches, he asked, "Shall we return to eat? My belly rumbles. And I've had quite enough of bees."

Merlyn noticed the ugly red swelling on his neck. She stepped nearer, straining to make out how many bites he had sustained without getting too close.

"*Alors,* if you must know," he added just a shade irritably, "my neck hurts like the devil. Worse than the scratch on my chest."

He swung toward the path, deciding to head for the village and, therefore, the river, for some nice cool mud to apply to his stings. The thought of it was even more appealing than refreshing wine for his parched throat and overheated body.

"Wait." Merlyn moved toward him and reached up to tip his chin aside and examine his neck. Red, angry welts proclaimed the determination of several bees to defend their hive; and not only were they in a tender area, but Merlyn could tell from Rolf's expression and actions that they bothered him a great deal.

Perhaps he even knew that a man could die from a

bee sting. In this instance, his throat could possibly close, cutting off his air.

"I can remove the stingers right here," she told him. "Then we can go to the riverbank. I know of a small tributary of the Tees nearby . . . 'tis only a trickle now, but at least it's still wet. Are you willing?"

"Anything."

The very answer indicated his desperation. Merlyn swallowed, then drew in a deep, sustaining breath before telling him, "Sit. Right where you are . . . sit."

You're addled, her cautious side warned. And surely, she thought, she must be, for never before would she have thought of using this method of removing a stinger from not only a stranger, but from a male stranger . . . and in such a place as his neck.

He sat obediently, placing his trust in her as he had once before, and Merlyn knelt before him. She placed her hands on either side of his head and tilted it for better access to the cluster of bites on one small patch of his neck. Her gaze met his, some kind of warning—and another, unnamed emotion—in her eyes. Her face came closer, until only the top of her dark head was visible to Rolf (if he cared to peer down from the corner of his eye until it felt uncomfortable).

Suddenly, he felt the silky rasp of her tongue touch his heated, hurting flesh. He started, a bolt of pure, erotic sensation shooting through his lower body. "What the—?"

"Hold still!" she interrupted her sweet torture long enough to admonish him. "I cannot find the stingers if you wiggle about like Gryff." Once again her tongue touched his neck. Rolf stiffened, sensing that she knew exactly what she was doing but wondering if she knew what *else* she was doing. . . .

Merlyn found the first barbed stinger and carefully

applied her teeth to it. It came free, and she removed it from her tongue with her thumb and forefinger and showed it to Rolf. "Here's the first."

Rolf glanced at her extended finger and nodded, barely noting the speck that had caused him such discomfort. His mind and body were a jumble of roiling thoughts and sensations. Witch! Was she trying to save him or seduce him?

Save you, fool. She cannot abide your very touch, hated Norman.

Merlyn looked into his eyes, a question in hers.

Rolf nodded and steeled himself for her next assault. By now, even the bee stings faded beneath the other, more exotic sensations strumming along his veins.

Her tongue again began its delicious foray of exquisite torture. Desire roared through Rolf. His fists clenched at his sides, his entire body tensing. Merlyn felt him swallow, and she realized with a small sense of satisfaction that he was not unaffected by her actions.

But the satisfaction was short-lived, for she realized belatedly that neither was *she* unaffected. As her tongue skimmed the smooth, muscular arch of his throat, an old and familiar sensation raced through Merlyn like a flashflood, leaving her even more shaken because she had never thought to feel this way with a man again.

And especially one of those who had been responsible for England's downfall, for the rape of her lands, her people, the slaughter of her family . . .

She came to the second stinger and nipped it carefully with her teeth just as she'd done the first. When she showed it to Rolf, however, his eyes were rigidly trained upon the forest before him. She lowered her gaze and flicked the stinger from her finger. It was then that she noticed the evidence of his desire beneath his tunic. His legs were crossed as he sat upon the ground, and the bulge that was clearly visible at the apex of his thighs beneath his clothing churned up a familiar alarm in Merlyn . . . and also a familiar arousal, reminiscent of the days when Stigand had loved her with his body.

One more, she thought. One more and 'twill be done.

With another glance up at Rolf's granite-struck profile, Merlyn touched her tongue to the corded column of his neck. The contact fairly sizzled.

He flinched, all but imperceptibly, proof of the stimulation of her touch and also the iron control he exercised over himself. In Merlyn's mind, the only favorable thing was that she was fortunate enough to home right in on the stinger, having already guessed where it was lodged from the pattern of the welts. At least this last time she didn't have to slide her tongue over hot flesh and pulsing vessels beneath for more than a few seconds.

Yet brief as was this venture, so was it all the more potent because of what had preceded it. Merlyn caught the stinger between the porcelain edges of her teeth and lifted her head . . .

Only to meet Rolf's warm, moist mouth as it closed over hers with a hunger that turned her insides to butter.

Chapter 12

Merlyn felt the world begin to spin, and a roaring sound filled her head. A sweet, sweet languor crept through her body, drugging her, wiping away all rationality for long moments.

His lips were warm and firm and moist. And incredibly sweet. No kiss had ever tasted like this, and in the back of her mind the remnants of reason waved their tattered warnings, but to no avail.

His hands cupped the sides of her face, gently, wonderingly, his callused fingers gliding lightly over the satiny skin of her cheeks and jaw. His mouth worshiped hers, the unexpected, exquisite gentleness deepening slowly to a more exploratory, demanding movement as his lips parted over hers.

"Merlyn," he murmured into her mouth, their breaths mingling as his tongue sought hers.

The gentle invasion, however, brought back ugly images burned into her brain by defilement and debasement. By brutality and sheer barbarism.

Merlyn pulled away, confused and torn. She put one hand to her mouth, the other to her chest, as she drew in a ragged breath and her eyes met his, clouded with pain and outrage. And dissipating desire.

"You wretch," she accused in a shaking whisper. "Is this how you thank me for saving your life?"

Rolf made an effort to rein in his reeling emotions. "Saving my life?" he repeated with a frown, totally uncomprehending.

"Aye!" She stood then, glaring down at him with blazing blue eyes. "You could have strangled . . . still may, if the gods of the forest heed my plea this day!"

Now it was Rolf's turn to leap to his feet. "Is that why you responded so ardently to my kiss? Hoping to keep me immobile here until I *did* strangle? Is that—"

As the word *strangle* registered, he sputtered to a halt. "What do you mean, *still may?*" he asked in a fractured voice, his words weighted with suspicion. What an ignominious demise, he thought . . . to die of a few bee stings.

"Your throat could swell shut."

He could only stare at her, dumbfounded with disbelief. Surely she was trying to frighten him out of spite. And yet, wouldn't it all be exactly in keeping with . . .

Save your pity for the English . . .

With a mental oath, he bridled the bent of his thoughts.

Merlyn was suddenly overcome with guilt, for she estimated that the danger of his having an acute reaction to the stings was past . . . at least as far as affecting his breathing. Yet, here he stood, sporting nigh on a dozen nasty bee stings (there were also several welts upon the back of his neck and, she suspected, his upper back as well) because he hadn't wanted her to go into the *weald* unescorted . . . and still bleeding from the slash across his chest for coming to her rescue against two—nay, three unforeseen assailants. True, the cut was superficial,

194

but the point was, he had been willing to risk his life to save hers. And if she hadn't chosen to slip into the woods unbeknownst to him . . . if she hadn't chosen to deceive Rufus, Rolf de Valmont wouldn't be in the possible danger facing him now. Nor would he have sustained the bleeding cut across his chest.

She'd also done a disservice to that silly puppy, as well, her conscience had the audacity to remind her in that brief moment of self-recrimination.

"Have you ever been stung before? By a bee?"

He looked at her askance. "Not in the neck." As her eyes narrowed at his tart answer, he added, "Aye. When I was a lad. Several times."

"How severe was your reaction?"

He shrugged and shook his head, eyeing her warily. "No more than any others I'd seen."

Merlyn nodded, her features relaxing somewhat. "Good." She swung away, unable to look at him any longer . . . from guilt, from undeniable attraction . . . in spite of the blood and the sweat and the dirt. And that sulky, little-boy-wounded mouth . . . "Come with me," she ordered him over her shoulder.

Before he could refuse, she was hurrying away toward the small creek that she knew still trickled nearby.

Rolf stood unsure for a moment, then decided the desire to be alone with her was too strong, no matter what the circumstances. There was virtually no privacy in the manor house, nor would there be any until the second floor was completed. Even then, retainers and servants would be constantly at the bedchamber doors seeking advice, direction, or complaining.

He found her kneeling beside a drying-up stream. The water might have been almost gone, but there was still plenty of mud along the banks. Merlyn motioned for him to join her and he did so.

He might as well make the best of the situation, for just watching her move was soothing to him. And not only were her movements graceful and fluid, but when his gaze was drawn to her face, it was like looking at what Rolf thought would be the quintessential woman: calm and soft-spoken, sweet-tempered and concerned, and infinitely lovely. Even her hands, soiled as they were, were beautifully formed, her fingers soothing and gentle against his hot skin as they did their work.

How could he ever have thought her a crooked-fingered crone?

At Merlyn's order, he removed his chainse and tunic. She helped him (to facilitate the process, he guessed with disappointment, rather than for any other reason) and then applied the cooling, soothing mud to the tops of his shoulders. He felt it begin to draw almost immediately.

As she moved around to his neck, his eyes alighted on her face and his breathing seemed to slow almost to a halt as he studied her most thoroughly, half afraid to say or do anything that would call her attention to him and his rapt perusal. He felt his traitorous loins tighten with desire.

There had to be a way to make her agree to be his wife. There just had to be. But how? For only the second time in his thirty winters, Rolf de Valmont found himself up against a solid wall of frustration where a woman was concerned. And not just any woman. First, it had been Brenna. That had been sheer folly to ever allow his feelings to grow. But now, with Merlyn, how could he not eventually win her over? She was without a man. He knew she was lonely, she had to be, especially with most of her family, her entire way of life, destroyed.

His very stillness caught Merlyn's attention. Her gaze lifted to his, suspicion in her eyes. Sure enough. She caught him red-handed in his ruminations, his unguarded look full of what appeared to be pity . . . and open yearning.

He certainly didn't look as if he were at death's door from lack of air.

She slapped the next dollop of mud against his neck with a vengeance, her contrition over her earlier behavior dissolved.

Rolf virtually levitated off the ground with the unexpected force of her hand, the pain she caused him swallowed in the face of his surprise, together with years of suppressing any outward sign of discomfort on a battlefield or while tangling single-handedly with an adversary.

He jumped to his feet, smarting pride and stinging skin doing equal damage to his temper. "Enough!" he roared, sending birds scattering through the trees above with a cacophony of flapping feathers. "I've had enough of your ministering to last me a lifetime!" And without a backward glance, he stalked through the trees toward Renford, half hoping that another renegade Scot would appear out of nowhere and take her off his hands.

"All you need is the garlic."

Hugh de Conteville grinned good-naturedly at Rolf and earned a warning look for his levity.

"And longer hair, of course," Roger added, then turned his head to hide a smile.

"Come now, Valmont," Hugh continued, laughter lurking in his eyes. "I couldn't have done better tending myself. A wandering swarm of bees, you say?" He shook his head as Rolf poured himself a good portion of fresh apple cider and slammed the wooden ewer back down on the table.

"And then, Hugh tells me," said Roger with a straight face, "that you single-handedly took on three Scots who tried to surprise you."

"It appears the bees got the better of you," Hugh said.

"Send out six men," Rolf said tersely. "We'll rout out any—"

"'Tis done already," Roger told him. "They have not returned yet."

"I believe 'twas a random incident. But I'll feel better—"

"My lord Rolf," Father Francis called, entering the hall and hurrying over to them. He opened his mouth again as he neared, but his tongue seemed suddenly paralyzed as he got a good look at Rolf.

The Lord of Renford was, literally, a sight. Drying mud was spattered over his face, neck, and shoulders. His clothing was damp and dark with dirt, his hair matted with sweat. Blood stained the rent front of his tunic.

The priest's hurried stride toward Rolf halted abruptly. "Are you hurt, my lord Rolf?" he inquired in a thin voice.

Rolf wiped his mouth with the back of his hand and shook his head. "Only a few bee stings," he admitted with a scowl as he set down his empty cup. "Is there something amiss?"

"Let me see to this," offered Roger.

"Nay. Any problem he has is mine as well. I am lord here, and I'll see to my responsibilities."

He sounded rather like a man determined to perform an unpleasant task at any cost, and his expression reflected his purposefulness. "As you can see, Merlyn tended to my injuries." He looked meaningfully at Hugh. "I would see you encouraging the completion of the fortifications, Hugh, after you eat, rather than administrative tasks."

Hugh nodded and exchanged a glance with Roger, as Rolf turned aside and listened to Father Francis speak to him in low, agitated tones.

"There is someone . . . er . . . skulking about at night, I believe, my lord, near the church."

Rolf resisted the impatience that rose in him, the urge to sigh and ask the clergyman if he had nothing more enlightening to tell him. "There are people, no doubt, hiding all over Northumbria, Father, as you of all people surely know."

The priest nodded. "Aye, but several villagers have told me of this, fearing 'tis a Saxon and that one of your men may mistake him for an . . . adversary and put an end to him."

Rolf raked his fingers through his tousled hair. "Give us more credit than that, Father," he sighed. "Has someone told you of this . . . ah . . . person, rather than me or one of my men, out of fear?"

The priest nodded. "One claims this person—if 'tis who they think—was thought to be dead, along with his family, and never joined the others from Renford living under Merlyn."

"And how the devil does he get into Renford at night?"

"If he lived here at one time, who would know the village better?"

Rolf motioned to Father Francis to follow him from the hall. "Tell me," he said as the clergyman made haste to keep up with his distance-eating strides, "why this man would sneak into Renford at night, only to disappear during the day?"

Rolf realized how silly the question was as he uttered the words. For the word *food* came to him just as Father Francis opened his mouth to pronounce it. "Well, if he can enter Renford to steal food, then he may as well remain here and earn his keep!"

Father Francis pointed out the spot where fresh blood blotted the ground . . . and feathers. Rolf dropped to a crouch to examine it. "He killed one of our *hens?*" Rolf asked in the tone of a bishop speaking of blasphemy. Even with his limited knowledge of farming and raising poultry, he could guess how precious the loss of a single chicken could be. So many less eggs for propagating chickens and for eating . . .

He stood after a few thoughtful moments, shading his eyes from the sun with one hand as he surveyed the area west of the church. "He could conceivably sneak in from the orchards, then through yon grazing field. . . ." He shook his head. "I cannot stretch my men so thin. We need them for labor if we are to make good headway before winter sets in." He looked at Father Francis. "God's blood, but 'twould be easier to join us than to do this!"

But he read the eloquent answer in the priest's eyes. Father Francis evidently knew more than he was telling.

Rolf made an instant decision. "Merlyn. Merlyn would know," he mumbled more to himself than to the clergyman. The thought came to him so naturally that he didn't even question or take note of what some may have considered an absurd idea. He had looked to Merlyn, it seemed, almost from the very beginning.

He found her outside the hall near the granary, fussing over Gryff with Raven, more for the child's sake, he guessed, than for that of the hound. "'Tis only a bump on the head, Raven. He's already looking for his next meal." She kissed the pert little tip of her daughter's nose, closing her eyes for a moment as she leaned her cheek against Raven's head. Rolf said nothing, unwilling to interrupt them and chase away the ache tugging at his insides at the tender picture they made.

All they need is you.

Fool, he thought. Are you mad?

"Gryff's a brave hound, is he not, Mamma?" Raven inquired.

"Aye, that he is. He tried to protect me."

"He'll make a good bandog . . . guard the village at night against wolves and other pred—"

"Predators."

"Aye. Them."

"We'll need more like him," Rolf said as he moved toward them.

Both mother and child looked up at the sound of his voice. Raven's features lit with pleasure, Merlyn's expression turning distant beneath a slow blush that burned her cheeks.

"I must speak to you," he said to Merlyn.

Raven pried Gryff from Rolf's foot and moved away with him, as if sensing the Lord of Renford's desire to be alone with her mother.

"Do you know of anyone who would shun the village—someone who once lived here—but steals food during the night?"

At her frown, he added, "Someone, mayhap, who is injured or disabled in some way and cannot procure his own food through other means."

"What means are left to any of these people after what William does to our forests?"

Rolf sighed. His chest burned, his stings hurt, more than a few muscles ached, and he wanted nothing more than to soak in a warm tub with a goblet of wine in one hand. A willing wench in the other would have completed the picture, but that was out of the question. Unless, of course, he wanted Marthe.

"The laws are similar to those of the Saxon kings before my lord William, Merlyn, and well you know it. He merely seeks to increase the Royal Forest. Traps . . . even spears or clubs . . . can get a man a hare or a pheasant. He can fish, as well."

"You just said yourself that you think this man is disabled."

"Or lazy. If he were desperate enough, his wife could procure food."

"Provided she were still alive."

"The other possibility is that he is too lazy to do aught but steal the meager pickings of his own people."

"He is stealing from his enemy, as well . . . the Normans," Merlyn defended this phantom thief, suspecting she knew exactly who it was.

Rolf narrowed his eyes at her. He was learning to gauge her meaning, ferret out her inferences, anticipate her moods. Somewhat at least, he mused wryly, suppressing his discomfort and irritation and summoning his patience. This latter was beginning to become habit. And he was learning to stretch his limited patience (at least in *his* mind) to heretofore undreamed-of lengths.

"What do you know, Merlyn?" he asked with a sigh of surrender.

"Shall I prepare your bath, my lord?"

He almost went slack-jawed at her offer. Almost. This proved that she was, indeed, trying to hide something, protect someone.

Tempting as was her offer, Rolf knew her information was more important. He shook his head. "I like the sweet air I breathe," he said, "and would prefer it to drowning under your tender attentions . . . wondrous as a warm bath sounds." Before she could retort, he continued, "Now, Merlyn, you must know by now that I am a fair man. No one will come to any harm from what you reveal to me. So . . . tell me."

She studied him, trying to discern the sincerity of his words. "Will you swear it?"

His lips thinned. "Very well."

"Say it."

"I swear no one will come to any harm from what you reveal to me." *I need people for my village too badly—need to win the trust of those I already have—to be too severe over something like a starving man stealing to stay alive.*

Merlyn nodded and gazed past him to the *weald*, as if envisioning the secrets it held. "Arthur the tanner was a fine man. Loyal, hardworking, and a good husband and father. He was injured at Stamford Bridge fighting against Harald Hardrada. But he insisted 'twas a minor hurt and followed King Harold to Hastings before he was properly healed. 'Twas his left arm, he said, and he was right-handed. He could still wield a club or pitchfork."

"And then?" Rolf got the distinct feeling that he wasn't going to like what she was going to tell him.

"He lost his left arm completely, fighting for England," her voice turned bitter, "and also the sight in one eye, for he was maced in the side of the head. Maced like Bryan."

Rolf ignored her thinly veiled accusation regarding Bryan. "And you think our nightly caller is he?"

Merlyn shook her head. "I know not. I thought he was dead. We heard naught of him or his family while we lived in the forest. If he were alive, why wouldn't he have joined us?"

Rolf pursed his lips thoughtfully. "Then we still don't know who 'tis, do we?" He felt suddenly disappointed, cheated, for he thought Merlyn could solve the mystery. Well, she'd told him what she knew, and perhaps it was, after all, this Arthur the tanner. He—or whoever it was—was very clever and stealthy. Rolf realized, also, that it could very well be a Scot or lone Norman deserter obtaining food the easy way.

"Not really."

Something in the tone of her voice gave him pause . . . and made him wonder if she'd truly told him what she knew or was hiding something. He stared into her face, trying to delve into her innermost thoughts, as if by sheer dint of will he could reach in with his mind and pull out everything he could find behind those lovely eyes of hers.

"What would you have me do then, Merlyn?" he asked softly. "Set a trap for one of your own, or go out and find him before he sets his mind to filching one of our hens—or worse—again?"

Her mouth twisted with disdain. "You vowed that no one would come to any harm only moments ago, Norman. Now you ask me to specify the manner in which he should be apprehended? So that you and your men can—"

"I gave you my word," he interrupted with a scowl. "I cannot do any better than that! If you won't trust my promise—and we must start somewhere—then you can be sure that I won't bother you with such matters again."

He watched with a secret satisfaction as doubt crept into her expression. He'd counted on her reaction to the threat of being left out of decisions concerning her people.

"Very well," she relented, her expression anything

but gracious. "But I've told you everything I know . . . for the moment. I'll make inquiries among the villagers and see what I can discover."

Rolf nodded, thoughts of a bath invading his concentration, beckoning without mercy. "Mayhap the party sent out has already caught the culprit."

Merlyn had bent to brush at a spot of dirt on her bliaut, but his words brought her head snapping up, accusation in her eyes.

"I couldn't give them any instructions concerning our nocturnal caller, Merlyn. I wasn't here to give the command. Rest assured, however, that my men aren't butchers. They were told to bring in anyone they could capture alive. And," he added, "they can tell the difference between a Scotsman and an Englishman."

Merlyn said nothing, but she thought how difficult a task it could be for an arrogant Norman warrior to distinguish between the two. The English hiding in the countryside looked as wild and uncivilized as their northern neighbors. And surely most Anglo-Saxons would be reluctant to give themselves up to any Normans. That meant they would be forced to flee . . . and more than likely be killed in the process.

As a new bleakness settled over her, Merlyn conceded that there was nothing to be done now.

"And now I want naught more than a hot bath and a good meal." But he didn't swing away. He hesitated, his gaze lingering on her face. A sweet, ineffable yearning filled him unexpectedly, and he had the strongest urge to take her in his arms and reassure her . . . to tell her everything would be righted in Renford, if he had his way, and she would never know want or pain again.

Of course, that was ridiculous. No one could ever

make and keep such a promise; even Rolf de Valmont, invincible warrior, knew that.

Instead, he heard himself saying, "Is it safe to wash away the mud now?" He raised one eyebrow in self-mockery but felt rooted to the ground, unable to pull himself away from her.

"Aye. I think so." She drew a deep breath and returned his gaze. "I never thanked you for saving my life, my lord," she told him quietly. "You have earned my admiration in thus exhibiting your physical skills."

She glanced up at the man putting the finishing touches on one chimney of the manor house as it poked the cloud-strewn sky, hoping Rolf would leave her and relieve her from all the unwelcome feelings churning within.

"You are most welcome, *madame*. And I trust I can add this newfound admiration to the gratitude you felt when you tended my arm." But the fact that she couldn't look him in the eye for more than a moment as she'd said the words indicated just how grudging was her admission. He also sensed that he had said exactly the wrong thing—enumerating her positive reactions toward him as if he were keeping count on a tally stick.

Merlyn gave him a look that told him exactly how hollow his victory really was and moved away.

You did it again, Valmont, a voice admonished him. *Why is it that you cannot win over this particular woman? Is it because you wish it above all else?*

Rolf watched the regal lift of her head and shoulders, the gentle sway of her slim hips, the smooth stride of her legs that set her skirts aflutter as she walked away. He told himself, as a sop to his pride, that although there were other things he would have had from her as well, gratitude and admiration were a solid beginning.

After the evening meal, Rolf took a walk through Renford alone. He was satisfied with the progress he saw; the second story of the manor was close to being completed. The fence about the village lands and the palisade around the lord's estate were repaired in all but a few places. Most of the cottages were livable, if still awaiting the finishing touches inside. And doors. Now, more than ever, he thought, doors with drop bars were essential to a village that lay awake half the night in apprehension, wrenched from what little sleep they managed to catch at the slightest unfamiliar sound.

Also, the time was nearing for the Conteville brothers to depart for their own respective responsibilities. They had agreed on Michaelmas for their leavetaking, and it was less than a sennight away.

Eh bien, they cannot stay forever, Rolf mused, and put the unsettling thought from his mind.

As he reached the northern end of the village, the wind carried the smell of the Tees to him, cool and fresh. An odd satisfaction settled over him. If only things could be put wholly to rights and remain that way . . .

You must be getting old, Valmont, to think of being content with a half-populated Anglo-Saxon village at your command and another that is deserted altogether. With little food to last you through the winter, and fear and hatred coming at you from all around . . .

He turned on his heel and strode swiftly back toward the manor, searching among the people scattered here and there for a friendly face . . . a diversion from his unsettling thoughts.

"Friendly face?" he muttered under his breath as he glanced at Derwick from beneath his lashes. He received a fleeting look of vehement dislike before the Saxon smoothed his expression and nodded in acknowledgment. "I should have let his leg rot and drop off," Rolf grumbled. "Ungrateful wretch."

As he neared the manor, he spotted Elsa opening the crude gate on the byre to herd the two cows inside. He seized his chance with a kind of desperation.

"Elsa!" he called to her.

The old woman, still spry and willing to work at her advanced age, turned at the sound of his voice. She stood and waited with the patience of the aged for him to approach her; the gate was half open, the cows standing nearby, their tails swishing now and again at some pesky insect, real or imagined.

Rolf felt the squish of something unpleasant beneath one shoe, but he ignored it, as he did the odor of warm manure as the brindle raised her tail and let go her load. "Elsa," he said in a low voice (and could have sworn that he caught a twinkle of laughter in her eyes), "I . . . will you show me how to pen the cows?"

Without hesitation, she nodded. If she thought it a strange request from the Lord of Renford, she gave no sign. "Aye, my lord Wolf. 'Tis but a simple thing." She pushed open the gate fully and explained, "The lead cow is the key. If you can get her into the pen, the other will naturally follow." She slapped the brown cow on the flank and stood back to watch it lumber into the pen, then the byre. The brindle followed docilely.

"'Tis as simple as that? You don't have to speak to it (he was beginning to feel very foolish) in Cymry?" he finished, irritation creasing his brow.

"Cymry?" Then, evidently realizing where Rolf had obtained that tidbit of false information, Elsa grinned. "These are English cows, are they not? From Lord Roger's village in the south of England? How would they understand the tongue of the Welsh?"

"You can imagine from whence I got my information," he said darkly. "Let me try it."

Elsa shook her head, sending her wispy white hair a-waving in the evening breeze. "Nay, lord."

At his even darker look, she said, "Would you appear the fool again? 'Tis almost impossible to get them out of the shed at dusk. 'Tis the end of the day . . . time to sleep, and well they know it." She paused and tipped her head to study him. "Come at sunrise, Lord Wolf. Then you may try it."

Rolf didn't know whether to throttle her for calling him a fool or to kiss her for preventing him from making another blunder before anyone who cared to watch.

He bowed to the more gallant inclination. "My thanks, old woman, for the advice."

He was about to turn away in the face of what he could have sworn was another unborn grin, when she spoke once more. This time, her words stopped him cold and sent an icy chill through him. "Beware, Lord Wolf from Normandy. I can feel it . . . smell its evil scent, yet I cannot identify it. But 'tis near . . . almost in our midst."

He stared at her expectantly, not particularly eager to hear what he sensed would be some dire pronouncement.

"Something wicked comes this way. To Renford. To us all. You must be on your guard. You—*we*— must be prepared."

"What?"

"That is all I can tell you because that is all I know. But you are forewarned, and you must shield those whom you would now call your people . . . and your very life."

Wondering if this woman were a witch (they seemed to abound in this part of England, he thought wryly), he asked, with a half-serious lift of his brows, "Could it possibly be Arthur the tanner?"

The old one shook her head. "Nay. 'Tis much worse."

Chapter 13

"I think we've found our man."

Rolf looked up at Roger, his forehead glazed with sweat, his face smudged with dirt where he'd attempted to wipe it away with one hand. He sheathed Death Blow and signaled to Bryce that their swordplay was at an end.

"The whelp is getting good enough to send me diving for the ground to save my skin." But pride in his young squire permeated Rolf's words.

He turned to Roger expectantly, noting the grim set of Conteville's features. His jaw was rigid, his eyes dark as slate with anger.

Rolf suddenly forgot his sword, his practice session, and his pride in Bryce's performance. Roger's words came homing in suddenly and sent alarm buzzing along his veins. "Who?"

"The man, I think, who has stolen twice from us and has attempted again . . . this time in broad daylight."

Rolf handed his sheathed sword and his shield to Bryce. "Good! His increasing boldness has finally cost him. Where is he?"

After searching fruitlessly for two days, Rolf's men

had found only the cold remnants of campfires, which could have been made by anyone. After their last search—within a radius of half a league of Renford—Rolf had recalled them, saying that he needed every one of them to help finish the reconstruction, and that he believed the Scots' attack on Merlyn and him had been a random incident. As for the one who had stolen from the village, Rolf didn't think the man constituted a real threat, and he put off a more intense search for him in favor of the more pressing task of completing the work on Renford . . . and drilling both men and women in self-defense.

"Rolf," Roger said in a low voice as they left Bryce and moved toward the pen where the horses were kept on the side of the manor nearest the river, "Hugh is with him, you must keep your wits about you, no matter how angry you are. He—"

Rolf halted mid-stride and faced Roger. "What exactly has he done this time? Has he harmed anyone?"

The bleak look in Roger's eyes raised his hackles, sending his heart sinking to his feet with dread.

When Roger didn't answer, Rolf turned and began to move more quickly toward the barn. "Judas, but he didn't steal one of the horses, did he?" he asked, half in grim jest.

"Nay. 'Twasn't stolen."

By the time they were halfway to where the horses were kept, Rolf was running, all kinds of horrible images flashing across his mind's eye—but nothing quite as grisly as what he found upon reaching the large penned area.

His back-up destrier, not Charon but the gray named Ombre, lay unmoving upon its side, blood

212

streaking its pale hide and pooling beneath it. Hugh was speaking in a low voice to a stick of a man, who was also bloodied . . . especially around his mouth and on his hand. One hand, Rolf noticed with one part of his mind. Several of Rolf's men stood round, their hands upon their sword hilts, anger and contempt scrawled across their faces, an undercurrent of tension in the air.

"Sweet Jesu!" Rolf exclaimed aloud. "What have you—?"

Roger's hand on his arm and the warning look on Hugh's face as he looked over at him had little effect on Rolf's dawning comprehension . . . and the outrage that exploded within him.

The blood-spattered culprit merely stared at Rolf with lifeless eyes and mumbled something, which Rolf couldn't (nor would he have cared to in that moment) understand.

Rolf strode over the gray's body and stared down. The animal's throat had been slit—*hacked* was more like it—and . . . He looked up at the Saxon beside Hugh. His stomach turned, his gorge rose, and it was all he could do not to lose his morning meal.

"Hungry," mumbled the man. "Feed the others . . ." He licked at the blood around his lips, although it appeared an empty, reflexive gesture. Hugh hastily swiped at the man's mouth with his tunic sleeve, obviously sensing how adversely the man's gesture would affect Rolf . . . or any of his men.

A sepulchral silence swirled around them, until the buzzing of an increasing swarm of horseflies invaded the tense quiet.

"You killed a valuable war-horse for *food?*" Rolf finally managed in a strangled voice. His face was very pale. "The animal was worth one hundredfold more than your miserable hide!"

"He has only one arm, Rolf," Hugh began, "and is blind in—"

"*I . . . care . . . not!*" he snarled through his teeth. He gulped in several breaths of air, trembling with rage. He still couldn't quite believe it. "You could do no better than murder a priceless destrier, *Arthur the tanner?* Could you not distinguish with your one eye that 'twas a *destrier* you killed?"

Arthur's eyes briefly came to life when he heard his name spat like a curse. "What know you of hunger?" he asked with a boldness Rolf would not have credited him with up to that point. "My children are starving, the wee babe all but lifeless these few days past." The gleam of comprehension in his eyes died, and his voice faded as he uttered the last words.

"That gives you no right to carve up my horse! Hens . . . a pig . . . I can overlook; even a boar or buck from the king's forest. But—" he glanced over at the dead horse—"Ombre?" The name emerged as a whisper. He wanted to weep with disbelief and frustration. Ombre was a fine, fine animal. Rolf had planned to breed him, along with Charon, with his two mares, once settled in England.

Charon.

"Where's Charon?" he cried suddenly, spinning around toward the barn as uncharacteristic panic surged through him.

"In here, lord," Hugh's squire Eric answered as he emerged from the stable. "He is unharmed."

"How will I feed them?" Arthur asked with a soft, dry sob as Rolf breathed a shallow sigh of relief.

His question only exacerbated Rolf's wrath. "You'll not have to worry about *that*, you butcher," he said in a terrible voice. "For at first light on the morrow, you will hang for your crime. You'll have no more earthly concerns. I swear to you before these men present."

No one spoke, for the sentence was just. A good destrier was worth a small fortune, and woe to the man responsible for the deliberate injury or demise of one.

"How will I feed my family?" Arthur repeated, rubbing his stained hand on his threadbare braies, as if totally oblivious to Rolf's pronouncement.

"He's mad," Roger said. "Mad with hunger. Mayhap 'tis why he committed such an unthinkable act."

For a moment, Rolf's eyes met Hugh's. *Save your pity for the English,* the latter seemed to repeat. Rolf looked away.

"Then let him eat the stallion's heart, for in doing so, 'twill give him the attributes he utterly lacks!" His voice was frigid, bereft of pity or compassion as he glared at the miserable wretch before him. "Throw him in the granary . . . and no food or water." With one last glance at the dead stallion, he swung away. "And bury the horse," he threw over his shoulder before striding toward the river.

Someone was behind him . . . Rolf heard the sound of snapping twigs beneath someone's tread. He didn't move from his position atop a boulder overlooking the Tees, however. The murmur of moving water was somehow comforting, and he was too absorbed in his contemplation of it to stir.

He also knew that an enemy would never be so careless.

"Don't tell me what I already know," he said.

"You mean that a man's life is more important than that of a horse?" Hugh de Conteville asked.

"You know the penalty for stealing a horse." Rolf

215

shook his head, his fingers clenching against his updrawn knees. "There is no punishment severe enough for killing one."

"I disagree."

"You spent almost half your life in a monastery, Hugh. Of course you wouldn't agree!"

Hugh came from behind him and sat down. Instead of gazing out at the river, however, he fixed his regard on his friend's countenance.

"What else could I have done?" Rolf asked, his gaze resting briefly upon the bloodstain on Hugh's tunic sleeve. "Let him go unpunished? What a fine way to establish my authority here!"

Hugh drew up one knee and rested an arm upon it as he, too, turned his gaze to the meandering Tees. "These are unusual circumstances, Rolf. You need every man, woman, and child you can find to contribute to your success here. As far as I can see, no one doubts your authority or your ability to act as *seigneur*."

Rolf scowled at this and muttered, "Except for Merlyn!"

"Punish him, aye, but don't kill him for trying to feed himself and his family. Make him see just how serious was his crime—take away his status as a freeman, if you will—but otherwise see to his and his family's needs, and no one will be able to fault you . . . not even the English."

Rolf's jaw remained rigid, his posture tense with underlying ire.

"And remember one thing, *mon ami:* This Arthur is more than likely a kind of hero to his fellow Saxons, for he fought at both Stamford Bridge and Hastings . . . against two formidable foes in the service of his king. Didn't Merlyn tell you so?"

Rolf turned to him. "So now you'd have me spare

216

him because he might die a martyr for England?"

"Partly."

Rolf shook his head and listened to the river's song as it eddied about the banks and a fallen tree that spanned it; as it splashed over rocks in the shallows, scenting the air with wet earth and pungent flora. "Even if I agreed to all that you've said . . . even if I could come to terms with his having killed a prized war-horse, I vowed before my men that he would hang. There is naught to be done about it now, for I will not lose face for one pitiful excuse of a man."

"But he actually . . . ate part of the flesh. He really didn't attempt to steal the stallion, merely killed it to eat. In this part of England, men are being driven every day to such desperate acts."

Rolf's chin only firmed further, jutting out as he clamped his jaws together. "Merely?" he asked in a low voice. "He merely killed it to eat, as opposed to trying to steal it?" He emitted a low growl of anger. "'Tis worse to have killed it, any wantwit would know that. And you heard him . . . he would have taken what he could to feed his family. Stealing a horse or stealing its flesh is one and the same in my mind." He looked at Hugh then. "And even if I wished to change his punishment—which I do not— 'tis impossible now. As I said, I swore before witnesses. My own men. Your and Roger's men. And the villagers. To relent now would be to appear weak and indecisive, and that I cannot have."

Hugh held up his gaze. *"Eh bien,'* tis your decision to make." He shook his head and put one hand on Rolf's shoulder. "But I sincerely hope that it will not set you back in your efforts to win over these people."

"We are truly blessed," Merlyn said, surprising

217

Cedric and Elsa. "The mill is undamaged. We will one day have flour for bread."

Merlyn couldn't help but feel a lifting of her spirits this morn, for the small mill on the Tees, just north of Renford (and where Rolf sat brooding) had been one of her favorite places. "And the miller from Lexom survived. He can run it . . . teach others his skills."

Cedric nodded as he pulled away overgrown vines all but covering the small stone building. Merlyn lent a helping hand, and he moved toward the door to the interior of the mill. "Now all we need is grain to grind."

"God will provide," Elsa said as Merlyn's expression sobered. "As will the Wolf."

"This miracle we must see to believe," Merlyn said with irony. "I cannot picture Rolf de Valmont behind a plowshare, urging on a team of oxen."

Elsa gazed at the moving paddles of the mill wheel, her faded blue eyes distant, and said softly, "I can."

"You don't have to, Merlyn," Cedric reminded her as she followed him into the mill. "Valmont has another role beside that of tiller of the fields. His task is to lead and defend. Who would put an able warrior behind a plow and oxen when there are others to do it?"

Merlyn stared at Cedric, momentarily silenced. Could it be, she wondered, that Rolf had won the taciturn Cedric's grudging trust? Oh, he hadn't always been cynical and withdrawn, but surely he wouldn't be the first to leap to the Norman's defense. Or did he see something in Rolf de Valmont that she, Merlyn, refused to see? Or to acknowledge?

And Elsa . . . She, right from the beginning, had appeared to grant the Norman credibility.

Merlyn mentally shook her head. Nay. A broken

218

man and an old woman were fair game for the charm of one like Valmont.

Cedric may be disabled, but he's not stupid. And you know very well that Elsa has seen much during her long life. Neither of them would be easily gulled.

Merlyn pushed aside the bothersome voice, refusing to heed it, and inspected the huge millstones, which appeared undamaged. The large room was dishearteningly empty, and a coating of flour and dust lay everywhere. As Merlyn searched every nook and cranny, Cedric thumped the wooden floor in one shadowed corner with his crutch. "Here," he said. "Come help me with this trapdoor, Merlyn."

Merlyn dropped to her knees and did as he bade her, then thrust a torch down into the hole. Beneath the cleverly concealed door in the floor, a ladder led down to a cool and dark hidden cellar. On the dirt floor below rested what were apparently three huge, bulging sacks of flour.

By this time Elsa had fought her way through the encroaching foliage and entered, at the same moment a grin spread across Cedric's face, lighting up his features.

"Flour!" Merlyn exclaimed as she handed Cedric the torch and gingerly descended the ladder to examine the sacks. With a natural sensitivity, Merlyn had made it a habit of unobtrusively lending a hand to any of Cedric's efforts that were impeded by his handicap—in this case having him help her with the torch as she did the footwork. He never indicated resentment toward or irritation with her, and Merlyn attributed that fact to a new healing within him and his growing acceptance of his lot. She couldn't help but notice his improved disposition and his more enthusiastic outlook.

And then, too, Rolf had asked Cedric earlier that morn if he would consider taking on the position of reeve or steward of the manor. Merlyn had been present when Rolf had made the request. Surprisingly, it had been a request and not a command, and even more surprising were Rolf's exact words to Cedric: "If you decline because you do not wish to serve me, I will accept your refusal. If, however, you decline because of your disablement, I will not agree to that."

Cedric's gaze had locked with his, and for a moment Merlyn held her breath, fearing the one-legged man would say something to insult or anger Valmont. But, as she discovered, she had underestimated both men. As Cedric stood undecided for a few, taut moments, Rolf had added, "You possess courage and intelligence. I also suspect you are capable of unquestioned loyalty. If you can direct that loyalty to me, then you need nothing more to be my steward."

Cedric couldn't possibly have refused, Merlyn thought, before such a proposition, unless he were fool enough to admit that he would not accept Rolf de Valmont's authority, thus going against his oath to Rolf. The longer Merlyn knew Rolf de Valmont, the better she understood his ability to handle men. He had a way of bringing out the best in them—call it charm, or flattery, or cajolery. Or simply a rare and valuable talent, she thought in all fairness.

So Cedric had accepted, yet asked that he be allowed to accompany Merlyn to inspect the mill, for it had been his brother John who had run it in the past. Whether for sentimental reasons or other, Merlyn couldn't tell, but the Lord of Renford gave Cedric leave to go.

After confirming that the sacks, indeed, contained

flour, Merlyn stood and brushed off her hands, a thoughtful look on her face. The horn signaling the nooning pulled Merlyn from her musings, and she looked up at Cedric as she began to ascend from the cellar. "We'll send someone back for these."

He nodded and backed out of her way; but beneath his elation, his look was apologetic. "I'd forgotten about this," he explained, his expression turning serious once more. "In my sorrow and self-pity, I had completely forgotten about this hidden cellar. John kept a secret supply in here—separate from the main cellar and revealed only to my lord Stigand and myself—as a last, desperate resort." He shook his head. "We could have used this weeks ago."

The corners of Merlyn's mouth curved. "And we can still use it now. We've a long winter ahead."

They left the mill and returned across the Tees to the village. Autumn was at hand, the leaves on some of the trees already turning and the breeze bearing a hint of the change. A new, light layer of multicolored leaves carpeted the ground in places and rustled beneath their feet.

A strange silence greeted Merlyn as she entered the manor . . . no babble of voices as everyone ate, no boisterous badinage among the Normans. Even the hounds seemed subdued as they lounged among the rushes or beneath the trestle tables.

She paused a moment to adjust her gaze to the dimness of the hall. The shafts of sunlight pouring in through the unshuttered windows set high in each of the four walls highlighted certain areas of the hall, while leaving the corners of the cavernous room shrouded in layers of shadows.

As Merlyn washed her hands in one of the bowls of water set near the door for that purpose, she saw Marthe sidle up to Cedric and whisper something in

221

his ear. He appeared stunned for a moment, looked briefly at Merlyn, then lowered his gaze.

Cedric wasn't easily shocked anymore, Merlyn knew, and unease trickled through her. But it was as she straightened to make her way to the head table that she noticed Rolf wasn't there. Everyone else was present, she saw, as she scanned the tables, except for Myles. And Rolf.

Hugh mustered one of his sweet smiles for her from across the room as she moved forward, although it was short-lived. Roger nodded in acknowledgment, but none of the other men would meet her gaze.

Puzzled, she turned to Cedric, pushing aside her annoyance at Marthe, who, she felt, should have come to her directly with any news. Cedric was about to move away. "Cedric, what is amiss?" Merlyn asked, the words sounding to her like the tolling of bells in the quiet hall.

"Marthe says that they've found Arthur the tanner. He is to be put to death at sunrise," he answered in low tones.

Merlyn tried to absorb the meaning of his words. She glanced about the hall again, noting now the grim expressions on the faces of her people who were looking directly at her. Many were staring down at their trenchers . . .

Why wasn't Rolf here? she wondered. It was just like him, she thought waspishly, to avoid her—and everyone else—in the wake of such an untenable decree. What in the world could Arthur the tanner have done beside steal a hen or two as Merlyn had suggested to Rolf?

And, more importantly, what of Rolf's promise to her?

Suddenly, her appetite dwindled, and a growing

sense of foreboding settled over her as she seated herself at the board.

At first no sounds came from the granary. And then, after an hour or so, the occupant began pounding feebly on the walls. "My family! Hungry . . . need me . . . need me . . ." His pitiful shouts were unnerving to those in the immediate area, and passersby gave the small storage area a wide berth.

"Where is my lord Rolf?" Merlyn demanded of Hugh de Conteville in the manor yard when she could stand Arthur's cries no longer. "Why is this man locked up when he but sought to feed his family? And what is this I heard about Valmont's decree that Arthur be hanged?"

She'd sought out Hugh for answers, even though she held no official position of authority. These were her people and she had an obligation to stand up for them.

The Norman's eyes were very somber as he spoke to her. "Arthur killed Rolf's destrier, Merlyn."

Horror transformed her expression. "Charon?" She felt her stomach flutter sickeningly at the thought, for Charon was Rolf's prized possession, a magnificent animal.

"Nay, his other stallion, the gray."

Either way, she thought, as disbelief vied with shock inside her, it was truly a mad and wanton act. The sentence was just, however, by all the laws with which Merlyn had ever been familiar.

"I—I don't understand," she whispered, shaking her head in bemusement. "Why would Arthur kill? . . ." Her question trailed off. Of course. Why else in these times?

Her eyes met Hugh's. "Nay. It cannot be."

"The man is beyond desperation, as you can guess, if he's committed such an act. He has sight in but one eye and lost an arm in battle. He cannot procure food for his children as easily as a man whole."

These things Merlyn knew, yet she remained silent as he spoke, one rational part of her mind taking careful note of the compassion that darkened his eyes, that softened his handsome features.

"Are you certain? How in heaven's name could he have dragged an entire horse through the village, even if he had two arms?"

Hugh's gaze went past her, to the granary. "I don't think he intended to attempt such a feat. Rather, his plan had been to . . . take what he needed."

In the midst of her churning thoughts and ambiguous emotions, the sick feeling that welled up into her throat at the thought of Arthur's foolhardy action, it came to Merlyn that Hugh de Conteville might side with her if she pleaded for the tanner's life. And she needed every ally she could muster before Rolf de Valmont's wrath.

"And where is my lord Rolf?"

"He and Myles are searching for Arthur's family."

A sudden thought occurred to Merlyn. "If Valmont had been more thorough in his search of the area, this wouldn't have happened. I cannot believe that a capable warrior and his men couldn't ferret out one Saxon family from the surrounding *weald*."

Hugh looked down at the ground between them for a moment, as if choosing his words with care. When he finally looked at Merlyn, he caught her off guard with his query. "And if they were so easily found, why did you and your band not do so before we ever arrived?"

Color delicately tinged her cheekbones. She had no answer for that, especially when put to her by Hugh

MORE PASSION AND ADVENTURE AWAIT... YOUR TRIP TO A BIG ADVENTUROUS WORLD BEGINS WHEN YOU ACCEPT YOUR FIRST 4 NOVELS ABSOLUTELY *FREE* (AN $18.00 VALUE)

Accept your Free gift and start to experience more of the passion and adventure you like in a historical romance novel. Each Zebra novel is filled with proud men, spirited women and tempestuous love that you'll remember long after you turn the last page.

Zebra Historical Romances are the finest novels of their kind. They are written by authors who really know how to weave tales of romance and adventure in the historical settings you love. You'll feel like you've actually gone back in time with the thrilling stories that each Zebra novel offers.

GET YOUR FREE GIFT WITH THE START OF YOUR HOME SUBSCRIPTION

Our readers tell us that these books sell out very fast in book stores and often they miss the newest titles. So Zebra has made arrangements for you to receive the four newest novels published each month.

You'll be guaranteed that you'll never miss a title, and home delivery is so convenient. And to show you just how easy it is to get Zebra Historical Romances, we'll send you your first 4 books absolutely FREE! Our gift to you just for trying our home subscription service.

BIG SAVINGS AND FREE HOME DELIVERY

Each month, you'll receive the four newest titles as soon as they are published. You'll probably receive them even before the bookstores do. What's more, you may preview these exciting novels free for 10 days. If you like them as much as we think you will, just pay the low preferred subscriber's price of just $3.75 each. *You'll save $3.00 each month off the publisher's price.* AND, your savings are even greater because there are never any shipping, handling or other hidden charges—FREE Home Delivery. Of course you can return any shipment within 10 days for full credit, no questions asked. There is no minimum number of books you must buy.

4 FREE BOOKS

TO GET YOUR 4 FREE BOOKS WORTH $18.00 — MAIL IN THE FREE BOOK CERTIFICATE T O D A Y

Fill in the Free Book Certificate below, and we'll send your FREE BOOKS to you as soon as we receive it.

If the certificate is missing below, write to: Zebra Home Subscription Service, Inc., P.O. Box 5214, 120 Brighton Road, Clifton, New Jersey 07015-5214.

FREE BOOK CERTIFICATE

4 FREE BOOKS

ZEBRA HOME SUBSCRIPTION SERVICE, INC.

YES! Please start my subscription to Zebra Historical Romances and send me my first 4 books absolutely FREE. I understand that each month I may preview four new Zebra Historical Romances free for 10 days. If I'm not satisfied with them, I may return the four books within 10 days and owe nothing. Otherwise, I will pay the low preferred subscriber's price of just $3.75 each; a total of $15.00, *a savings off the publisher's price of $3.00.* I may return any shipment and I may cancel this subscription at any time. There is no obligation to buy any shipment and there are no shipping, handling or other hidden charges. Regardless of what I decide, the four free books are mine to keep.

NAME

ADDRESS   APT

CITY   STATE   ZIP
(   )
TELEPHONE

SIGNATURE   (if under 18, parent or guardian must sign)

Terms, offer and prices subject to change without notice. Subscription subject to acceptance by Zebra Books. Zebra Books reserves the right to reject any order or cancel any subscription.

GET
FOUR
FREE
BOOKS
(AN $18.00 VALUE)

ZEBRA HOME SUBSCRIPTION
SERVICE, INC.
P.O. Box 5214
120 BRIGHTON ROAD
CLIFTON, NEW JERSEY 07015-5214

de Conteville, for his words held nothing of accusation or challenge. Only logic, calmly pointed out to her.

"My lady Merlyn," he addressed her in a soothing voice, according her her old title, "do not add to Rolf's burden. Give him a chance, I ask of you as one human being to another." His eyes were a warm silver-gray, seeking her trust.

By all the saints, she lamented silently, were they all beguilers like their leader? Was every man among Valmont's group versed in sincere-seeming, insidious seduction of the soul when he so chose?

She belatedly remembered the taciturn, cynical Myles, the easily angered Rufus . . . and her theory disintegrated as it formed.

". . . you've all been ill-treated by Normans in the past," he was saying. "That is not Rolf's way. Surely you've seen this time and again."

"Aye," she murmured, holding his gaze. "But even given that the English are the best in Christendom at hiding from friend and enemy alike, that does not change Arthur's fate."

He shook his head, pursing his lips thoughtfully. Then his eyes narrowed and his gaze went beyond her, to the south, where a commotion was building at the edge of the forest. "I believe only you have the power to change Arthur's fate."

Merlyn swung about, watching as Rolf and Myles emerged from the shadow of the trees, a woman and a child behind them, an infant in Rolf's arms.

Merlyn had no time to ponder Hugh's words. They sank into the dim recesses of her mind like pebbles in a pond as she was caught up in the events immediately following.

The woman recognized Merlyn as the latter ran forward toward them. "Merlyn . . . oh, Merlyn!" She dropped on her knees before Merlyn, a filthy, scrawny representation of humanity, and clutched at Merlyn's hands.

"Margaret? Is that you?"

Silly, inane words. Who else would she be? If Arthur had been close, no doubt his family had been as well. And Merlyn knew Margaret's voice, even with the rasp of hardship and despair edging every word. And the once flaxen-gold hair, now looking worse than had Merlyn the crone's . . .

"Merlyn . . . what of Arthur?" she asked, looking up at Merlyn through her matted hair, her eyes sunken into her skull, her once-fair cheeks now skeletally hollowed to the bone. "The Norman"— she pronounced "Norman" *sotto voce*—"would tell us naught but that he was their prisoner."

The child beside her, dragged forward in her mother's headlong rush to Merlyn, whimpered softly. "F-f-father," she whispered, fat tears forming in her sky-blue eyes and trickling down her pale cheeks.

"He—he's not right in the head, Merlyn," Margaret said in a pitiful voice, "He . . . sometimes does strange things, then remembers naught." Her hands tightened over Merlyn's with viselike strength, communicating fear. "He made us shun all others . . . even you, for he trusted no one. And he berates himself—punishes himself—for his injuries."

Before Merlyn could do more than stroke the distraught Margaret's head, Rolf had come striding up to them. He handed Merlyn the dozing baby. "See to them," he said tersely, and moved away before Merlyn could say a word.

Merlyn looked at Myles, but the Vikingesque chevalier's face was shuttered. Then he, too, moved away toward the manor, leaving only a small group of villagers, who crowded around their former neighbor.

"We thought you dead, child," said Elsa, and Margaret began to weep.

"May as well have been," Marthe muttered. "Look at them!"

Merlyn rounded on the woman, babe in her arms and all. "You hush, Marthe!" she commanded in a sibilant voice. Marthe stepped backward, her mouth falling open at the fierceness of Merlyn's expression.

"Merlyn," Margaret attempted again through her tears, "where is Arthur?"

Merlyn adjusted the sleeping infant in her arm and helped Margaret to her feet with her free hand. Raven, who'd been close behind her mother, moved toward the older child and stretched out her hand. "Come, Edwina, do you not remember me?"

The joy that lit up Edwina's face was instantaneous, and her tears stopped abruptly. Surely, Merlyn thought, these people were as greatly starved for the sight and sound of other human beings as they were for food.

"Merlyn?"

Margaret's voice intruded upon her thoughts, quietly insistent, desperate, as Merlyn turned toward the manor. Elsa stepped to the other side of Margaret and put an arm about her shoulders, guiding her unsteady steps.

Mother of God, Merlyn thought, Margaret's query echoing through her mind, *how will I find the courage to tell her?*

Chapter 14

There was no guard posted at the granary. In his supreme confidence, Merlyn thought, Rolf de Valmont obviously believed no one would defy his orders.

Well, he was wrong.

With half a loaf of bread and a chunk of roasted boar meat under her arm, a flask of water clutched in her fingers, Merlyn fought to lift the bar with her free hand. As the door opened, letting in a shaft of daylight, she called softly, "Arthur? Arthur, 'tis I, Merlyn. Be not afraid, for I've brought you—"

An arm clamped about her neck from the darkness within the tiny hut, setting her off balance and causing her to drop the food. The pressure across her windpipe was enough to make it impossible for Merlyn to speak, and she began to cough with a choking sound, even as she struggled to free herself.

The man had surprising strength for one supposedly weakened by hunger and disabled by battle.

"Arthur!" she rasped, and suddenly the pressure on her throat was gone.

She stood a moment, pulling in huge gulps of air, half expecting him to bolt through the unbarred door. But the shadows around her remained dark and unmoving.

"Arthur?" she ventured again, then slowly, carefully, stooped to retrieve her offerings.

"Aye."

The voice came from behind her, a husky sound and certainly bearing little resemblance to the Arthur she once knew. The odor of sweat and an unwashed body permeated the air. And fear. Merlyn could almost taste the fear, so thick was it around her.

"I've brought you food and water. You've naught to fear from me, Arthur . . . surely you remember me, Stigand's widow Merlyn?"

She turned slowly, squinting against the darkness. To her surprise, however, she heard a soft sound near the door. Her first thought was that he was going to flee and Rolf would have her head for that.

But when she glanced around, she saw the outline of his form close by the partially open door, the knife-edge of light spilling onto the dirt floor and limning his long hair and profile. He dropped to a crouch within less than an arm's length from the door and stared at her.

"Here." She stooped beside him, setting down the food and now half-empty flask. "Eat, Arthur." As she studied him, her heart went out to this man, for his eyes were lucid enough, although the affection with which he had once regarded her was gone. He hardly looked a man mad enough to kill a Norman warhorse.

He looked at the food for a long, quiet moment. "What use to eat now when I am to die for trying to feed my loved ones? Can you tell me that, Merlyn?"

"You are not going to die, Arthur. I promise you that."

He canted his head at her, his sightless eye

apparent with its lack of focus, the left side of his head, which had been struck with a Norman mace, slightly concave, although his hair covered most of the disfigurement. "Have you some influence with these invaders?" he asked, bringing a host of emotions surging to Merlyn's breast. "Not for my life, but for the sake of Margaret and my children?"

He seemed so rational, so sound of mind in those moments, that before she could answer his query, Merlyn was moved to ask, "Why did you do it, Arthur? Why did you kill the horse?"

He shook his head slowly as he reached for the water. "I don't remember what was in my mind then." He took a long draught and held the flask between the fingers of his hand. "I can only remember finding myself sitting upon the ground with the taste of blood on my lips"—he suddenly looked genuinely repulsed by the thought—"surrounded by Normans."

Merlyn reached out to put a hand on his shoulder. "I will not let him harm you," she pledged again in a low but steady voice. "Do you hear me?"

Without warning, Arthur's shoulders began to quiver and silent sobs shook his frame. "There, there," she soothed, as with a child. "You and your family are safe now."

He raised his head to the sliver of light, and Merlyn could see the tracks of his tears through the dirt and blood on his face. His eyes held a faraway look. "I killed the war-horse because 'twas Norman. And *they* killed my lord Harold." Fresh tears sheened his eyes. "I could not help him . . . He lay helpless, his housecarls fighting to the death for him, and I had naught to give him but one arm . . . one eye." He shook his head pitifully. "Would that I could have given my life for his! Would that I could have saved

England as well as Harold!"

The bitterness, the acrid self-recrimination, were keen-edged with anguish that was rational enough.

Merlyn swallowed past the clot of emotion paralyzing her throat. "A man can only do so much," she said quietly as they stood there in the dimness, save for the sunbeam nudging through the slightly open portal, "can only give so much. Your family needs you now, Arthur, and you must not despair. I will—"

The door suddenly lurched open, showering them both with brilliant sunlight. Merlyn took a step backward in reaction, squinting against the light. She knew, however, even before her eyes adjusted, who was looming before her like some avenging Norse god.

Arthur, seemingly still lost in his own private hell, never moved.

"I might have known," Rolf de Valmont's deep, angry voice charged. He reached in and grabbed her forearm, pulling her out through the open door. The tone of his voice, the strength brought to bear upon her arm, and his words themselves were enough to caution Merlyn against exercising her first reaction—struggling against his physical handling of her.

Shading her eyes, she tilted her face toward his until their gazes locked. "Do what you will to me," she said through set teeth, "but *don't shut this door!* He's not an animal . . . Even an animal would have food and water. And light."

And to prove her determination, she reached for the crude jamb, so that Rolf would have had to crush her hand between the door and the frame in order to close it.

"What are you *doing?*" he gritted back, a blood vessel pulsing in one temple. "Making me look the

231

fool before everyone?"

The look on his face was one of pure rage and made her reconsider. Her fingers slackened on the door frame of their own volition. Realizing she was backing down in the face of his authority (and thinking it might be the wise thing to do, considering the situation), Merlyn resorted to the only weapon left her.

"Please?" she whispered, her eyes beseeching him as they had not done before.

Fleetingly, he was taken off guard. Never had she pleaded with him.

He suddenly found himself torn between the urge to ignore what he saw as the plying of her womanly wiles and the urge to give in to her heart-wrenching plea, so unexpectedly and appealingly offered.

As he hesitated, Merlyn pressed her advantage. She released her grip on the doorway and dared to touch his arm. All her compassion for Arthur of Renford and her expectations of Rolf de Valmont were, in that moment, shining in her very fine eyes.

Angry as he was, Rolf felt the heat of her fingers through his tunic and chainse, and he couldn't help but think thoughts that had nothing to do with anything outside of a bedchamber.

He stared at her hand, battling to retain the anger that was his most effective shield against her.

"Fetch Myles," he said then, to Merlyn's surprise.

Before either of them could think about it twice, Merlyn fled, ready to turn Renford inside out to find the chevalier before Rolf could change his mind.

Myles was (and Merlyn began to suspect that Rolf knew all along where he was but deliberately said nothing) on the new upper floor of the manor, helping one of the men fit the heavy oaken door for the lord's bedchamber to its hinges.

It was the first time that Merlyn had ventured up to the newly completed floor, but she gave the sights and smells scant notice.

With a few short words to Myles, she turned and retreated back down the stairs and across the hall toward the yard, praying that the blond giant was behind her.

Nothing had changed in the tableau before the granary, except that Rolf was studying the man crouched at the base of its doorway. The lines of his profile were taut, yet pensive, and before he glanced up at Merlyn, she silently sent a prayer heavenward on Arthur's behalf.

Roused from his contemplation of the prisoner, Rolf directed Myles, "Stay here with him until I return. Leave the door ajar as it is, and let him eat and drink what he has been given, as he will. And as far as you are concerned, *I* gave the order for food and water for him."

Myles nodded and took up his post immediately before the open door, casting Merlyn a brief but piercing look in the process.

"I won't be long," Rolf added, and indicated to Merlyn to follow him toward the manor.

With one last look at the stern-faced Myles, Merlyn swung away and hurried to keep up with Rolf de Valmont's long steps, feeling the responsibility for Arthur the tanner's life—and the welfare of his wife and two children—bearing down upon her shoulders with crushing weight.

Rolf indicated that she precede him into the largest bedchamber, then closed the thick wooden door behind them. The workman had recruited another to take Myles's place and they were working on the next door.

Rolf leaned against the portal and watched her take in the room with its stone fireplace and the chest containing his belongings. Two small square windows were unshuttered, letting in the fresh September air and light. There was no bed yet, no rushes spread over the new wooden floor.

Just as Merlyn turned to him, Rolf spoke. "Now, explain to me how it is that you took it upon yourself to defy my specific orders."

Merlyn noted that the hectic color had left his face, but his mouth was still taut and his eyes still held anger.

She drew in a deep, sustaining breath as she allowed her eyes to meet his. "I cannot allow you to put him to death," she said quietly but with conviction. "The man was a loyal English subject . . . gave his arm and part of his sight for king and country. You cannot treat him like an animal."

Rolf folded his arms across his chest and pushed away from the door. "'I cannot allow . . . ', 'You cannot treat him . . .'" He shook his head slowly, emphatically. "You are not the thane's wife now, Merlyn. The thane is dead . . . your king is dead . . . your very existence changed forever. Yet you take it upon yourself to issue orders in direct contradiction to mine?"

Merlyn couldn't hold his gaze, for it was disturbing in many ways aside from the anger. She swung away and walked to a window. It was set high enough in the wall so that she couldn't see much more than the sky, but it was something to gaze at besides Rolf de Valmont. She needed to keep her own anger before her as a defense against him, for his pull on her senses was as potent as the strongest mead.

And she certainly couldn't allow him to charm her into forgetting that a man's life depended upon her success.

"I meant no real harm, my lord," she said over her shoulder. "'Tis just that Arthur is a good man . . ."

"*Was* a good man, now gone awry. By all the saints, Merlyn, he killed my horse! Do you know how much a good destrier is worth? And, God forbid, what if something happens to Charon? A chevalier is lost without a good mount."

Merlyn pivoted from the window. "And what of Arthur's worth? His importance to his children? His importance to Renford? He did wrong, aye, but he's not himself." She looked away, fighting the sorrow that threatened her composure before this man. "The whole of Northumbria is but a shadow of itself, because of rebellious earls, I do not deny. . . . But what would *you* do, Rolf de Valmont, were the shoe on the other foot?"

Her gaze clashed with his, and it was naked with pain.

He suddenly wanted, in the worst way, to console her. To tell her that he would take care of her and Raven. The villagers. To assure her that they would survive the winter and early spring; that the crops would be bountiful at harvest; that there would be no more attacks from ravaging Scots or Norman outcasts; that life would be peaceful and full of joy forever.

But those were assurances that no human being could ever make to another. And he was only a puny mortal, like herself, caught in the web of life's capricious whims and God's inexplicable machinations.

He unconsciously shook his head at his thoughts, but to Merlyn it was a negative answer to her plea.

She stepped toward him, one hand held out to him, her eyes glittering with the first tears he'd ever seen from her. "Surely you have a heart? Surely you cannot take a father from his—"

"I cannot grant your request, even were I so inclined, Merlyn. My men were witnesses to my decree. Roger and Hugh, Myles and the others . . . many villagers as well. My credibility—my very authority—would not only suffer, it would collapse. A responsible leader cannot act in so irresponsible a manner." Frustration and the faintest hint of regret edged his voice, but in the mute cacophony of Merlyn's thoughts and feelings, she only heard the negative, only saw his shaking head.

Acknowledging that he was right and, in the process, according him a new respect, Merlyn suddenly realized what she had to do. It was the only thing left to do to save Arthur.

And she had to propose it to him before her courage deserted her . . . before she had time to think of the personal repercussions of such an offer.

She drew a sharp breath and said, "If you'll spare Arthur's life, I'll wed you." The word *wed* was barely audible, evidence of the abhorrence of the very idea to her . . . selling herself like a camp whore to a Norman warrior.

Rolf looked stunned, turning his head aside with a frown, as if he couldn't believe he'd heard right.

Merlyn recklessly rushed on before he could refuse. "You asked me the other morn . . . and I declined. Well, I'm accepting now. I'll wed you."

Recovering from his momentary surprise, Rolf answered, "And you think yourself worth my risking my credibility, my authority?"

She ignored the slight to her person. He'd wanted her, surely that couldn't have changed so quickly.

His pride had asked that question. "You are lord here now. You have the power of life and death over us all if you go by Norman law, as you've told me before. What you say will stand. I'm merely striking a bargain with you. People have married for less."

His eyebrows tented to a devilish angle, but she saw no anger in his eyes. Rather, a reluctant levity. "Ah, I see. Merlyn the martyr."

She spun away in annoyance, staring sightlessly at fat-cheeked white clouds frolicking across a cerulean sky. She told herself that, in spite of his words, he would take her to wife. She had no doubts about her effect on him as a woman. And not only would she be saving Arthur's life if he agreed, but she could also do more for her people as the lord's wife.

It would be a bargain, pure and simple; and Merlyn and those she loved would be the better for it. So she told herself. Surely his change from anger to amusement was an indication of his delight with her proposal.

"Very well, Merlyn. I accept your offer."

Merlyn swung around to face him, her expression a mixture of suspicion and irritation, rather than relief. The female in her told her she should have been flattered, but he'd certainly thrown over his fear of losing face before those over whom he ruled with sudden, careless-seeming ease! And after she'd pleaded with him . . . shed *tears* before him.

It was a far cry from his fervent and totally unexpected offer to her the other day.

"And when will you do me the honor? Perhaps on the morrow?"

Merlyn looked stricken. The morrow?

Reading her expressive features, Rolf said, with a half-smile, "I would have Hugh and Roger here for the wedding, and they are to leave the day after Michaelmas."

Merlyn did some calculating and discovered that Michaelmas was about a sennight away. She swallowed, hoping he wouldn't notice her cowardice.

"As you wish," she whispered. Then, straightening and mustering the scattered scraps of her dignity, added, "And will you free Arthur? Lift his sentence?"

At the mention of the man who had killed Ombre, Rolf's mien darkened. "Aye." He pointed a finger at her as he stepped closer. Merlyn stood her ground, even when he tipped her chin toward his face with that same accusing finger. "And you will kiss your betrothed to seal the bargain, *oui?*"

She stiffened and drew back her head.

"Ah, ah, ah, my little pagan. You made a pledge, and I will hold to my part of the agreement only if you hold to yours."

He drew her chin toward him and loosely encircled her shoulders with his other arm. As his mouth descended toward hers, his hazel eyes were bright with triumph, along with something more subtle, yet infinitely more profound.

Merlyn held his gaze, unable to look away. His lips touched hers, warm and firm but gentle. Gentler even than the first time. They brushed the silken surfaces of hers in light, tentative exploration.

So delicate was his touch that Merlyn's own mouth relaxed, quite against her will. He whispered her name before his tongue slipped into her mouth the tiniest bit, all the while his lips nibbling at hers.

This approach, Rolf could only hope, would not conjure up ugly memories of debasement or invasion as had the hunger in his previous kiss. No, there was no desperation or overt persuasion in this kiss, for he was not without experience with women and learned quickly; he merely wanted to seal her sacrifice. And taste of her lips as he'd yearned to do for what seemed like forever.

After his tongue wet Merlyn's lips, Rolf fixed the warm adhesion of his mouth to hers for a few blissful moments, feeling desire shoot through his midsection with all the potency of a lance . . . a lance of purest pleasure instead of pain.

Merlyn, too, felt the power of his mouth flitting over hers, his tongue teasing hers, and she had to dredge up the sight of Arthur the tanner's face in order to find the will to pull away. "I—I must tell—" She stopped mid-sentence, the smallest bit flustered in the wake of his kiss and her words. After all, *he* was lord. It was up to him to inform Arthur of his newly won freedom.

"You may tell him, Merlyn." His arm fell away, a frown creasing his forehead once again. "He and his family may live in their former home, and he may do what he can to serve me and his fellow villagers. But I will require of him some recompense for my horse."

Merlyn's look turned guarded.

How little she trusts me, he thought with a mental sigh.

"He will make replacement arrows for my hunting bow—and those of my archers—in any spare time he has. Michael will teach him, for not only is he skilled in that particular work, but he is a patient young man, as well, and will encourage the tanner to make use of what physical resources he has left to him."

Merlyn felt her throat tighten at his words. Whether he realized it or not, Rolf de Valmont had once again revealed a soft heart beneath his tough exterior, his ready temper.

Mayhap Elsa's good feelings about him were valid . . .

Don't be a fool. He's a murdering, marauding

239

Norman, usurping your lands, everything that you've cherished all your life. How could you ever harbor good feelings toward him?

"Michaelmas, then," he said, chasing away her darker thoughts.

Merlyn nodded, the word *aye* stuck in her throat like a splinter of bone.

He walked into their lives on a sunny September day, two days before Michaelmas, to be exact, and exuding a confidence and determination that drew many to him immediately.

He wasn't emaciated as the rest of them had been before coming under Rolf de Valmont's protection. Nor did he appear acrimonious or surly in light of England's plight.

He took an immediate interest in Merlyn, much to Rolf's annoyance.

And Merlyn returned the interest, furthering Rolf's annoyance.

"I come from west of here," he told them, "looking for a new place to settle. My village, too small and distant to be known to you, was destroyed by the Normans"—the barest change in his voice here—"and nearly everyone killed or scattered."

Rolf, who had been watching him through assessing eyes, asked, "And a heathly one you are, too. Just how have you managed that?"

Edward Smithsson shrugged, then pulled a knife from beneath his overtunic. "I am good with a dagger." He tossed it up into the air and caught it before whisking it back into the sheath at his waist. "Fish . . . hares . . . even a boar now and again." He looked at Rolf as he said the last words. "I don't think your duke will miss them, considering his occupation with his enemies across the Channel."

Rolf held out one hand, palm up. "You will give me your weapon, until I deem it safe to return it."

Edward shook his head. "That I cannot do. 'Tis my only defense, my only way of obtaining a decent meal."

"I will defend you while you live here," Rolf told him, "and you will be provided with three meals every day."

Edward ignored the outstretched hand. "Still, you will understand, I hope, if I cannot comply?"

Myles, who'd been standing behind Smithsson, surprised him and removed the dagger in question from its sheath before the Saxon could put up more than token resistance.

For the first time, Edward Smithsson frowned. Merlyn stepped forward then and put a hand on his arm. "'Tis for the best, Edward," she told him in an attempt to avoid an altercation. "You can trust these men."

She was surprised at her own words but even more uneasy at the look that entered his eyes. It seemed somehow to register disappointment in her, as his eyes slitted a fraction and the blue irises darkened.

But then it was gone as his face cleared. "And who are you, lovely one?" he asked.

"Merlyn. I bid you welcome to Renford and hope you'll stay."

Rolf just stared at her for a long moment, unable to fathom her warm and congenial welcome to this perfect stranger . . . English or not.

"Just who *is* this Edward Smithsson?" he grumbled to Hugh that night in the great hall.

"A good-natured fellow who appreciates your bride-to-be," Hugh said with a half-hidden grin from behind his cup of wine. "Don't tell me you're jealous, Valmont," he chided. As Rolf gave him a sour look, he added thoughtfully, *"Eh bien,* he is pleasing enough to look upon . . ."

"What?" Roger said in mock horror. "My brother is now admiring a man's looks as opposed to those of a woman?"

"Only from a woman's perspective," Hugh explained, unruffled. "There is no crime in that."

Rolf looked at him askance. "No doubt 'tis Smithsson's long hair. With his features, he might remind some of us of a female."

"With a beard?" Myles threw in, using a falsetto voice.

Hugh grinned, and Roger conceded, "You've a point there."

"Easy on that wine, *mon ami,*" Rolf warned Hugh, "else we have none for my wedding." He was drinking cider instead, not having anticipated another celebration to use up their precious, dwindling reserves.

"One cup only, I told him," said Roger. "He pines for the lovely Brenna and would use the wine to soothe his heart . . . and the itch in his braies."

They all laughed at this, Myles included. The latter was involved in a game of dice with Rufus and Michael. Bryce, Eric, and Roger's squire were teasing Gryff with a wooden ball one of them had carved, throwing it over the pup's head or almost to him before one of them stepped in to snatch it before the animal could pounce on it.

Others were already abed about the perimeter of the great hall or in the cottages and outbuildings throughout Renford. A light September rain began to patter on the dry ground outside.

Rolf stretched his arms high over his head, flexing his fingers and marveling at the fact that the mention

242

of Brenna of Abernethy only stirred fond memories, nothing more. "Then he'd better guard his scrawny neck," he said, referring to Edward, "else I throttle it."

"His neck is hardly scrawny," Hugh reminded him. "And he is possessed of a nimble tongue and sweet words to match his looks. 'Tis just as well that you are taking Merlyn to wife with him around."

Rolf's eyes narrowed as he glanced about the hall, trying to pierce the gloom around the walls.

"He cannot hear us," Roger said. "He chose to spend the night with the tanner and his family." Rolf and Hugh looked sharply at Roger as he continued. "Now, does that mean that he is kindhearted and generous-spirited? Or is he up to something?"

"Up to what?" Hugh asked. "Can you not give him the benefit of the doubt?"

"Nay," Rolf growled.

"What bothers me," Roger said, "is how he knows of my lord William's 'enemies across the Channel.' What would the average Englishman know of that?"

"And he's too friendly for an Englishman," Myles added, looking up from his game.

"Keep an eye on that one," Roger said in agreement. Hugh nodded.

"Rolf is naught if not a good judge of men," Michael defended Rolf. "And we will watch this Smithsson, Roger, do not doubt it."

Rufus grunted his assent before they returned to their dice, muttering, "No doubt he has his eye on the tanner's wife."

Gryff came scampering up to Rolf, in obvious search of relief from the teasing of the three squires. Rolf scratched the pup behind his ears. "And why aren't you with Raven, eh? What kind of bandog are you, anyway?" He scooped the pup into his grasp and stepped over the bench upon which he'd been sitting. "I'll take him to Merlyn," he said, drawing raised eyebrows and knowing looks from the others. "And I suggest you all get to bed. We comb my entire holdings thoroughly in the morn. I want no disruptions at my wedding. I want my people to have a full day of celebration . . . God knows when the next will be." He grinned then, raising a finger into the air for emphasis. "'Twill also ensure a proper send-off the morning after for my best friend and his brother."

With the wriggling Gryff beneath one arm, Rolf swung away and strode toward one of the great doors. He paused, peering out into the light drizzle of the overcast night. As he stepped over the threshold, feigning interest in the weather, he was so acutely aware of the impending departure of the Conteville brothers and their men that the words he'd uttered, thus overtly accepting the English of Renford as his own, with all their profound implications, never even registered.

Chapter 15

Rolf met Merlyn at the church door, then they proceeded inside the cool, dim chapel. He wore his family colors of emerald green and gold; Merlyn wore her yellow bliaut. Her thick, dark hair was neatly braided and coiled about her head, emphasizing the pure lines of her profile, her slender neck and smooth throat. The women had made a garland of wild flowers for her hair, lavender and yellow and orange against a background of shiny green myrtle placed upon her crown.

They had also decorated the church with wildflowers and greenery, and Merlyn felt warmed inside by their efforts. Word had raced through Renford like wildfire, Merlyn knew, even before the announcement had been made. This show of support for her was welcome, soothing stuff, for it showed that her people loved her . . . cared enough to attempt to make it a real celebratory affair.

It also meant, she suspected, that many of them were accepting Rolf de Valmont. About this, she had mixed feelings.

She tried to lose herself in the mass being said by trying to interpret the little Latin she understood, willing her mind to blankness, refusing to think of what would come after. The exchanged vows, the celebration, and the bedding . . .

As Father Francis said the mass, the scent of lavender drifted up to Rolf, and with a poignant pang, he was reminded of the day he'd made Merlyn bathe and don clean clothes. As he glanced down at her through the cover of his lashes, he was still amazed that although he'd suspected she wasn't what she'd appeared, he hadn't imagined the true extent of her virtues, physical and otherwise; that here, in desolate and depopulated Northumbria, he should find so precious a jewel. So precious, in fact, that she had, quite literally, stolen his heart as he'd never expected to happen again.

Unexpectedly, his eyes misted, and Rolf forced his attentions to those around them, lest anyone see a warrior's tears and deem him little more than a babe. Some of the people looked grim, but more of them wore a look of calmness . . . a good sign, Rolf acknowledged. He would protect these people who were beginning to look to him for just that, and he would provide for them. There would come a day when they would be clothed in decent garments, not the rags most of them were now wearing.

He had such plans for his barony! The thought of all the work, the challenge involved, was almost intimidating . . . almost but not quite, for Rolf had never been one to shrink from a challenge—at least not on the battlefield. As he covertly studied the people present, he determined again to do his best for these, his people now.

Hugh had been right. It was a perfect—*eh bien,* almost perfect, he silently corrected—opportunity to settle down and assume responsibility for something more than his horse and sword. Responsibility for men in battle was important but short-lived. This, however, was as permanent a situation as life could offer. And the fact that he had less to work with now than the average baron in a less strife-torn area did not dampen his enthusiasm as it had only weeks ago. With Merlyn at his side, he could do anything.

His thoughts surprised him. He glanced down at her bowed head, the tenderness in his eyes hidden, and his gaze was then drawn farther downward to sweet pink toes peeping from beneath the hem of her gown. He would one day shod her feet with the softest kid leather from Córdoba, he swore silently. He would one day dress her in the finest fabrics his gold could buy.

He heard someone clear his throat nearby and, roused from his ruminations, glanced up to find Hugh looking at him, one corner of his mouth lifted wryly. He tipped his head toward Father Francis and the altar, and in the sudden silence Rolf realized that the priest was waiting for him to lead Merlyn forward.

Neither Rolf nor Merlyn heard a word Father Francis uttered as he blessed the marriage, so engrossed was Rolf in Merlyn and so suddenly apprehensive of her bargain was Merlyn. What was she getting herself into? she thought in sudden, insidious panic.

You're saving a man's life.

She dared to glance up at Rolf then. The hue of his tunic brought out the green in his hazel eyes. The gold trim around the neckline, sleeves, and hem emphasized the soft golden gleam in his sable hair, a reflection of the lighted candles set around the altar, the softly hissing flames of the torches in newly remounted wall brackets.

Handsome he was, by any standard, she acknowl-

247

edged, but could he run and defend the village and surrounding lands? Could he act as arbiter of disputes for her people? Or would he ruthlessly squelch any complaints . . . crush them with an iron fist of cruel authority.

She thought she was beginning to know him better than that, but one never knew with certainty until one actually lived with a man—or woman. Perhaps Rolf de Valmont had been putting his best foot forward (and the thought actually made her smile inside as she thought of his natural, negative reaction to several situations) with the intention of winning her over all along, in order to encourage her people to accept him.

Don't flatter yourself. You were an unsightly, irritating crone, deliberately thwarting him.

But his behavior had changed toward her the moment she had emerged from her forced bath.

Father Francis joined their hands and sprinkled holy water over their heads. Then he gave Rolf the kiss of peace, and Rolf turned to Merlyn. In the brief time before he gave the same to her, her expression was suddenly wary with the suspicion that he had schemed from almost the beginning to accomplish *this.*

Her gaze fused with his, hers accusatory, his inexorable. His lips touched hers, and suddenly all thought fled, leaving only dizzying sensations whirling through her midsection . . . and lower.

Does it really matter? one last vestige of reason queried softly. *Rolf de Valmont got what he wanted, and you did, as well. You not only saved Arthur's life, but you are now in a position from which you can better see to the needs of your people.*

But the bargain was all but forgotten in the warm, wonderful feeling of his lips over hers, his strong, capable body a hairsbreadth away from the slightness of hers. And the light in his half-hooded eyes promising things that had nothing to do with material bargains . . .

Well-wishers lined the path from the church to the manor. A handful of children, accompanied by a number of adults (who were obviously daring to feel confident enough under Rolf de Valmont's protection to display open happiness), cavorted about the churchyard, laughing and singing and dancing.

It warmed Merlyn's heart to see this, along with the many smiling faces of others, even though these latter were more hesitant to let go their inhibitions before their new Norman lord and his men.

Hugh and Roger de Conteville were resplendent in scarlet and gold, and most gallant, stealing Merlyn away for quick congratulatory kisses before Rolf could object, then laughing uproariously when Valmont refused to grant the same privilege to his other men.

"Do you know, Merlyn," Hugh told her just before they ascended the stone steps of the manor, "that Rolf was so drunk when he toasted Brenna and me at our wedding, that as he stood on the board, he lost his balance and fell into the crowd?"

With sweet-scented skin and pretty names like . . . Brenna . . .

The words flashed through Merlyn's mind. Her smile died aborning as the name Brenna registered. It was the name Rolf de Valmont had uttered with such reverence when she'd tended his arm.

"Merlyn?"

She pushed aside such silly thoughts. If Rolf had

249

been in love with Hugh de Conteville's wife, that was no concern of hers. Obviously, Hugh was happy with the fair Brenna.

'Tis a Scots name, one more devil taunted her, but she shook her head to clear it of the voice and smiled up at Hugh. "I don't believe we have quite enough Norman wine for him to imbibe . . . although he may turn to the lady Liane's mead."

They laughed together at the shared merriment, but Merlyn's was cut short as Rolf came between them suddenly and swept her up into his arms. "The groom carries the bride, lout," he said to Hugh with mock sternness, "and especially when his best friend would steal her attention." He moved past his grinning friend and entered the manor, noting once again that Merlyn's feet were unshod. "And you'll not have to go barefooted for long, if I have any say about it," Rolf pledged in her ear before setting her down.

It occurred to Merlyn, as she saw the laden tables, that Rolf had outdone himself for his own wedding. The boards were equally full, if not more so, than for the modest celebration after Merlyn and her followers had sworn fealty to him. And what had he said then? *We'll not be able to do it again until after spring.* Yet here they were, presented with tempting displays of food, a commodity more precious than gold in this part of England.

She decided he was either truly wasteful . . . or determined to do them both proud on this their wedding day. The second thought brought a queer little pinch near her heart, but before she could examine it, Rolf was at her side, looking down at her with expectancy in his eyes.

She suddenly felt awkward, even shy. Shy? Merlyn? With a mental shrug, she dismissed her unease and said, "So much food, my lord . . . Will we not suffer later?"

His lips curved softly, sweetly, into a smile that quite unexpectedly caused her breath to freeze in her lungs, as it was meant to do. He wanted to banish that hungry, worried look that shadowed her eyes all too often. And that was only one of many things Rolf de Valmont wanted to do for Merlyn of Renford. "But no Michaelmas goose, I'm afraid." His voice was full of rue. "I only intend to wed once, Merlyn," he continued. "You would begrudge me this?" he inclined his head toward the tables. "And after I spent half a day and an entire evening hunting? When I should have been celebrating Michaelmas *and* my wedding the night before? And then having to cajole Agnes to be generous with the flour Cedric found for us?"

Habits died hard, and memories of near-starvation were still quick to surface in her thoughts, influence her behavior. "But what of the winter? The early spring . . . until crops come in?"

His expression grew sober. Michaelmas was the official end of autumn and beginning of winter. As the seigneur, Rolf should have been totaling up his accounts from rents. That was not the case this Michaelmas. These people could not feed themselves and their families, let alone spare him anything.

"You will not worry about such things right now. 'Tis our wedding day, and I would have everyone enjoy it." He put his lips to her ear, "And especially you, wife, for you'll not wed again, either."

It was his pledge to her, not of love—he did not dare—but rather of security. He knew it was a pledge that was impossible to ensure, but he would have said anything in those moments to bring a smile to her face. A smile like the one she had given Cedric at

251

another celebration . . . and unwittingly stolen Rolf de Valmont's heart.

Rather than smile, however, Merlyn was instead reminded of how the marriage had come about, and smiling was suddenly the farthest thing from her mind. "I find a marriage under these circumstances as abhorrent as a forced marriage, my lord. Perhaps one day I *will* wed again . . . and then, I pray, by choice."

The smile slid from his features at the damning reminder, and Merlyn turned away, ignoring him . . . and a tiny voice that whispered she was being unduly cruel. If he thought to charm her into his bed this night, he would learn differently. She would submit to him, to be certain, but only as part of the bargain. Nothing on this earth would ever allow her to be willingly bedded by a Norman. And especially one who spared a man's life only at such a cost to her personally.

What would Stigand have done?

Stigand's gone!

Aye, but he was a good man, and wise. He would have spared a man's life if he could have thought of a means to do it without undermining his own authority.

Well, probably so, she thought stubbornly, but I'll not go crawling to Rolf de Valmont with an apology.

"Mamma, my lord Hugh is going to play 'is lute!" Raven said excitedly from beside Merlyn.

Merlyn looked into her daughter's eager little face, feeling like a traitor. She dropped down and took her hands. "Do you understand why I had to marry Sieur de Valmont, Raven?"

Raven's smile dimmed a little. "Aye. Renford needs a new thane, and *he* needs a wife. *I* will be his child now, and Gryff 'is hunting hound."

"Stigand was your father!" Merlyn said sharply, alarmed at the ease with which the little girl had so totally accepted Rolf.

The smile faded completely. "I know, Mamma. Can I not have two, then?"

Merlyn suddenly hugged Raven to her, clutching her as if she would never let her go. "Forgive me, child," she murmured into her ear. "Of course you can. I just don't want you to forget your natural father."

"I would never forget my lord father."

Amidst the noise in the hall, the sweet strains of a lute permeated the air and the crowd began to quiet. "Go," Merlyn said, patting Raven on her bottom, "and sit at my lord Hugh's feet so you can better see and hear him."

Raven's face lit up, and she turned and scampered off, dark curls bouncing. Others had quickly gathered around him, Merlyn noticed, as if more in need of entertainment than food and drink . . . an indication that Rolf de Valmont had at least succeeded in keeping their bellies filled since he'd come to Northumbria.

Merlyn looked about her. Many of her own people were gathering around Hugh de Conteville, seemingly mesmerized by his deep, soothing voice and the beautiful sounds coming from his lute, which seemed to be an extension of himself rather than a separate, inanimate wooden instrument.

Marthe was staring up at Hugh agog, as if he were the embodiment of the Norse god Odin himself. For once she hid behind no man and sat at his feet, utterly entranced.

"My brother has that effect on people," Roger said to her quietly. Merlyn turned aside and looked up at him.

"He can soothe the savage beast, as they say, in anyone. He was, at one time, seriously considering becoming a monk at Cérisy-la-Forêt in Normandy."

"I can well believe it," Merlyn said with a smile. She glanced at Rolf, who stood nearby with Cedric and Myles. The latter two were intent on Hugh's performance, but Rolf's expression was closed, his thoughts obviously elsewhere.

He's hurt, she thought with some surprise. *And I am the cause of it.*

She deliberately hardened her heart against him. It was a dastardly bargain, her darker, unreasonable side maintained, which could have been avoided if he'd only exercised a little compassion for a sick man.

As if reading her thoughts, Rolf turned and caught her looking at him. Face stern, he strode toward her, acknowledged Roger with a brief nod, and said, "And where is the one for whom you made this supreme sacrifice?" One dark brow arched questioningly, but there was no gleam of amusement in his eyes.

"Arthur?"

"Bien sûr." The words were clipped, his tone grim; and although Merlyn knew next to no French, there was no mistaking the translation: *Of course. Who else?* Even Roger threw him a puzzled glance before moving to join the others who'd gathered around Hugh.

The very fact that he'd spoken in his native French revealed Rolf's agitation, if his actions did not.

"Why . . . I don't know. In his cottage, I would think."

"Rather foolish behavior, would you not say, my lady wife, since I gave specific orders for everyone in Renford to attend our wedding?"

"I—I'll fetch him," she said without hesitation,

254

glad for a reason to escape his somber scrutiny. As she swung away, he touched her arm.

"Send someone else," he said. "Nay, better yet, I'll go."

"You?" The word was out before she realized she'd uttered it, real doubt etched across her features.

"You are concerned about something? Surely our Arthur would not dare raise a hand to me after being spared. Therefore you must be concerned for *him*." His mien darkened with silent umbrage. "I assure you, I am no barbarian, *madame*. I wouldn't spare a man only to kill him a sennight later over a much lesser . . . slight."

But Merlyn did not quite believe him. Arthur's mind was delicately balanced between the present and the past. A past in which he believed that he'd failed his beloved king and might do anything to make amends. He was often unpredictable in his words and behavior.

In actuality, she was concerned about both of them, even though she cared not one wit about Rolf de Valmont's safety in and of itself. It was only because he was, for now at least, their protector and provider.

She opened her mouth to speak, but he spoke first. "And I notice Smithsson is not here, either. Only Margaret." He indicated Arthur's wife, helping her daughter and herself to food from one of the tables, while Elsa stood by, holding and cooing to the baby. "I will send Smithsson to the hall, where he belongs. Then I will speak to Arthur. 'Tis as good a time as any."

He turned on his heel without giving Merlyn a chance to reply and strode from the hall.

*   *   *

They sat together, head to head, deep in low conversation . . . Arthur and Edward Smithsson. From Rolf's position just inside the partially opened door, Arthur appeared perfectly lucid, intent upon what his fellow Englishman was saying.

Smithsson's long, fair hair shielded most of his profile from Rolf's gaze, but it was obvious he was speaking in earnest if low tones.

"The Lord of Renford requires his people to attend his wedding celebration."

Both men looked up, Edward reacting more quickly, one hand going to his waist where his dagger had been.

"What do you here?" Rolf pressed, keeping the advantage.

"I was trying to persuade Arthur to join me in going to the hall," he said smoothly, ". . . my lord." The last two words sound just the slightest bit forced. "He's . . . hesitant, in light of what he did."

Rolf continued to stare at Edward consideringly as he moved inside the cottage and stopped before the two men seated on a battered settle. "'Tis over and done with. There is no need for you to feel unwelcome," he said to the tanner as his gaze switched to him. "Do you understand, Arthur?"

Arthur continued to stare at the floor between his feet, but his mouth was a mutinous line. He seemed agitated and a flush was creeping up his drawn cheeks.

"Leave us," Rolf commanded, feeling a nasty urge to put his fist smack in the middle of Smithsson's fair face.

The Saxon stood and looked Rolf straight in the eye, his own burning blue, his lips twitching ever so slightly beneath his moustache.

Something wicked comes this way . . . You must

be on your guard . . .

Elsa's warning came to Rolf like a searing bolt of lightning, every bit as illuminating, as stunning. It caused his heart to skip in its otherwise steady cadence, combined as it was with his own sharp intuition.

His eyes still locked with Rolf's, Smithsson reached down to place a comforting hand on Arthur's shoulder. He squeezed it, then nodded at Rolf with a flicker of movement and left the cottage.

Rolf glanced around, spotted a stool in one corner near the cold fireplace, and pulled it over and placed it across from Arthur. Its legs scraped over the straw-strewn wooden floor with a dull, vibrating sound in the otherwise silent room. Rolf sat, and its wobbly legs creaked warningly.

In the middle of his ambivalent feelings toward this man, he hoped it wouldn't collapse beneath his weight and rob him of what little dignity he could command under the circumstances.

He turned his full attention to Arthur, putting the stool out of his mind. He had the distinct impression that the tanner was angry . . . and that that anger had been deliberately stoked by Edward Smithsson. He remembered Derwick's bitter words: *a lowly tiller of the soil who failed his king in protecting his country . . .*

It came to Rolf then that he'd chosen to avoid coming to his own conclusions about the conquest of England because it had been easier to follow William of Normandy without question. He still remained absolutely loyal to William, but now, face to face with the repercussions of Hastings—and in love with one of the vanquished—Rolf realized that he had done the conquered English, and himself, a disservice. He also knew that it was now his responsibility to help these people heal in every way.

For once, he didn't wonder how Hugh de Conteville would have handled this delicate situation. The words just came, from the part of Rolf de Valmont that was noble and compassionate and just.

"Whatever you may think of me," he said quietly, knowing not why it should matter to him what this muddle-minded man thought, "I did not kill your king. Nor did I directly engage the housecarls surrounding him." He paused, searching for the words that would bring the tanner out of his silence. "I would have you know that."

Rolf had heard the tanner's anguished words to Merlyn just before he'd burst into the granary, but he'd been too angry at the time to pay them much heed. Too angry at the senseless loss of a destrier, and then at Merlyn's disobedience, to allow them to soften his heart in the smallest way toward this man. Yet Merlyn had mentioned Arthur's love for and loyalty to Harold Godwinson, and what Rolf had heard the tanner say to Merlyn in the granary now came back vividly. It happened often among the vanquished.

Arthur would not meet Rolf's eyes. "It means less than naught, Norman," he muttered. "You cannot win over every Englishman just because you won the battle." His words were heavy with hatred.

"True. But neither can you wallow in self-pity . . . live in the past while life goes on, while your wife and children, your friends and neighbors, try to rebuild their world. I saw where you had hidden your family beneath the riverbank . . . an all-but-fool-proof hiding place, Arthur of Renford, and very clever. I need clever men such as yourself to help me rebuild Renford's future . . . England's future; to pick up the pieces and carry on; to make the fields ripe with harvest; to keep the land safe from thieving Scots and Danes and would-be mischief makers. You are of no use to me sulking here in this room, reminiscing about what is no more . . . and with the likes of Edward Smithsson."

If the tanner heard him, he didn't acknowledge it. His eyes still on the floor at his feet, he said, "You butchered him like an animal, my king. I lay there, my arm hanging by a thread, helpless to go to his aid."

Rolf had heard of Harold Godwinson's horrible death, but he felt that it might ease some of this man's festering memories to speak of it.

". . . blinded in one eye by a Norman arrow," Arthur was saying, the acrid words pouring out in an emotional deluge. "A man with an arrow in one eye surely cannot see with the other, either. So he crouched there, helpless, his housecarls being cut down as the battle raged around him. He could not see, let alone move to retreat. 'Twas too late by then, anyway, for the Bastard saw my lord Harold's plight and came charging up to him with three other knights." Tears were streaming down his face now as he floundered helplessly in the past. "And hacked him—to pieces."

Eustace of Boulogne (Rolf remembered the story well), with Hugh of Ponthieu, son of the man who had imprisoned Harold Godwinson on an earlier trip to Normandy. The third knight was a man by the name of Giffard. But Rolf would not reveal any of this to Arthur. To what purpose?

"He was a courageous man, your Harold," he said without thinking. Rolf had dealt with men who'd suffered emotional injuries from battle, and his instincts served him well now. "And as I am loyal to my duke, so can I understand your loyalty to and

259

grief over the loss of your king, Arthur."

The tanner began to rock back and forth on the settle in obvious anguish. The empty sleeve where his left arm had been swayed slightly with the movement, a mute reminder of the horrors of war.

"But in spite of everything, life continues, unfair as 'tis. And in the end, I believe it offers more joy than despair." He paused. "Look at me," he said softly. Arthur was slow to act. He stared a while longer at the floor and then slowly lifted his chin. His right eye met Rolf's gaze unflinchingly. "I cannot say that I did not believe in my duke's cause," Rolf continued, "but I can say that there are others who did not . . . but would never have dared oppose him. Ask Roger de Conteville, one of the Norman twins with our group. He had no wish to fight Harold Godwinson, for Godwinson had saved his life several summers earlier when he was on a mission in Normandy for King Edward."

"'Twas no mission!" Arthur fired back, his eyes bright with sudden fury. "He was but on a fishing expedition when his boat was blown off course. He had no mission in Normandy."

Rolf nodded, but his expression did not change. "That is the English version. But I didn't come here to argue a moot point. Harold Godwinson pulled Roger de Conteville from quicksand and carried him upon his own back while dragging another Norman to safety.

"What I would have you know, Arthur of Renford, is that there are two sides to every story . . . to every disagreement . . . to every battle. If I had been in a position to take on Godwinson man to man, I would have done so in the name of my duke. But I was fighting in William's left division under Count Alan Fergant."

"So you would absolve yourself of my lord Harold's death."

Rolf released his breath with a soft, drawn-out hiss of air. Was the Saxon really missing the point? Or was he refusing to accept Rolf's implication that he had had nothing to do with Harold Godwinson's shamefully achieved death? "Nay. I would only tell you that as life changes, so must you change accordingly, tanner. Otherwise you may as well lay down and die . . . and leave your family to struggle on without you." He leaned closer, his forearms braced on his knees. "I would wager anything I have that you alone could not have saved your king, even had you had the full use of both arms. And if you think about it, you will see that I speak the truth."

They sat there, their gazes linked, for long, quiet moments, one searching for tentative acceptance, the other struggling to tentatively accept. Only the faint sounds of revelry coming from the manor disturbed the heavy stillness.

Finally, Rolf added. "Is this how you repay the lady Merlyn for wedding me to save you? By sitting here and commiserating with Edward Smithsson?" He watched the expression on Arthur's face change to unwilling surprise before he stood. "Come, Arthur the tanner. Show my lady wife that you are worth her noble sacrifice."

Chapter 16

When Rolf returned to the hall with Arthur, he found that Edwin Smithsson had borrowed Hugh's lute and was playing what sounded like a Welsh love song to . . . Merlyn. She sat upon the bench beside him, every bit as enthralled as Marthe. Garth was playing along with a reed pipe, and a woman whom Rolf recalled as Mary was attempting to keep up with Smithsson's nimble fingers on a small harp resting in her lap.

A slow, seething anger began to build within Rolf. He quickly indicated to Arthur where his family was seated, before searching the crowd for someone not under the Englishman's spell. Rufus was juggling empty cups for several children opposite Rolf, and near one of the great stone hearths Michael and Bryce were whittling furiously, obviously in a race, to the delight of several other youngsters.

Roger and Myles were deep in conversation to one side with Cedric, seemingly oblivious to the activity around them; while one little boy, gnawing on what looked like a venison bone, had gathered a following of hounds in his wake as he tottered about the hall. But it was the impetuous—and rather bad-mannered—Gryff who leaped up and snatched the toddler's treasure, causing the latter to look down at his empty hand in bewilderment before he started wailing. As Gryff scuttled away, the child's mother came to the rescue, scooping him up into her arms and scolding him at the same time. The look she threw the fleeing pup was enough to coax a half-smile from Rolf.

"He'll earn his keep tenfold by summer next," Hugh predicted with a wry twist of his mouth. "Along with his audacity, he has cleverness and courage . . . if still a bit foolhardy."

Rolf nodded, his attention returning to Edward. "I spoke a bit to Smithsson before he sweet-talked my lute from me."

Rolf's eyes narrowed.

"Oh, have some faith, *mon ami*. He cannot charm *me*."

"I ken that, Hugh. 'Tis just that he walked into Renford like the king himself, and his behavior still borders on the arrogant."

Hugh put an arm about his shoulders. "Smile, friend. 'Twould not do to rouse his suspicions, now, would it?" He led Rolf toward food and drink. "Come. Have a draught of wine with me to improve your disposition."

"'Twill take more than a mere draught to chase the frown from my face . . . and the murderous thoughts from my mind."

Hugh shook his head and poured wine from a ewer into a horn cup, then handed it to Rolf. "He hails from somewhere in Herefordshire, so thinks Roger from his accent and his knowledge of Welsh . . . not from a village just west of here as he contends."

"He never said which one, did he?"

Hugh shook his head. "It doesn't matter. Even if

263

he lied, no one here would betray him. Yet. Even though many are beginning to depend on you, even grant you a grudging respect, you are still the enemy. They would never betray one of their own without just cause."

"Herefordshire, you say? Roger told me 'twas a den of rebellion." Rolf's dark brows drew together over the rim of his cup as he watched Merlyn join the others in applauding Edward's performance, then lean toward his ear to say something.

"Aye. Some years back Edric the Wild enlisted the aid of several Welsh princes to rebel, and now 'tis rumored there is growing discontent again." Hugh hunkered down to stroke one of the hounds who'd approached. He looked up at Rolf, his wine still in one hand. "And the second son of William fitz Osbern, Roger of Breteuil, is Earl of Hereford."

Rolf frowned. "But fitz Osbern was the king's friend."

"And so he was. But Earl Waltheof of Northumbria is English, not Norman, even if he is married to King William's niece."

"What has that to do with Roger of Hereford?"

Hugh shrugged and stood. "I just want you to be aware of the possibilities for trouble. It could come from anywhere."

Comprehension dawned suddenly. "You mean to say your brother is connecting Edward Smithsson to Hereford . . . and Earl Roger?"

Hugh drained his wine and set his cup down. "Anything is possible. You, yourself, don't like Smithsson, and you are usually a fair judge of men."

"*Merci*," was the ironic reply. "And also, of course, for dropping this into my lap on the eve of your departure."

Hugh put one hand on Rolf's shoulder and looked

deep into his eyes, all trace of his wonderful humor gone now. "'Tis conjecture only. But Roger and I want you to see just how chaotic and dangerous things could become if you aren't watchful. Continue to win over these humble people, even if you must swallow your pride. Their side of the story, to them, is just as valid as ours is to us . . . maybe more so. If you would seek to stay out of any political collusion, you must not increase enmity between you and them, but rather learn their ways. Learn to care for *them*, take on their sorrows and their joys, and they will learn to respect and obey you. By the rood, Valmont, they may even learn to love you!" Humor replaced his somberness as he broke into rich laughter, his silvery eyes asparkle.

Rolf smiled back. He couldn't help but acknowledge to himself how much he loved Hugh de Conteville. And how much he would miss him. Not Brenna so much now, but Hugh. It would always be Hugh, his brother in every way but blood. "But now I must win over my wife, methinks, to begin properly."

Hugh leaned close. *"Eh bien,* I think you already have, *mon ami,* although she may not be ready to admit such an unthinkable thing." He winked. "You can regale me in the morn."

One of Rolf's brows lifted with a demonesque tilt. *"Regale?* What manner of bridegroom do you think me to be?"

Hugh shrugged in feigned dismissal. "As you wish. But we will know if you loved or fought by the smile—or lack thereof—on your face." He poured himself a small amount of wine and offered the ewer to Rolf.

As Rolf held out his cup, he lamented, "I shall miss both you and Roger immensely, you know." He shook his head forlornly, appearing close to tears. "But my wine! My precious, heady, and soooooothing red wine . . ."

The feasting was over much too soon for Merlyn. As the women escorted her to the bedchamber upstairs, she dimly realized she had drunk too much mead. Her cheeks were flushed like those of a new bride—a bride innocent in the ways of love. Distant echoes of resentment still flared within her, along with fear.

Elsa and Marthe and Margaret undressed her, unbraided and brushed her hair, and tucked her beneath the cover after Mary placed a cup of mulled wine in her hand. Merlyn felt the room begin to sway. Clutching the cup with both hands, she downed the warmed, spiced wine in three gulps, like the antidote to some poison she'd drunk.

Coward! accused a voice. But if she'd had the necessary items at hand, Merlyn would have reverted to the grimy, bent, and garlic-reeking crone who had shielded her from Rolf de Valmont's attentions in the very beginning.

Now look where she was. In the middle of his great, soft mattress . . . his wife, no less. Soft, soft mattress, she thought dreamily, as she began to drift off. A down mattress, she guessed, the likes of which she had never experienced. A bubble of laughter rose in her throat, and she buried her head in the softness beneath her to stifle it. How ludicrous . . . such luxury in the middle of Northumbria . . . in Renford.

She began to hum the Welsh tune Edward Smithsson had played for her, the sweet notes from Hugh de Conteville's lute dancing drunkenly about her head.

"Child," Elsa murmured to her, smoothing away a shiny sable lock that shielded her cheek. "Your groom approaches. Wake up." The old woman shook her gently. "Merlyn?"

Merlyn smiled in her half-sleep from the depths of the downy pallet beneath her, her fingers slipping from the empty cup that had held the wine. "Ummm?"

"What are we to do?" Margaret asked, a worried look on her thin but pretty face. "He will be furious with us for . . . this."

Elsa straightened slowly and looked at Margaret. "You know him not yet, Margaret. He will be good for Renford. For all of us." She looked down at the slumbering Merlyn. "And especially for Merlyn here, for he is a good man."

"But he will be insulted when he sees her burrowed beneath the covers and sound asleep," whined Marthe, her fish-eyes wide with worry. Then of a sudden, her seeming concern changed to a sly smile. "I would be happy to take her place."

Not even in your dreams, Marthe, Elsa thought. She refused to validate the audacious offer, however, and said instead, "Help me prop her up. At least when his men deposit him at the threshold, she will be sitting up."

The three women worked to turn Merlyn over—with little cooperation from her—and brace her against the wall that served as temporary headboard. They tucked the cover modestly around her ribs and spread the glossy ebony tresses about her shoulders and over her breasts. Her head, however, would not remain upright.

Margaret sighed as she stared at Merlyn. "'Tis the best we can do, I think."

"Aye," agreed Elsa.

"Here." Mary came forward and dabbed a bit of lavender water on Merlyn's throat and behind her ears. The delicate scent wafted upward and enveloped Merlyn. She smiled in her sleep, a soft hiss of contentment escaping her rosy lips.

"There's naught more that we can do—except waylay him for the night," Elsa said with a humorous twitch of her lips. Her pale eyes were lit with amusement. "Our poor bridegroom is in for a surprise."

"Merlyn is the one in for a surprise," Marthe said sharply. "She'll be sorry she drank herself senseless when he beats her before the entire village on—"

"Marthe!" Elsa said in genuine irritation. Elsa suspected that Mary knew better, but Margaret's eyes were suddenly shaded with apprehension.

Before she could say any more, however, the laughter and tromping of masculine feet came to them from directly outside the door.

Mary bent to place a cup of the mulled wine on the rush-covered floor beside the mattress for Rolf, then retreated quickly with the other three women.

The door crashed open, and as the four women scuttled out, Rolf was unceremoniously deposited on his feet after being carried on the upturned palms of Hugh, Roger, Myles, and Rufus. Several other Norman men milled around and strained for a peek at the bride, but Rolf, upon seeing the unnatural downward dip of her head, sized up the situation in the blink of an eye.

He spun about and spanned the doorway with his arms, forbidding entry with his most charming grin to any who would have followed him. "No one may see my bride but me," he said with a wink. "You know how jealous I am."

"But—"

"*Eh bien*—"

"*Mais*—"

"What the—?"

"Now, now, now, *mes amis*, we are in England . . . specifically, in Renford. And I'm told things here are done a little differently," he bluffed. He raised his shoulders in a sheepish shrug without letting his hands drop from the door frame. "And since I am Lord of Renford, I must attempt to abide by some of the Saxon customs here." His grin widened. *"Bon soir, mes copains. Dormez-vous bien."*

He reached for the door and quickly closed and barred it, more than a little relieved that no one had really pressed for entry. The situation was far from the normal, to say nothing of ideal, but Rolf knew he could trust Hugh to take care of the others if the need arose.

He turned about and crossed his arms, taking in his new wife on his new down mattress—a gift from Roger and Liane—and the telltale position she'd achieved. He pushed away from the door, fighting the annoyance that the Rolf de Valmont of a month ago would have felt. He walked to the bed and stared down at Merlyn. The scent of lavender drifted up to him, reminding him of the bath he'd made her take in the kitchen weeks ago . . . and what it had ultimately revealed.

Her raven hair shielded the portion of her canted face closest to him, but the firelight obligingly played across the other side, tingeing her cheek, part of her throat, and the tops of her breasts in warm, rosy hues. Color and shadow played about her features and form, most definitely in repose save for the steady rise and fall of her chest.

Had she deliberately overimbibed, or was it

because she was unused to mead and wine in the months immediately preceding their arrival? And would he ever know for certain?

What does it matter? She's yours now.

He sat down beside her and reached for the brimming cup of wine. Without touching or disturbing her, Rolf sipped and studied. She was more than a match for any man, he thought. One moment a cackling crone, the next a lovely, intelligent noblewoman. She certainly had more than her share of courage and tenacity. And determination. She put her people before herself, as any good leader would do. She had even wed him to save a broken man's life. And it was nothing short of a miracle that she still retained her wits.

Rolf thought of the cowardly yet sly Marthe and the pretty but painfully timid Margaret, both obviously adversely affected by recent events. Others seemed to have weathered this series of catastrophes, but they had not been looked to for guidance as had Merlyn. The burden had been primarily on her shoulders, whether she'd wanted it to be or not. And the only chink in her armor was Raven.

A fierce protectiveness rose in Rolf. He would kill anyone who dared to touch a hair on the child's head, for not only had he grown to love the little girl, but he sensed Merlyn's destruction would be imminent in the wake of Raven's. And he loved this enigmatic Saxon woman with Welsh antecedents too much to even contemplate her demise, physically or mentally.

Rolf finished the wine and began to undress. He made a neat pile of his clothing near his side of the mattress, then walked over the fresh-laid rushes to stoke the small fire against the night chill. He carefully and quietly barred the two windows, catching a breathtaking glimpse of thousands of stars, pinpoints of light in the dark fabric of the night sky. A harvest moon sat sentinel above the earth, a silvered, shining disk of contrasting radiance against the Stygian vault of the heavens.

He retreated to the bed and slid in beside Merlyn. She was finally roused enough by his movement to ease herself downward into a supine position, turning onto her side to face her new husband. Soft breaths escaped her lips and feathered through the strands of dark hair webbing her fair cheek like the sheerest gossamer. Rolf watched her rhythmic breathing, willing the tautness in his loins to subside for now. He gently took one of her hands in his, enfolding her slender fingers in his own.

Trustingly as a child, her hand nestled naturally within his while she slept on.

They were coming again.

Oh, God, was there no end to them? Merlyn thought in horror.

She grabbed Raven's hand and pulled her along toward the safety of the weald. "Come quick, child. Hurry!" she urged. But Raven's legs were so short that Merlyn literally had to drag her away from the marauding men.

Scots, Normans, and Danes . . . they all rushed into the village like so many hordes of demons, wielding swords and lances and axes and torches and . . .

"Hurry," she pleaded. "Hurry, Raven, or—"

She ran straight into a wall of solid muscle . . . and came up short. Her breath burst from her lungs with the impact. Tentacle-like arms wound around her, pulling her closer, smothering her . . .

"Let me go!" she shrieked, but her voice was suddenly gone. She could only mouth the words ineffectively. Her warning to Raven never sounded,

and Merlyn felt the small hand in hers slip away. Was the child fleeing to safety. Or had she met with . . .

"Merlyn, *chère*. 'Tis a dream . . . a bad dream, nothing more."

The voice came from the man imprisoning her. His grip relaxed as she came awake, jerking upright, her eyes straining against the darkness.

"Merlyn?" he said softly in her ear. "You're here, with me. You're safe, *mon coeur*."

She perceived the glow from the scarlet blanket of coals in the hearth, and recognized Rolf de Valmont's deep and soothing voice. What was she doing here in bed with him? she thought wildly, her heart still thumping triple-time, alarm still spilling through her limbs.

He touched a finger to her cheek as she sat there attempting to reorient herself. She had a death grip on the blanket, and her skin was covered with gooseflesh. She trembled slightly in the wake of retreating terror, drawing in great gasps of air, unshackled by the man in her dream, for it had been Rolf, she guessed, who'd held her. And certainly with no intent to harm her.

Yet as reality crept in, as remembrance dawned and the tremors began to subside, Merlyn remained unmoving, her gaze resting on the pulsing embers in the fireplace, awaiting his anger over her excess drinking, her cowardly descent into oblivion to avoid what she knew must come. Awaiting what she knew must come.

Her head ached, her mouth was dry, and she felt the barest bit woozy.

"Are you all right now?" he asked, concern making his voice infinitely gentle.

She nodded wordlessly. How much time had passed? If the embers in the hearth were any indication, much of the night was gone. Why hadn't he wakened her and demanded his conjugal rights? And what in God's name would he do to her now after her foolhardy behavior? After shaming him before her women and his men? Surely the entire village would know of it by morn.

She should apologize, she thought suddenly. She should turn to him and apologize for making him the laughingstock of the village. And after she'd insulted him.

But she couldn't.

"Merlyn?" he queried softly.

Slowly, reluctantly, she turned her head until her gaze met his in the dimness. Who was this man beside her? This soft-spoken, gentle, and more patient man? The Rolf de Valmont with whom she'd exchanged bitter words in weeks gone by, she could deal with. But this . . .

Callused fingers lightly touched her chin as he tipped her face further upward. "Talk to me, Merlyn. Tell me what—"

Her tongue suddenly came to life. Unsure of him and herself, she took the offensive. Angry with this new and tender man whom fate had decreed she loathe, Merlyn held his gaze as she exclaimed, "I'll tell you what's wrong, Norman. This—this *bargain!*"

His fingers remained caressingly about her chin, but his brows drew together a fraction. "'Twas your suggestion, Merlyn. Or have you forgotten?"

She brushed his hand away and gave him her profile. "I have forgotten naught. You are a greedy opportunist, just like your duke. Rolling in here with your food-laden carts and trinkets to win over my people after all that was done to England . . . acting the part of magnanimous conqueror with your

273

false kindness and generosity . . ." Her gaze locked with his again. "But your true colors were revealed soon enough, Valmont. You sentenced a man to death—a man injured in body and spirit alike—and then accepted my desperate offer as the only way to save him." She drew in a shaky breath, giving her unreasonable outrage free rein. "And you ask me to tell you what is amiss? That was what you were going to say, wasn't—"

His lips against hers put an immediate halt to her ranting. The contact was unexpected and caught Merlyn off guard. She did nothing for a moment, trying to gather her wits, a difficult enough thing even without the lingering effects of drink. But that moment of attempted wit-summoning was a mistake. Rolf's mouth wooed hers, his tongue teasing her lips to open. When she would have protested, halfhearted as it may have been, his tongue slid between her teeth, an unwelcome yet insidiously sweet invader.

As her anger was scattered to the winds, she found her senses, her body, responding in ultimate betrayal. Her anger—her only defense against him—melted like the morning frost beneath a scintillating sun.

She groaned in frustration, in protest, but it was only token. Fire streaked through her abdomen, surging through her loins, her limbs, and ultimately, her mind, wreaking sensual havoc wherever it touched its silken flame. As his tongue engaged in a dizzying clash and retreat, court and play, Merlyn's body leaned toward his, a flower offering its nectar to a honeybee.

Rolf was quick to sense her defeat, her compliance, her eagerness. He crushed her to him, his lips leaving hers long enough to lovingly pay homage to the high, delicate bones of her cheeks, the sweet stretch of her brow, the fine, downy hair nudging her temples, all the while his breath misting her skin. One free hand skimmed the hollow of her waist, the gentle swell of her hip, the smooth length of her flank.

She moaned again, but this time in pleasure instead of in protest. "Rolf." She murmured his name instinctively, her fingertips exploring the solid musculature of his shoulders, his neck, his back . . . satin sheathing steel.

The light scent of lavender enfolded them, combining with the faint drift of woodsmoke, and man and woman . . . a heady draught.

Merlyn found herself torn, physically yearning to unite with him, while mental images of a huge, rough Norman plundering her body rose unexpectedly to vie with her desire to join her body to his. She squeezed her eyes shut against the memories, concentrating instead on the man, the moment.

As if obliging her, Rolf's tongue wended its way down one side of her neck, arousing yet more intense sensations within her as it flicked a trail of wet fire over the pulsing hollow at the base of her throat, then down to the silken cleft between her breasts.

Her entire body hummed as he traced their tempting swells, first one, then the other. His teeth teased the nipples to life, while one hand continued its provocative stimulation up and down the length of her thighs, lingering teasingly at the downy entrance between them after each tender foray.

Merlyn could only reach his head and shoulders now, and in exquisite desperation she tangled her fingers through his thick sable hair, as if to prevent him from slipping away . . . while another part of her wanted him to move lower, ever lower.

He obliged her second wish, his tongue and lips delving straight down the valley between her ribs to sear the flat planes of her belly, then circle and dip into her navel.

Desire rushed through her, leaving her tingling and expectant. Merlyn moaned again, this time his name emerging from her lips on a sigh. "Rolf . . ."

He hovered over the soft, springing curls shielding her womanhood, before moving lower. . . .

Molten heat burst through her lower body and moisture sleeked the satiny cleft of her femininity like morning dew sheening the grass. All thought of rape left her mind. Merlyn wanted him to take her with all her will, his tender and tantalizing loveplay blotting out brutal remembrances.

Rolf sensed her readiness, her need; but he wasn't finished yet.

Holding his own rampaging desire in check, he moved his mouth back to her neck, tracing the fine blue veins along its smooth, velvet length, feeling them pulse with rising excitement, burning urgency.

"Rolf . . ." she mumbled in a ragged voice, suddenly impatient. "What—?"

"I but search for stingers, my Merlyn, as you once did for me." A soft chuckle escaped him. "'Tis your punishment for tormenting me so that day." He dragged his tongue over sweet flesh, then used his teeth to nip at imaginary stingers here and there, sending shudders rippling through the woman beneath him. "Or, if you will, I'm returning the favor."

Merlyn's body cleaved to his, inviting, then demanding, while he continued his sensual assault on her throat. Her fingernails raked over his back with increasing fervor, until he positioned himself over her, whispering French love words in her ear, as his tongue nipped and whorled about that delicate aperture as well.

"You will drive me mad, my little pagan," he whispered to her, his voice a breath of sound.

"Nay, enchanter," she returned. "'Tis you who are maddening. . . ." She wrapped her legs about his hips in wanton invitation, and he could no longer find the will to resist. His mouth returned to hers as he remained poised above her for a brief eternity, trying to gauge her reaction after having been raped.

Merlyn took hold of his hips with her hands, and his doubts vanished. An attraction turned to passion too-long-denied was consummated at last with their union. As he buried his shaft in the sweet sheath of her, Rolf softly declared his love in his own tongue, *"Je t'aime, ma chère, de tout mon coeur,"* knowing that she wouldn't understand, yet reveling in the whispered sound of the words.

Together they strove, rising toward bright and blazing heights. And Merlyn once more knew the wonder of physical union with a man who loved her . . . with a man so tender and considerate in his loving that he was able to erase the degradation that had blighted her mind and heart. For one magic moment, it mattered not that he was Norman . . . that he was Rolf de Valmont, enemy of her people at Hastings and thereafter. He was a man, she a woman, and their pleasure rose above the realm of such worldly concerns.

When her cry of exultation would have shattered the still night air, Rolf's mouth closed over hers, accepting her acclamation with joy as she sealed with her body the covenant that she had so vocally condemned.

Chapter 17

"I cannot find words to thank you both for . . ." Rolf faltered, seeking those very words, and failed, ". . . everything," he finished somberly. He'd anticipated with some relish carrying on the work they had helped him organize and begin; yet, at the same time, Rolf felt as if a lead weight were pushing down on his chest in the face of the Conteville brothers' departure.

"'Twas our pleasure," Roger said, obviously speaking for Hugh as well. He took Rolf's extended hand in his own hearty grip, then clapped him on the shoulder with affection.

"Indeed." Hugh ignored his friend's offered hand, clasping him instead in a generous and bone-crunching hug. "I wouldn't have missed your falling in love with a crone for aught," he said *sotto voce* in Rolf's ear before releasing him.

The Lord of Renford laughed softly. "The brightest benefit of being consigned to hell, no doubt," he returned under his breath.

Roger, obviously guessing the gist of their banter, grinned as he looked on.

"Cultivate your sense of humor," Hugh advised.

"'Twill serve you well here."

Rolf nodded in silent accord, his eyes holding Hugh's. In such circumstances, if they could not find humor in serious situations, life would be joyless, indeed.

They stood just outside the manor, the rising sun peeking between streaks of pearly clouds, bathing the yard and those within it in pale golden light and alternating shadow.

Their three squires led their mounts from the stable to join fewer than half-dozen others who were already mounted and waiting. It was unusually quiet; the retainers spoke in low tones, if at all, and the three chevaliers nearest the hall were not boisterous in their exchanges.

"You leave with fewer men than you brought," Rolf said with a slight frown as he glanced about the manor yard. He noticed that more and more of the people of Renford were quietly filing in through the gate.

"Did you think we would do any less?" Hugh asked him. He mounted and settled into the saddle. Styx tossed his great head and snorted, sending his shiny, silken mane rippling. "We allowed any man who so desired to remain in your service. That was our understanding from the beginning."

"Your understanding, not mine," Rolf said as his gaze returned to Hugh's. He found himself fighting the emotion that tightened his throat.

"*Eh bien*, you don't need to know all our business, Valmont. Twins do have certain privileges."

"And the actions of the men speak for themselves," Roger said.

Rolf put one foot in the stirrup, the rowel in his heel clinking softly as he swung onto Charon's back. He glanced around at the few who were leaving

Renford. "But how will I pay them—?" he began, more to himself than to anyone else.

"You have land aplenty," Hugh cut in. "They don't necessarily want gold. And they've seen firsthand what they're up against."

"My only regret is that we didn't get to bid the lady Merlyn farewell," Roger said as he glanced up at the new second story of the manor.

Rolf grinned slyly. "She's exhausted from all the wedding festivities. You understand . . ." He trailed off, his eyes widening suggestively.

Everyone laughed at that. Even Elsa responded, standing beside Cedric and watching the leave-taking. Raven stood beside her, her eyes round with wonder at the sight of the great destriers. "Our Merlyn is no such thing, my lord Rolf," Elsa said with good-natured affront. She bent and whispered into Raven's ear, and the child skipped away and disappeared into the hall.

Merlyn burrowed deeper into the pallet, snuggling among the blankets as if it were the middle of a bitter winter. But something was different.

She came awake slowly, her body missing the warmth of Rolf beside her before her mind could form the thought. First her hand crept from beneath the bedclothes, seeking. When it encountered only emptiness, her eyes opened but she remained prone, allowing the memories from the night before to filter into her mind, bringing a blush to her cheeks and a curling heat to her midsection.

"Mamma?"

Raven's voice roused Merlyn from her contemplations, and she looked over at the half-open door. "Aye, child." She smiled at her daughter, then sobered at the anxious expression on Raven's face.

"What is amiss?" She sat up, willing away the bleariness of mead and sleep and lovemaking.

Remaining in the doorway, as if she couldn't wait to leave, Raven told her, "My lords Hugh and Roger are leaving this morn, Mamma. Now."

Now.

Merlyn sat straighter, everything suddenly soberly clear. How could she have forgotten? After all they had done for Renford and its people . . .

"Are they still in the yard?" she asked the child, scrambling to leave the warmth of the covers. She reached for her undergarments and chainse.

"Aye. Elsa bade me fetch you."

Elsa? Of course, she thought as she dressed and Raven disappeared. Elsa had been lady of the manor in her time. She knew the protocol for guests, even if they were uninvited Normans.

Merlyn quickly donned her yellow overgown, wishing she had another decent bliaut and some shoes. And time to wash her face and brush her hair. Running her fingers through her sleep-mussed mane and jerking at the many snarls she encountered, she hurried after Raven, wondering why Rolf hadn't wakened her. Had it been out of ignorance? Or consideration?

After last night, she felt she could safely conclude it was consideration. An inconsiderate man did not make love like Rolf de Valmont had. But it was only proper, as lady of the manor, that she bid farewell to her guests.

She flew down the stairs, through the sparsely peopled hall, and paused on the threshold. The brightness of the morning stung her eyes, and they narrowed in reaction. Sunlight struck the men in their armor in a vivid and blinding tableau, bringing

281

back a flood of unpleasant memories.

These are good men.

Merlyn tried to hold to that thought, even as she took in their great war-horses, their shimmering steel mail and war accoutrements. The pride and confidence that made them sit their mounts as if they unquestioningly owned all of England stirred up old enmities and emotions.

Hugh and Roger had left their mail coifs settled upon their shoulders, as had Rolf, Myles, and the others. They each carried their helm beneath an arm. Bareheaded as they were, they were not quite as forbidding as when they'd first ridden into Renford, yet Merlyn felt awed. And self-conscious. And, strangely, insignificant.

Ridiculous, she thought, as a cloud spread across the sun and cast them all in more human form. You need not new clothing and perfect grooming to prove aught. You are still Merlyn inside, and nothing can change that.

With a toss of her head and a straightening of her stance, Merlyn stepped out into the yard. "My lords?" she queried, confidence and authority infusing those two words, in spite of the warmth in her cheeks.

Every man in the yard—Norman and Saxon alike—turned at the sound of her voice. She felt all eyes upon her. Oh, yes, she thought, they want to see how Merlyn will react . . . the crone, the widow, the bride, the former lady of the manor now restored to that status by a Norman baron.

She moved forward with the smooth, sure stride of a Cymry princess, her undressed hair spewing down her back like molten onyx in the play of clouds across the sun, her gown swirling about her bare feet and ankles.

"Forgive me for oversleeping." She nodded at

282

Rolf, her cheeks heating a fraction more, then moved to stand before the two mounted Contevilles, a slight smile curving her lips. "I would not have you think me remiss by failing to bid you Godspeed."

She did not make the mistake of approaching the horses too closely, as upon their first meeting. Rather, she looked up at them, her good wishes apparent in her clear, direct gaze, as well as in her words. "On behalf of my people, I thank you for what you've done for Renford." She glanced about at the other mounted men. "All of you. And for the help you've been to . . . my lord husband."

Both Contevilles nodded, returning her smile. "We wouldn't have had it any other way," Hugh responded. "We are old friends—Rolf is like family—and know that we can all count on one another. If you need anything that is within our power to give, Merlyn, know that we stand prepared to render it."

"And Liane and I aren't so very far away," Roger added, sending a meaningful look Rolf's way. "At least we are here in England and not across the Channel."

"An accident of circumstance, I assure you," Hugh countered. "Had I not a grant of my own, with those dependent upon me and my protection," he said with gallant sincerity, "I would gladly remain in England."

He seemed about to say something else but held his silence, and Merlyn suspected that he had belatedly evinced some qualm about her reaction to his obviously well-meant words regarding Normans in England.

"You are all welcome in Renford . . . anytime." Merlyn was struck by her own sincerity, and she suddenly felt an impending loss in the face of their leaving.

There was an odd silence in the yard, then. The chink of mail and trappings, birdsong, the stomping of a hoof, the creak of shifting saddle leather, accompanied the morning breeze as it rustled through the turning leaves in the trees. *Farewell, farewell*, the wind seemed to whisper, and a bank of clouds scudded across the eastern sun, increasing the chill in the air . . . and in Merlyn's heart.

It portended ill, Merlyn felt, and she glanced over at Elsa. The old woman's eyes were on the skies, then they moved to Edward, who had just entered the open gate with Margaret and Derwick. A thoughtful frown settled between her snowy eyebrows, then eased when she looked back at Merlyn, but didn't quite disappear.

"It grows late," Rolf said into the silence. "'Twill soon be time for the nooning if we sit here and stare at one another." He nodded at Merlyn, a warm look in his eyes. "Myles and I will be back well before the horn sounds." He urged the restive Charon forward and toward the gate. The others filed out behind him, and Merlyn noted more than a few of the silent villagers raising hands in farewell.

Of course. The men leaving may have been Norman, but they had contributed to the rebuilding of the village and the lives of its people during the past month. And especially Hugh and Roger de Conteville. Then, too, life under these particular Normans had been incomparably better than immediately before they had arrived.

An unwelcome heaviness invaded her throat, burned the backs of her eyes. Under different circumstances, she would have regarded them as friends—competent, trustworthy, compassionate. Even as the vanquishers, they had appeared good men, in every way. But what would happen now?

Why must you *remain here?*

As Rolf disappeared around the palisade, her long-ago words returned to flay her. Would she still, even now, have preferred one of the fair-haired Norman chevaliers to Rolf de Valmont?

Aye! her stubborn side reaffirmed.

But her heart was strangely silent. And Merlyn refused to examine that damning silence.

During Rolf's absence, Merlyn made a point of circulating around the village, ostensibly to stop and speak with as many people as she could, but also to discreetly see exactly what kind of security measures were in place during his absence. As she made her rounds, however, Merlyn realized belatedly that it would be not only to Rolf's benefit, but to theirs as well to protect his fief. She also acknowledged that the very fact that she wondered about Renford's safety when he was away represented two conflicting thoughts: She had confidence enough in Rolf de Valmont to feel secure in his presence, yet she didn't trust the system he had put in place if he was not in Renford to head it.

With such confusion increasing her frustration with the whole situation, Merlyn decided to focus on her people. She was especially concerned about Arthur, and when Margaret had appeared in the yard earlier with Derwick and Edward, Merlyn wondered about him. What had Rolf said to him to make him come to the hall the day before for the wedding celebration? True, the tanner had kept to himself, refraining from participating in any of the revelry. But he had made a showing, and that in itself seemed little short of a miracle. Merlyn wanted to know exactly what Rolf had said to him if she could discover it.

She entered the tanner's cottage with a brief knock on the partially open door. "Arthur?" She moved into the dim, one-room dwelling, allowing her eyes to adjust to the interior. Soft cooing noises came to her, and she recognized the sounds of a happy infant responding to another.

Her mood lightened.

There, before a small crackling fire, Arthur sat on a rickety settle, cradling his baby son in his right arm and making absurd sounds and faces at the child. He'd move his face close enough to touch the babe's tiny nose with the tip of his own. The child would grab at his father's long, shaggy hair with one hand, then chortle with glee as the tanner quickly pulled away. His legs worked visibly beneath the blanket.

Reluctant to interrupt, Merlyn stood where she was, enjoying the sight.

After a few moments more, Arthur raised his head and stilled, as if listening. He slowly turned toward Merlyn, who was on his right, until he saw her. He frowned, as if making a concerted effort to identify her, and Merlyn felt the heaviness return to her heart once more.

He obviously didn't recognize her. . . .

"Is that you, Merlyn?"

"Aye." She moved forward into the flickering firelight, a half-smile softening her mouth as the baby made another sound of delight.

"Would that we all could be so content with so little." His words were blunted with bleakness.

Merlyn looked up at Arthur. "So little to some is everything to others. Being among one's family, safe and healthy, is more important than aught else. Is that not why you went to such pains to hide and keep your wife and children secure beneath the river-bank?''

His mood of introspection disappeared as he caught sight of her bare feet. His eyes met hers. "The lady of the manor should never be without shoes to protect her feet. You were never without shoes when Stigand was thane."

"There are more important things to attend to, Arthur, than shoes for me," she answered, wanting to pull back her bare feet beneath her skirts but resisting the urge.

He looked up at her, his head angled slyly, his good eye focusing on her face. "I ken where there is enough leather to shod the entire village."

"You do?" She was taken off guard by the unexpected revelation.

The slyness faded from his features and he shrugged, lovingly smoothing a knuckle down the babe's cheek. "I wouldn't have told anyone but you, Merlyn, for you saved my worthless life. 'Tis little enough I can do to repay you." He glanced up at her. "I meant to tell you last eve, but I . . . couldn't."

Merlyn went to stand before the settle, bending to better see the child as Arthur carefully laid it down beside him. "No life is worthless, Arthur," she said quietly. "And the fact that you made a showing at the wedding feast was thanks enough. I would have done the same for any of the others. . . ."

"He bade me come to the hall," Arthur interrupted her.

Merlyn slowly lifted her gaze to meet his. "Did he force you?"

And what if he did? her dark side queried. *As your husband, he is your master even more so than to the others now.*

Arthur was silent a few moments. Then he shook

his head. "Nay. He used no force. Only words."

At Merlyn's frown, he added, "He said that there are two sides to everything, be it a tale or a battle; that while he would have engaged King Harold fairly had he had the opportunity, Roger de Conteville would not have raised a hand to the king because he'd once saved Conteville's life in Normandy."

Merlyn was stunned. Yet she could believe such a thing of either Roger or Hugh de Conteville. And she doubted that Rolf de Valmont was so well practiced in prevarication that he would have made up such a tale merely to persuade a Saxon (who had killed a prized destrier, no less) to attend his wedding celebration.

Here was a side of Rolf de Valmont that was becoming more and more apparent to Merlyn as the days and weeks went by; a side of Rolf that stood him in good stead with men—and women—in general, not just his own retainers and fellow warriors. Here was innate if latent sensitivity; a growing willingness to see the other side, even if he did not agree with it.

Merlyn was no fool. Combine that sensitivity and attempted objectivity with his skill as a soldier. Then add his courage in the face of an enemy, his tenacity when he felt he was right, and his growing concern for her people, whom he now apparently considered his own, and you had the makings of a good leader.

It once would have been nigh on impossible for Merlyn to acknowledge it, and it still went against the grain. If Renford had to have a Norman overlord, then, she conceded, better Rolf de Valmont than someone else. He had his faults (an understatement!), but who didn't? And mayhap, just mayhap, if Merlyn sincerely threw in her lot with him because every other avenue to freedom for the English had been destroyed . . .

Nay, she thought. She wasn't quite ready for that yet. Sharing his bed was enough humiliation for now, she acknowledged with pink cheeks, and heard her own scornful laughter echoing through the dim recesses of her conscience.

". . . Edward can help us, and Derwick," Arthur was saying.

Merlyn looked at him, dragged from her thoughts. "Help us?"

"Retrieve the leather I've hidden," he repeated patiently. "I had thought, in my more hopeful moments, that if we survived, we could have either sold or bartered that leather to other villages . . . or at least used it for our own needs."

"Where is it?"

"I can lead you there," he answered, his expression growing guarded. "I would not have any Norman taking his share first. It represents years of work, on my own time and with my own share after I paid my yearly rent to Stigand. I would give it to you, Merlyn, and only you."

"With Rolf gone, now's the perfect time," she said, thinking aloud.

Arthur said nothing, but bent over his son and pressed his lips to the little one's forehead.

"But you do Rolf an injustice," she began without thinking.

"Only you," he repeated.

"We cannot leave here without an escort—at the least for safety's sake."

"Edward Smithsson is quite capable of defending us, as is Derwick."

"Without weapons?"

His eye met hers. "Believe me, there is naught out there more dangerous than the Normans. Valmont has seen to that."

He sat back on the settle then, his splayed fingers resting on the sleepy child's swaddled frame, and lapsed into silence as he stared into the flickering fire.

"Arthur . . ." But Merlyn knew he would not answer her. His mind had apparently retreated, dwelling somewhere in the past now . . . or his own purgatory between then and now. Whether he'd done it deliberately was impossible for Merlyn to determine. Her gaze returned to the child. Would it be safe alone with Arthur like this? she wondered.

Merlyn reached to touch the babe. Arthur's fingers appeared to tighten, spanning the little one's fragile form without exerting uncomfortable pressure as his body shifted slightly toward it in a protective attitude.

She withdrew quietly, deciding she must trust Margaret's judgment . . . and that part of Arthur still responsive to the world around him.

The longer that Rolf was in Renford, the less reason he had to mistrust Merlyn or the other villagers. If any of them wanted to leave, they were free to go, although he had not exactly come out and made the announcement. He had decided (and told his men) that anyone not intelligent enough to realize that they were safer under his aegis was welcome to return to the *weald*.

There was also the mystery of Bryan's murder. It would have been foolhardy to trade the security of Norman-ruled and restored Renford for the hardship and danger of the forest in the aftermath of war and sporadic rebellion.

Therefore, when Merlyn, Edward, Derwick, and Arthur left the village an hour later (each from a different point), their furtive foray went unnoticed. Almost.

Only Elsa watched with worried eyes as Merlyn slipped into the wooded area leading to the river. . . .

As they entered the forest, as the living wall that was the *weald* closed around them, Merlyn briefly had second thoughts. They hadn't told a soul where they were going. In fact, Merlyn didn't even know for certain. Perhaps it had been rash to leave the sanctuary of the village on the word of a man who was not only filled with bitterness and hatred toward those who ruled over them, but could not seem to maintain contact with reality, either.

Mayhap he told Edward, her sensible side suggested. Surely Edward Smithsson was intelligent and trustworthy. She strained to catch sight of him as they headed south, parallel to but just out of sight of the Tees. She couldn't see much, however, in the dense brush and branches; mostly the tall Smithsson's fair head and Arthur's back as he limped along, every step seeming painful. Derwick walked behind Merlyn, bringing up the rear.

An odd feeling settled over her, a sense of wrongdoing . . . of guilt. They weren't doing anything wrong, she insisted to herself. They were retrieving a cache of tanned hides that Arthur had hidden. The entire village would benefit from the leather, Norman and Saxon alike. If they were rather secretive about their methods of obtaining it, then so be it. The end would justify the means.

Merlyn's unease receded a little but didn't completely disappear.

Arthur led them a fair distance south of Renford, and finally to a well-covered depression to which he pointed when they finally halted on the west bank of the Tees.

"I wouldn't have noticed it," she admitted aloud.

"Nor I," Edward agreed. He gave her a measuring look, then went down on his knees and began scooping the debris of autumn from the top layer of deep brown soil. Derwick dropped beside him, and Merlyn did the same.

Arthur's hand on her shoulder restrained her for a moment, however. "Let me," he said. "You keep watch."

He knelt stiffly then, across from Edward, and began scrabbling at the dirt with the broken trowel Merlyn handed him.

Merlyn bit back the question "For whom?" realizing that not everyone had as much faith in Rolf's ability to make safe the lands around them. And somehow, as the minutes passed, she had a feeling that the enemy was here in their midst and not out in the forest.

Or did Arthur mean Rolf himself?

"Here," Edward exclaimed, and pulled a crude burlap sack from the loosened soil. He shook the dirt from it and set it on the ground before him. He glanced up at Merlyn. "Would you like to do the honors, lady of the manor?"

Merlyn caught the unmistakable ring of sarcasm in his words, but no one else seemed to notice.

"There's another," Arthur told them as he recommenced his digging. Derwick followed suit. Merlyn, however, nodded at Smithsson and moved to open the sack, aware of his steady gaze. Inside was a good supply of leather, almost enough, as Arthur had said, for the entire village. Merlyn sat back on her heels, wondering at the stroke of good fortune.

"Here . . . help me," Arthur ordered Derwick, and the two of them unearthed the rest of the fabric sack the tanner had so carefully buried.

"This is too good to be true, Arthur," Merlyn said. "Surely Rolf will pay you in gold for—"

"What good is Norman gold to him?" Edward cut in, his expression unpleasant. "To any of us, except to pay . . ." He trailed off and looked away from Merlyn, obviously unwilling to continue in her presence.

"You forget that I'm English, too," Merlyn objected, for some reason wanting to prove to this particular Englishman her loyalty to England.

"You gave that up when you crawled into his bed." Derwick had spoken, but everyone was looking at her. Her face grew uncomfortably warm, and her annoyance only increased the hue of embarrassment. "It matters not whom I sleep with. Nor even whom I wed. I am a loyal Englishwoman. Every bit as loyal as any man among you."

Her gaze was caught and held by Smithsson's. The bright blue of his eyes seemed to singe her, to bore into her, searching for feelings, motives.

"The lady Merlyn isn't to blame." Arthur's words skidded into the strained silence. "What matters now is making our people decent footwear for the coming winter. These"—he indicated the two sacks—"are for Merlyn from me . . . and Margaret," he added softly.

"Thank you," she told him, trying to muster a smile. For some reason, she felt as if she were among enemies, except for the tanner. That was absurd. So absurd, in fact, that Merlyn, in her hasty attempt to prove her love for and loyalty to England, blurted out something quite off the top of her head. "What chance have we now of sending the Normans from our land?" she asked Edward, a challenge in her dark blue eyes. "And especially from Northumbria? We are decimated . . . the few of us left barely surviving. Better to seek to thrive—even heal—under the

Bastard's rule than rashly sacrifice lives and resources we can ill afford.''

The wisdom of her words caught Smithsson by surprise. His eyes widened slightly as he acknowledged that perhaps Will had been right about her. Except that she now seemed willing to wait until a more opportune time—if at all—to consider going against their Norman subjugators.

God only knew when that would be—and they couldn't afford to wait until the Normans were so deeply entrenched that *no one* would ever be capable of driving them back into the English Channel, their bones paving the bottom, where they belonged.

Chapter 18

The earsplitting squeal of a pig was unmistakable.

Rolf reined in Charon, his head angled toward the sound. "Listen!"

Myles obliged, pulling in beside Rolf and halting, his eyes scanning the *weald*, straining to determine from whence the sound was coming.

Rolf slid from the stallion's back. "Help me." He looped his shield strap up over his head, unbuckled his swordbelt, and struggled impatiently with his coif. Myles dismounted and went to unlace his heavy mail hauberk.

As Myles tackled the bindings, he offered, "If you wish to go swine hunting, I'll guard your back."

Rolf caught the rare hint of humor in his tone and slanted him a quick look over his shoulder. "What a sight, I wager . . . a Norman baron in pursuit of a pig." His eyes sought the sky, whose blue-gray brightness was scored by hundreds of half-bare boughs. But his determination overrode any remaining reluctance he might have felt.

The fastenings undone, Rolf hunched his shoulders forward with a shimmying movement. The long, myriad-ringed coat with its slit up the front and back for riding cascaded toward the ground. It pooled about his feet with a noisy *chink*. Rolf stepped over it and pointed in the direction of the sounds still coming from the woods.

"There," he said softly, plunging through the trees just off the path with all the enthusiasm of a child jumping into a pool of water on a sizzling summer day, knowing that Myles wouldn't be far behind.

He paused briefly, allowing his eyes to adjust to the lower light level, listening for the sounds that would lead him to the animal. It sounded like there was more than one, he thought, but couldn't be certain. With the instincts of a hunter, Rolf guessed that the animal was being chased. His hand unconsciously moved to an extra dagger tucked into the waist of his braies. It had better not be a Scot. Or anyone else bent upon mayhem on *his* lands.

He heard Myles's careful movements behind him and surged forward again. Just as he took his fourth stride ahead, something small darted past him in a flurry of light and shadow. Rolf hurled himself at the small animal, praying suddenly that it wasn't a skunk or something equally disagreeable, and trusting in Myles to take care of anyone else who might be after the pig.

He landed right on top of it in his exuberance, setting it to squealing at the top of its lungs. Clutching the piglet to him, he rolled over, relieving it of his weight. *"Tais-toi, fou,"* he said through set teeth. "You'll attract every hungry man from here to York."

He received a porcine grunt in seeming response as he heaved himself to his feet. The frightened creature shrieked a few more times in short staccato bursts, finally stilling when Rolf placed his other hand over its snout.

The brush behind Rolf rustled noisily, and Myles

emerged. He eyed the piglet in Rolf's arms. "Hardly enough for a decent meal," was his only comment before he swung away, obviously eager to return to the horses.

Rolf grabbed at Myles's arm with his free hand. "*Attends*," he said. "Wait. You take him"—he held out the squirming swine—"and I'll hunt a little further. I think there's at least one other."

"But the horses—"

"—will be fine. Who would they allow to approach them? Certainly not a timid Saxon peasant—or a stinking Scot." He noted Myles's disgusted look as the latter held the pig with all the enthusiasm of a man embracing a privy pot. "You don't like pork?" he said, one eyebrow lifting.

"I like it roasted on a spit and set on my trencher."

"*Eh bien*, let me search . . . Stay right behind me, if you can keep up in your mail, and I promise we'll not be long."

Myles mumbled something under his breath but nodded his assent. His fair skin looked flushed to Rolf, and he was about to ask him if he found swine hunting to be more arduous than battle.

He thought better of it, however, and merely said, "What good is one piglet?" He moved to turn away. "We can't breed it if we've only one."

"And who's to say the other will be a female?"

Rolf shook his head, a smile quirking his lips. "Chevalier," he said over his shoulder, "you can't be a farmer without pigs . . . or a little faith."

"Would you put a price on the liberation of England?" Edward pressed Merlyn, his voice calm and quiet. "Who can say how many lives and resources must be expended in the name of freedom?"

Merlyn read a challenge in his eyes . . . and a

warning. Somehow, she felt as if he were testing her. He was an Englishman, she thought, who obviously put his homeland before anything else. She had been that way once . . . before a man named Rolf de Valmont had ridden into her life and played havoc with her emotions—and many of the convictions she'd held for a score of years.

Staring at him in the hushed quiet of the *weald*, with only the gurgling of the Tees in the background, the rhythmic click of Arthur's trowel as he mindlessly stabbed at the dead leaves and partially packed debris to his one side, Merlyn wondered if perhaps she weren't being a traitor. It had been no easy thing, accepting Rolf and his men, yet he had been their savior. And except for the incident involving the destrier and their marriage, Valmont hadn't really given her anything to resent.

Nay, he only helped subjugate your homeland . . . and kill off the flower of England at Hastings. Now you are like warm clay in his hands when the candles are doused at eventide.

Derwick and Arthur were silent as Merlyn briefly shifted her gaze to them. They also avoided her eyes.

But Edward's eyes remained on her face as he stood before her, tall and proud and challenging. His height and bearing, his fair hair and beard, his penetrating blue eyes, all reminded Merlyn of Harold Godwinson. Although she'd never seen the late king herself, Stigand had fought with him at Stamford Bridge in September before the great battle at Hastings. Her husband had returned home briefly before the desperate cry for men had gone out once again, as word reached Harold that William of Normandy had landed at Pevensey, only days after the Stamford victory. But Stigand of Renford's description had been detailed and full of admiration and awe.

Edward Smithsson seemed a man cut from similar fabric to Merlyn. As he stood there, she could easily envision him leading a contingent of Saxons in rebellion against any interlopers. And specifically, Rolf de Valmont.

She could also envision him as thane of Renford.

"What are you saying?" she asked him quietly.

"Must anything be said. *Dare* anything be said?" His words were soft but fervent. Challenging.

Or was it her own writhing conscience?

"Are you implying that I cannot be trusted?"

He shrugged with the barest of movements. "Can you?"

Before she could answer, the relative quiet of the forest was shattered by an inhuman scream rending the air. All four of them turned toward the sound immediately, Edward's hand automatically going for the dagger that had been confiscated. "Get behind me," he commanded Merlyn as he roughly shoved her, with a backhanded motion of his arm, in that direction. He and Derwick dropped to a defensive half-crouch.

Merlyn barely glanced at Arthur, but noted on the periphery of her chaotic thoughts that he remained frozen where he still knelt.

"Give me back my pig!" roared a deep, familiar voice. A man came sprinting through the trees behind them, his brown hair flying, his short legs working as if all the demons of hell were after him. A shrieking, snorting pig was trapped in his embrace.

Merlyn could only stare, shocked, as a larger body came hurtling through the dying foliage behind the stranger, straight for the latter's legs. In spite of his size, the bigger man was faster. He caught the first man behind the knees with one long, darting dive, sending them both tumbling to the ground . . . and the piglet flying through the air to land, stunned, at Merlyn's feet.

"By the rood, you thieving Scot, I'll skin your filthy hide for this!" Rolf de Valmont declared through gritted teeth as he raised his dark head and watched the pig struggle frantically to its feet.

Edward whirled toward the creature, swiftly stooping to sweep the bewildered animal off its unsteady legs before it could gain its bearings.

"I'm no Scot, you idiot!" snapped the brown-haired man in English as he tried to push himself to his knees. Ignoring him, Rolf maintained his hold on the man's legs as the sight of the other four people suddenly snagged his attention.

Just as Smithsson straightened, Myles emerged from the forest behind Rolf, in full mail from the neck down. A fringe of his normally neat, white-blond hair hung over his forehead, a grimace splashed across his features. Another protesting piglet was manacled to his side by one stiffly held arm. Without hesitation, he unceremoniously smacked it on the snout, and it immediately fell silent.

Merlyn had the wildest urge to laugh. She bit the inside of her cheek to hold her ill-timed merriment in check. Now was not the time for levity but, rather, quick thinking.

Rolf leapt to his feet, hauling the first man up with him by the back of his tunic. The Lord of Renford's brief look of satisfaction as Edward had retrieved the runaway pig immediately changed to one of surprise, then bemusement.

Then Merlyn's worst fears were realized as it turned to an expression of downright suspicion as he eyed the four from Renford. "God's wounds!" he rasped, his voice taking on genuine menace as it increased in volume. "What the devil are you *about* here?"

Even as he uttered the words, one part of him realized how ridiculous he must look tackling a man for a lowly pig, as if it were worth its weight in gold. But, even more significant, was the gravity of the discovery of Edward Smithsson and *Merlyn* standing there with Derwick and the tanner . . . half a mile from the village and obviously up to something clandestine. Merlyn looked as guilty as the cat with the mouse's tail protruding from its clenched jaws.

And she appeared to be struggling with a bout of mirth when, to Rolf, the situation was suddenly anything but amusing.

"Judas," he muttered as he brushed himself off, his anger growing by the minute. "I turn my back for half a morn, and here you are . . . *plotting*, no less."

He watched with extreme disappointment as color splashed Merlyn's cheeks, indicating guilt . . . at least to him.

Myles let his swine tumble to the ground as he drew his sword and moved forward. As the piglet scrambled away in newfound freedom, Rolf commanded, "Catch it!"

Merlyn herself bent and snatched at one hind leg as it brushed by. The frightened creature shrieked as though about to be slaughtered. Forgetting her dignity, she yanked it back toward her, clutching its body to her own as she straightened. Its wails increased to an earsplitting pitch.

It was a cacophonous tableau: two Norman chevaliers, one in full mail with sword drawn, the other disheveled and dirty, stiffly stanced and furious, and the four Saxons—two holding squirming swine—staring at them while porcine squeals shrilled and echoed through the *weald* like Armageddon itself.

"'Tis not what you may think," Merlyn said, muffling the piglet's squeaks with one hand. Edward looked about to say something, as well.

In spite of the noise, Rolf heard her words. "And just what do you *think* I think?" he growled, his eyes boring into hers before they flicked to Edward, then Derwick, then back again.

Unexpectedly, Arthur came to life and spoke as the squealing began to subside. "I asked them to come here," he said. His eye met Rolf's and held the latter's angry gaze without flinching. "I wanted to give the lady Merlyn a gift—for the entire village, and not to be coveted by you and yours."

Myles snorted in obvious derision, and Rolf's eyes narrowed. "You—all of you—*are* me and mine."

As soon as the words came out, Rolf knew he'd made a mistake. Derwick's head jerked up as he bristled visibly, and Edward's expression turned to one of cold outrage. Merlyn's lashes lowered, shielding her reaction.

It was Arthur, again, who spoke. *"Never."* The word was low, fervent, and summed up the anger, resentment and hatred that would exist between most Normans and English for generations to come.

"If any one of you possessed one bit of intelligence, you would understand the honor he has bestowed upon you," Myles interjected in sour tones.

"And how easy for you to say such a thing, standing there in your armor and with your weapon drawn!" Edward charged. High color spotted his cheekbones.

In an effort to avert further verbal animosity, Rolf asked the tanner, "Exactly what did you wish to give Merlyn?"

Arthur touched the sack he'd unearthed, then jerked his head in the direction of the other. "Leather for shoes and belts and—"

"I see," Rolf cut him off. "But not for my men. They are to go shoeless and bootless—unable to mend bit and bridle, repair fastenings on weapons and shields—in return for protecting you. In payment for helping you restore Renford—your very lives . . ."

"We did not *ask* you here!" Edward hissed.

"Nay. But here *you* are, Smithsson, accepting food and shelter from the likes of us. Now, I wonder who is the hypocrite?" Rolf taunted softly, ominously.

"I am not the one threatening a man's life for a pig. Why don't you let him go and prove your . . . largesse?" Edward's words were mocking, challenging.

Remembering belatedly the man whose tunic he held in an unflinching grip, Rolf spun around to face him. "Who are *you* if not a Scot?" His frown deepened as he added, "And I am not fond of being called an idiot, especially by a thief."

Will showed no sign of recognition as his gaze briefly scanned Edward and the others. "I wasn't stealing. I am Will, and I was procuring food for myself. That pig"—he indicated the one Merlyn held—"was running free. In fact, both were loose, and I but wished to eat. They are domesticated pigs and not part of the Royal Forest."

Rolf loosened his hold. "Nay, and so they are not. But my villagers are allowed to let their swine roam the forest in search of acorns and the like. You were stealing their—and therefore *my*—property."

"Swine? Since when do you have—" He snapped his mouth shut, obviously having second thoughts about what he'd been about to say.

"We were not about anything treasonous," Merlyn said, having brought her telltale blushing under control. "We saw no need to include further escort, my lord husband—" (how formal that sounded, one part of her thought, after the intimacies they'd shared the night before), "only to collect Arthur's offering. Can we not settle this back in the village?"

Given the fact that Smithsson was present—and Derwick, no especial friend to Rolf—Valmont's suspicions were still rampant. Yet there were, indeed, two sacks apparently containing leather and obviously having been buried in the nearby depression, their existence and whereabouts apparently known only to Arthur.

Rolf made a decision then. "Can you return to Renford without an escort?"

"We got here, didn't we?" Derwick muttered under his breath, which Rolf chose to ignore. His underlying, unspoken question had nothing to do with finding their way back.

"I was concerned about the lady Merlyn."

Edward said, "Of course, we'll see to her. What manner of men do you think we are?"

"And what manner of woman think you that *I* am," Merlyn asked acerbically, "that I cannot find my way back to Renford . . . with or without these others?" She swung about, still clutching the piglet, and moved back in the direction from which they'd come.

"If you need a home, you are welcome to abide with us in yon village of Renford," Rolf said to Will. "Otherwise, if you plan to continue stealing from us, you'd better be on your way."

Without further ado, he nodded at Edward, turned, and moved past Myles toward where they'd left the horses.

Merlyn was torn by conflicting loyalties.

All the way back to the village, she ignored the wriggling creature she carried, the murmur of the men, her thoughts awhirl. She'd just lied to Rolf. She *had* been listening to what Edward had to say, even if she hadn't wholly agreed with him, and had righteously emphasized her loyalty to England. She'd even implied they wait until the time was right to rise up.

And why wouldn't you be loyal?

Yet her precariously balanced position had been brought home keenly by Edward Smithsson's beliefs. And now she was truly caught in the middle—an Englishwoman with people around her who were ready to rebel again. And she was wed to a Norman. No matter that it had been to save a life, or to stand as a buffer between Rolf de Valmont and her own. She had agreed to wed him . . . had shared the bliss of their wedding night like a new bride in love with the man of her fantasies.

And cunning, conniving Rolf de Valmont had shackled her as effectively as if he'd used iron fetters. That is, unless she threw her honor to the winds and followed her political beliefs . . . those very same beliefs that had moved thousands of men to sacrifice their lives.

Yet when all was said and done, did anything matter but life itself? A decent life, with love and a little happiness thrown in before death claimed the inevitable victory? And England had seen its share of conquerors, Merlyn knew . . . Celts, Romans, Angles and Saxons, Vikings. And now Normans. Her homeland was a virtual melting pot, with so many Danes and other Vikings settled in northeastern England that two hundred years ago Alfred the Great had established the Danelaw, a boundary to help keep the Scandinavians from penetrating further south and creating havoc elsewhere in England. And these Vikings, primarily the Danes, had remained peacefully and melded with the native Anglo-Saxons, enriching English culture with aspects of Denmark's.

If everyone could live in peace, without slavery and

unduly harsh inequities, what matter? Look at Elsa, she thought. The old woman had survived everything life had thrown at her, and she was healthy, wise, and resilient. Certainly a slave to no one. Perhaps that was the secret so many of the ancient ones seemed to possess: the ability to bend, to adapt.

Traitorous fool, her conscience taunted. *What would Stigand have said to that? And Harold Godwinson? And the thousands who died for England and the English?*

But they were gone. With all their strength and courage and determination, their wisdom and leadership, they were gone. She stumbled over a half-hidden fallen tree branch as her eyes filled. "And I am still here," she whispered in quiet anguish. "I am still here."

Rolf instructed Myles, and it was passed on from him, to keep a close watch—though not too obviously—on Smithsson, Derwick, and Arthur. Merlyn, Rolf decided, he could observe himself.

Had he taken a viper to his bed? he wondered in his darker moments. Was she truly a witch—a pagan like her druid ancestors—to pledge herself to him and then cold-bloodedly plot against him behind his back? To share her body with him willingly, and aye, joyfully, only to bring about his downfall and even death when his back was turned?

And if his suspicions were even close to the truth, how could he love this woman? How could he crave her beautiful but elusive smile, her touch, the sound of her voice? Sweet Jesu, even the very sight of her? And how could he have given himself to her so completely the night before?

Yet another side of him, the part of him that

wished, above all things, to trust Merlyn, urged him to follow that very trust. She had done nothing more than follow Arthur into the woods—at the tanner's behest, and Rolf could understand that—to procure a commodity that would benefit the entire village. By the grace of God, they now had a male and female pig—Elsa had assured him so—and enough leather for the immediate necessities and perhaps even a little more. If Arthur had been wary of Valmont's men taking the leather for themselves, Rolf couldn't really blame him. The man hardly knew him, and he was not entirely rational.

"What do you think?" Rolf had asked Myles on their return.

The blond giant was silent a moment, then said over his shoulder, "The tanner is harmless. . . ."

"Aye," Rolf interrupted with heavy irony. "He only slays and eats war-horses."

"Merlyn cares too much for the child and her people to jeopardize their safety," Myles continued, unperturbed. "'Tis Smithsson and Derwick that I question."

"Oh, aye," Rolf agreed bitterly. "'Tis as if they deliberately waited until Hugh and Roger left."

Myles glanced over at him without comment, but Rolf guessed what he was thinking. He reached down deep inside, searching for the strength and resolve that he'd so admired in his best friend all these years. Hugh believed he could do it, as did Roger. No one ever said that just because Merlyn had agreed to wed him everything would just fall into place. He'd made some progress in his uphill battle, but ultimate success was still a long way off, and he knew it.

Save your pity for the English . . . cultivate your patience . . . The advice swiftly came to mind when Rolf thought about Hugh. Yet Hugh had assumed that Rolf could take care of any treachery and collusion he might encounter, and therefore had emphasized the patience and compassion he felt Valmont must nurture.

With a mental sigh, feeling almost as overwhelmed and frustrated as when he'd first come to Northumbria, Rolf reaffirmed his commitment to his task here . . . if for no other reason than the untenable thought of being forced to return to Normandy, having been defeated by a motley group of Saxon farmers and his own love for the wrong woman.

One day at a time, he told himself. One day at a time.

"A contingent of Danes is setting sail for England."

Edward nodded. "I knew we could count on Cnut."

"They'll be here soon."

Edward shook his head. "There is no guarantee in the timing with the Danes. I wouldn't make any wagers on their arrival."

"Waltheof has men posted along the coast, and a vanguard of Danes is purported to have landed. Roger prepares to march out from Hereford even as we speak."

Edward nodded, then bent to help Will lift a bundle of thatching. "And you are needed more here with me?"

Will grunted beneath the weight of the bound stack of straw as they shifted together to heave it toward the roof of the cottage they were repairing. It was a cottage that Will was to occupy. He grimaced. "My longing for sizzling, spitted pork landed me in Renford, and not any deliberate plans. But now that I'm here, there's no turning back."

Edward stepped back to observe their handiwork. His words, however, were far removed from such mundane things as thatching a roof. "As soon as we get word that de Gael is moving, then we do the same."

Will nodded, and hands on hips, he, too, appeared to study their handiwork. "You must work on Merlyn. . . . You can already count on Derwick and Garth and the tanner, and I'm certain there must be others who are not yet enamored of Valmont."

"Aye. Like Marthe."

In spite of the gravity of the situation, Edward had to bite his lip to keep an absolutely straight face. He didn't know Will as well as he knew Marthe, but he suspected the woman would drive him into a mead barrel.

"The woman is an imbecile," Will said sourly.

Edward laughed softly, and Will realized that he had never heard Edward Smithsson laugh aloud before. "And so she is. But she hates Valmont. She is also too stupid to be of much use to us, but we know she will do anything for a man's attention. And," he raised an eyebrow at the disgruntled Will, "they must never suspect our connection, or we are finished. And Marthe, of all people, is too busy watching out for herself to notice aught but the size of a man's tool. You would do well to show an interest in her . . . invite her to share your lodgings."

Will cut him a look and grimaced, as if to say, "Some things are too much to ask of a man—even for the liberation of his homeland," but he didn't reply.

"And a man can always use a woman's body to forget his other concerns . . . if only for a few hours."

"Then *you* take her!" Will bent to pick up the stray straw strewn about the ground.

Edward shrugged and moved to view the front of the cottage from several angles. "She will be taken care of, one way of the other. Once she has served her usefulness and joins us—if she survives—we can pawn her off on someone else. Northumbria is full of men hungry for food . . . and a warm and willing wench."

"And if she proves to be a hindrance? Or even a threat?"

Edward's eyes locked with Will's. "Then she will be disposed of."

Will straightened and made for the cottage door, mumbling, "'Tis almost enough to make a man change loyalties."

This time Edward laughed loudly, part of it an act for the benefit of anyone observing them, and part of it genuine. "Almost, my friend. But there is so much more at stake here than any inconvenience caused you by a pesky female." His voice dropped as he followed Will only to the threshold. "And you know it as well as anyone."

Will nodded.

"However, there *is* one more option."

The smaller, dark-haired man cast Edward a skeptical glance before moving to shut the door with his foot.

"We can always give her to the Bastard."

Even Will's lips twitched, ever so slightly, at that.

Chapter 19

Rolf was in an uncharacteristically brooding mood the next morning.

He'd spent the night on his half of the bed, the emotional side of him aching to take Merlyn into his arms, every other consideration be damned. Reason, however, told him that he was a lovesick fool, and he would end up with his head on a pike at some obscure crossroads in the hell that was Northumbria as an example to any other Norman who dared let his heart rule his head.

After breaking the fast, he left the hall to make an early round of the village lands. On Charon's back, with the wind in his face, he felt secure, less vulnerable to anything fate chose to throw at him. People cut a wide swath around him as he encountered them scurrying to perform as many tasks as could be accomplished during the milder beginning of winter, but for the most part he ignored them, his mind occupied with Merlyn and what he suspected, but shied away from asking.

He rode alone, unafraid, unconcerned about anything but the possible treachery of his new wife.

'Twas a bargain struck, not a love match. Why wouldn't she plot if it would rid them all of you?

Rolf deliberately concentrated on the animal beneath him, reveling in the rhythm of bunching, then stretching equine tendon and muscle as the destrier moved with a graceful ease that belied the raw power of his awesome frame.

Rolf had planned to drill the men of Renford in defense, even those such as Cedric and Arthur (Arthur? he thought, with a mental grimace) who had sustained handicaps. But was he being a fool to put weapons, however crude, in their hands in light of this newest suspicion?

No doubt, concluded his fatalistic side.

Yet he also acknowledged that it was of tantamount importance the men be prepared for an attack, no matter how unlikely (which wasn't the case in this instance). In addition to the traditional oak staffs used for defense, Rufus and a young towheaded lad from Lexom by the name of Erik had begun work on repairing anything in the way of metal that could be used as a weapon—trowels, shovels, pitchforks. They were also working in conjunction with Michael on two plows to add to their existing supply of two others, one from Roger de Conteville and the other miraculously saved and brought to Renford from Lexom.

Little by little, they were making progress, and Rolf had evinced a growing pride in their movement forward, painstakingly slow as it was.

The last thing he needed was a raid on Renford and unprepared, broken-spirited men . . . or collusion from those within the village itself.

He dismounted at the river and let Charon drink. He stroked the huge animal's sleek, coal-black sides and spoke softly to him in French. It was somehow as soothing to Rolf as he suspected it was to the stallion . . . speaking the language of his native Normandy, and to an animal who was an irreplaceable extension of himself in his chosen (and natural) vocation, that of a chevalier.

"What am I to do, *copain?*" he murmured to the horse, as if Charon could give him an answer. He leaned his forehead against the destrier's shoulder, a gesture of purest resignation. *"Que faire?"* he repeated in French.

Treat her well and you'll win over the rest of them, also . . . Hugh's words came back to him.

"Hah! I never treated any wench better than I treated her on our wedding night."

If you want something badly enough, if 'tis important enough to you, then 'tis worth the effort and risk involved . . .

Rolf raised his head, the mere memory of Hugh's voice infusing new life into his flagging spirits. Merlyn, Renford, his own barony . . . it was all still worth the risk, wasn't it? Had he come all this way, left the familiar, the comfortable behind, only to give up the day after Hugh and Roger had left?

I'd not give you false hopes, ever. And my lord William would never have chosen you if he didn't believe in you as well . . .

Then Roger's voice, *But remember this, too. If you haven't the respect and affection of those you rule, you have nothing* . . .

Rolf shook his head emphatically, as if to rid his mind of his doubts. He mounted Charon with more enthusiasm than he'd dismounted. *"Eh bien, mon beau* Charon," he said to the stallion as he turned its head back toward Renford. "We may not be able to win their affection, but—*par Dieu!*—we'll win their respect or die trying!"

Charon pranced up and down the ragtag line of Englishmen, Rolf deliberately keeping a firm hold on the reins to keep the horse's magnificent head high in an effort to plant respect in their hearts, if not fear. The destrier snorted and shook his head in magnificent protest several times, but the movements couldn't have served Rolf's purpose better.

His aim wasn't to teach these men to fight a mounted knight but rather, initially, to get their attention; to effect the acknowledgment of his absolute capability at what he did best . . . and anything else he could garner in his determination to keep charge of his demesne against possible collusion to take it from him.

Yet as he caught the pained look on Arthur's face as he stood poised with his pitchfork, Rolf felt a spurt of guilt. Arthur had been at Hastings. The man was undoubtedly aware of the power and capabilities of a war-horse . . . had seen many at work firsthand.

The sight of Arthur's face moved Rolf to cut short his posturing. He stopped the great animal before the men. His own men-at-arms were scattered among the English to aid in the lesson, and several of the heartier women were, as well. Including Merlyn . . . and the indomitable Elsa.

"I've no intention of harming any of you," Rolf began in his sternest military voice. "I merely wanted you—*all* of you—to see how difficult it would be to attempt to engage a mounted chevalier, no matter how you were armed. And 'tis unlikely that we will ever be attacked by mounted men—my own countrymen."

A few grumblings could be heard here and there, as if they disputed his words, but otherwise the men were silent.

He mentally debated for the briefest of moments, then made an important decision. "If you or yours are ever threatened by a rider such as myself, you must remember to try and disable the horse first.

That will render the man riding it more vulnerable."
And I pray that you never use my own advice against me or any of my men, he silently added. "Slash a tendon in one of the lower legs if you can avoid being injured by that same leg and its lethal hoof. A destrier has been trained to lash out with these hooves and can crush a man's head in an instant. So beware."

He dismounted and handed the reins to Bryce, who led Charon back to the stable.

The villagers seemed to heave a collective sigh of relief.

"There is no reason for a man to let himself be cut down," Rolf told them as he stood before them in breeches and tunic, straddle-stanced, Death Blow clear of its sheath and resting, tip downward, against the earth. "Whether the opponent is better skilled, better armed, has the advantage of surprise, or outnumbers you, you can still do some damage to your enemy and possibly save your life. If another wants something you have and the odds are greatly against you, by all means 'tis no act of cowardice to allow him to take it. Your life is worth more than any possession." He paused, looking at specific faces in the group that seemed to leap out at him, noting their expressions—or lack thereof—before he continued. (He also noted with some acerbity that Merlyn was standing near Edward Smithsson: *And here is how to skewer your husband while he sleeps . . .*)

"Anything, of course, but your family," he continued, ignoring his gruesome imaginings. "But as long as you have a weapon of some kind—a pitchfork, a scythe, a shovel, a hoe, a dagger, a trowel, even a tree limb—you have a chance. If you want it. For the will to fight, the determination to hold onto your life and those of your loved ones, is the most potent weapon of all." He paused again, and the wind moaning through the trees seemed intensified

315

this time . . . as if no one were willing to make a sound as Rolf snared their undivided attention.

"But what of a man with one arm . . . one leg?" Marthe called out in a peevish voice.

Rolf slowly turned his gaze to her. How like the woman to remind a man of his infirmities, when she herself would know naught of the courage in a man's heart, sound of body or nay.

She stood apart from the row of makeshift weapon carriers, near Will. Rolf caught a fleeting impression of a frown from the man, but his attention was suddenly wholly focused on Marthe and the most important message he could impart to her—to all of them.

"A man's strength and courage reside in his heart and soul, woman, and not necessarily in his physical prowess. That inner, God-given strength is what makes a man adjust his balance if he is missing a leg; train his left hand if he is missing his right; depend upon his sense of smell and hearing if he has lost one eye . . . or both."

He looked away from her in dismissal. "Some of you were members of the *fyrd* under Harold Godwinson, while others of you saw actual fighting. I do not doubt your capabilities but would drill you occasionally to keep you prepared for the worst. Also, perhaps, teach you a thing or two in addition to what you already know." He looked directly at Merlyn for the first time. "You, my lady wife, and your partner"—he watched with secret satisfaction as color crept into her cheeks—"will be in my group, as will Elsa, Cedric, and Arthur."

Myles threw him a look that Rolf felt, rather than saw, but he knew what he was doing. If he didn't, then he deserved to die.

* * *

"Listen carefully to what he says," Edward muttered to Merlyn. Her eyes met his for a moment, and she knew exactly what he meant. *For you can use it against him when the time comes.*

Part of her recoiled at the implication, but another part of her, the part that was Welsh and Saxon and *English*, hearkened to that very subtly stated suggestion. Merlyn fought to remain neutral, lest Rolf, who could be so very perceptive, catch her dilemma.

If he hasn't already. The man is no fool.

Michael joined their group and worked with Elsa, Merlyn, and Edward. Rolf, it seemed, deliberately chose to work with Cedric, whom he evidently trusted, and Arthur. Both men were handicapped, and Merlyn wondered at Rolf's faith in their ability to defend themselves, let alone anyone else.

She was being mean-spirited, she knew, and furtively watched their progress as she listened to young Michael and Edward—who was obviously a skilled fighter, as well—with half her attention.

Give them some time, I say . . . Let's wait . . . and watch. If they are cruel and truly care naught about our people . . . I will show you myself how to get rid of them.

Indeed, Cedric was no coward, no man to allow himself to be paralyzed by the loss of a leg for long. . . .

When unexpectedly Elsa knocked Merlyn's feet from beneath her, sending her slamming to the ground, Edward said, "Pay attention. Your life could depend on it."

Merlyn caught Rolf watching her for a moment, concern flickering briefly in his eyes before he returned his attention to Cedric. But Elsa was the one whose look flashed some kind of warning to her before the old woman helped Merlyn brush herself off.

The air was suddenly thick with unspoken, clashing thoughts. . . .

Yet it was difficult for Merlyn to ignore her new husband, especially when she'd given herself to him on their wedding night as eagerly as any young bride. Whether she was willing to admit it or not, her attraction to him was as strong an emotion as she had ever felt for another man. Could her body have so deceived her? she wondered. Could her instincts have been so wrong? One did not give oneself to one's enemy the way she had unless there were redeeming qualities that manifested themselves, which made up—at least in part—for the original offense committed. Or if immense advantages were involved.

Rolf's presence was commanding, she admitted. He was in his element, training men to fight, and the fact that he didn't relegate another retainer to work with Cedric and Arthur said much for him. So many things about Rolf de Valmont were enigmatic, she acknowledged, and intriguing as well. Her disappointment in the face of his indifference toward her the night before made her face hot whenever she thought of it.

And whatever else it might have been, it was humiliating, too. After she'd thrown herself at him to rescue Arthur, then cuddled with him and cleaved unto him all night like an absolute wanton, he had turned his back on her the second night, and now obviously couldn't even bring himself to do more than glance at her.

You know why he's angry.

Merlyn ignored the voice. She glanced around. As she saw her people engaging strangers—*Normans*—an unexpected and ugly feeling rose up within her. Why shouldn't the villagers use the skills being taught by their masters to throw them off? Why shouldn't they follow the lead of determined and capable men like Edward Smithsson to chase the arrogant Normans from their land?

Such dark thoughts made it easy for shame and humiliation to sprout within her like some silent, insidious blight, her struggling emotions nurturing it and sending it seeping through like a slow-working poison.

Out of the corner of her eye it registered that Elsa was moving toward her again, taking advantage of her preoccupation. The woman's determination to participate certainly belied her age—or had she guessed the bent of Merlyn's thoughts in that uncanny way of hers . . .

Merlyn's musings scattered like foam before a hot burst of breath. She turned to meet the older woman head-on, dropping to a semi-crouch position in imitation of Edward and Derwick the day before, and raising her tightly held trowel.

Instead of needing to defend herself, however mock the attack might have been, Merlyn caught the flash of pain in Elsa's dim blue eyes as she raised the broomstick in her hand . . . the fleeting rigidity of her entire body before it began a macabre, boneless collapse in slow motion before Merlyn's stunned eyes.

She moved to break Elsa's fall, feeling suddenly as sluggish as in a nightmare; but in a blur of movement, Rolf was between them and scooping the woman into his capable arms.

"Elsa," Merlyn cried softly, reaching for a limp hand, "what is amiss?"

The pale, blue-veined eyelids trembled but didn't raise. "Naught to fret over," the older woman answered on a whisper of breath, her fingers lightly squeezing Merlyn's. "I just need to rest for a moment."

"I'll take her to the hall . . ." Rolf began.

Elsa moved her head from side to side in mute objection.

"Just lay her down here," Merlyn said, and Rolf knelt, holding Elsa as if she were of the most fragile constitution. He laid her carefully upon the ground, then jerked his overtunic from his belt and over his head. He covered her with it while Cedric handed him his own ragged overshirt to pillow her head.

"'Tis all your fault, Valmont," Edward accused him as Merlyn knelt beside the older woman and murmured something into her ear.

Rolf met his gaze head-on, his eyes kindling with ire.

"If you hadn't insisted on making an old woman learn to defend that which should be left to others . . ."

Rolf eyes glittered. "I did no such thing where Elsa was concerned. Her courage and mettle set an example for us all, for 'tis in expecting others to fight your battles that you ultimately lose everything."

Their deadlocked eyes held for a few brief moments. "Perhaps we wouldn't have lost at Hastings if that had been so . . . is that what you imply?"

Rolf glanced away from Edward's face, and his gaze encountered Cedric . . . and Arthur. After what these two men had willingly sacrificed in good faith, how could he ever condemn their late leader? Their actions and those of their countrymen? Then, too, it was high time he acknowledged something he'd never had reason to seriously contemplate before.

"Harold Godwinson and his army were the most formidable foe my lord William ever encountered. To this day, if you ask him, one man to another, he will tell you so." Rolf hadn't the foggiest notion if William would ever say such a thing to an Englishman, but he knew for a fact that the Norman duke had considered his victory at Hastings his most hard won.

What harm to conjecture for the sake of these vanquished but proud people? What harm to build up their pride when everything else had been taken from them?

Build them up too much, and you'll encourage ideas that are better left alone . . . ideas that can be replaced with alternatives equally satisfying. You don't need a rebellion on your hands, cautioned one part of him.

His words drew Merlyn's attention, along with that of many of the others who'd halted their mock engagements when Elsa had collapsed.

Rolf suddenly wondered if he were losing his wits saying such things. "Can we move her?" he asked Merlyn before she could speak.

"Nay," Elsa said emphatically. "I am better now."

Merlyn nodded at him, as if Elsa hadn't spoken. "If someone can take her to her cottage, she can rest in her own bed rather than on the damp ground." Rolf nodded. "Is your chest tight, Elsa?" she asked gently.

"'Tis eased up now, almost as if it never happened."

Merlyn nodded at Rolf and he slid his arms beneath the old woman. As he lifted her, he warned, "No more protests, wench, else I'll make you learn to ride Charon." He raised one eyebrow at her wickedly. "Even one such as you would be humbled by the experience, I wager."

"Mayhap," came the spritely enough reply, her eyes meeting his, "but the Wolf was humbled by a *cow*. Such is not the stuff of which legends are made." And Rolf could have sworn that a fragile eyelid dipped in a wink.

He grinned, in spite of himself, and as he moved through the parted men and women, Rolf acknowledged just how precious this ancient woman was to him—and to Renford, as well.

"You are a fool, Merlyn of Renford, if you think to plot against him. He is good. . . . He offers security and a decent life." Elsa paused and drew in a slow, shallow breath. "And love."

"Love." Merlyn's mouth turned down as she said the word. "Lust is more like it . . . and greed."

She felt Elsa's gaze on her as she warmed some Norman wine in a small pot over the periphery of a newly stoked fire, then mixed it with water.

"I saw naught of regret the morning after."

Merlyn knew exactly what she meant but said nothing.

"But you are different today. I think you each hugged your own edge of the pallet." Merlyn threw her a look askance, the fire casting her profile in tones of pink and rose. "And I cannot blame him. Who would wish to take a traitor to his bosom? Rolf de Valmont is no Holofernes."

Merlyn poured the warmed wine into a cup and moved over to Elsa, irritation shading her eyes. "I am no trai—" She stopped mid-word, her brow suddenly creasing in puzzlement. "Who?"

"Holofernes," the old woman said with conviction. "An Assyrian general who attacked the Jews and, while laying siege to the city of Bethulia, took the lovely Judith to his bed." She paused to take a sip of the wine as Merlyn supported her shoulders. "You see," she added, her eyes holding Merlyn's, "he was taken by her beauty. The price he paid for allowing his loins to rule his judgment . . . was his head. She cut it off while he slept, and his army fled."

Merlyn frowned. "That is—"

"You may be as comely as Judith, but your Wolf is

smarter than Holofernes, child. He does not trust you since he discovered you in the *weald* with Smithsson and the tanner. *Think* before you involve yourself with the likes of Edward Smithsson."

Merlyn raised the cup to Elsa's lips again. "How know you of Jews and Assyrian generals? Where did you hear that tale?" she asked, refusing for the moment to acknowledge the woman's warning.

Elsa grunted and narrowed her eyes at Merlyn, as if she couldn't believe that the younger woman had not known the obvious. "Lord Hugh, of course. He studied in a monastery, you ken. He knows all about the sacred writings of the Apocrypha."

Merlyn spread a blanket over Elsa, then offered the cup a third time. "None of that applies to me," she said. "Rolf is not my enemy . . . he is my husband."

Elsa nodded. "Exactly. Remember that, and do not seek to throw it all away for dreams of restoring the past."

Merlyn laughed bitterly. "Throw it all away?"

"Aye. The rebuilding of the village, the rising hopes of so many of our people here, the prospect of a normal life once again—even if 'tis under the Normans."

"Elsa," Merlyn said, her anger suddenly rising against the sage old woman whom she had always loved and respected, "who is the traitor here? You or me? How can you dismiss our irretrievable loss so lightly?" She lowered her voice. "How can you accept these—these butchers as our masters?"

"They can only be our masters if we allow it, child." She lay her head against the pallet again, her pale blue eyes fixed on the smoke-blackened beams overhead. "I have lived to see England survive every kind of adversity. But we always manage to survive . . . to prosper. And do you know why?" Her gaze flicked to Merlyn expectantly.

323

Merlyn shook her head.

"Because we have always assimilated our enemies, our conquerors. How many of our own villagers are pure 'English'? We—all of us—have mixed blood, whether it be Briton or Saxon, Angle or Jute, Danish or Welsh—"

"I have done naught!" Merlyn insisted. "If they talk of . . . things, I cannot help that. I did nothing untoward." Her eyes narrowed. "And do not tell me to say aught of their . . . *business* to Rolf."

Elsa let out a soft sigh. "I do not ask you to betray your own, Merlyn. Only to disassociate yourself from anything that could involve your own life. The lives of others who could be unwitting pawns. And of innocents."

Like Raven.

The unspoken words hung in the air between them as keenly as if they'd been shouted. Merlyn felt the blood drain from her face. Her heart lurched within her breast, too, like a stone tripping over the edge of a chasm.

But mustn't the liberation of England come before even her own child?

As if reading her thoughts, Elsa said softly, "Who decreed that you must even think of putting your daughter's life in jeopardy for a devil-spawned plot to liberate England? Don't ever be so foolish as to interfere with what has been ordained, Merlyn of Renford, lest you would suffer losses that would make your previous ones seem all but insignificant." She paused. "And are you willing to betray the man who took you to wife? Who loves Stigand's child? Who embraces your people as his own?" She nodded before Merlyn could answer. "Aye, even the Wolf's faithful men, who've done so much for Renford?"

She lay back on the pallet, appearing suddenly

very tired. And very old.

Anger and self-recrimination prevented Merlyn from responding to the questions about Rolf and his men, but she'd immediately caught Elsa's most important warning. The woman had been speaking as one mother to another. As one mother who had lost that which she'd valued most—her sons and daughters. Aside from the devastating blow of such a loss in itself, a woman also suffered the eradication of her husband through the death of his offspring. And memories counted for little when compared to living flesh and blood.

Merlyn's anger ebbed away. She tucked the blanket more securely around Elsa and then remained standing over her for long moments. Then she whispered, "I shan't make the mistake of sacrificing Raven, Elsa."

The ancient one did not stir, but Merlyn knew she slept because of her soft snores.

I shan't make that mistake, but neither will I betray anyone to Rolf de Valmont. For he is Norman and I am English. I am English before I am his wife. I am English before I am his subject. And nothing can change that.

Later, at dusk, Merlyn retreated to their bedchamber, having made certain that Elsa was resting comfortably. She restlessly paced the room, her pensive mood shifting to one of resentment, then back again to cautious introspection in light of Elsa's warning.

The woman had been right about many things. Yet Merlyn couldn't help but resent Rolf de Valmont. The man was just like his arrogant duke. He managed to obtain everything he wanted (at least what Merlyn thought he wanted): a title, lands, power. He'd helped win England, then took over Renford with almost no resistance; and now he'd managed to win the trust and respect of many of the villagers.

Her blood flowed hot and fast in anger. And he had almost—*almost*—won her over with his tender treatment of her on their wedding night, his affected emotion. She actually had *enjoyed* their shared intimacies . . . and worse, she actually *liked* him at times!

Don't be a fool, her conscience told her. *Any woman starved for love and affection would have been taken in by his winning ways.*

Aye, and while I'd lain moaning beneath him, brave men were choosing to stand up to him . . . to give their very lives in the retaking of England from Valmont and his ilk.

Shame rolled over her in great, engulfing waves. Her cheeks turned crimson with her humiliation and anger. "Nay!" she said in a low, fierce voice. "Rather cut out my heart!"

The soft creak of a door swinging on new hinges caught her attention. Her chin jerked upward, her eyes widening in startlement.

Rolf's impressive form filled the doorway, the evening shadows shading one half of his face, while the light from the nearest torch danced across the other, making one eye glitter like a winking emerald. "Why ever would you wish to cut out your heart, my lady wife?" he asked her softly.

Chapter 20

Remnants of her ire still shading her eyes to a smoky amethyst, Merlyn stared at Rolf.

He closed the door behind him and moved into the room. His expression was neither pleased nor displeased. In fact, his features were strangely lacking in emotion. Only the soft sibilance of his voice gave away anything he might have been feeling.

Merlyn had the distinct impression that she was dealing with a side of Rolf de Valmont she hadn't seen. Her gaze dropped, caution replacing her irritation.

His shoes came into her line of vision, and one finger lifted her face to his. "I ask you again, Merlyn," he repeated, his voice freighted with quiet determination, "what would ever make you want to do such a thing?"

Something in his eyes flickered briefly, something akin to hope—or so Merlyn thought. Then, in the face of her silence, it died, leaving only the unrelenting hold of his somber, green-brown eyes.

Merlyn felt, strangely, that she had somehow disappointed him.

327

She pulled her chin away, the mere scent of him, of horses and wine and work, clinging to him like an aphrodisiac. Damn him to hell! she thought in utter frustration, as her senses responded to his nearness against her will.

Before she could move away, he put his arms around her shoulders and pulled her to him, firmly, inexorably. With his eyes plumbing the depths of hers, his lips moved nearer and nearer. One hand slid up her spine to cradle the back of her head, making it impossible to move without a struggle.

"Is it my touch that moves you to threaten such bodily harm to yourself?"

His lips were a whisper away from hers, his gaze a hazel blur as it remained fused with hers. "I think not," he murmured, his warm, sweet breath caressing her mouth before he kissed her.

The man was an absolute master at loveplay, she told herself, attempting to conjure up images of him doing exactly the same thing with scores of other women, as an obstacle, however fragile, however fleeting, against his sensual domination over her.

And what should that matter to you? You hate him. He is the enemy.

Physically, she had no real inclination to move, however, as the sweet elixir of his kiss flowed through her lower abdomen, then her limbs, until she was clinging to him like . . .

A loud sob of despair sounded in the passageway outside the bedchamber. Rolf swiftly released her and spun toward the door. Raven burst through the unlatched panel and rushed into the room. Black hair flying, fat tears rolling down her flushed cheeks, she launched herself into Rolf's arms and clung . . . not unlike Merlyn had done only moments ago.

"M—m—m'lord," she sobbed into his shoulder as

he lifted her high and held her to his chest.

"What is it, precious one?" he soothed in unconscious imitation of Hugh de Conteville as he stroked her hair. He felt a profound sense of protectiveness toward her as she wrapped her short legs about his waist in an obvious quest for further security.

"G—Gryff," she sputtered against his blue wool tunic. "H—he ran into the s—s—stable and—"

"And what are you doing up past dark?" Merlyn snapped, feeling overwhelmingly resentful of the child's obvious trust in Rolf . . . and oddly let down, even as her concern for Raven fought to the fore. "If that pesky cur chooses to hie himself into the stable, then he deserves what he—"

Rolf looked at her sharply over Raven's dark head, his expression absolutely forbidding. Even as she caught his eye, Merlyn realized the folly of her reaction. She had been too concerned over the appearance of the Normans, and Raven's subsequent disobedience, to heed the child's grief over the fatally injured Thor, what now seemed aeons ago. As Raven peeked at her from Rolf's shoulder, her red-rimmed eyes and tear-splashed cheeks attesting further to her agitation, Merlyn broke off her reprimand.

Not, she told herself, because of any look Rolf de Valmont could level at her, but rather due to her own decision.

"*Tais-toi, ma petite,*" he murmured to Raven. "Gryff's in the stable?"

"Aye," came the wobbly reply. "He heard s—something and woke me up. He was s—scratching at the door. I followed 'im out."

Rolf set her down. "I'll fetch him, *chère.* Stay here with your mother." He was at the door in an instant . . . and halted a nose short of colliding with Bryce, who'd appeared out of nowhere with Gryff cradled in his arms.

Not again, Rolf thought as he steadied his squire by the shoulders and stepped back, his gaze on the pup.

"His curiosity will get him killed yet," Bryce said with a rueful movement of his lips, "but he is unharmed, I think."

Raven ran over to them. "Gryff," she lamented softly.

At the sound of what he obviously recognized as his mistress's voice, however, the object of her pity opened his eyes and raised his head. He instantly began to struggle against Bryce's hold, whimpered softly, then quieted.

As Raven took the dog from the youth, Rolf said, with a quirk of his mouth, "Sly devil. He knows how to get pity rather than a kick in the backside for disobedience."

Raven clutched the animal to her, and he let out a yelp. She looked up at Rolf in surprise before carefully setting Gryff down.

"He might yet be injured," Rolf said. He knelt to probe the puppy's sides, but not before saying something to Bryce *sotto voce.* "Come, Merlyn," he invited as the squire retreated. "We need your skills." He had no desire to stir any more of Merlyn's resentment by leaving her out of the goings-on that included her daughter.

Merlyn moved foward, more for her daughter's sake than for the dog's.

You love animals. Why such an aversion to this one? You cannot nurture a dislike for Valmont through a hound.

Rolf allowed Merlyn to brush his hands away from Gryff as she knelt before the pup. He watched with a kind of wonder as Raven lifted her face, eyes shining with hopeful expectation and trust, to her mother's. "Will he live, Mamma?" she asked softly, her voice much too solemn, in Rolf's opinion, for a child her age.

As Merlyn's fingers gently explored Gryff's body, she encountered what felt like an injured rib. Gryff's whimper confirmed it, yet he did not try to bite her, as a wounded dog might if someone inadvertently intensifies its pain. Instead, he licked her hand with a quick swipe of his tongue and watched her, his head cocked, his ears alertly forward.

Merlyn finished her examination and scratched him behind the ears . . . for the first time since Rolf had given him to Raven. She looked at her daughter. "Aye, child. He has only injured a rib, as far as I can tell. But you will have to be very careful with him. No lifting him until he heals."

"And no letting him out at night without telling an adult," Rolf added, ruffling her feather-soft hair.

Raven nodded, her expression still solemn. Then she asked a completely unexpected question. "May I sleep here this night? Gryff an' me will be good, I promise."

Merlyn was momentarily taken aback, but it was Rolf to whom Raven had addressed the question. He smiled at her innocent wheedling and nodded without hesitation. *"Mais oui."*

Merlyn started to speak. "Just for—" she began, then quickly bit back the words. Rolf might be less inclined to approach her intimately if Raven was in the same chamber—not only this night, but every night. Not necessarily, however. Privacy was at such a minimum that it was not unusual for children to sleep with their parents.

But Rolf had never before married, and he had never (as far as Merlyn knew) had children. He was also, evidently, accustomed to bedchambers above the manor hall. Perhaps in Normandy the children were kept separate from the adults . . .

Aye, commented a scornful voice, *and perhaps he does not consider himself a newlywed . . . and perhaps his healthy appetite for his bride has vanished.*

As Raven looked to Merlyn for additional consent, a cursory rap on the door heralded the entrance of two youths hefting a wooden tub for bathing. Merlyn looked at her husband questioningly, but Rolf was occupied with Raven. She had somehow crept into his arms again and was snuggled cozily against him. As he stood up, she asked drowsily, "Where shall I sleep, m'lord?"

He considered this a moment, with great concentration. "Why, you'll have to sleep on the bed with your mother . . . and me. And," he added, "you must call me Rolf."

Raven appeared agreeable to this. In fact, her eyes positively lit up.

"But," he added with a mock-stern frown, "you must promise not to kick me in my sleep. And the hound," he glanced down at Gryff, "will sleep on the floor, of course." He glanced at Merlyn. She looked away, afraid that he would see the relief—and the barest trace of damning disappointment, too—in her eyes.

"Would you not like me to bathe you?" Raven inquired as the men returned with steaming buckets of water. "I helped Mamma bathe guests—and sometimes Papa, too," she explained.

Rolf, dismayed at the thought of the child helping him wash, quickly shook his head. "Your rest is more important, *mon enfant.* All I ask if that you go quickly to sleep, for we have another full day ahead of us on the morrow. You must help gather beech-nuts and acorns to feed our new pigs. 'Tis a very important task, you know."

Raven brightened, obviously at the chance to be of some help in the morning if she could not be so this night. "Aye, m'lord."

Rolf set her down as he corrected her. "Rolf. And perhaps you would like to help me name the pigs on the morrow."

She smiled shyly and answered, "Oh, aye . . . Rolf!" then went right to one corner of the chamber and quickly made a bed for Gryff. Then, without a word, she crept onto the soft down pallet and shimmied beneath the covers until only the crown of her dark head showed, her back to Rolf and Merlyn. Within moments, she was still.

Merlyn, meanwhile, was setting out toweling on the floor and beside the round wood-slatted, padded tub. Four additional buckets of water had been brought in, two hot, two cold. As she poured the water into the tub, Merlyn refused to meet Rolf's eyes. Relieved that Raven was in their bed, Merlyn was once again afraid to let that relief—and anything else that might appear, however unwillingly—color her expression. She rose without looking at him.

"But I would like you to help me," he said in a dangerously dulcet voice, "for I am tired and aching from teaching self-defense to our men."

It was a blatant lie, for he felt wonderfully rejuvenated physically from the activity he loved so well—even if he was in an emotional maelstrom.

"And women," Merlyn corrected, to hide her dismay at his request, although such a comment would not have been out of the ordinary for her. And to rob the words *our men* of their obvious significance . . . a significance that would make her sympathy for Smithsson and his followers even more traitorous. If one looked at it from the Norman point of view, of course.

"And women," he agreed softly as he unbuckled his belt, his gaze fixed upon her averted face. Merlyn took it, placed it aside, and knelt before him to wait as he unfastened the cord that held up his braies. She reached up and helped ease them down over his hips and flanks, all the while conscious of his nearness, his growing state of undress . . . and the heat searing her cheeks.

She could have refused. Merlyn doubted that Rolf would have forced her to perform the task. Yet guilt, and the fact that it *was* a wife's place to go along with her husband's wishes, especially in so mundane a matter, made her comply. Also, the more cooperative she was, perhaps the more inclined Rolf would be to dismiss his suspicions.

And what about coupling with him? sneered a voice.

The very thought, along with the fact that his maleness was exposed to her now and a hairsbreadth from her face, renewed the heat in her cheeks. It crawled down her neck and reached up to her hairline, insidiously revealing.

Rolf watched her lashes lower before his burgeoning desire, the intensifying hue of her skin, and ached to bury himself within her . . . in spite of the fact that she might have had no qualms about sticking him with his own dagger.

He loved her more than ever, even as reason—his every instinct—laughed at him silently and told him that, in his own way, he was as witless as Marthe; as lost in useless fantasy as Arthur. Yet no matter how much Merlyn might take it into her head to plot his downfall, nothing could change her physical reac-

334

tion toward him. Of this he was certain. The fact that he had detected emotion as well as desire on their wedding night—and on other occasions, as well— only fueled his hope, cast aside his caution.

Quos deus vult perdere prius dementat.

The words came to him out of nowhere, in the calm but rich register of Hugh de Conteville's voice. *Those whom God wishes to destroy, he first makes mad.* Surely Hugh had quoted those words to him sometime in the past, for now they skimmed across the surface of his mind as if in warning. It surely was an ill omen, for he knew no Latin, yet to remember Hugh's quote exactly . . .

"Then so be it," he whispered to himself with quiet desperation. "I must be mad." He pulled Merlyn upright by her elbows until she was leaning into him with the extraordinary intensity of his obvious hunger for her.

Gone was his earlier control, the restraint he'd used before Raven had come flying into the room. The touch of her hands, the elusive scent of lavender from her glossy black hair, the sight of hectic color in the fine, fair flesh of her face . . . And also, the thought of everything she was . . . had been . . . and could be . . .

"Merlyn. Ahh, Merlyn . . ." he sighed into her mouth before he kissed her, an unwitting declaration of love striving for acknowledgement, a paean of adoration that only a fool could have missed.

And Merlyn was no fool.

It came to her in that instant that Rolf de Valmont was in love with her.

The memories of their wedding night returned in newly enlightening detail. . . . *You will drive me mad, my little pagan. . . . Je t'aime de tout mon coeur. . . .* She hadn't understood the last words, but

335

everything he'd said that night had sounded tenderly endearing.

In spite of her own driving desire, in spite of her own inner turmoil, Merlyn recognized the note of anguished passion in his voice for what it was . . . the anguished passion of a man in love. And against his will.

She unconsciously stiffened at the realization, several new and unexpected feelings suddenly sprouting and rising above all others: surprise and triumph. Cautious triumph, but triumph all the same.

Rolf felt her slight withdrawal and, pulling back on his runaway desire, cursed himself silently in the basest terms. Had he given himself away somehow? *Dieu me sauve*, he exhorted, if she'd guessed, for Merlyn of Renford wasn't ready to understand his feelings for her. And love was the most potent of weapons, if unreturned; especially by one who had every reason to consider you the adversary.

Merlyn slipped from his embrace and caught the hem of his tunic. Her breathing was noticeably heavier, her voice breathier as she said, "You cannot bathe in your clothing." Her eyes avoided his as she tried to deal with this newest revelation without letting on. Here was an unexpected advantage, if she was right . . . and if she chose to use it.

As Rolf raised the garment over his head, he felt her hands repeat the procedure with the edge of his chainse. How removed she seemed suddenly, he thought, and irritation began to temper his arousal as she stood expectantly before him then, waiting for him to step into the bath.

Why, she looked guilty! he realized as he turned from her; and the suspicion that had been weighing on his heart and mind, that had been slowly sapping him of his newly burgeoning hope and happiness like a leech from the unwary, suddenly left him physically shaken.

He reached out a hand for the tub, ostensibly for balance. Under normal circumstances, it would have been totally unnecessary, for he was a man in his prime; a conditioned warrior who could have leapt over the tub from a complete standstill without so much as touching it.

You are reading too much into this, his reasonable side warned.

Since when can a wench turn a warrior to whey? taunted another.

The warm water touched his foot, rising up his leg like a caress. Rolf sank into it with relief, allowing it to enfold him, to relax him, to return him to a more normal state of mind. God's wounds, but he'd never been reduced to such a level, even on a battlefield! It was a helpless feeling.

He closed his eyes and heard Merlyn move away. *Good*, he thought. *Let her leave . . . pray let her leave Renford, the witch!*

His curiosity—and distrust—made Rolf lift his lashes a fraction. He saw her moving toward the iron-bound chest that held his belongings. What was she about? he wondered with a frown. He quickly did a mental inventory of the contents of the chest. A weapon. She was undoubtedly searching for a weapon. . . .

He tensed, just as Merlyn swung back toward him, a bar of French soap in her hand.

Imbécile. The word danced through his head like a grinning devil.

If embarrassing relief sifted through him in that moment, immediately in its wake came irritation; extreme annoyance caused by her unwitting power

337

over him. The power he allowed her to have over him.

Rolf watched her through the tangle of his lashes, clearing the last remnants of fog in his brain with an effort and doing some quick thinking.

As Merlyn reached into the tub to wet the washing cloth, Rolf unexpectedly grabbed her wrist, pulling her against the side of the tub.

She looked up into his face, startled at first. His eyes were narrowed at her, denuded of passion and tenderness . . . and most certainly anguish.

"My entire body aches, wife. What can you do to ease that?" he demanded in a low but gruff voice.

The cough and crackle of the fire nearby grew louder in the silence that followed.

"Perhaps you'd rather hold my head under the water until I relax . . . forever?"

What was he about? Merlyn wondered, puzzled by this odd behavior. Was he angry because she had pulled away from his rising need? Typical man, she thought with acerbic sarcasm, allowing his loins to lead his thoughts.

"Let go of my wrist."

"Or perhaps you'd prefer to use yon dagger," he inclined his head to where his swordbelt lay, ignoring her command. "Quick and easy."

Her eyes met his. "You still don't trust me."

"Give me a reason to trust you, Merlyn, and I will gladly do so," he answered, his body taut as a primed bowstring. "Give me a reason to dismiss the sight of you conspiring with Smithsson and his pitiful followers, and I will fall on my knees before God in thanksgiving."

His fingers tightened around her wrist with the intensity of his words, and Merlyn once again felt the pull of his physical hold over her as their gazes locked, melded; as he drew her nearer, like a cobra luring its mesmerized victim.

As her lips met his, Merlyn realized with a kind of despair that she could never harm him in any way. Not for Edward Smithsson. Not even for England. Elsa had been right. Rolf was no Holofernes, but neither was she a Judith. She could never harm him herself, although that didn't mean that she wouldn't allow another to do so. . . .

As their kiss deepened, Merlyn gave in to the desire building within her like the steam under a cauldron lid, allowing her physical need to shove aside all thought of collusion and traitors and vanquished and conquerors; of terrorized children, confused women, and maimed men. Of burnt crops, slaughtered flocks, razed villages.

This was now, this was real, this was welcome. For now, she was his wife, and he inspired a primal need deep within her that cast aside all others in these mad, mindless moments.

He lifted her into the tub, heedless of soaking her clothing, and smothered her soft sound of protest with his mouth. They hardly made a splash, Rolf and Merlyn, as the tension burgeoned, not only out of fear of waking the sleeping child across the room, but also as an admission that the intense emotion, the raging hunger, did not exist between them.

It was lust, nothing more unless he so chose, Rolf lied to himself. If he could control every other aspect of his life, he surely could control his heart, as she obviously did hers.

It was only the need for physical pleasure, Merlyn deceived herself, and from such a wizard as Rolf de Valmont; for she could never love a Norman, could never allow herself such a fatal flaw in her defenses.

Rolf spoke no more to her but rather communicated unconsciously through his actions. His one hand glided up and down her spine, then to her hips, pressing her to him, letting her feel his need. Her breasts crushed against his bare chest, even though through her clothing, was arousing to him as wet wool gently abraded his flesh.

Merlyn, too, felt the strangely erotic sensations of warm water and clinging clothing against nude skin, and she also found it oddly stimulating. Or was it just because the man beneath her was Rolf de Valmont?

As he lifted her skirts, an unexpectedly revealing thought struck Merlyn. A thought that, if she had allowed it, would have indeed led her to further explore what she considered only a powerful physical attraction for her husband: If he'd been wearing chain mail, she would have been just as stimulated; her blood would have poured through her veins with just as much heat, her muscles would have turned equally as languorous as they were now. For it was the thought of the man beneath the barrier of her bliaut and undertunic, the man beneath the armor, who fascinated her as no other had, who drove all rational thought from her mind when he so chose.

Surely I am addled, she had the presence of mind to think just as he lifted her to fit her silken heat to his arousal. *Lost* would have been a more appropriate word, but Merlyn would not even contemplate it . . . could not contemplate as she slowly, smoothly sheathed him, feeling as if impaling herself upon a spear of lightning, so bright and wondrous were the added sensations bursting through her.

Rolf swallowed his words of endearment, groaning against her temple, her closed eyes, then her sweet mouth as they established an exquisite rhythm within their warm, wet bower.

When it was over, they lay still, reveling silently in the aftermath, the wondrous feeling of their bodies still entwined, until even the heat from the hearth could not counteract the cooling water, the receding ardor.

Merlyn stood then, rather awkwardly, and stepped, with his aid, from the tub onto the toweling she had laid over the rushes. He followed her, glancing toward the bed. Satisfied that Raven still slept, Rolf slowly peeled Merlyn's clothing from her shivering body and moved her closer to the fire. He lay her down, allowing the leaping light and shadow from the hearth to bathe her nude form. With extra toweling, he dried her from head to toe, taking and giving exquisite pleasure as he moved over her breasts and abdomen, then lower to her thighs and legs and back up again.

With soothing movements, he dried her hair, then ran his fingers through its satiny length, marveling at its texture and rich onyx hue as he curled a tress about two fingers.

Merlyn began to move beneath him, desire stirring her once again to new warmth, renewed need. The sweet-scented rushes surrounded them with their faint fragrance, their prickly presence erotically adding further to the growing urgency.

They joined more leisurely this time, without the fear of splashing and rousing the child; without the desperate urgency of trying to prove something to themselves.

There was nothing to prove now. All antagonism, all suspicion, had been erased, at least for this night, in the magic of their first joining. Now they explored and worshiped slowly, thoroughly, and with wonder lighting their eyes. Skin to skin, they savored each other: Merlyn the latent power beneath Rolf's

341

surprisingly smooth flesh, and Rolf the supple firmness of the woman who had almost convinced him that she was a dried-up, ancient crone. Almost, but not quite.

Now he knew the courageous folly of her charade; yet, as they rose once again past all mortal concerns, he managed to vow to himself never to underestimate her, in anything, again.

Afterwards, Rolf carried her to the bed and placed her beside Raven. He eased in on the other side and they slept, sharing the bond of love for the child between them—the one thing of which each was certain—as they shielded her small form between them.

Chapter 21

The weather began to turn ugly.

"'Twas milder in Normandy," Rolf complained to Myles in late October as they trudged toward Renford, carrying a stag between them. "Even the grass was greener." His chief occupation lately had been hunting for game to get Renford through the winter. He was growing weary of slogging through the bare-branched *weald*, with its soggy carpet of dead leaves, branches, and mud, much as he loved the chase.

"We left Normandy before the grass turned brown," the blond chevalier reminded him with a lift of his fair brows. "'Tis almost blood-month now."

"Oui, but this weather is drear . . . chilling right down to the bone. And we have no animals we can afford to slaughter."

"Look at the bright side," the normally taciturn Myles advised him. "Renford fares better than many we saw on the road from the south. We have a growing supply of salted meat from the *weald* and fish from the Tees; apples and cider coming out of our ears—"

Rolf made a face at this. "Cider? Judas! A man

needs good red wine to thicken his blood."

"We have enough flour to get us through until first harvest if we use it wisely," Myles continued, obviously unperturbed.

"Aye. And a growing population to feed, as well." Rolf shifted the stag's hindquarters across his shoulder. "Why, of a sudden, does every Englishman around wish to make Renford his home?"

Myles, who led, supporting the weight of the stag's head and shoulders, turned his head aside as he spoke. "When first we arrived, I seem to remember a certain disappointment at the paltry number of humanity here. Now you lament your good fortune?"

"Aye. The more people here, the more to rebel when the time comes. If I am killed, Myles, you are welcome to Renford and all its . . . treasures."

Myles halted abruptly. Rolf almost lost his end of the stag with the unexpected cessation of movement. "From whence comes this concern?" Myles asked as he set down his load and swung to face Rolf. "Don't you think 'tis unjustified now? Don't you think you've won the goodwill of these English?"

Rolf, pulled precariously forward in the wake of Myles's action, was forced to set down his burden. He met his retainer's look steadily. His face was streaked with dried sweat and dirt, his cloak and tunic with the stag's blood. He felt like anything but a baron now, but he welcomed Myles's talkative mood. "Will any Norman ever win the goodwill of an Englishman? Nothing is ever a sure thing. Nothing."

Myles shrugged, then brushed off his hands. *"Bien sûr,* but what a dull existence without uncertainty. There would be no surprises, no challenges."

Rolf frowned at his friend and peer. "You've been away from Normandy too long, *copain.* You sound suspiciously like Hugh, except you speak nonsense. What man wouldn't want peace and tranquility . . . and security?" His eyes narrowed. "Do you know something that I don't? Has Smithsson suddenly disappeared? And his cohort in collusion, Will, as well?"

"Will?"

"They're thick as thieves when they think they're unobserved . . . except that I wouldn't have thought Will to be such a lackwit as to invite Marthe to share a cottage."

"You cannot call a man lackwit for inviting a woman to warm his bed and maintain his home."

Rolf nodded. "True. I'd not have thought you noticed. . . . You've become so complacent that you notice naught . . . except for the comely Margaret. Another man's wife, I might add."

A bright flush climbed up Myles's face. He opened his mouth to retort, but Rolf added quickly, "Forgive me. What man wouldn't notice a fair wench? I meant nothing by it." He bent to lift his end of the deer. "I'm in a foul mood this morn," he muttered.

"'Twill pass." He attempted to smile, but it looked more like a grimace.

Myles bent to his task. "Mayhap you should devote more of your nights to sleeping. Your mood might sweeten." Rolf caught the irony in his voice and acknowledged that he deserved the chevalier's retort. "And I think that you have little to worry about. If there is aught afoot, we are on the watch for it." His lips tightened with determination. "There is nothing they can do that we cannot deal with . . . you know that in your heart as well as I."

Rolf nodded, yet he silently asked, *But what if the entire village rises up against us? Then do we just slaughter them all for essaying to regain what they*

345

once had? Cedric and Elsa and—God forbid!—Merlyn . . .

To Rolf, of late, things were no longer simply black or white. There was a shaded area in between now, he admitted to himself, that blurred the boundaries between right and wrong. And the longer he was in England, the more deeply involved he became in the affairs of the area and its people, the more complicated things became. And the more uncertain he felt at times.

Why couldn't he shake this feeling of foreboding? And why couldn't he shake the echoes of an old woman's twice-repeated: *Something wicked comes this way?*

He and Merlyn had established a truce at night. Things that were difficult to ignore or put aside during the day were easier to discount at night. Yet during the day, the trust that he'd begun building in her—and others, as well—was not as firm as it once had been . . . and ever since the incident in the forest with the pigs.

Everyone was busy, what with salting and preserving any leftover fresh meat; scouring the forest for mushrooms, seeds, wild herbs, and edible plants, the charred fields for any onions that still might be hiding beneath the earth; making cider and mead; fashioning footwear (under Arthur's direction) and other leather goods needed for mending tack; getting the smithy going to repair and make new farming equipment under Erik's and Rufus's supervision; and continuing general repairs on the minor details in the village. There was plenty to do and enough people now to do it, yet Rolf still worried about keeping their bellies full. He knew, whether it was warriors or villagers, that empty bellies led to discontent, among other things. . . .

"What if Smithsson were to meet with an accident?" he wondered aloud so Myles could hear him. "A fatal accident?"

"Then you take the chance of making him a martyr," Myles threw over his shoulder.

"I was hoping you wouldn't say that," came the reply. "There isn't room for the spirit of 'St. Edward' in Renford while I am yet alive."

Myles threw back his head in laughter, almost unbalancing them both, and Rolf joined in, his spirits considerably restored.

Arthur carefully made his way to Will's cottage. The night sky glowed as a result of bright banks of snow clouds, even though they obscured the moon and stars. Frustration grew within him at his awkward progress away from his sleeping family. Oh, it was swift enough progress, he thought, but between his ungainly balance and his obstructed vision, he felt like a much older man.

Smithsson would already be there, he knew. They all took a chance by meeting in one place, and in the village yet, beneath Valmont's very nose. But it was worth the risk . . . any risk.

His head began to ache suddenly, and the familiar but dreaded ringing of distant church bells sounded in his left ear—a repercussion of the blow to his head. To his added annoyance, words began to dance in his mind: *I did not kill your king.*

"Ah!" he murmured with not only the physical pain of the memory, but with the emotional pain, as well. Those words were the words of a good man.

Nay! 'Tis the devil testing you, tanner.

Arthur paused in the shadow of the cottage before Will's. He covered his ear with his right hand. "Go

347

away," he whispered.

He was a courageous man, your Harold.

"Begone!" he snapped, more loudly than he'd intended.

The door to Will's dwelling opened and someone called softly, "Who's there?"

"Me. Arthur," he whispered fiercely, the sound of Smithsson's voice giving him added strength in his struggle to dismiss the unwelcome, disturbing voice from his mind.

Instantly, Edward sidled through the door and along one cottage to the next, where Arthur stood, rooted. He took hold of the tanner's elbow. "Come along," he muttered in an undertone into his ear. "Quietly, or we'll have every Norman in Renford at our throats."

When they were inside, the door closed and latched behind them, Arthur could make out the pale-haired Danish boy who operated the smithy, dark and diminutive Will, Derwick, and Garth. They sat cross-legged in a tight circle by a small fire in the hearth. Marthe was evidently abed behind a patched, threadbare privacy curtain to one side of the one-room dwelling.

Arthur lowered himself beside Derwick without a word.

". . . cannot overpower his trained men," Garth was saying in a low voice. "Even were we to get others to join us, we have no real weapons, no horses—"

"We have what we need," Derwick interjected. "A love for England. A passion to regain what is rightfully ours."

Erik spoke then, his blue eyes lighting with excitement. "We can take Valmont! If we kill him, his men will leave Renford, for the land was granted to him alone, was it not?"

Derwick cast him a disapproving glance in the soft glow from the fire. "Were you at Hastings, boy? There are a hundred more landless Norman sons who are waiting in line for a piece of England."

Smithsson, who had been quiet since Arthur's entrance, was listening with half an ear, or so it appeared. The firelight turned his long blond hair to red-gold, his beard to a darker shade. When he spoke, however, it was obvious he hadn't missed a word. "Mayhap, but if we dispatch Valmont and his men, I can lead the villagers in a stand against any others myself. We'll have their arms and their horses. . . . Why, Valmont is training us himself, the *nithing!*" He spat toward the fire, and the hot stone sizzled ominously.

For a few moments a profound silence gathered in the room. *Nithing* was the worst insult in the Saxon tongue.

"All of England," he continued into the quiet, "village by village, will do the same!"

All faces turned toward him, with varying degrees of hope and enthusiasm in their expressions.

"Earl Roger marches out of Herefordshire even as we speak," Will informed them in a low but steady voice, "and seeks to join Ralph de Gael, Earl of Norfolk, and his fellow Bretons established in England. De Gael's fellow magnates in Brittany stand ready to revolt against Count Hoel or to raid into Normandy itself. The Bastard's other enemies on the continent are watching developments carefully."

"Their help, particularly in tying William of Normandy's hands in the duchy itself, and coming aid from the Danes under Cnut all but guarantee the success of this uprising," added Smithsson. "But we *mustn't* balk. Only the boldest of action, without hesitation, will allow us to wrest England back from the usurper. Do you understand?"

Everyone except Arthur nodded in agreement.

"Arthur," Derwick whispered to him, "do you ken?"

Arthur nodded, a distant look in his eye when he raised his head from his contemplation of the floor, his distorted face obviously a potent reminder of what they were up against . . . and the consequences of their failing.

"They butchered him," he murmured in a broken voice. "We demand retribution . . . for what they did to Harold!"

Edward nodded. "And we shall have it, Arthur, this I pledge to you." He bowed his head in silent contemplation for long moments. No one spoke or moved. A faint snore sounded from behind the curtain across the room, causing Edward to smile to himself. That wretched excuse for a woman was totally, blissfully unconcerned with what they were about, he'd have wagered his very life.

His inner smile moved to his lips as he raised his head and looked at each man in turn. He spoke slowly, emphatically, as he said, "And we cannot count on Merlyn. She is a lost cause. Any man who forgets that will pay a high price, mark me."

Will stiffened, obviously at Edward's decision, but then lowered his gaze.

When Edward continued, his smile was a predatory grin as he finally said, "And now . . . for a strategy."

Arthur suddenly put his hand over his ear, as he had earlier outside the cottage. His jaws moved, his eyes closed; through lips drawn with pain, if the light had been better, if anyone could have looked closely enough, the name *Merlyn* would have been discernible upon his lips.

Over and over again . . .

As October turned to November, Merlyn was forced to spend more time indoors. She was thus provided the opportunity to see Rolf deal with complaints of Renfordites firsthand. Many times he asked her to listen to individual grievances right along with him, which gave Merlyn immense satisfaction. After all, she told herself, that was one of the reasons, aside from sparing Arthur's life, that she had agreed to wed Rolf de Valmont: to ensure her involvement in village affairs.

The fact that she enjoyed being in his company more and more—actually scoured the hall with her gaze for a glimpse of him many times in the course of a day—had nothing to do with it, she told herself obstinately again and again. It was due only to the residual if powerful effect of night after night in his arms.

And, of course, anticipation of the nights to come . . .

Rob, a sullen and belligerent Saxon who'd materialized from the woods with a timid wife and two little ones, requested an audience with Rolf one November morning. The Lord of Renford was sighting newly made arrows and making adjustments as needed in the shafts or feathers. Now that Arthur's skill and knowledge were needed to fashion and repair leather goods, Michael had his hands full with arrow-making.

Cedric approached him. "My lord, Rob Longtooth seeks an audience with you this morn." He spoke *sotto voice* and immediately caught Rolf's attention.

He looked up at Cedric and caught a rare gleam of

351

amusement in the Englishman's eyes. The two of them had secretly nicknamed the man "Longtooth" because of one missing eyetooth. The other, as if to make up for it, was unnaturally elongated, lending his smile (when he grudgingly gave it) a lopsided, comically villainous appearance. They'd agreed, in a moment of shared mirth, that Rob looked as if on one occasion at least, he'd carried his belligerence too far and someone had planted a fist smack into his mouth.

Rolf acknowledged Cedric with a nod, one side of his mouth crescenting slightly. "Send him to me."

Merlyn was walking toward the kitchen just then. "My lady wife, if you would do me the honor of hearing out the man known as Rob?"

Merlyn paused, an involuntary shiver sweeping through her at the sound of his voice, the sight of his dark, thick-lashed eyes crowned by those devilishly tented eyebrows, especially when he was frustrated . . . or up to mischief.

"Certainly, my lord." She went and sat beside him at the head table, waiting for Rob to approach.

The man and woman with whom Rob and Aleen shared their cottage followed close behind them. The second couple looked irritated, yet also ill at ease. But not Rob. With the shy Aleen in tow—and looking like she wished she could be anywhere else—Rob appeared ready for battle, his eyes dark with anger, his normally sullen expression grim. Rolf noted their two children huddling in the shadows near the closest door.

"What is your grievance?" Rolf asked Rob when the latter reached the high table.

"The *Dane* here stole one of our eggs," he charged without ceremony.

352

Immediately, Merlyn bristled at Rob's singling out Bjorn Fairhair as anything but an Englishman. Such blatant prejudice had had no place in Renford when Stigand was thane, and Merlyn hated hearing it crop up now. Elsa had been right: England was a mixture of many peoples, although as people gathered in Renford from other destroyed villages, a certain amount of rivalry and animosity would be only natural. Now Merlyn wondered if Rolf would think anything of Rob's attitude.

"The Dane?" Rolf asked innocently.

Rob jerked his chin over his shoulder. "Aye. Blondie, there. He stole an egg from the mouth of my babes. God's blood, but I cannot turn my back without one of 'em pilferin' something!"

Rolf looked over at Bjorn, whose face was bright red. His wife stared at the floor, color touching her cheeks as well.

Eggs were scarce, and Rolf allowed the ones that were not being hatched to be divided among the families as they became available. A boiled egg in Renford was a prized delicacy.

"I see. Have you aught to say in your defense, Bjorn?"

"I—I was just looking at it, my lord." His face turned magenta, obviously in the wake of this lame-sounding excuse. "Me an' Ingrid here haven't had eggs in months, and I was just admiring it. Didn't mean aught—"

"'Twas *my* wish, my lord," Ingrid spoke up then. "I asked Bjorn if those eggs weren't the prettiest things in all England. He—he took one for me to look at, nothin' more. And it . . . slipped and fell to the floor."

"An' *broke!*" Rob jeered.

An unholy light suddenly appeared in Rolf's eyes,

and he had an all but uncontrollable urge to throw back his head and have a good laugh. *Go suck it up from the rushes,* he silently ordered the outraged Rob. *Or cook it into a rush stew.*

Out of the corner of his eye he saw Merlyn lower her chin.

A suspicious cough sounded from Cedric nearby. *Damn the man,* Rolf cursed his steward. *He's no help at all.*

Don't blame it on Cedric, Valmount. 'Tis one of the greatest honors bestowed upon a baron, this dividing up of the eggs.

In a desperate attempt to curb his galloping urge to laugh, Rolf quickly pushed himself to his feet, placed one hand upon the board before him, and vaulted over it to land lithely before Rob.

His lightning movement shifted his concentration to the physical feat and also caused the complainant to jump backward in surprise, slamming into Aleen and eliciting a gasp from her. Apprehension transformed Rob's features as he found himself almost nose to nose with the Lord of Renford.

The sight of Rob's very real fear also helped sober Rolf.

"Let us put this in perspective," he said matter-of-factly, not wishing to frighten the man and his poor wife any further. "You cannot accuse a man of stealing aught if he but wishes to admire it, although"—he looked meaningfully at Bjorn—"'tis courteous to ask permission before touching anything that does not belong to you."

Bjorn nodded. "Aye, my lord," and Rolf could have sworn he saw a spark of answering amusement in the man's blue eyes.

In that moment, Rolf decided Bjorn would be an ally in time of need, while he'd think twice before giving his back to Rob under the same circumstances.

Merlyn spoke from behind Rolf. "If 'twill satisfy you, Rob, I will give you my egg. Especially if it was meant for one of the children."

Rob grudgingly nodded in her direction, but it was Aleen who said, "Thank you, my lady," and put her hand on her husband's arm as if to urge him to leave the hall without further ado.

"And," Rolf said more loudly than necessary, "you may have *my* egg as well, for I would not want to overindulge myself while your children go without." Before anyone could answer, he said to Bjorn, "You will receive your share when 'tis your turn, for 'twas an accident and I see no need to punish either of you."

Bjorn nodded. "Yes, my lord. Thank you for your generosity." He swung away. Ingrid dipped her head toward Rolf and Merlyn and followed him.

"Is there aught else?" Rolf asked Rob.

The man shook his head, looking suspiciously dissatisfied.

"Then I would suggest," he said, leaning even closer to Rob, "that you learn to tolerate those with whom you share a home. If it came down to drawing straws, you could just as easily have to leave the cottage as Bjorn and Ingrid, until another can be built."

"Aye, my lord." The sullen look was back.

"And, Rob . . . Bjorn is of Danish descent, but an Englishman all the same. Just, I suspect, as you consider yourself such, although of Saxon descent . . . ?" He raised a quizzical eyebrow and Rob nodded. "When you speak of a man in his presence, have the grace to call him by his name. Will you remember that?"

"Aye."

"Good!" He inclined his head toward the back of the hall. "I believe you can wheedle two eggs from Agnes if you tell her of my decision."

It had been their habit to waste little time in preliminary talk at bedtime, for both Rolf and Merlyn discovered it was far easier to succumb to the sensual enchantment between them behind closed doors. Questions didn't arise, suspicions were held at bay, only the potent attraction of the physical could blot out all else before slumber overcame them.

Merlyn was more than a little relieved that Edward had not approached her again concerning rebellion. Her feelings were so mixed, so difficult to sort through and come to one solid conclusion, that a respite from the emotional dilemma with the issue raised in the *weald* weeks earlier was welcome.

It was not fair, Merlyn acknowledged with one part of her mind, to either her husband or her people, yet she eagerly sought the haven of the physical in Rolf de Valmont's arms, deliberately ignoring the distant if persistent reverberations of her conscience.

The fact that she strongly suspected he loved her didn't enter into it now, either. She basked in long overdue male strength and guidance, ignoring the seething issue just outside the bedchamber door. It was too easy to allow all responsibility to remain squarely on Rolf de Valmont's shoulders—a task to which he rose most capably, even admirably, in spite of her first impression of him.

Hugh de Conteville would have been pleased and proud, she found herself thinking more and more. . . .

She glanced up at her husband as he stood looking

into the fire, obviously in thought, his profile to her. As he slowly slid his tunic over his head and dropped it to the floor, Merlyn could have sworn he wore a smile. As he reached over his head to pull off his chainse, she found herself admiring the flat planes of his stomach, the strong, beautiful lines of his chest. . . .

He threw back his head for a moment as the chainse climbed up his neck and chin, and Merlyn caught the proud cut of his Adam's apple in the corded column of his neck. Giddiness glided through her like melting butter . . . but there was more. Not for the first time, she found herself yearning to discover something of his mind. His thoughts, his feelings, his plans for the future . . .

She shied away from the very word.

"Merlyn?"

He'd caught her in her rapt contemplation of him. She didn't realize that she was suddenly wearing a faint frown.

"Is aught amiss?"

Rather than reveal what she'd been thinking, rather than delve into issues she stubbornly wished to avoid, she quickly replied, "I thought I saw you smiling, my lord. Have you some jest you'd like to share?"

He looked surprised for an instant before answering. "Why, yes . . . there is a jest, but 'tis of my own invention." He grinned.

Merlyn tipped her head aside in expectation, and the silken sweep of her hair swayed softly to one side of her face.

Like the graceful undulation of a falcon's wing on the wind, Rolf thought . . . "I was thinking of Rob."

An answering bubble of merriment rose in Merlyn's throat. "You handled the situation very well," she told him, "considering you were bursting with mirth inside."

Rolf opened his mouth in halfhearted denial, then decided it wasn't necessary. "And just how did you know that, my lady wife?" He approached the bed slowly and with feigned thoughtfulness. "I neither smiled nor laughed."

"But I saw Cedric's face. He would never have come so near to losing control if he hadn't sensed your reaction. He's a very observant man . . . with a wonderful sense of humor that has been buried for months. And you helped him retrieve it."

"At Rob's expense, I'm afraid," he said with rue, but Merlyn wasn't fooled.

"And you loved every minute of it. Admit it."

He dropped down beside her on the bed, clad only in his braies, and set his chin in the heel of his hand. There was only an arm's length between them. "I admit to nothing of the sort." But his eyes were alight with mischief, something Merlyn found captivating.

"Tell me your acrobatics weren't to prevent your merriment from surfacing and ruining the . . . *gravity* of the situation," she demanded. "What were you thinking? Tell me truly."

"What am I thinking?" He thoughtfully stroked one side of his clean-shaven face. "Why, I'm thinking just how enchanting you are."

Her lashes lowered momentarily, a gentle blush bathing her cheeks. "What were you thinking *then?*" she insisted when she finally allowed her gaze to return to his.

He sighed and lay back, his hands crossed beneath his head, his eyes studying the freshly cut beams in the ceiling.

"Rolf!"

After a time he cleared his throat. Eyes still on the

ceiling, he said, with great solemnity, "You won't tell Rob, will you? For if you do, you'll absolutely destroy the growing consensus that I am wise as Solomon."

"'You may have *my* egg as well'?" she laughed. "I believe Solomon would have sheared it in two."

"Eh bien . . ." he began slowly, deliberately drawing out the moment. "I thought to tell him to . . . go suck it up from the rushes."

After a flash of stunned silence, Merlyn broke into a heart-stopping smile (which Rolf missed in his effort to remain sober). "Rolf . . ." she began, the sweet sound of her jubilation singing through the room as the healing elixir of laughter chased away old fears and concerns, "'twould have been the p— perfect answer for s—someone with a sense of humor." She tried to catch her breath. "But not Rob!"

Suddenly, Rolf could keep silent no longer. The woman beside him was metamorphosing right before him and he was not only delighted, but he wanted in the worst way to share the moment with her.

His mouth began to quiver. The quake moved down to his chest, then the entire pallet, before he gave in to a bout of hearty laughter.

Merlyn's laughter renewed at the sound of his, and he turned over onto his stomach less he choke from such hearty merriment. He buried his face in the covers, afraid the entire village would hear him.

After a time, he recovered himself and raised his face. He swiveled his head aside and captured her gaze. The atmosphere was very relaxed and easy in the aftermath of their shared levity.

In the sudden intensity of his unwavering regard, Merlyn sought something to say to keep the mood light, for she was in awe of this side of Rolf de Valmont—a side that was in perfect accord with her own ability to enjoy the absurd. "You have no board to leap over now. How will you contain your laughter the night through?" she asked with a smile that made his heart trip drunkenly through his breast.

He lowered his mouth toward hers, his breath brushing across her cheek like the sigh of a zephyr. "I have better things in mind to absorb . . . my energies this night."

With the warm adhesion of his mouth sending tremors of delight through her, Merlyn acknowledged that, indeed, there were other, more pleasurable ways to divert one's laughter.

Chapter 22

"He'll never learn to be a bandog if you coddle him so," Rolf told Raven as the child clutched the growing mastiff pup in her arms. His increasingly long legs dangled down to her knees, his little potbelly protruding like that of any healthy, growing puppy.

"But he follows Mamma *everywhere*," the little girl complained, "especially into the *weald* . . . and there are pred—" She paused, her small brow knitted in concentration as she obviously searched for the elusive end of the word.

"Predators," he replied absently, his mind dwelling on the fact that Merlyn was still going into the woods when the weather was getting so cold. True, he was still learning many things about the running of a manor, but the unwelcome, insidious doubts that began to sprout anew would not give him any true peace of mind.

On one hand, he was ashamed of himself. On the other, he could not afford to ignore his warrior's instincts. Not even for Merlyn.

"Aye." Raven kissed the top of Gryff's head, then set him down. He wandered around the yard near them, nose to the ground, tail swishing nonchalantly.

"But he must learn not to fear those very predators, *petite*, or he'll never be of any use other than a lapdog. One day he will grow to be very big—twelve or thirteen stone—and the purpose of such a dog is to keep away enemies, human and otherwise, at night when we are sleeping."

"And he must be tied during the day?"

He began to answer in the affirmative, then changed his mind at the hope in her eyes. "Only if you wish him to be." The child unknowingly had him wound around her finger in a manner he dared not allow her mother. "If you wish, *chère*, he can just be your pet."

"Oh, nay! Gryff must earn his keep, like all the other animals. He cannot lay eggs or pull a plow or give milk, but he can guard the village when he grows up," she explained proudly.

Rolf nodded in complete agreement, a smile in his eyes. "*Oui*. Then so be it."

Later that morning, when everyone was occupied and the manor gates opened, no one noticed the subtly scattered trail of tidbits leading from the edge of the road into the woods.

An hour or two later, a worried Raven sought out her mother. "Mamma?" she asked as she approached Merlyn, who was in the kitchen showing Agnes exactly what "secret" flavorings—and the approximate amounts—she normally added when brewing honey-ale or mead.

"Aye, sweet?" Merlyn straightened from the vat of the amber-colored liquid and wiped her hands on her skirts, glad for a break. Ribbons of creamy froth trailed through the brew like lace, and the smell it gave off was intoxicating in itself. "Would you like to help us? . . ." Her question trailed off at the worried look on the child's face. "What is it?" she asked, sharply enough so that Agnes, too, raised concerned eyes from her work.

"Gryff is gone." Tears welled in her great blue eyes. She blinked them back in an obvious attempt to be brave.

Merlyn reached to smooth her daughter's dark, tangled curls from her cheeks, unmindful of how Raven was a tiny replica of herself. "Now you remember what Rolf said, do you not? The dog must be allowed some freedom to roam, or he will never find his way back to the village from his nighttime duties when he's grown."

Raven nodded, but the tears didn't stop. Merlyn knew that the child had learned long ago not to bother an adult with little things in the wake of other, more serious problems—like finding food and shelter. So in the face of Raven's continued distress, Merlyn began to feel genuine concern. "How long has he been missing?"

"A *long* time, Mamma," Raven said, her lower lip quivering.

A long time to a child wasn't necessarily a long time to an adult. Nonetheless, Merlyn put aside the stained apron that protected her bliaut and headed toward the yard with Raven close behind.

"Did you tell my lord Rolf?"

"I couldn't find him, Mamma."

"Fetch my cloak, will you?" Merlyn asked as they passed through the hall, and Raven quickly did as she was bid.

As they left the protection of the palisade, a wicked wind buffeted them from what seemed like all directions. Merlyn glanced up at the winter sky with a frown. Bright, snow-laden clouds burst across it,

363

threatening to unleash their frigid burden over the earth below.

At the edge of the road across from the south side of the manor, Merlyn halted and instructed Raven, "Stay here, child. In fact, go back into the hall or the manor yard until I return." The wind was whipping her skirts about her ankles and trying to pry its way beneath her heavy woolen mantle. She shivered and hugged it closer to her body. "Go," she repeated in the face of Raven's apparent struggle between obedience and her concern for the dog. "'Tis too cold for you to remain here. I'll bring him back with me, I promise."

Raven nodded, relief kindling in her eyes. She turned away and ran toward the manor yard, looking back once and waving just before she slipped around a corner of the stone wall and toward the higher wooden stockade.

As Merlyn crossed the road and entered the forest, she marveled for the hundredth time at the unshakable faith children had in adults . . . an absolute belief that a grown person could make everything all right, whether it was mending a nicked finger or finding food where little was available.

Merlyn knew she couldn't solve England's problems, but she was determined to find the animal who meant so much to her daughter.

"Marthe!"

Marthe was squatting beside Gryff, who was licking the palm of her hand. With the other hand, the woman held the dog's collar in a death grip. At Merlyn's exclamation, Marthe looked up guiltily.

Food!

Merlyn suddenly envisioned Marthe making a

meal out of Gryff. . . .

Absurd. She wasn't starving now.

"How . . . what are you doing here?" Merlyn asked, relieved to find Gryff unharmed, but puzzled as to why Marthe, of all people, would be out in the cold *weald* and hanging onto Gryff as if he were of great value.

At first Marthe seemed to have lost her tongue, but not for long. "I was rescuing the stupid hound," she explained, frowning in irritation at Gryff when, at the sound and sight of Merlyn, he began to struggle against her hold. She reached for a length of cord at her feet and secured it to the pup's collar, just as a man emerged from the trees behind her.

Merlyn's eyes widened slightly in surprise, but she wouldn't allow her sudden and extreme unease to show in her expression as she recognized Edward Smithsson.

"Are you ready to rid Renford of Valmont?" he asked bluntly, the wind blowing his blond hair about his face. His eyes were narrowed against the cold and hard as stone. Once again, Merlyn was reminded of Harold Godwinson, at least outwardly . . . tall and fair, strong and confident. He was also regal . . . yet unyielding, with nary a glint of compassion in those frigid blue eyes.

She could understand why men—and women— were eager to do his bidding, for not only did he possess a magnetism and that all-important quality of leadership, but he no doubt reminded many an Englishman of the late, beloved Saxon king. Echoes of the past . . . what could be again if a miracle were to occur . . .

"I thought not," he said with derision, looking pointedly over her head and beyond her.

In spite of the wind rattling through the bare

branches overhead, Merlyn caught the snap of dry debris underfoot and swung about. . . .

"My lord!" she cried softly.

Waltheof, Earl of Huntingdon, son of the late Siward of Northumbria and husband to Judith, niece of Duke William of Normandy, came toward her. Two men flanked him protectively, but Merlyn could not at first grasp the significance of that.

What was the earl doing *here?* An English earl, high in the Bastard's esteem, in the *weald* with the likes of Edward Smithsson?

Without ceremony, Waltheof addressed her in urgent tones. "What is this Smithsson tells me, Merlyn? That you would rather live under Norman rule than see England freed? How can that be?"

It struck her then: Waltheof was consorting with Smithsson. Waltheof was part of the conspiracy.

For the space of several heartbeats, Merlyn was struck dumb as the implication of this sank in.

"What would Stigand think? Did he throw away his life for naught? And all those others—"

"But—but I didn't know, my lord," she blurted out when her wits returned, "that the movement Edward spoke of was supported by men like yourself!"

"Nay, of course not," Edward said, his voice freighted with irony. "Only rabble like ourselves would dare perpetrate such a bid for freedom, isn't that so, Merlyn?"

She shook her head, but Waltheof spoke again. "There is no time for quibbling now. You have always been a fine example of leadership to your people here; Will said that only recently you told him and Edward you were every bit as loyal as any man among us. Then prove it, Merlyn. Show me that my trust in you is merited."

She stared at him, myriad voices chasing through

her head—Elsa's, Rolf's, Derwick's, Edward's, Waltheof's . . .

"What . . . am I to do?" she whispered, her face pale, a sinking feeling within her.

"I think you know."

"Someone approaches," one of Waltheof's men warned in a low voice.

They melted back into the trees as silently as spirits, leaving only Merlyn, Marthe, and Edward.

"I smell something," Rolf threw over his shoulder in a low voice to Rufus, who was close behind. "And 'tisn't a boar." He readjusted his swordbelt at his hips, one hand patting Death Blow reassuringly, then moving to rest on his dagger hilt.

"Then let's go back," the red-haired Norman said, "for more men."

Rolf came up short, putting out a hand to halt Rufus in his tracks.

"*Qu'est-ce que c'est?*" the shorter, stocky Norman asked.

Rolf silently pointed to a mound of dead leaves and brush to one side of the path. The wind had scattered some of the debris . . . enough to expose the bottom of a shoe.

Rolf held his finger to his lips and indicated for Rufus to remain where he was. He approached the half-scattered mound and squatted to inspect it. He paused to listen for a moment to the sounds of the forest, then bent cautiously and brushed aside some of the leaves. He moved up an ankle, then the rest of the leg to the bloody torso of . . . André, one of the two men who patrolled the *weald* regularly.

More frantically then, Rolf scraped away the leaves and pulled the body toward the path. "*Merde!*" he cursed with soft virulence. When Rufus made a move to help, he ordered, *"Reste-là!* Stay where you are; it may be a trap."

André was dead, and a deep sense of loss moved through Rolf. But now was not the time to mourn, and he allowed outrage to invade his mind, pushing aside his sadness for the time being. As I live and breathe, he thought, is there no end to this? Was there ever to be any security for him and those who were starting to look to him for protection here in northern England?

"I'm beginning to understand how they felt when first we came here," he muttered, a savage note in his voice. "Like rabbits awaiting slaughter from any direction."

"André?" Rufus asked in surprise as he allowed himself a quick glance at the body Rolf uncovered.

"Aye. And if we look long enough, I wager we'll find Sweyn, as well."

"Shall I go back for—"

"Nay. We'll *both* return for more men. 'Tis suicide for anyone to be alone out here right now. . . ."

"But my lady Merlyn is out there. . . ."

Rolf stood and turned on Rufus, unwisely dropping his guard for a moment. But the look that flashed across his man's face was one of genuine concern . . . Rufus, the stoic, the stern. But he was definitely not stupid. In spite of his concern for Merlyn, he knew better than to do something foolish.

What he did not know, Rolf acknowledged bleakly, was that Merlyn was capable of treachery. And much as it might make the new Lord of Renford appear the foolish, lovesick male, he had to inform his men—every one of them—of her possible involvement in anything that was anti-Norman.

He opened his mouth to speak. Just then, a shriek

was carried to them on the wind: *"Naaaayyy . . ."* Faint, thready, but definitely feminine and fraught with fear.

It had to be Merlyn, for Raven had told him her mother had gone after Gryff. Merlyn . . . who couldn't stand the sight of the hound, or so it seemed . . . going after the animal she despised?

She's softened toward the hound, and she would do anything for Raven. "You go back, get help," Rolf ordered Rufus, lest he was walking into a snare. His instincts were screaming in warning, but his feelings for his wife—the desperate hope that she might merely have run into a problem—were suddenly overwhelming. He could handle an angered boar or bear, a hunger-crazed Saxon, a renegade Scot . . . anything but her betrayal.

If Merlyn was in trouble, he would go to her; would willingly, gladly sacrifice his life to save hers. It was that simple.

He pointed emphatically in the direction of the manor before Rufus could protest. A grim look on his face, the Norman spun on his heel and moved swiftly toward Renford, sword drawn.

Rolf shoved aside the implications of André's half-hidden corpse and moved up the path and in the direction of the scream he'd heard.

Edward roughly clamped his hand over Merlyn's mouth. "Fool!" he snarled in her ear. "'Twas a threat to ensure your cooperation; she is unharmed."

Merlyn's eyes were huge with terror for Raven. She began to struggle. Damn them all! She would side with the Normans before she would ever allow harm to come to her daughter.

"Be *still!*" Smithsson hissed in her ear. "Naught

has befallen the girl." Merlyn relaxed somewhat, although still trying to twist her face from beneath his palm. She could hear the smile in his voice as he added, "Although, perhaps your scream will serve to benefit us, rather than the opposite."

Merlyn yanked her chin from his grip. "Quiet!" he ordered in a low voice, and grabbed one hand to drag her into the woods. "You are a disgrace to your people. Will was so wrong about you . . . and so was Waltheof, as he saw."

Merlyn jerked her face up to his, her eyes flashing. "I'll show you what a disgrace I am," she vowed, her eyes dark with outrage. "Leave me here . . . Stay here with me, if you dare to face Rolf's fury, and see whose side I am on."

Before Edward could answer, Rolf came plunging up the trail and into view. Marthe sat still as a stone, holding Gryff by the rope, her startled, myopic gaze upon Rolf. But it was the couple behind her who riveted Rolf's attention: Merlyn, standing straight and regal, beside Edward Smithsson. Two native English, bonded by the same cause, facing him, the Norman adversary, with a strange calm . . .

Rolf's worst nightmare was realized.

His fear for the woman he loved was transformed into shattering disappointment. Instantly, adrenaline began pumping through his body, churning up an icy rage. He drew his sword, his features suddenly freezing into the mask he wore into battle: cold, expressionless, save for grim purpose. When he knew many comrades around him would fall and that every breath he drew could be his last . . .

"Move aside, Merlyn," he ordered through set teeth, "lest you get caught in the fray when I kill this snake. He'll not live to strike down another of my men, I swear to God!"

Edward unsheathed the sword at his waist. (Sword? Merlyn thought with one part of her mind.) Unsure as to what to do next, Merlyn was suddenly reluctant to leave his side. Not because she feared for him but, rather, because she believed Rolf would not attack with her so close . . . no matter how he thought she'd wronged him.

What is it, precious one? Rolf's tender query flickered through her mind, bringing a wealth of emotion to constrict her throat.

Suddenly, the blinders fell away, and it came to Merlyn like a miraculous vision that Rolf de Valmont was a good man, just as Elsa had told her. And, more importantly, not only did he love her, but she loved him.

She loved him.

Why, in the name of all that was holy, had she obstinately refused to see what was before her nose?

Fear for her Norman husband held Merlyn immobile when he commanded her to move away . . . and not a desire to stand beside Edward Smithsson for his cause.

She had different commitments, different responsibilities now. This cause was no longer hers.

For what seemed an ephemeral eternity, Merlyn stood rooted to the spot, unable to help Rolf or herself. And in that brief forever, Rolf knew that he had lost her . . . that he'd never really *had* her, and he'd been a fool to even think it could ever be so.

As it was, no one could have helped Rolf in those strained seconds.

He heard the snap of a stick underfoot behind him and whirled, knowing he was presenting his back to Edward Smithsson's blade. As he swung around, he arced Death Blow about and, with great satisfaction, felt the blade bury itself in flesh. An animallike groan

371

of pain met his ears, and he recognized it as a death song.

If he had to go down, he would take at least one of them with him.

Merlyn cried out as Rolf pulled the sword from the Saxon who'd emerged from the forest behind him. He whirled about again, his body acting as a pivot point for his final, wild swing of Death Blow with both hands, striking the man who was about to strike him.

He had the immense satisfaction of seeing his attacker literally cut in two at the waist as a result of his last supreme effort . . .

Before he was dealt a stunning blow to the head.

The world exploded in a thousand pinpoints of light, then spun drunkenly about him. Blackness closed in, obliterating his vision and threatening to take him into the nether region of death.

But not before Merlyn's image flashed before him, cruel in its vividness, standing proudly beside his enemy, Edward Smithsson, grim purpose lighting her eyes.

If acting the crone had been difficult, it was nothing now as Merlyn fought to suppress her concern for Rolf. She was paralyzed inside with the fear that he was dead.

"Sweet Jesu, but he took two of my men!" Waltheof growled as he bent to examine the first man Rolf had downed.

"He wasn't sent to England for merely his looks," Will replied from beside the earl, shaking his head. "But we have no time to mourn their deaths. We'll avenge them later."

"What would you have me do?" Merlyn asked,

tearing her eyes from Rolf's body and willing her wooden lips to work.

Edward bent to the fallen Norman. "Good. He still lives." He looked up at Merlyn. "I doubt there is aught you can do for us, traitor."

Exquisite relief flooded through Merlyn, and as her cheeks filled with color once again, she feigned indignation. "Only I can convince those in Renford to follow you and Waltheof."

"The earl could do it so much better, even were you sincere," Edward contradicted her nastily.

"There will be no division among us," Waltheof said as he straigthened from examining the second man on the ground. "Will believes it, and I believe it. Merlyn is in our camp. Her late husband was one of Godwinson's most trusted. 'Tis inconceivable that she would betray us, you've just had proof of that. Surely she can return as our messenger—and to prepare the villagers to rise up."

"Erik and Garth are still in Renford, as is Arthur," Will reminded him.

"Aye." It was Edward who answered. "But only one of them is dependable—Garth. Erik is an untried, overexuberant youth, and Arthur of little use."

"However you feel about them," Will reminded him, "they are with us. And," he added, looking directly at Merlyn, *"you* must not betray them to the Normans." He took the rope securing Gryff from Marthe's hand and untied it. The dog immediately went to Rolf and sniffed his bloodied head as he lay unmoving upon the ground. The mastiff whined softly, then trotted over to Merlyn to sit at her feet, uncharacteristically subdued.

Merlyn, still feeling faint from relief, wondered at Smithsson's easy dismissal of Arthur. "What would you specifically have me do, my lord?" she asked

Waltheof to hide her thoughts.

"Tell them we've taken Rolf and will release him only when they leave Renford for Normandy. If they are foolhardy enough to try and rescue him, he will die."

"So that is the reason you didn't kill him?" she asked, her insides atremble, for it was obvious that Waltheof had instructed Will, who had dealt Rolf the blow to his head, to spare him if possible.

"Exactly. If they are willing to leave in exchange for their leader, then our task will be simple." What he didn't tell her was that he planned to slaughter them all as they departed, lest they one day return under a new leader. "If they are stubborn," Waltheof added, "we'll kill Valmont and eliminate the rest of them with the help of the villagers. Then we'll join the other armies gathering across England under Ralph de Gael and Roger of Breteuil." He shrugged. "Who knows? Cnut and his army could arrive at any moment." He looked around the small circle of men. "We are all agreed, then, to let her return?"

Heads nodded and grunts of assent sounded. Except for Edward. He didn't look convinced. But Waltheof was the only one whose trust Merlyn felt she needed.

"Tell them to leave," Waltheof ordered her. "They can collect Valmont on their way out. Otherwise he'll die . . . and so will they."

Will laughed softly and without humor. "They will anyway," he muttered.

Edward, his narrowed eyes on Merlyn, said nothing in response.

"Go now, before they all come charging through the *weald* in search of their precious leader," the earl told her.

"But where will you be? How will I communicate

with you?"

Edward shook his head. "There will be no need. Just give the Normans the message. And tell the villagers to be prepared."

Refusing to allow her gaze to touch Rolf, Merlyn nodded and stooped to pick up Gryff. Holding onto him as if he were the most precious thing in the world, she backed away a few steps, then turned and hurried into the forest.

"I say we kill him now," Edward said when Merlyn was gone. "Send his corpse in pieces back to Renford."

Waltheof put a hand on his shoulder. "He is our guarantee that Merlyn will fully cooperate. If you are right about her, my friend, if she is with the Normans, she won't be so eager to sacrifice Valmont now, will she?"

Two more earls were raising armies? Merlyn thought in consternation as she stumbled through the woods toward Renford. And the Danish king was on his way to help the uprising?

Yes. And Rolf is wounded . . . and in the hands of English rebels.

She had wondered, over the weeks and months before Rolf and his men had come to Northumbria, if her life could have been more shattered, more uncertain or chaotic. The answer was an unequivocal no.

Until now.

The ghastly image of Rolf's crumpled form, his blood-matted hair, filled her vision, and her mind reeled. She clutched Gryff tighter, as if for security, and plunged onward, tears filling her eyes for the first time she could remember, blurring the pathway

375

ahead to a kaleidoscope of black and brown and dullest gray.

Merlyn stumbled over something sticking out into her path, and she went down onto her knees. Gryff flew from her arms with a yelp, lay still a moment as if to regain his wind, then scrambled to his feet and trotted over to where she knelt.

But Merlyn forgot the dog for a moment. Before her, between her braced arms, rested a man's leather-shod foot. Her eyes moved up the ankle and calf, to encounter the other leg, bent at a grotesque angle at the knee. She forced her eyes to travel farther until she recognized him.

It was André. And he was dead.

Merlyn cried out softly in horror and pushed herself to her feet. Like a recurring nightmare, her world was disintegrating around her, only this time she wasn't prepared to deal with it.

Raven!

Letting Gryff run ahead of her, Merlyn fled up the trail toward the manor once again, praying that Raven had obeyed her and was still in the hall.

Panic made her clumsy, terror made her queasy. And heartbreak made her tears begin to flow like rain. Once again, she couldn't make out the path clearly. A stitch zigzagged up her side, her breath came in gasps, her limbs felt like stone.

And then she ran smack into what felt like a wall. Big, powerful hands took her by the shoulders. A voice spoke to her in a language she didn't understand, then the hands shook her when she didn't respond.

"Merlyn!" the deep accented voice rasped in her ear.

She raised her tear-tracked face to that of her captor. It was the Viking colossus, Myles de Mortain.

Chapter 23

In spite of Merlyn's insistence—and to her dismay—Myles and his men did not go racing through the *weald* in search of their fallen leader and his abductors. They collected André's body and hurried Merlyn out of the forest and to the manor.

A distraught Merlyn was ready to thrash the taciturn Myles in frustration. If Rolf de Valmont had driven her to anger, this man was enough to drive her to attempt bodily harm. He said nothing after her brief explanation of what had happened with Rolf earlier, ignoring Merlyn until they reached the hall.

Extra sentries were posted around the village and two men sent to incarcerate Garth and Arthur in the granary.

At first she could only cling to Raven, her bout of weeping renewed at the sight of her daughter safe and sound.

Know you that even now her throat may have been slit by one of our own in Renford . . .

A shudder moved through Merlyn at the memory of Edward's ugly threat.

"Where's Rolf?" Raven asked as she disengaged herself from her mother's embrace and bent to hug

Gryff. "Thou art naughty," she scolded him in somber, formal tones, although relief was evident on her small features. Then she imitated Merlyn's scowl and shook a finger at him. "My lord Rolf went after you and Mamma, and you show naught of being sorry." She looked up at Merlyn. "Where *is* Rolf?" she asked again. "And why are you weeping if Gryff is safe, Mamma?"

Merlyn drew in a shuddering breath and wiped her eyes. It was as if all her unshed tears had been waiting for the right moment to burst forth . . . in an endless, unwelcome torrent.

"He—he's been abducted . . . taken, child," she began, then found she couldn't finish for the look of dawning horror on Raven's face—a look that Merlyn had once vowed she would never again allow to cross her daughter's features. Or those of any other child in Renford . . .

It gave her strength now. And purpose.

"Is he . . . *dead?*" Raven whispered, her own eyes glistening suddenly with tears as Merlyn's own began, finally, to recede.

Merlyn hugged her tightly once again, this time more for the child's reasurance than her own. "Nay, sweet," she answered, trying to minimize the situation without lying. "Only hurt."

"Then we must get him back . . . and make him better," Raven said in a muffled but confident voice from her mother's shoulder. She pulled away and looked into Merlyn's eyes. "Won't we? We got Gryff back. Then we can get Rolf."

Before Merlyn could answer, Rufus came striding up to her. "Myles would speak to you, my lady," he told her, his bleak look extremely disturbing to Merlyn.

"Take Gryff to the kitchen and ask Agnes if she can

378

spare some scraps. We'll talk later."

As she joined Myles and the other men around him, Merlyn wondered if the white-blond Norman harbored the same doubts about her as had Rolf. Myles was Rolf's trusted retainer, a knight like himself. No doubt they spoke of personal things, too. Yet Merlyn had had little to do with him. He was definitely a man's man, and not the easiest to engage in conversation.

Cedric numbered among them, and this fact was comforting to Merlyn.

"What do you know about all this?" Myles asked when she stood before him near one of the great hearths. A shield and several gleaming weapons, newly placed upon one stone wall, were caught in her peripheral vision, vividly reminding Merlyn that the owner of those weapons was not there . . . was in mortal danger. "And tell me everything, Merlyn, for Rolf's life hangs in the balance. If that means aught to you."

His words were stern but neutral, revealing nothing of his opinion of her. Perhaps Rolf hadn't told him of what he obviously had considered his misplaced trust.

Surely it was misplaced until you realized you loved him.

Her chest constricted at the implication of that thought.

"My lord Waltheof—Earl of Huntingdon—was there. He, Edward, Will, and several others were there, as far as I could tell. And Marthe. Waltheof said that all of England is rising up—"

"We've heard that before," he growled, cutting her off.

"But he also mentioned other armies grouping across England under Ralph de Gael, Earl of

Norfolk, and Roger of Breteuil, Earl of Hereford. And Cnut of Denmark is bringing ships and men—"

"What of Rolf?" he interrupted her again, obviously unimpressed.

"I told you before: He will be allowed to go free when you and your men leave Renford."

Myles's eyes slitted, his narrowed gaze carefully assessing. "And do you believe that?"

Merlyn's gaze shifted to Cedric. The look in his eyes was reminiscent of the bitter and disillusioned man who had lived in the forest with her before these Normans came to Renford. Bryce, Rolf's squire, looked stunned, disbelieving, as did Bjorn Fairhair, who had come, so he'd told Merlyn, to once again express his gratitude to Rolf and herself.

Was it that bad? she thought, panic threatening to override reason. Could it be that Cedric—all of them—knew something that she didn't?

"Why shouldn't I?" she whispered, the trace of color in her cheeks waning.

"Because you are in league with them. You know they lie."

She shook her head in vehement denial. "Nay!" Tears threatened again, but she would not allow them to betray her before these men. "I heard them talk, but I thought 'twas only talk. Surely they will keep their word and release Rolf if you leave . . ." She didn't think of the significance of Rolf—or all of them—leaving England. Uppermost in her mind was saving his life.

"Did any one of them give you his word?"

They will anyway. The words leapt to life in her memory. *They will* die *anyway.*

"Of course not," Myles continued inexorably. "And even if one of them had, it would mean less than nothing. They'll kill Rolf no matter what we do, you can be sure of that."

Disbelief assailed Merlyn. Those were good men, the English with Waltheof, weren't they? Her own people. Why would they slaughter a man if he and his followers did as they were instructed? Especially when he'd done so much to restore Renford and help its people recover?

Rolf is Norman. What care these English rebels about what he has or has not done here? He and his fought for the Bastard . . . overran England. Any means will justify ridding our land of them forever.

She shook her head at that reasoning. Hadn't the English rebelled before? Hadn't they failed abysmally? The devastation of Northumbria was the latest example of William of Normandy's determination to hold England. He had been in control for over nine years, and with every year that passed, England's chance to throw off Norman domination diminished.

And remember Bryan. Who killed him if not your noble English?

". . . foolish enough to think they will spare him?" Myles was asking her in the wake of what happened to be her gesture of denial.

Her eyes met his. "Then what can we do?"

"Move the villagers into the manor . . . and wait. 'Tis what Rolf would have done; we discussed it many times."

"But what—what of *Rolf?*"

"Rolf knew of the risk when he agreed to hold these lands of my lord William." It was Rufus who spoke.

Michael and John returned to the hall just then. "Myles," Michael said as they approached the others, "the tanner is gone. And so is Garth and the youth who works the smithy."

This was no surprise to Merlyn. "I think we are rid

of any who would betray us from inside the village," she said.

Myles gave her a long, level look, obviously deciding, behind those ice-blue eyes, just how much credence to give her words. "You know of no others?"

"Outre la ville entière! Aside from the entire village!" Bryce blurted out, thrusting the fingers of one hand through his hair. His agitation over the plight of the man he served was evident. "Mayhap we would be better off if all of Renford disappeared into *la forêt!"*

"Rolf would have been the last to give the order to desert his barony—and we'll not do any differently," Myles declared. "If there are any villagers who would side with their fellow Englishmen against their lord, they may leave. The granary will hold only so many, and I cannot spare any of my men to watch over prisoners. Those who are loyal to Rolf may seek the safety of the manor as long as we can manage." He looked at Merlyn again. "Will you tell them, or shall I?"

It sounded like a direct challenge.

"How long can we last?" she asked in reply.

"As long as we must. Surely word has gotten out to Lanfranc and he is dealing with this uprising—if 'tis truly such. I doubt there are enough men left in Northumbria willing to revolt again in the face of William's retaliation earlier. I believe we are not up against great numbers." He paused, glancing down at the floor with a thoughtful frown. "We will not budge from here; we will hold Renford for Rolf." When he looked up again, his expression was stony—as grim as any she had ever seen, on Norman or Saxon. "Though I would give my sword arm for the chance to spare Rolf's life," he added softly, "he would not want us to risk Renford and its people—

382

his wife and child—to save him. He considers himself your protector and provider now. Unconditionally."

His wife and child.

The words hit Merlyn like physical blows, and for a moment, she could not speak. Surely Rolf had communicated this belief to Myles if the man had spoken the words with such conviction. And there she'd been vacillating between Edward Smithsson and Rolf de Valmont—the man she'd married, no matter the reason. The man who, her intuition had revealed, loved her. And Raven, as well.

Still unwilling to accept the inevitability of Rolf de Valmont's death, Merlyn raised her gaze to Myles's, conjuring up the fortitude that had sustained her through the long weeks when she had lived in the *weald*, acting as leader and inspiration to her people. "We will go together, you and I, and tell all of Renford what has happened . . . and what you intend to do."

Rolf regained consciousness slowly, swimming upward from its murky depths like a sluggish fish toward daylight from the shadowed, muddy bottom of a pond. When he came fully awake, however, it was not daylight he encountered but continuing darkness. A terrifying darkness, for although he was gagged, his eyes were not covered and he could see nothing but blackness.

He jerked his head off the ground, straining to see, and was instantly rewarded with a bolt of excruciating pain tearing through his cranium. He groaned softly as the pain encompassed his entire head and increased in its pounding tempo.

As he remained absolutely still, waiting for the

hurt to subside even the smallest bit, he realized that he was also stiff and cold. The air he breathed was stale, dank. He lay on his right side, his cheek against the ground, and could feel a dirt wall behind him with his bound hands. But all these added discomforts were nothing compared to the agony in his head.

Sweet Jesu, where am I? In my grave? he had the presence of mind to wonder with a grimace as the throbbing slowly lessened to a tolerable level. He wanted to sit up but feared another burst of pain.

You can't just lie here like a beaten dog.

The thought roused him. Mentally bracing himself for what was to come, Rolf attempted to heave himself sideways to a sitting position. And failed. As he lost his balance and toppled back over, his head felt like it was exploding and he lay still for long moments, panting from his exertions. The skin on one side of his face and neck felt stiff, as if some substance had congealed upon it . . . like blood.

He tried to remember what had happened after he and Rufus had discovered André's body outside the village. The image that dominated his clearing mind was of Merlyn standing beside Edward Smithsson, her eyes communicating resoluteness to him.

At the memory, the pain from his head filtered down to his chest and threatened to cut off his breathing. He immediately attempted to clear his brain of everything but the will to sit up. In the void he tried to make of his mind, however, an idea came to him without warning.

He took a deep breath, set his teeth against the coming pain, and drew his knees up as close to his chest as possible. Before he could change his mind, he rocked sideways to his knees, braced his aching forehead against the ground, then heaved himself upward until he could sit.

He fell back against the rough wall, swimming in and out of consciousness from the crushing pressure inside his skull. His head lolled sideways before he fully came to again.

Why didn't they just kill me? he thought with a flicker of contempt for his attackers.

Because this is worse than death, he reasoned, playing devil's advocate.

Footfalls sounded on wooden floorboards above him, alerting him to the fact that not only was he about to have company, but also that he was beneath a building of some kind. He remained perfectly still, straining to identify the sounds overhead. Whoever it was, was none too stealthy.

The grating sound of movement above him and to his left reinforced his belief that someone was coming to him. He slowly raised his head and tried to focus on the source of the disturbance. The screech of hinges rusty from disuse came to him, but he could make out nothing save impenetrable gloom; and the harder he tried, the more his head hurt.

Rolf strained for a glimpse of some kind of light, but although the sound of the trapdoor slamming backward against a wooden floor came to him . . . although, from the awkward, careful movements of shoes scraping against wood, he could hear the tread of someone slowly descending what was more than likely a ladder, Rolf saw nothing. No brightening of the blackness, no movement of any kind.

The thought that he was blind came to him like a punch in the gut. The shock surpassed his wary curiosity as to who was approaching him. It surpassed even his feeling of doom as he sat there, helpless against being slaughtered like a trussed pig.

"Valmont?"

The voice penetrated his roiling emotions and distracted him for a moment. At whose mercy was he? Who had spoken?

He wouldn't give the man the satisfaction of grunting his acknowledgement through his gag, but rather sat silent and unmoving. Blind, injured, bound hand and foot, he'd never been in a sorrier situation in his life; never been on the losing side of a battle or defeated in any sort of altercation. If only Duke William could see him now. Degraded so by a motley bunch of Anglo-Saxons . . .

Self-pity, Valmont?

He stared in the direction of the person clumsily descending the ladder, suddenly discerning a faint and formless glow. Nebulous, blurred, but a definite brightening all the same. His spirits lifted a fraction.

"Are you still alive?" asked the voice. Rolf angled his head to better catch the sound, trying to ignore the discomfort the slight movement caused.

The voice was familiar. The odor of pitch, the soft hiss of fire, came to Rolf, and he realized the man held a torch. *That* was the pale beacon within the darkness around him.

Footsteps approached, and his gag was jerked loose. Rolf tried to lubricate his dry mouth with an equally dry tongue. "Is that you, Arthur?" he rasped, his voice hoarse from disuse.

"You don't recognize me?" The tanner chortled unexpectedly. The sound was strange to Rolf's ears, for he had never heard Arthur laugh. Unease skittered through him, but he suddenly wasn't sure it would be wise to reveal his disability. Perhaps, if he allowed his eyes to follow the pale glow of the torch and the direction of Arthur's voice, the man wouldn't catch on.

He may have been half blind, he may have been

wounded in the head, but if Arthur was the only one with him, he had a chance to find his way out of wherever he was if he could overcome the tanner. And then, by some miracle, he might be able to find his way back to Renford without encountering any other of Smithsson's band.

If the tanner knows you cannot see, he may be less vigilant.

True. It didn't seem to Rolf, at that point, that he had much more to lose.

"I cannot see."

Indeed, he couldn't see Arthur's reaction, but there followed a long silence. Sensing some kind of indecision, or even confusion, on the tanner's part, Rolf took advantage. "Where are we, Arthur?"

Arthur finally broke the silence. "Beneath their very noses."

Rolf stared in the direction of the torch, trying to think above the pain in his head. "The mill."

"Aye. But they'll never find you, even if they think to search upstairs."

"You left Margaret and the children to . . . guard *me?* A man bound and blind?"

"England's liberation is more important than . . . family concerns."

"Is that why you hid your family so well when first we came to Renford? Is that why you killed my destrier to feed your family?" Playing shamelessly on Arthur's obvious love for his wife and children, and the debt he owed Merlyn, Rolf continued, "Is this how you pay the lady Merlyn for saving your life?" His words were quiet, softly condemning.

The question was a gamble, for if Arthur knew Merlyn was in league with Smithsson, he, Rolf, was only reminding the tanner that she wouldn't care what happened to him one way or another.

His chest began to ache again, the open wound that was his heart throbbing almost as tremendously as his skull.

"Is this how you repay me for putting food on your table?" Rolf pressed. "For giving shelter to your wife and children? For protecting them from harm?"

If Arthur were the least unstable, Rolf reasoned, then perhaps he could use it to his own advantage. It certainly was worth a try. . . .

Rolf couldn't see Arthur, but the tanner was suffering in his own way.

The sight of a helpless Rolf de Valmont vividly reminded him, for some strange reason, of Harold Godwinson as he'd fallen at Hastings. Blinded, wounded, shamelessly being butchered . . .

Except that Valmont wasn't being attacked as he sat there, and only Erik and himself were around at the moment to do the Norman any more harm.

He held the torch higher, noting the caked blood on Valmont's face and neck, the way he stared sightlessly ahead, speaking *toward* Arthur, not directly at him.

The dreaded, familiar ache began at the back of Arthur's head. Images flashed before his mind's eye: five men and himself sitting by the light of a fire and plotting against a man who had helped Renford rise from the ruins. And then Valmont sitting before him, speaking to him, persuading him to attend the wedding celebration after he, Arthur, had killed a prized war-horse.

As Rolf's lips moved, Arthur heard words that the Norman had uttered to him weeks ago: *As I am loyal to my duke, so can I understand your loyalty to and grief over the loss of your king. . . . There are two*

*sides to every story. . . . Neither can you wallow in
self-pity . . . live in the past while life goes on; while
your wife and children, your friends and neighbors
try to rebuild their world. . . . I need you to help
me rebuild Renford's future—England's future. . . . I
did not kill your king . . . your king . . . your king . . .*

"Arthur!" a voice called softly but urgently from
above him, rescuing him from the haunting echoes
of Rolf de Valmont's words. And the shattered
remnants of his conscience.

He looked up at Erik, hovering over the edge of the
opening above him. The torch cast flickering
shadows upward and across his young face, gilding
his white-blond hair. "Is aught amiss down there?
Do you need me to watch over him?"

"Nay. Go back to your post . . ."

The creak of the ladder rungs under Erik's weight
was his answer. Only Erik was cautious enough to
close the trapdoor behind him.

To Rolf, it sounded like the door of a stone
sepulchur slamming shut forever, sealing him in his
own tomb.

Easy now. All is not lost . . . yet.

"Who comes now?" Rolf demanded of Arthur.

Erik had reached the bottom of the ladder. "I see
he's still demanding as ever, even though he's naught
more than a prisoner."

The voice was familiar, but Rolf couldn't quite
put it with a face yet. He needed to hear more, and
Erik obliged. "'Tis Erik, the smithy and loyal
English subject. Are you blind?"

Ignoring Erik's scornful question, Rolf asked,
"Just why am I here, Arthur? Why didn't you kill me
while you had the chance in the forest?"

He sensed Arthur's uncertainty, whatever it meant
for him, and determined to elicit any information

389

about their plans that he could.

"All of England is rising up, Norman," Erik answered before Arthur could speak. If Rolf couldn't see the excitement in his eyes, he could surely hear it in his voice. "Even the Danes are coming to our aid. When your men agree to leave England forever, you may go with them. But not until that time."

It sounded ludicrous to Rolf. Surely the youth was uninformed . . . or the men behind such a plan were idiots. "My men won't leave Renford. They have my direct orders never to do such a thing . . . *no matter what.*"

"Then you are a dead man," Erik told him after a moment of silence, his attitude not quite as bold as before. "And we will attack. . . . My lord Waltheof brought two score of men with him to take Renford."

Waltheof, Earl of Huntingdon? Rolf thought, more than a little surprised. It couldn't be. The man was held in high esteem by none other than William himself.

Rolf kept his gaze down, trying to hide a half-smile at the thought of Smithsson and his band trying to take Renford . . . Waltheof be damned. Myles would never give up Rolf's barony, even in the event of Valmont's death, until William himself sent orders. And even were Waltheof actually involved, as Erik had said . . . even if he'd brought men with him, Archbishop Lanfranc, in whose hands William had left the administration of England while he was in Normandy, was no fool. He was clever and capable and would crush any revolt by summoning not only Norman lords established in England, but also English lords who'd accepted Duke William's rule.

The only blight on Rolf's thoughts was that he undoubtedly wouldn't live to see the uprising crushed. And that Merlyn, the woman to whom he'd knowingly, foolishly, given his heart, had thrown that love in his face and betrayed him.

It was bitter, bitter gall. Worse than the thought of death.

But didn't you know all along that it might come down to this?

"What do we do . . . just wait like sitting ducks?" Merlyn demanded of Myles. She hated the way her concern for Rolf made her sound like a shrew. But she couldn't help it.

They were in Rolf's and Merlyn's bedchamber, along with Michael, for the hall below was crowded with villagers. The yard held all the village livestock—though not much, still enough to take up some of the space. No one besides the small group in league with Edward Smithsson (except for Erik and, to Merlyn's disappointment but not surprise, Arthur) had elected to leave Renford. This provided a great measure of comfort for Merlyn. Yet, she thought bitterly time and again, to what purpose without Rolf? She had Raven, safe and sound, but she loved Rolf, as well. And as long as she lived, she would never shed the heavy burden of guilt she now carried.

Margaret, the tanner's wife, had been beside herself with worry—as much for Arthur as for what Myles might do to her as punishment for her husband's traitorous disappearance. "And after you saved his life," she'd lamented tearfully to Merlyn. "He even told me once that perhaps my lord Rolf was right . . . rebuilding our home and providing for our family should be the focus of our lives now." She'd begun to weep anew.

"A man must do what he must. Arthur followed

391

his beliefs," Merlyn told her in an attempt to comfort her. "And we don't know for certain that he is on the other side," she offered. Yet she could see that Margaret wasn't any more convinced than she was by this reasoning.

". . . we wait, for the hundredth time," Myles was saying, breaking into Merlyn's thoughts.

"Like cowards!" she cried, frustrated. "We hide behind the palisade and do nothing!"

Myles looked up from a crude map of the surrounding area he'd been studying with Michael. "You would have us go blindly charging into the forest? We have no idea where they are or how many there are." He shook his head. "My task is to hold Renford secure . . . to wait for reinforcements, which will surely be here soon. Lanfranc will swiftly put down this rebellion."

He didn't mention Rolf, and that was extremely disturbing to Merlyn.

"And what of your *friend*? Your *ami*!" she shouted, using one of the few Norman French words she'd bothered to remember. "Would the Conteville brothers have left him out there to be slaughtered?" she waved a hand agitatedly toward the window behind her. "I think not!"

Myles's eyes turned icy, his expression taking on the appearance of carved bedrock. "That cannot be helped. I am under orders not to sacrifice *one* life, not *one* bit of land, not *one* animal by walking into a trap to spare Rolf's life. Do you understand, woman? I am under orders from Rolf himself, and he knew exactly what he was doing when he issued them . . ."

A knock sounded on the door. "Merlyn?" came the muffled call. "Merlyn!"

Merlyn walked to the door and opened it. Elsa stood before her, her eyes alight with a secret excite-

392

ment that unexpectedly sent hope careening through Merlyn.

Don't be a fool.

Merlyn stepped into the passageway and closed the door behind her. Elsa grabbed her arm and pulled her into a shadowed corner of the corridor, breathless from climbing the stairway.

"Elsa, someone could have fetched me for you. Why did you take the stairs yourself?"

"I'm not dead yet," the older woman replied, a trace of contempt in her voice for any such weakness. "And I have news that is more important than my health. 'Tis worth ascending a hundred steps to tell you"—she directed a furtive glance about them—"and only you. No one else must know, or all could be lost."

Merlyn's heart thudded against her ribs in reaction. She opened her mouth to ask what Elsa had to tell her, but the old woman was already speaking.

"The Wolf is alive . . . wounded, but alive. I can feel it here." She touched a palm to her heart. "I know it here." She touched a finger to her head. She lowered her voice even more, so that Merlyn had to bend her head to catch the last words. "We are almost certain he is nearby . . . so close that you won't believe it!"

Chapter 24

The messenger was exhausted, barely able to speak. He was also wounded in his side. It looked as if an arrow had hit him and, fortunately, struck a protecting rib. How he'd managed to get to Lexom, Edward Smithsson could only wonder.

"What news?" Waltheof asked, his face taking on a bleak cast.

"They say—say that Wulfstan, b—bishop of Worchester . . . and Aethelwig, abbot . . . Evesham . . . have stopped Roger of B—Breteuil . . . from advancing out . . . of Herefordshire to meet—meet d—de Gael." He paused, gasping in air, his face pale as chalk.

"From whence do you come? To whom did you speak?"

"Stamford. A . . . m—messenger from Norwich."

The man had come all the way from Stamford? Edward thought, more than a little astonished.

They were in one of the few remaining cottages in Lexom, the second of only two buildings that were salvageable. With some patching and propping, they made it into a serviceable shelter against the bitter November winds and sleet, while the other served as cramped sleeping quarters for Waltheof's men, six or seven a shift.

A few hearty souls who had remained hidden among the ruins at Lexom rather than going to Renford were interested in joining up with an English earl . . . especially allying themselves with Waltheof, who was the son of the late Siward, English Earl of Northumbria.

"And de Gael?" Waltheof asked sharply as Edward and Will helped ease the wounded man to a pallet of straw upon the earthen floor and gave him water. The messenger choked, earning an "Easy now" from Smithsson.

"Barred same way . . . by Bishop Odo . . . Geoffrey of C—Coutances . . . Richard, son of Count Gilbert. And . . ." he coughed again, then added, "William of Warenne."

Waltheof's lips thinned, and Edward's somber look turned maniacal. "It cannot be!" the latter said, still holding the messenger up with an arm braced beneath his shoulders. He motioned Marthe over from the pot she was attending by the fire.

"Where is de Gael now?" pressed Waltheof.

"Retreated. Norwich."

"I cannot believe so many Englishmen would be so solidly behind the Bastard!" Waltheof hissed, pacing the room with jerky, agitated steps. "Traitors—all of them!"

"'Twould seem they are cowards, as well," Edward added, lowering to the floor the man he'd been tending. He cast Marthe a dubious look through his lashes before he relinquished his care of the messenger. "They fear for their precious hides too much to leave the side possessing the advantage."

Edward stood, his eyes narrowed in thought. "That doesn't mean the uprising has been crushed.

Anything could happen now. What we need to do, my lord earl, is take the manor at Renford. Send proof of Valmont's imminent demise if they won't surrender the village."

Waltheof looked at Edward, obviously formulating his own plan. "Aye. Shall we send them some gruesome token from their great leader to prompt them to move? A hand? An eye? Mayhap his heart?" He shook his head at his last suggestion. "Nay. We'll save the heart for last. Let them know he suffers as they remain obstinate, and send such parts without which he can still survive . . . in agony."

"With more than two score of men, we should be able to take the village even if they refuse to budge in the end," Edward said.

"I cannot believe that more of the villagers have not shown up to join us," Waltheof mumbled to no one in particular.

"They may be held against their will in Renford, or by some kind of threat to a wife or child. There is no level to which the Normans will not stoop."

Waltheof began to pace again. When he stopped before Smithsson, he slammed one fist into his palm and said "Aye" in a savage voice. "But time is on *their* side . . . not ours."

Rolf lost track of time in his Stygian-black prison. Only when Arthur came to see him did he catch glimpses of light of any kind through the haze of his impaired vision. The tanner gave him water once a day and one meager meal. He also gave him a blanket, scant but welcome protection against the cold dampness that seeped into his very bones.

A normally active and extroverted man, the incarceration, the inactivity and cramped position, and the lack of companionship worked detrimentally on him. Even though the pain in his head eased a little with each passing day (or what seemed like passing days to Rolf), his constantly agitated thoughts, mostly of Merlyn's perfidy and the fate of his men and the people of Renford, did nothing to help the healing process. Even his dreams were confusing, frightening, and increased his sense of helpless frustration.

The only ray of hope was that he noticed his sight was slowly improving, as if, now and again, a layer of fine linen were being unwrapped from around his head and face, rendering the images before him in the torchlight increasingly clearer. Far from what it had been, but better than the near total blindness that had afflicted him right after he'd been struck in the head . . .

One day (Rolf guessed, after wheedling a bit of information from Arthur and doing some of his own calculations, it was about a sennight after his imprisonment) the tanner opened the trapdoor and descended the ladder in his usual ungainly-sounding manner. Rolf knew the sounds—the clumsy cadence of Arthur's shoes shuffling against the rungs, the creak of the wood beneath his weight, the sibilant song of the lighted torch—by heart.

He looked up at the tanner when Arthur finally stood before him, squinting against the remaining haze impeding his vision. The flare of the brand hurt his light-sensitive eyes, and his shoulders and arms ached from always being in the same awkward position. In fact, every muscle in his body ached. And Judas, but he stank! The stale air in the crude underground cell was rank enough to cause a man coming in from the fresh outdoors to reel, Rolf was certain, even though he himself was accustomed to it.

The pain, the filth, his weakness from inactivity and lack of proper diet, did nothing to improve his spirits.

He stared up at Arthur for a long moment, then looked directly past him to the opposite dirt wall. "Why don't you just seal the trapdoor and be done with it?" he asked in a voice empty of expression.

"They won't let you die so easily. They want to send proof to the village that you are still alive." His voice was utterly lifeless, as reft of emotion as if it hurt to move his lips and make a sound.

Rolf looked up at him. "By all means, Arthur, give them my breeches—soiled and stinking as they are—and no one will doubt that I am very much alive and . . . functioning." He had the maddest urge to laugh, but not the energy, so he gave the tanner a grimacelike grin.

"You don't understand. They want me—us—to lop off your . . . hand."

Nausea spiraled up from the depths of Rolf's empty belly. Not so much at the thought of the pain of such an injury, but rather at the prospect of getting deathly ill at the sight of gore from his own severed limb . . . and before the two men who held him captive . . .

You'll die anyway from loss of blood, so what difference if the entire village—the entire English army of rebels!—learns of it?

The little color in his face drained away at the thought of his bleeding to death . . . *after* fainting from the very sight. How fitting, he had the presence of mind to think. The final degradation.

He dragged his gaze back to meet Arthur's in the flickering light from the flambeau. The man's features, skewed unnaturally under the best of circumstances, took on a pitiful expression now, and

Rolf got the distinct impression that Arthur the tanner had no liking for the task he'd been assigned.

Raising shaky, bound hands (which had been brought around from behind him a day or so before) and managing to inject just a hint of irony in his voice, he said, "Lop away, tanner, if that is what you must do . . ."

"You must create a diversion of some kind," Merlyn whispered to Cedric. They were in the shadows of one corner of the cow byre. "There is no way I can get out of the manor yard. . . . There are armed men at regular intervals about the palisade and wall." Her breath made puffs of vapor in the cold night air, and she drew her woolen mantle more snugly about her body. "I would have to be invisible to scale the stockade or the stone wall . . . and 'twould be even more difficult to open a gate."

Cedric shook his head, leaning closer to one of the oxen in obvious search of warmth. Merlyn could just discern the movement. "You cannot go alone in search of my lord," he whispered urgently. "We cannot be certain he is even *there* . . . in spite of what Elsa says. And even if you get out of the yard, 'tis folly for a woman to go alone!"

She couldn't believe the sudden obstinacy of the man.

"You didn't always think that way, Cedric of Renford. Have you of a sudden lost your trust in me? The faith you put in me when you were hurting so?" The words sounded harsh to her own ears, but that had been the way of it only months ago. She couldn't afford to let him forget that fact, when Rolf's life might be hanging in the balance while Cedric decided whether or not to shed his male pride.

He lowered his chin and stared silently at the ground between them. An ox lowed. Then he said, very softly, "I'll go."

"Nay! He's my husband. *I* harbored traitorous thoughts toward him and his men. I *must* go . . . or I'll never be able to live with myself, don't you see?"

"Then let me go with you. We can create some sort of diversion and . . . oh, God, I owe you so much, Merlyn. And *him* as well."

Merlyn heard the anguish in his lowered voice, and she put a hand on his arm. "Surely you realize, Cedric, that you cannot go." She couldn't bring herself to say any more. He knew there were certain things he could not do as well as a man with both legs; slipping softly through the forest was one of them.

Before he could answer, Merlyn said, "Bryce! Bryce would go against Myles's orders if 'twas to save Rolf, I would wager aught! Bryce can go with me while you create a diversion."

She turned her face up to his expectantly in the darkness, her spirits lifting, for Bryce was young but capable . . . and certainly loyal, above all, to Rolf. Only a youth might do something as rash and risky as this, and Merlyn was counting on that.

"Aye. Bryce would be the one," Cedric murmured. "He can help get you over the wall, offer you some protection while you search the mill. . . ."

No one thought anything of it when, long past midnight according to the time-keeping candle that burned in the hall, Elsa moved out of the manor and into the yard like a wraith. Over the past dozen or so days it had become the old woman's habit, when she couldn't sleep, to wander about the yard, staring up at the moon and stars, or training her gaze on the *weald* with rapt attention, head canted slightly. Sometimes she would enter the barn or the byre, the small henhouse or the pigsty, seeming to communicate silently with or to take comfort from the animals therein. No one knew exactly why, and no one particularly cared.

But this night she had a mission as she entered the crudely enclosed pigsty. When she emerged moments later, the light wind billowing out her skirts and mantle with chill but gentle puffs, there was nothing to indicate that she concealed beneath her clothing the two piglets Rolf had caught in the woods.

She turned slowly and walked south, past the empty sheep's pen and the henhouse, to where the high stockade gave way to the lower stone wall. To where existed a small hole burrowed beneath the stone by a persistent puppy, who was wont to explore the forest across the road that wound past the manor.

She stood for a while, her face lifted to the overcast sky, thankful for the absence of celestial light this night. An armed Norman walked by her and nodded in her direction. But Elsa appeared to be elsewhere, and the guard didn't disturb her. He moved on and stopped to speak in low tones to another Norman, just the other side of the henhouse.

Elsa glanced sharply farther north, to where the wall angled east to parallel the road for a ways. The other guard at the southern end must have been patrolling farther east in those moments, for there was no sign of him.

After a surreptitious glance over her shoulder to make certain the other two men were still on the opposite side of the henhouse, Elsa marshaled all her energy and surged toward the burrowed hole beneath the wall to her right. She loosed the first sleepy piglet from beneath her mantle and shoved it through the opening. Before it could even let out a squeak, with surprising swiftness, she did the same to the other. Only this time, she jabbed a thorn in the animal's behind, sending it squealing into the night, causing its companion to emit a similar cry of fright and increase the speed of its unexpected flight to freedom.

At the same time, she heard the whiz of an arrow, saw the burst of flame arcing overhead and toward the trees west of the wall.

Cedric, she thought with an inner cackle of jubilation.

As the sky briefly lit up above her, she felt the first pain shoot through her chest. At first she thought it was exultation, as she heard the whoosh of flames from the burning arrow that landed and fired the dry carpet of leaves on the forest floor a good stone's throw west. But the white-hot stab cut off her breath, much as it had when the Wolf had carried her to her cottage that one day.

And Elsa knew it was her time.

In one last calculated attempt to lure the Norman guards away from the half-hidden but incriminating burrow, Elsa threw herself to the ground. With the last of her fading strength, the old woman rolled toward the henhouse like an ancient dervish . . . until her failing heart stopped beating and she could move no more.

The shrieking animals, the shouting of men, and the crackling of a growing conflagration came to Merlyn on the wind. She and Bryce were huddled among several bales of hay at the north wall of the manor yard. They watched as men from the yard itself and others from the hall emerged into the cold night in response to the commotion.

As figures moved swiftly toward the west stockade, she and Bryce crawled toward where the northern stockade turned into a lower stone wall. After a quick look behind them, Bryce whispered *"Allez-y,"* and linked his hands to boost her to the top of the wall. He vaulted up after her, glanced over his shoulder again, then grabbed Merlyn's hands and lowered her to the other side and the refuge of the trees. He quickly followed, dropping lightly to his feet.

"At all cost," Merlyn warned into his ear, *"be silent."*

He nodded, although Merlyn could feel the movement rather than discern it in the darkness, and they carefully crept along the wall toward the Tees to the east. They reached the river without incident, the commotion they'd left behind fading into the distance. As they turned north to follow it, however, Merlyn suddenly halted, squeezing Bryce's arm to signal him to do likewise. A man, limned by the faint glow from the opening in the trees above the river, knelt on the riverbank, drinking from his cupped hands.

Bryce motioned for Merlyn to remain where she was and crept up behind the stranger. It seemed to take forever to Merlyn, but Bryce was being slow and very cautious, a credit to the youth. In fact, he moved so slowly at first—being in training as a chevalier rather than as a man who would fight by creeping stealthily through the woods—that the stranger finally shook the water from his hands and moved to stand.

In that moment Merlyn watched, her heart jumping into her windpipe, as Bryce attacked the man from behind and slit his throat. She let out her breath, relief seeping through her at the efficiency with which the squire executed the move. Bryce motioned for her to continue on toward the mill.

Rolf watched as Arthur retreated into his own world, his face in his hands as he rocked back and forth. Rolf could feel pity for him, even now, as he raised his bound wrists and finished his daily ration of water.

You softhearted fool. He'll maim, then kill you.

The tanner obviously was in pain, having suffered a blow to the head. Rolf wondered if he, likewise, would experience such debilitating pain for the rest of his life.

What life? 'Twill be too short to matter now.

He pulled his gaze from Arthur and his silent struggle and stared at his own bound wrists. The cord was frayed a little but otherwise secure. He'd earned scraped and bleeding wrists for his attempts to work the knot loose. He glanced down at his ankles. He was so stiff that he could barely reach them, let alone attempt to untie them. He had tried several times since they had been so foolish—or was Arthur being compassionate?—as to have rebound his wrists in his lap as opposed to the exquisite torture of behind his back. But to no avail.

With a mental sigh, he carefully set down his cup and slowly bent forward, his gaze going to Arthur. The tanner was still preoccupied, and just as Rolf's fingers made contact with the rope he was struck, once again, by the thought that Arthur often acted more like his protector than his guard.

True, the tanner only gave him his one meal and cup of water, but from what Rolf had observed, the man didn't eat much more himself. Erik didn't look any too robust, either. And Arthur hadn't yet done him any injury, as he'd warned Rolf earlier.

Had something possibly gone awry in Smithsson's plans?

Perhaps the tanner didn't have the nerve—who knew what went on in the man's mind?—and was waiting for the eager Erik to do the grisly work. If that were the case, Rolf thought with a twist of his lips, he didn't have much time. Once they began chopping him into pieces, he had no doubt it would be the beginning of the end for him, for there was no way they could return him in such condition to Renford without Myles and his men wreaking bloody vengeance on them all.

It was difficult to get any leverage from his fingers alone. His bottom was numb, and it hurt his back to bend stiff muscles so far forward. He'd acquired the habit of tightening the muscles in each part of his body for several moments, then relaxing them, in an effort not only to pass the time, but also to maintain some sort of strength and suppleness. Nonetheless, his back and leg muscles protested every inch of the way to his ankles.

After what seemed like hours, Rolf gave up. He slowly pulled his torso upright, waited for the ache in his head to subside, then leaned back against the cold wall.

His spirits were at a dangerously low ebb.

He looked over at Arthur, who was asleep. Then, exhausted, Rolf dozed, too.

The sound of the trapdoor rudely jarred Rolf from fitful slumber. He started and straightened, his hurting body forgotten, just as Erik descended the ladder. Arthur, too, sat erect, as the youth skipped the last four rungs and landed on the ground. He spun around, a dagger in his hand.

"We've got to kill him. *Now.*"

Arthur heaved himself to his feet, his expression wary. "Why? Who gave the command?"

Edward Smithsson's head appeared in the opening above. "*I* did."

Without warning, a body was shoved into the cell below, tumbling to a halt at Erik's feet.

Rolf could only stare, squinting to focus against the haziness that still refused to disappear. . . .

Merlyn.

As Edward nimbly descended the ladder and came to stand before them, horror washed over Rolf. No matter what she had done, even betrayal, he still loved her. And the sight of her lying unmoving in a heap on the dirt floor made his chest constrict with a shocking surge of uncharacteristic fear and denial.

"She's not dead yet, Valmont," Edward told him, a gleam of triumph lighting his eyes in the wavering torchlight. He jerked his chin toward the ceiling. "But your squire lies above in his own blood. 'Twould seem the young fool came along with your loving wife in search of you."

Slowly, steadily, rage invaded Rolf's brain, dispelling the mind-numbing fear. It gathered speed, sweeping through every part of him until he was tingling for action, hungering for vengeance, physical pain and weakened state not gone yet all but forgotten.

Arthur moved over to Merlyn and carefully turned her onto her side. "My lady?" he queried softly, his face close to hers.

"Leave her, tanner, for she's of no use to anyone," Edward growled.

It was as if Arthur hadn't heard him. He pushed back her hair and stroked her pale cheek, crooning softly, unintelligibly.

"This is almost too convenient," Edward said to

Rolf. "Now we can kill you both."

"Your hostage ploy didn't work, I see. What kind of milksops do you think my men to be?" Rolf's tone was one of pure contempt. "You can cut me up limb by limb, kill me a thousand times, but 'twill change naught. You haven't a chance, Smithsson, and you've no right to disillusion these people who look to you for guidance. You've no right to lead them to their deaths for a lost cause."

Rolf watched with a niggling satisfaction as Smithsson's face turned red with anger, before he delivered his final salvo: "And I think most of the people of Renford know that I am a better thane than you. Look at the pitiful following you have . . . where *are* they? *Who* are they besides a boy and a man injured in his mind by war?"

"You are *no thane*, Norman *nithing!* How dare you compare yourself to an English thane?" He drew his dagger, and Erik, from behind him, did likewise.

"Wake up, my lady," Arthur murmured to Merlyn in the background. "Wake up!"

In that tension-fraught moment, the tanner's words seemed to come from another world, but to Rolf's relief, Merlyn stirred in response.

"Merlyn?" Arthur said to her, seemingly oblivious to everyone else present. He helped her to sit up.

The first person she saw, sitting across from her, was Rolf.

The confusion clouding her eyes cleared, and her lips formed his name.

"I suspect you'll have to kill all three of us now," Rolf said to Edward when he'd dragged his gaze from his dazed wife. "Arthur may not care about me, but he is loyal to Merlyn."

Edward glanced at Erik, then said to Rolf, "Gladly. I'll take the English whore first. . . ."

"Something reeks here," Myles said to Cedric, his eyebrows drawn together in a fierce frown. "Elsa found dead, her body still warm . . . a fire started in the forest . . . where *pigs* were heard shrieking in the night . . ." He leaned toward Cedric, who stood before him, balanced on his crutch and looking both guilty and defiant at the same time. "Although I can understand the rebels firing the trees across from the manor to draw us out, I doubt they would waste two precious pigs to add to the confusion. And I doubt Waltheof would have gone to the trouble of bringing live pigs along for food when he can readily hunt game."

"And the old woman . . ." added Rufus. "*Our* pigs are gone, and not far from her body John found a small burrow beneath the wall." He shook his head and pursed his lips, a suspicious look in his eyes. "And the fire was barely started . . . too easy to put out . . ."

"Where's the lady Merlyn?" Myles asked Cedric tersely, cutting Rufus off.

"And Bryce is missing, as well," Michael threw in before Cedric answered, his face smeared with soot, his cloak, tunic, and breeches looking as if he'd been through a battle. "We cannot find him."

"What is afoot here?" Myles demanded of Cedric. "What do you know of this?"

Cedric's features hardened with determination. "Naught. I am just as concerned about Merlyn as you . . . and Bryce, as well, for I have no idea—"

Myles grabbed a handful of the Saxon's tunic and jerked him closer. The crutch fell to the floor, its landing muffled by the rushes to a soft *thunk*. As Myles's gaze knifed into his, Cedric knew he couldn't buy much more time, for it was quite apparent this man was a capable leader. He was less inclined to leniency or tolerance than Rolf de Valmont, and was obviously dead serious about getting to the bottom of this latest string of strange events.

"You're lying," he snarled softly into Cedric's face.

His balance totally dependent on the Norman who looked ready to slay him, Cedric was at a definite disadvantage. And he was beginning to feel like a fool, as well. "What if it meant the difference between life and death for my lord Rolf?"

Myles gave him one brain-scrambling shake with his mighty sword arm. "In all likelihood, Rolf is dead. My concern now is for his wife and squire, two of those he entrusted to *my* care." He shook Cedric again, holding him up like a rag doll at the same time.

The humiliation was bad enough, but Cedric pushed that aside as he assimilated Myles's words. If they couldn't save Rolf, might they not at least attempt to rescue Merlyn and Bryce?

What a coil! he thought with self-reproach. And all because he had helped Merlyn in her very risky—if not impossible—bid to find and free Rolf.

"Well?" Myles repeated, nose to nose now with Cedric . . .

Chapter 25

"Get away from her, tanner."

Arthur looked up, turning his good eye toward Smithsson. "She needs me."

"She'll need no one where she's going," Edward said, and motioned Arthur aside impatiently. "Move and let's be done with this."

Arthur slowly shook his head. "Merlyn will always be one of our own. And she saved my life." He glanced at the floor with a thoughtful frown.

Erik went to take the tanner's arm, but Arthur jerked it away and looked up, his eyes suddenly narrowing with irritation at the youth.

"She didn't wed Valmont to save your life, fool," Smithsson said. "She wed him to share his bed every night. To help him convince our people that he was their master . . . that he could help them." His mouth turned down at the corners, his nostrils flaring with contempt. "She is a traitor to her people—just as she was a traitor to the Normans when she thought *we* would prevail. She changes her allegiance as easily as the wind changes direction. Now move aside, Arthur, else you die with her."

As Arthur slowly stood, Rolf said, "Let her go! Kill

me, rather. What use to kill a woman? She has a child—daughter of Stigand, no less—to raise. Surely the child will be an asset to the English . . ."

But Rolf was not only attempting to bargain for Merlyn's life, he was also trying to divert attention from Arthur, who appeared to be groping for something beneath his tunic. His dagger?

Rolf was taking the enormous chance that the tanner would side with Merlyn when it came right down to it. And, like the fool he was, he acknowledged, her life was still more important to him than his own.

Erik, once again, moved to take Arthur's arm. Rolf caught the gleam of a dagger blade as it fell to the ground behind Arthur.

Merlyn saw it as well. So, evidently, did Smithsson, for when Merlyn moved to grab it, Edward raised his own weapon and lunged toward her.

Several things happened simultaneously: Rolf, helpless where he sat, cried out his warning *"Merlyn!"* as he futilely tried to fling himself toward her; Erik hesitated a heartbeat, as if having second thoughts about what he was to do; and Arthur, taking advantage of Erik's indecision, pulled away from him and flung his body protectively before Merlyn's.

He took the savage blow meant for her between the shoulder blades and, with a low cry, slumped over her, blood staining his tunic in an obscenely spreading blotch.

Edward wasn't finished with her, however. He moved for her throat, wrapping his hands around her windpipe and squeezing. . . .

Merlyn felt the hilt of Arthur's weapon beneath her left hand, and she clamped onto it with a death grip. As Rolf's warning echoed in her mind, as the world began to turn black around the edges, she summoned

411

a last, desperate strength, fear boiling through her blood and propelling her to shove the blade into Edward's chest, between his ribs and into his heart.

He died instantly, a look of surprise frozen across his features forever.

As he dropped to the ground, Merlyn pulled herself from beneath Arthur and crawled toward Rolf. Her tunic was bloodied, but she appeared unharmed.

"Rolf . . ." she cried softly.

"Stay where you are!" Erik commanded from behind her. There was a note of panic in his voice.

She froze.

Rolf looked up at him. The youth looked poised to dispatch Merlyn with his dagger. The desperation on his face frightened Rolf more than the dagger he held high.

"If you touch one hair on her head, I'll personally see you strung up like the traitor you are and left for carrion."

If the youth had experienced any hesitation earlier, Rolf hoped he might yet be dissuaded, either by a dire threat or by the offer of leniency, to refrain from harming either of them.

"Cut me loose, then drop the dagger. If you do that, as your lord I'll spare your life, Erik . . . *do you hear me?"*

Heavy footsteps sounded on the mill floor above them, startling them all.

Erik looked up at the trapdoor, and Rolf knew exactly what he was thinking. Was it Edward's men or Rolf's?

"Join me and fight like a man. Or, if 'tis Waltheof's men, I'll tell them you betrayed them. And you'll die, just like Smithsson here."

"And if 'tis not?" Erik whispered, the expression

412

on his young, vulnerable face suddenly genuinely fearful.

"Your life will be spared."

The footfalls were almost to the trapdoor; muffled voices could be heard.

"Quickly! Make up your mind!"

Erik leapt across the space between them, cut the ropes that bound Rolf, and dropped the dagger into his lap. He flattened himself against the wall then, his eyes going to the closed door above.

Arthur groaned softly, and Merlyn turned her head toward him.

"Later! Come here!" Rolf commanded softly.

Just as she reached his side, the trapdoor was thrown open with a clatter. A torch was thrust inside and Myles's blond head appeared above it, his eyes going to the two bodies directly beneath the door. "What the devil is going *on* down there?" he demanded when his gaze alighted on Rolf and Merlyn, his expression as ferocious as the dragon on the prow of a Viking longship.

Relief—even a sliver of joy—threatened Rolf's composure at the sight of Myles's face. And he could just imagine how grimly determined he looked . . . filthy, disheveled, and clutching Arthur's dagger like a madman about to take on an entire army. "Come down and get us out of this cursed hole, Mortain," Rolf answered. "There is no danger from anyone down here now."

Myles descended the ladder and stepped over the bodies until he was before Rolf, who was attempting to get to his feet. Merlyn took him under one arm, and Myles under the other. "*Dieu,* but it stinks like a cesspit down here!" the blond chevalier commented, wrinkling his nose.

"What did you expect?" Rolf replied, gingerly

413

stretching cramped muscles. "If you'd come for me sooner, 'twouldn't have offended your sensibilities so."

"He wouldn't *allow* anyone to leave the manor grounds," Merlyn said darkly, casting Myles an accusatory look rather than one of gratitude. She was also glad for a chance to concentrate on someone other than Rolf, who wouldn't look directly at her now. "Bryce and I had to sneak away—"

"He was following my orders," Rolf told her, avoiding her eyes. He was afraid she would see exactly how desperately he loved her still. "And," he added, "no doubt was afraid you'd go running to Smithsson."

Guilt colored Merlyn's cheeks, yet she was also taken aback by the bitterness in his voice. Hadn't she come after him, at risk to her own life? Hadn't she left Raven?

She saw a flutter of movement out of the corner of her eye and suddenly remembered Arthur as they moved toward the ladder. She left Rolf to go to the downed tanner, rescued from her dark ruminations. As she gingerly turned him onto his back, he mumbled, "M—Margaret . . . children . . ."

From the bleeding through his mouth and nose, Merlyn knew he was mortally wounded. "I . . . we shall see to them, Arthur, I give you my word." She sat beside him and held his head in her lap. "Now you must be quiet. Save your strength to heal."

Rolf pushed away from Myles, dropping to his knees beside Merlyn and the wounded man. "You are a brave man, tanner," he said softly. "You saved your lady's life. Harold Godwinson surely was fortunate to·have you on his side."

Arthur opened his eyes and stared ahead unseeingly for a moment. Then he groped for Rolf's hand.

414

When he couldn't quite reach it, Rolf extended it and closed his fingers about Arthur's. "Good . . ." the tanner mumbled. "Good man . . ."

Blood bubbled from between his lips and Merlyn told him, "Do not speak, Arthur. Later you can—"

"R—regret . . . the horse . . ." he muttered, then grimaced in obvious pain. "Hungry, my lord. Soooo . . . h—hungry . . ."

"Speak of it no more. 'Tis over and done with." Rolf looked up at Merlyn, a question in his eyes.

She shook her head, an all but imperceptible movement. Her gaze fell before the unexpectedness, the steadiness of his.

"Thank you for saving Merlyn . . ." Rolf's words died off as the tanner gave a last gasp and his head lolled to the side.

"Rolf," Myles said, "Bryce is outside the mill, wounded. We cannot tarry. . . ."

Rolf nodded and released Arthur's hand. He stood stiffly and automatically offered Merlyn his hand. His eyes, once again, would not meet hers. The moment of shared sorrow over Arthur was gone.

"Erik . . ." Rolf looked at the youth, who was still hovering in the shadows. "Take Arthur to the village. Can you do that?"

Erik nodded and stepped forward, his gaze going briefly to Myles.

"Smithsson can rot down here for all I care," Rolf added coldly, and swung toward the ladder.

They managed to get back to Renford unchallenged, Bryce proving to be less of a burden than anyone would have thought before closer examination of his wounds. Just before dawn, however, a hail of arrows was directed at the manor itself. The weapons did little damage—it was obvious that most of them were not loosed by skilled archers—until the men in the shelter of the *weald* lighted them and aimed them at every thatched roof in Renford. The sight of fire in the village was nightmarish for its occupants.

Rolf consulted briefly with Myles before directing as many men as he could spare to put out the fires. If he could help it, the people of Renford would not have to see their village destroyed again. "Put on your mail," Rolf had ordered them, "and your helms as well. We'll see how effective these arrows are against moving targets."

Many of the Englishmen volunteered to risk their lives to save the village, including Erik. "They'll have no protection," Myles warned.

"They'll have their pride. Their need to protect what is theirs." Rolf shook his head, biting his lower lip thoughtfully. "I have little faith in these rabble warriors who hide behind trees."

He ordered one retainer to fetch his own mail, but Myles cautioned him, "You can do more good here, giving us cover from the palisade and putting your skill with a bow to good use."

"Oui," Rolf agreed bleakly. "I'm weak as a babe. How can I help put out fires, let alone support the weight of my mail? Judas, but 'twill be a miracle if I can even pull back a bowstring!"

As he looked at Myles, Hugh de Conteville's face materialized before him. *Save your pity for the English . . .*

". . . matter your condition, you'll still serve better as an archer," Myles was saying.

Rolf stood, took a long draught of mead, and answered, "Aye. That I will."

*   *   *

Merlyn had seen to Bryce's wounds and was preparing Elsa's body for burial. Margaret had helped her with Arthur, infinite sadness etching her face. A rush of vivid, ugly memories had assaulted Merlyn as they worked over the tanner . . . thoughts of other skirmishes, other bodies, other burials.

She took comfort, nonetheless, in the fact that Raven was safely at her side, and also, ironically, that they were protected by Norman warriors, no less.

Discreetly, Merlyn followed Rolf to the manor door and watched as he was assisted up to a simple platform behind the stockade to help defend those who were to leave the safety of the yard and put out the fires. Several of his best bowmen were already stationed along the palisade and essaying to pick off those who were shooting from the periphery of the forest.

Within a few hours the fires were put out, and any English rebels left alive in the *weald* had disappeared. Rolf had his men collect the bodies of those who had died for Edward Smithsson, including that of Garth, suspecting that Waltheof and his men had deserted them for whatever reason.

They remained within the shelter of the manor palisade for two more days, before returning to their homes. Rolf slept much of the time and, when he was awake, fed his increasing appetite. On the third day, Rolf, Myles, Rufus, and two other Normans rode to Lexom.

"They were here," Rufus observed, "but 'tis deserted now."

Rolf looked about the building that had briefly served as Smithsson's base. "I would wager Death Blow that Lanfranc put down the uprising. Waltheof got wind of it and fled." He walked over to the table, where sat a cold, empty pot. He sniffed it. "Rabbit stew. How fitting for Smithsson and his ilk—killers of women." He was thinking of how willing Edward Smithsson had been to kill Merlyn. An involuntary shiver moved through him at the thought of how close he had come to losing her. In spite of everything . . .

He moved to the cold hearth and, with the tip of his sword, lifted a charred remnant of what looked like a woman's overtunic.

"It could be Marthe's," observed Father Francis, who had accompanied them in case there were any wounded survivors in need of his services. His frown turned troubled.

"Aye. Will had no use for a wench who would only slow him down in his flight," Rolf said with a distasteful twist of his lips, "nor did the hate-filled Derwick."

"We've not heard the last of this," Myles predicted.

"Eh bien," Rolf agreed, "I wouldn't be surprised if my lord William came here himself to make certain all is quiet now. And I wager he'll not be so lenient as in the past with any English baron or earl who sided with the troublemakers . . . including his niece's husband, Waltheof of Huntingdon."

But even as he uttered the words, Rolf wondered how he would deal with Merlyn's treachery before William of Normandy . . . if he came to Northumbria. Even to hide the fact that Merlyn had conspired with Smithsson and Earl Waltheof would be treason, and there was no guarantee that if William of Normandy discovered it, he wouldn't put her to death. Or put them both to death . . .

He could only hope he wouldn't be placed in such a situation. His own feelings regarding Merlyn and

418

her vacillating allegiance were disturbing enough.

As if reading his mind, Myles had said to him the night before, when the hall was empty and he'd found Rolf sitting staring sightlessly into the blazing fire in one of the great hearths, "She risked her life to seek you out. . . . She even led Bryce to disobedience . . . the old woman to risk her fragile health. That should prove her loyalty."

Rolf had looked up from his blind contemplation. "I *saw* them in the forest that time she swore she was only following the tanner's wishes concerning the leather."

"And you should know how highly she regarded him. She sacrificed herself to save his life."

One side of Rolf's mouth crescented with rue. *"Merci, mon ami,* for the compliment."

Myles waved a hand in dismissal. "That's not the point. . . ."

"And what about her stand with Smithsson less than a fortnight ago? I *saw* the look in her eyes. There's no doubt in my mind: *She was with them.*"

Myles shook his head and turned away. "What happened to the gray area between right and wrong, Rolf? She is only human. . . ."

Rolf's expression turned angry. He stood to face his man, his fingers curling at his sides.

"She came to us, told us everything," Myles added before Rolf could speak, "then left the safety of the manor . . . left her *child,* to find you."

"I see, Mortain," he said with soft menace. "And she is just to be forgiven everything because she knew when to choose the winning side?"

"I didn't exactly say that . . . but then I'm not lord here, nor her husband . . ."

A commotion at the door of the cottage brought Rolf back to the present and the matter at hand.

Geoffrey, one of Rolf's retainers, dragged in a reluctant peasant and released him before Rolf. The man fell to his knees, his hands together in supplication.

"What is this?" Rolf asked, motioning Father Francis to his side.

"We found him outside, hiding behind a—"

"I was *not* hiding, my lord," the man said rather indignantly, in spite of his humble pose. "I was waiting to see who you were. . . ."

"A sorry excuse," said Geoffrey.

Rolf raised a hand to silence him. "Whatever your reasons, you are here now, whether you wish to be or not." He leaned to take an elbow and lift the man to his feet. "Tell us what you know of the English who were here in the days past . . . er . . ."

The peasant met Rolf's steady regard. "Harold, my lord. You see, I was bringing my family to Renford— I'd heard of the new Norman lord there who was helping the people rebuild—when we stumbled upon Lexom and the men who were here a sennight ago."

"And, of course, you sided with them," Geoffrey accused.

. . . because she knew when to choose the winning side . . . Myles's words came back to Rolf. Who was he to condemn this man for doing the same thing to protect his family? Yet, with Merlyn, it was different. She was his wife.

"Enough, Geoffrey," Rolf said curtly. "If you feared for your life, the welfare of your family, you couldn't very well tell them you were going to Renford of your own volition. I understand that." His voice lowered. "As long as you didn't kill any of my men . . ."

Harold shook his head emphatically. "Nay, my

lord. I did not."

"What happened to them? To Waltheof and his men?" Rolf pressed.

"They left one night. I heard them arguing . . . Edward Smithsson and Earl Waltheof. Later, one of Smithsson's men told me that the earl had heard of the scattering of two other armies advancing out of Hereford and Norfolk . . . that Archbishop Lanfranc was putting down the uprisings."

"Just as I thought," Rolf said, looking over at Myles.

Myles nodded and looked at Harold, openly suspicious. "You were *seeking* out Rolf de Valmont and Renford? A Norman lord in an Anglo-Saxon village?"

Harold looked at Myles, then Father Francis, then finally Rolf. "I am sick of war and death. I want naught more than to keep my family safe, to watch my children grow, the crops yield their bounty. I can accept, now, that which I cannot change."

Rolf studied him . . . his tattered clothing, his long, matted hair and beard. And the hope, the pride in his eyes. Here might be a man worth having on his side . . . a man to help Renford prosper.

"As Myles said, I am Rolf de Valmont. If you are willing to swear fealty to me, you and your family may accompany us back to the village and consider it your home." Harold looked relieved. "And if there are any others out there willing to do likewise"—he inclined his head toward the door—"you may tell them what they must do."

"Aye, my lord." Harold knelt before Rolf and Father Francis for the oath-taking.

An uncomfortable truce developed between Merlyn

and Rolf. Merlyn knew why (although she thought it unjustified) Rolf was cool but polite toward her, why he deliberately held her at arm's length. And Rolf was both relieved and disappointed that Merlyn didn't draw him out, didn't bring up the subject of what was keeping them apart physically . . . tearing them both apart inside, as well.

Merlyn felt that the very fact she had risked her life to find him was proof enough of her affection and loyalty, while Rolf felt she owed him an explanation and an apology. He literally expected her to beg his forgiveness for her connections with Smithsson and Waltheof, however transient.

One day in mid-December, Merlyn found Rolf standing before the cow byre, lost in thought. The wind whipped his mantle about his long legs, but his head was bowed in contemplation. He seemed oblivious to the cold, to the snowflakes that gently touched his dark hair, momentarily spangling it to silver in places.

In spite of herself, Merlyn was driven to enter the pen. She moved to stand beside him. "Elsa . . ." she mused aloud. "You miss her, too."

He looked up at her, startled by her presence . . . and the name of the wise old woman about whom he'd been thinking. He nodded, looking over at the two milch cows contentedly chewing their cud within the three-sided byre they shared with the oxen.

"She warned me of Smithsson's coming . . . several times."

Merlyn stole a glance at him through ebony lashes tipped with snow, but remained silent.

"She also told me your secret," he added in a low voice.

"My secret?"

"Aye." The corners of his mouth softened to a sad smile. "You once told me you spoke to the cows in Welsh. But Elsa showed me how to pen them."

The look on her face turned disbelieving. "You asked Elsa to show you how to pen the cows?"

"Mais oui. Wouldn't a good farmer know of such things?"

The disbelieving look turned to downright doubt. "You are a chevalier—a warrior, not a farmer."

She said it with such conviction that he unexpectedly felt the cold fingers of doubt skitter down his back. And, certainly, not for the first time. Maybe she was right. Maybe he *didn't* belong here. Why, he couldn't even win the respect and loyalty of his wife. And he certainly wasn't a farmer, no matter what he told himself.

Would he ever be?

What you don't know, your people will teach you.

Hugh's words, as they rarely failed to do, buttressed his flagging confidence. But he didn't answer Merlyn, turning his gaze back to the cows instead.

She walked away, wondering why she'd said such a thing aloud. And too proud to apologize.

As Rolf stood, lost once again in thought, a familiar sound came to him from the *weald.* He lifted his head and listened. He heard nothing but the low and lonely whip of the wind in the naked branches of the trees. He turned and left the pen, latching the crude gate behind him as he'd seen Elsa do scores of times.

As he walked toward the hall, he heard the sound again . . . and recognized it this time. Unexpectedly, it was like a bright and beckoning beacon in his dark thoughts. He grabbed Bryce, who was walking past carrying several bridles, by the arm. "Help me!" he said, his eyes alight with excitement like those of a child. "Come with me now . . ." He turned and strode toward the southern end of the manor grounds, then began to sprint toward the low stone wall that stood parallel to the road skirting that side of Renford and the woods beyond.

As he reached the wall and vaulted over it, Bryce, who'd dropped the bridles in a heap and was now nearing the wall in his attempt to catch up with his master, panted, "What is it?"

"Pigs!" Rolf shouted over his shoulder as he ran across the road, forgetting that Bryce was still healing from his wounds. "*Our* pigs!"

Merlyn, having seen Rolf and Bryce racing across the manor yard like two madmen, immediately informed Myles. The knight grabbed his swordbelt and ran out the door, mantleless . . . and smack into Bjorn.

"What's amiss?" the latter asked, alarmed.

"Rolf and Bryce . . . may need help," Myles said, and pushed past him. The big-boned, blond Dane followed Myles like a shadow across the yard.

"Hurry . . . here!" Rolf shouted to Bryce as he disappeared into the trees.

Myles's long legs swiftly ate up the distance to the wall, over which he leapt, and then the road. He followed Bryce's retreating back into the forest, with Bjorn in his wake.

Ten minutes later, the horn signaled visitors. Cedric hobbled down the stone steps and into the yard to see who was being admitted through the gate. Merlyn watched with a worried frown from the manor door, certain it had something to do with Rolf. Something that boded ill . . .

He was either madder than Arthur . . . or sadly in

need of diversion, Rolf thought with acerbity as he pursued the piglets who, through some minor miracle, were evidently alive and whole and still in the vicinity.

Yet by now, if nothing else, Rolf de Valmont definitely understood the value of pigs. And as he tramped through the mud and forest detritus, stinging branches whipping across his face, strangling vines winding around his arms and legs, more than anything he wished he had regained all of his old strength and fleetness. Much of it was restored, as was his vision, but he was not in the excellent physical condition he'd commanded before he'd been taken hostage. And his head still ached whenever he moved quickly. . . .

Well, whatever his disadvantages, he thought, he had no desire to fail at so lowly a task. And the animals were desperately needed to breed more of their own. So he pushed on, squinting against the tumbling snowflakes.

He could hear Bryce close behind him, hindered also, he guessed, by the brush and branches tearing at his skin and hair and clothing as they crashed through the woods.

They seemed to be making a half circle, Rolf realized, as the sound of the others in the trees behind him registered. Good, then the entire village could help round up the troublesome twins—as he was beginning to think of them—if they headed back toward the road on the south side of Renford.

Certainly a pair of piglets couldn't elude an entire village.

But these are Anglo-Saxon pigs, elusive and obstinate, like the men and women who bred them. . . .

"*Bien sûr*," he muttered under his breath as he felt a stitch begin to prick his side.

Suddenly, the trees thinned, and he caught sight of one of the creatures as it burst onto the road, its short legs pumping furiously.

And that wasn't all . . .

Pandemonium exploded on the rutted road that ran past the normally quiet Renford.

As Rolf came to a bone-jarring halt at the edge of the *weald*, through the shifting curtain of snow he saw at least a score of mounted Normans in full mail, destriers screaming as they reared and plunged beneath their riders while two piglets wreaked havoc between their platter-sized hooves.

Rolf put his hands to his head in frustration, his eyes closing for a fraction of a second. His piglets were going to be trampled before his eyes, wouldn't you know it. *"Dieu nous sauve,"* he appealed under his breath.

One of the little creatures, obviously possessing a better sense of direction than his companion, managed to dodge and dart his way back toward Rolf. The other tried to follow.

Before more than a score of Norman soldiers, Rolf de Valmont flung himself at the animal coming his way, pouncing on it with as much determination as if it were a fleeing cask of jewels. The other piglet, finally emerging from the hellish chaos of the road, followed pell-mell.

From farther back, a pale and overexerted Bryce could only stare, slack-jawed, at the prancing, plunging horses in the road. Myles, coming up behind him, did likewise, although he had the presence of mind to snap his mouth shut.

And so it was left to Bjorn, with the instincts of the true farmer, to regain his senses and snag the other panicked piglet before it disappeared into the forest behind them.

The squealing increased before it slowly began to subside; horsemen worked to regain control of their destriers. Rolf came to his feet cold, wet, and filthy, but evincing a sense of satisfaction nonetheless.

Until, through swirling snowflakes, he squinted up at one particular Norman moving toward him on his great war-horse . . .

And into the shrewd and piercing eyes of William, Duke of Normandy and King of England.

Chapter 26

"You've become quite the farmer, I see," William of Normandy said over a cup of wine.

Rolf, needing all the wine he could swallow to deal with his duke in the wake of the uprising, nodded, drained the cup, and helped himself to more.

Quite unexpected—and a pleasant surprise in an anything but pleasant situation—was Roger de Conteville's presence. Roger's appearance was not only one of the best things to happen to Rolf since the brothers had departed, but, bless the man! he'd thought to bring a few extra casks of Norman wine with him. In fact, as if that weren't enough, Roger had brought a small cart laden with goods, including several bolts of badly needed woolen cloth. And (Rolf's eyes had filled with very un-warriorlike emotion) four lovely sheep.

"He's becoming very adept at chasing pigs, my lord," Myles said, straight-faced, in answer to William's comment.

"Pork is scarce in Northumbria," Rolf, summoning his wits, said in his defense. "One day we'll have enough to feed the entire village through the winter. I am sick to death of hunting!"

William raised a dark eyebrow, obviously thinking about his own passion, the chase, and perhaps the fact that Rolf de Valmont had just admitted to hunting in the Royal Forest.

If William of Normandy was angry, he said nothing.

"Did you ever think you'd see the day when Rolf de Valmont would say he was sick of hunting?" Roger asked with a grin.

The duke shook his head. "Just so he doesn't lose his taste for protecting what is his . . . *ours*." He turned his head aside, and Merlyn, who'd been standing just outside the circle of Normans, caught the strong, aggressive lines of his jutting jaw. He was a tall, powerfully built man, with an aura of power and command about him that Merlyn recognized as that of a natural and successful leader. Also, there was a pent-up energy and a ruthlessness about him, as well.

Merlyn found herself hating him as much as ever. Seeing him in the flesh did nothing to endear him to her.

"We'll not remain here long," William told Rolf, "for I'm disinclined to be a burden to your scant resources."

Merlyn bristled. Now he was insulting their hospitality? How the villagers had contributed enough food to feed The Bastard and his men a substantial meal while they did without? . . .

"Although," he added, as if sensing the offense taken, "'twas one of the best meals I've had since returning to England." He looked at Merlyn, his piercing eyes drilling into hers. "And we appreciate your sacrifice, Lady Merlyn."

She nodded in acknowledgment, with as much grace as she could command under the circumstances;

but in spite of his words, a shiver moved through her. He was a formidable opponent, that much was apparent. But his next words made her earlier frisson seem like nothing compared to the fear and sense of loss he evoked in her.

"The Bretons here who supported de Gael are being dealt with ..." he trailed off, leaving no uncertainty in anyone's mind as to just how severely they were being dealt with, "while de Gael himself is hiding in Brittany. Roger of Breteuil has been captured, and Waltheof ..." his jaw grew rigid, "Waltheof is in prison outside Winchester. He will be executed for his treachery."

Merlyn felt sick inside. Waltheof, friend to her late husband, champion of the English ...

And fool enough to wed into William of Normandy's family and then betray his trust ...

"I would see what you have done in Renford, Valmont," William told Rolf, "and meet these villagers of yours. Have you executed any for collusion?"

Executed. The word ricocheted through Merlyn's brain.

Rolf shook his head. "Any who plotted with Smithsson or Waltheof were either killed in the fighting or disappeared."

Merlyn listened, stunned as Rolf lied to his lord. Not only was he protecting her, but the youth Erik, as well. That in itself was considered treason; punishable, she did not doubt, by death.

William nodded. "Then I would ask that you accompany us in our brief inspection of Renford and what you've done here before we leave."

Rolf nodded and stood. "If I may have leave to make myself more ... er ... presentable?" he asked with a wry slant of his lips.

William nodded, and as Rolf went upstairs, Roger de Conteville said, "You can only imagine the devastation we found when we arrived here only a few months ago, my lord. Rolf has risen to the task admirably," he smiled, obviously at the memory, "grumbling only now and again."

William gave him a hint of a smile in return. "So, one of my prized chevaliers has taken to farming, 'twould seem, in spite of his true preferences. I had thought to offer him the opportunity to return and fight on the continent with me, he's so superb a leader in battle. I can always find land-hungry men to take his place, but perhaps not . . ." He trailed off and glanced about the hall, at the few servants hurrying to and fro to refill empty cups and clear away empty trenchers, and at Merlyn who was now speaking quietly to Cedric, several tables away.

"Who is that man she speaks with?" he asked Myles.

"Cedric of Renford. An Anglo-Saxon who lost his leg at Hastings. He is Rolf's steward, and most capable . . . and loyal."

William nodded, stroking his clean-shaven chin as he studied the pair through assessing eyes. "Rolf, it seems, knows a man's strength does not necessarily lie in his limbs . . . a far cry from the warrior of a winter ago, eh, Mortain?"

"You do not give him enough credit, my lord. He was not quite that *obtus*."

"Dull-minded?" William shook his dark head. "I never thought such a thing, but mayhap I didn't give him enough credit in that respect." He eyed Merlyn one more time. "It seems he discovered something precious among the ruins." He stood and stepped away from the bench. *"Allons,"* he said. "We don't wish to wear out our . . . welcome here." His features hardened. "A few weeks in England, then back across the Channel to prepare for the war in Brittany."

William waited for Rolf in the yard, then mounted his horse, flanked by Roger de Conteville on one side and Rolf de Valmont on the other. Myles followed on foot, as did several other of Rolf's men.

Rolf had caught the look in Merlyn's eyes as he walked past her, in full mail, to mount Charon. It made him cringe inside, yet he'd wished to accord William the respect he was due and, for once, felt an inexplicable need to feel in command again. . . .

Like a respectable chevalier rather than a lord of farmers? mocked an irksome voice from some dark niche in his mind.

Guilt flickered within him, until the practical side of him came up with the best reason of all: He wanted to look like a loyal Norman; wanted William to believe him a loyal Norman baron should anything happen during the ride through Renford to hint at what Rolf considered his betrayal of his duke. A score of things could go wrong . . . and get one of his villagers severely punished. Or, God forbid, even his wife.

Without warning, Rolf found himself floundering in doubt . . . uncertainty about *everything* in those moments. And his biggest fear was not that his outright lie would be discovered but, rather, that *his* villagers would reject him . . . would lump him along with all Normans, rather than see him as a man who'd changed over the months, who'd sincerely tried to help them restore their lives. More for their own welfare, he realized with a jolt, than even for his own gain. Perhaps he hadn't even really succeeded at anything here . . .

So you hide behind your armor, chevalier, so no one can see your fear of failure ... and the possibility of severe discipline measures by William should he discover your soft heart ... coward!

The last word sliced through his heart with scarifying pain. He'd been called many things in his life, but never coward.

The sun broke through the clouds above, shining down on them and melting the light dusting of snow that had rested, briefly, like a sparkling white blanket over the ugly mud beneath. The interlocked rings of their mail glinted in the sunlight, flashing silver here and there like lightning.

"Your people are in need of clothing," William observed as he obviously noted many wearing skins (skins from animals that Rolf had killed in the Royal Forest) for warmth over their ragged garments. "But I also see," he added, a perplexed look crossing his face, "that they are well-shod."

Rolf couldn't help but smile slightly at the memory of the one responsible for that. Not the Arthur who had mindlessly slain Ombre, but the man who'd sacrificed his own life to save Merlyn. "Our tanner was excellent at his craft," Rolf answered in a strong, firm voice. "He not only had secreted away a cache of leather, but also taught others to help him—he'd lost an arm, you see—fashion shoes and the like."

William looked directly at him, as if awaiting an explanation of how the tanner had lost an arm ... perhaps in which battle against the Normans. But Rolf only said, "He was a good man," unknowingly echoing some of Arthur's last thoughts.

William nodded and returned his gaze to his surroundings. The people of Renford wore mixed expressions: some suspicious, some apprehensive, some curious. But none were hatred-filled, to Rolf's relief. Perhaps it was because although he was mounted, although he wore mail, his head was bare, and the people could see his face, his expression, as he looked at each and every one of them. There was much of the familiar in the foreign, enough so that even if the younger children hid behind their mothers' skirts, the adults appeared less intimidated and more at ease.

"You have chosen a site for a keep?" William asked.

"*Oui*." Rolf pointed north. "On yon rise this side of the Tees . . ."

Suddenly, Erik was there, standing alone before the cottage that had housed Edward Smithsson and Will. And the hapless Marthe. His blue eyes were filled with hostility and Rolf tensed, wondering if the lad would be foolish enough to attempt an attack on William of Normandy. Rolf put his right hand to his sword hilt, praying that Erik wouldn't make him regret the fact that he hadn't incarcerated him. Praying that the youth wouldn't betray them both . . .

"Some rebellion left in this one," William commented.

From behind them, Rolf heard Roger de Conteville say, "Hotheaded youth, my lord. We've all had our days of folly."

Erik's gaze dropped just then, as if he remembered his pledge to Rolf in the hole beneath the mill, and he retreated a step. Rolf could have kissed Roger. The tense moment was diffused.

They came before the tanner's home, and the pretty flaxen-haired Margaret stood before the doorway, the babe in her arms and the older Edwina by her side. Raven stood beside her friend.

Why, the little devil! Rolf thought with some consternation. She'd just been in the hall with Merlyn. What was she doing . . .

His thoughts halted abruptly for, bold as brass, she stepped forward without warning, her eyes brimming with tears. Rolf halted, and the others did the same.

"*Reste-là*," Rolf ordered her, his voice sharp with urgency. One simply did not step into the path of a battle-trained destrier . . . and especially if one knew nothing about war-horses and was only a mite of a girl.

Raven obediently stepped back, the tears spilling over her lower lids. "What did we do to you, my lord," she began, her mouth quivering, "that you leave us?"

Like a runaway boulder, Rolf's heart tumbled through his chest. She stood so bravely, futilely fighting her distress. . . .

Forgetting everything else, he dismounted, unthinkingly tossing Charon's reins to the Duke of Normandy. "*Jamais, petite!*" he pledged softly as he swept her small body into his arms and high against his chest. "I'll never leave you." His mouth was against her sweet-smelling hair . . . glossy and dark like her mother's.

Raven hiccoughed on an indrawn breath and clung to him for a moment. A brief but awkward silence reigned. "B—but when last you were dressed s—so, you left Renford with yon Lord Roger and his b—brother."

Rolf held her away from his shoulder and looked into her eyes . . . Merlyn's eyes. The Merlyn of years ago. The Merlyn he longed to possess heart and soul . . . to comfort and shield and defend to the death. And to trust.

"But I came back, did I not?"

Raven gnawed on one small knuckle as she regarded him through tear-sheened eyes, saying nothing.

"Je te promis, ma chère . . . I'll—" He stopped mid-sentence, suddenly remembering Merlyn's long-ago question: *Pretty words, my lord. But were you even half what you pledge, what happens when you're gone?*

The thought of life's unfairness and uncertainty struck him like an unexpected kick in the middle. He felt his insides wrench. How could he promise her— or anyone else—he would never leave them? One never really knew. Life was unpredictable at best.

Raven seemed to catch his hesitation, the shadow of uncertainty that passed through his eyes. Her tiny winged brows drew together.

"I'll never leave you *willingly*, I promise," he told her, then hugged her quickly once more and set her down. Margaret stepped forward to take Raven's hand and draw her back out of the way.

Rolf turned, caught Charon's reins from William, and vaulted astride the great black courser. He didn't look at Raven again but lightly rowled the stallion forward, his own eyebrows now flattened by a thoughtful frown.

"She is the picture of her mother," William commented, "and claims your heart into the bargain. You'll have your hands full, even in the best of times," he added with a half-grin.

"Mamma!" Raven cried, and threw herself against her mother. "He's *still* gone! Rolf still hasn't come back and—and he took Gryff with 'im . . . and he's *not* coming back!"

436

Merlyn stiffened, then held her small daughter away from her to look into her eyes. "Who told you such a thing?" she asked sharply, even as one part of her mind acknowledged how brave the child could be under the worst circumstances. Yet now she was genuinely shaken . . . terrified, even.

Cedric emerged from the shadows in the dim hall and limped up to them as they stood at the bottom of the stone steps leading to the chambers above. He looked slightly ill at ease, but Merlyn didn't notice.

"Did Rolf *tell* you, child?" Merlyn asked, suddenly feeling a twinge of apprehension. In the silence that followed her question, Merlyn looked up at Cedric.

"I beg your pardon, my lady, but I fear the child may be right."

Merlyn's look turned sharp, bemusement stunning her into silence for a moment. She knew Cedric had been close to Elsa but, sweet heaven! that didn't give him the Sight as the old one had claimed she possessed. What was he talking about?

"'Tis said that Duke William intended to offer my lord the chance to return to Normandy with him."

"Nonsense," Merlyn said with a wave of her hand. "Even Rolf de Valmont wouldn't leave without telling anyone. . . . He's only gone to accompany the duke and his men to the boundary of his lands."

Cedric shook his head slowly. "'Tis well past the nooning." He glanced pointedly at a time-keeping candle nearby. "He's been gone an hour longer than my lord Myles."

"Myles? He's returned?"

She hadn't heard him return. Where was he?

And, more importantly, where was Rolf?

"Aye. I believe he's at the tanner's . . . er . . . Margaret's."

"Stay right here," she told Raven. "I'll get to the

437

bottom of this." And grabbing her mantle from near the door, Merlyn swirled it about her as she left the hall, her thoughts bouncing through her mind like bats trapped in a belfry. She raced down the steps to the yard and across it, heedless of anything but finding Myles.

Of course, her conscience told her, *why wouldn't he prefer to return to Normandy if he had the chance? Who wouldn't after discovering the devastation here? And who wouldn't after almost losing his life because his wife lied to him . . . betrayed him, if only for a few but significant moments?*

Rolf de Valmont had more than enough reason to leave. She had seen to that.

You did what you had to.

Running through the village with a sudden, alarming urgency, Merlyn didn't heed the mud that sucked at her shoes, the wind that whipped wisps of her hair into her face. But the warmth and brightness of the sun felt good, like the soothing presence of a friend, a fragment of security by virtue of its permanence, and heartening at a time when her confidence suddenly needed shoring up.

As she neared Margaret's cottage, Myles emerged through the doorway. She slowed her steps just as he looked up at her.

"Is aught amiss?" he asked, his features revealing nothing of his thoughts.

"My—my lord Rolf," she said, breathless from exertion . . . and more than that. "Where is he?"

Myles adjusted his mantle with maddening deliberateness, then shrugged. "Mayhap down by the river."

"The river? But why? Is he . . . has he . . . did William? . . ." She couldn't finish any of her thoughts aloud.

438

"My lord William is gone," he told her calmly. "He left Rolf with some . . . decisions to make." His gaze dropped momentarily, purposely, but the significance was lost to Merlyn. "No doubt he is thinking over his . . . options." His gaze met hers, full of meaning.

"Options?" He'd said it so nonchalantly, as if none of Rolf's decisions would affect the entire village . . . the lives of many people beside herself. Perhaps, even, the fate of Northumbria itself . . . England!

Ire rose within her, lifting her chin, darkening her eyes to the deep violet of irises in spring and pushing aside all her other emotions, all other considerations. How *like* him to take William up on his offer . . . to just leave the area as breezily as he'd arrived. And break Raven's heart in the process.

Other voices vied with her anger, clamoring for acknowledgment within the jumble of her thoughts. With a vengeance, Merlyn ignored them as she whirled away from Myles de Mortain and marched east toward the Tees.

He sat astride Charon, lost in thought as he gazed over the river. The sun in the southern sky dappled his bare head and shoulders. It bathed one side of his face in tones of muted gold and limned his beautiful profile. It burnished his chestnut hair to deep auburn; and the proud carriage of his torso, the set of his splendid shoulders, brought to Merlyn's mind a dark-haired forest deity. Like one of the many worshiped by her Druid ancestors.

Why don't you just prostrate yourself before him in utter adoration, as no doubt scores of others have before you?

Lest she heed the ludicrous suggestion, she drew in

a breath and assaulted him verbally. "What do you *here?*" she demanded as she emerged into the clearing where the great Charon stood patiently.

The stallion's ears pricked forward, and in unison with his master, he swung his perfectly formed head toward the sound of her voice.

"Merlyn?" Rolf asked in surprise.

"Who else did you think it to be, my lord *husband,*" she answered with unmistakable sarcasm.

"You do remind me of someone I once knew." A reluctant smile suddenly tugged at one corner of his mouth. "Especially with your hair as tangled and full of burrs as a crone's . . ."

Merlyn looked down at herself, having forgotten in her haste and angry preoccupation that she must, indeed, look much like the Merlyn he had first met.

He was trying to distract her from her purpose, she thought then, narrowing her eyes at him; attempting to make light of her seeking him out. "You didn't answer my question." She stepped forward, conscious of the *squish* of mud in her new shoes. "Why are you here when Myles is back in the village?"

He quirked an eyebrow. "And since when are you so concerned as to my whereabouts?"

"Since you're breaking Raven's heart because she thinks you are never coming back!" She hadn't meant to say it with quite so much fervor, but that's how it came out.

As if on cue, Gryff came trotting into view from the trees that lined the riverbank, tongue lolling. He made right for Merlyn, obviously having no trouble identifying her in her dirty and disheveled state.

"Gryff!" Rolf commanded. The pup skidded to a halt, panting as if the devil had been chasing him. "Sit!"

Gryff sat.

Again, refusing to be swayed from her purpose, Merlyn looked expectantly at Rolf. He frowned and, throwing one leg over Charon's saddle, dismounted in a smooth, single movement. Leaving the horse to drink, he moved toward Merlyn, his mail chinking softly. "What is this about Raven?"

"Would that you were so concerned about all those others who depend on you!"

Including her mother, something deep within her echoed.

"What do you mean?" His frown deepened, and Gryff, obviously tired of sitting still, wandered off unnoticed by either Rolf or Merlyn. "Who said I'm not coming back?"

"Cedric!" she blurted out, feeling suddenly, to her chagrin, the press of tears behind her eyes.

Rolf noted the gleam of moisture along her lower lashes and almost moved to take her into his arms, for he couldn't bear to see her cry. She'd done it so infrequently that it tore him asunder inside to see it now.

He caught himself, however, as an idea popped into his mind. His first reaction had been to curse his loose-tongued steward, but the more he thought about it, the more certain he was that the wily Cedric had known exactly what he was about when he'd told Merlyn of William's offer. Something, no doubt, Myles had told *him,* with the same end in mind.

Then and there, Rolf de Valmont decided to take the gamble of his life.

"Leave Raven out of this," he said softly. "What if I *do* leave Renford? What is there to hold me here? Elsa is dead. She was a valued friend. She had faith in me . . . which is more than I can say for you, Merlyn. Even Arthur seemed to respect me, or what I was trying to do, in the end. He's gone, as well." He grimaced. "So I am left—aside from Raven—with Gryff here"—who had returned from the woods and was circling Rolf's booted feet, nose to the ground—"and a wife whose noble sacrifices do not extend to me . . . unless I am on the winning side."

"That's not fair! I had a child to think of. . . ."

"Then you were not really loyal to England, Merlyn, because king and country should come before anything else."

"To you, a chevalier . . . a man of war who knows naught—"

"To *anyone*," he told her. "If there is no leader at the helm, everyone suffers, and security, even in its most fragile and fleeting form, disappears completely."

He stepped closer to her, his hazel eyes bright with his own frustrations and disappointments. "And your daughter's welfare was safer in my hands than in those of any other! Did you ever think of *that* while you were plotting against me with Smithsson . . . supposedly digging up leather? And then with Waltheof?"

She shook her head, unable to answer around the tightness in her throat.

He furrowed his fingers through his short hair, then sighed . . . a calculatedly resigned sound. "You must admit, even aside from all that, there is more to farming than the ability to pen a cow or understanding the value of a pig."

"You need not be a farmer, proud, foolish man," she told him flatly. "You never had to be."

He looked up at her again, aching to crush her to him. But he couldn't. Things weren't settled by any means.

"What do you mean?"

Merlyn drew in a sustaining breath, in control,

once more, of her treacherous tears. "You are lord here, sworn to protect and defend. Why do you think William sent you here? He deliberately sent a capable warrior, not a man of the soil. The villagers know the business of farming and you that of fighting . . . and you are learning to rule fairly."

He moved closer to her, his eyes plumbing the luminous amethyst depths of hers. "Is that why you've delighted in reminding me all this time of what a failure I am?" he asked in a low voice.

Merlyn shook her head, realizing her mistake . . . a mistake caused by resentment and bitterness and fear. "You cannot go," she said in a quaking voice. "*I* won't let you."

Anticipation buzzed along his veins, sending hope sweeping through him like wildfire, until he had to consciously call into play every scrap of self-discipline at his command. "Why is that, Merlyn?"

She shook her head, biting down on her lower lip, unable to say the words that one tiny part of her still felt would brand her a traitor.

"I need a reason, Merlyn. A *good* reason."

"They need you! Everyone needs you . . . Raven and Cedric—he'd lay down his life for you!—and Bjorn and Margaret and—"

"I need more."

She looked bemused. "I cannot promise the love, or even the respect, of each and every one—"

He stepped closer, until he was only an arm's length away. "There is one thing I need above all else."

The tears began anew, and Merlyn found herself losing control in the face of his nearness, his unwavering pursuit of what she still refused to grant him freely. She latched onto anger like a lifeline. "All right! *I* need you! There. Are you happy?" She spun

443

away, staring blindly through waves of emotion, into the woods.

"Nay. 'Tis not enough," he said from very close behind her. His warm breath brushed her cheek, but he did not touch her.

The silence gathered between them, and Rolf began to think he'd failed. Perhaps he *should* return to Normandy, for living with and loving Merlyn without anything but physical reciprocation would slowly kill him. He could never settle for one-sided love without shriveling inside. He knew instinctively that he would end up a miserable, bitter old man, showering his unrequited love on Raven instead of his wife.

The hope that had been burgeoning within him suddenly began to dissipate. . . .

And then she slowly turned to him, her face lifting to his as tears tumbled down her cheeks. "I love you, Rolf de Valmont," she whispered. "Please . . . stay with us."

He took her, then, into the welcome haven of his embrace, crushing her to him, his lips at the sweet curve of her temple. *"Mon Dieu*, Merlyn, I've waited so long to hear those words!" He buried his face in the beautiful tangled mass of her hair, black as Charon's but infinitely softer and sweeter.

"'T-tis treason t-to love the enemy," she stuttered softly into his chest.

"My stubborn, stubborn Merlyn," he admonished with a smile. "I am not your enemy. I love you . . . have from the time you emerged from that bath, transformed from crone to nymph . . . and your people as well. *My* people now."

"I'm so sorry I wavered in my loyalty." She pulled back to look into his eyes. "I was confused, you see, but I vow on my daughter's soul, I never plotted with

Edward that time in the *weald*. I told him . . ." she hesitated and pulled in a ragged breath, "that 'twas better to seek to thrive under William's rule . . . and heal. That was all, I swear."

The relief brightening his expression spurred her on to one more admission. "And the time I went after Gryff, when I saw Earl Waltheof . . . for one mad moment I thought there might have been some substance to Smithsson's belief—to the uprising itself. But when you appeared, I couldn't bear to see you harmed. I realized in those moments that I loved you, Rolf. But it was too late."

He stared at the faint imprint of his mail on her fair cheek, and felt a new and powerful rush of emotion surge through him. "I . . . think I understand, *mon coeur*, and I ask not that you give up your loyalty to England, but rather transfer some part of that loyalty to me, nothing more."

"And you'll not leave?" She reminded him of Raven for a moment, so small and vulnerable.

He shook his head. "Not unless 'tis in a shroud . . ." At the look on her face, he smiled tenderly. "We cannot be certain of anything, Merlyn, save our love for one another." His tone lightened. "However, I do pride myself on my ability to keep my hide in one piece."

"Not recently," she reminded him, one hand moving to caress his cheek. "I—we—almost lost you."

"But you didn't, and I'll do my damnedest to see that it never happens again." His mouth descended to meet hers, his deep yearning for her seeping through him like an aphrodisiac.

"Rolf?"

His lips hovered a heartbeat away from hers, and with a husky breath of sound, he answered, *"Oui?"*

445

"Were you *really* going to leave us?" She stared at his mouth, mesmerized by the sight . . . and the thought of the exquisite pleasure that was coming.

But he didn't answer her. No, he thought. Mayhap another time, when she was ready to hear the truth. When she was ready to understand just how desperately he loved her and needed her love in return. But not now. Now was the time to make her forget everything but his love for her . . . and her newly declared love for him.

His mouth captured hers with all the longing and love in his heart, forcing her thoughts to scatter like smoke on the wind.

Later, he thought. One day, he would tell her: but he had better things on his mind just now. . . .

Author's Note

In 1069, the combined forces of the Danish king, Sweyn Estrithson, and a number of powerful Saxon magnates in England presented the most serious and coherent threat to William of Normandy since he'd conquered England at Hastings three years earlier. The center of the crisis was the north, and although other revolts were thus triggered throughout England, the most serious threat was to northern England. Yorkshire was lost, and in the "whirling chaos" north of the Tees, Malcolm, King of Scotland, became the emerging authority as he threw in his lot with William's opponents. Thus faced with the possibility of the establishment of a Scandinavian kingdom in northern England, or a realm created for Edgar Atheling and supported by Malcolm and Estrithson, William acted with vigor and at great risk to regain control in the north.

The end result was, in an age of accepted brutality in war, a terrible retaliation (which would still be felt twenty years later) that included the destruction of prosperity in Yorkshire for more than a generation. The total campaign, which went as far west as Merseyside and as far south as Derby, was to be ranked as one of the outstanding military achievements of the age, but at a terrible price. Its savagery was condemned even by those who were otherwise ardent admirers of the Norman king, leaving in its wake unnecessary death and destruction, and subsequent pestilence.

This was the northern England to which Rolf de Valmont was sent. None of the circumstances described in *Tender Warrior* are exaggerated. In fact, many of the more gruesome details were avoided.

The revolt of the earls—Waltheof of Huntingdon, Ralph de Gael, Roger of Breteuil, etc.—in 1075 was also an actual occurrence. It was trivial compared to the uprising of 1069 and never really had a chance. At Christmas 1075, William returned from Normandy to a pacified England thanks to the capable Archbishop Lanfranc, to mete out punishment to the rebels. While Ralph de Gael fled to Brittany, the Bretons in England who supported him were "savagely dealt with," "Earl Roger was thrown into captivity," and Earl Waltheof was beheaded in May of 1076 just outside of Winchester. By that time, William had returned to Normandy to prepare for the war in Brittany.